The Shadow Chaser

As well as being a novelist, John Matthews is an experienced journalist, editor and publishing consultant, though after the success of *Past Imperfect*, which became an international bestseller, he has devoted most of his time to writing books. He lives in Surrey with his wife and son.

D1445502

The Shadow Chaser

JOHN MATTHEWS

MICHAEL JOSEPH
an imprint of
PENGUIN BOOKS

MICHAEL JOSEPH

Published by the Penguin Group

Penguin Books Ltd, 80 Strand, London WC2R 0RL, England

Penguin Putnam Inc., 375 Hudson Street, New York, New York 10014, USA

Penguin Books Australia Ltd, 250 Camberwell Road, Camberwell, Victoria 3124, Australia

Penguin Books Canada Ltd, 10 Alcorn Avenue, Toronto, Ontario, Canada M4V 3B2

Penguin Books India (P) Ltd, 11 Community Centre,
Panchsheel Park, New Delhi – 110 017, India

Penguin Books (NZ) Ltd, Cnr Rosedale and Airborne Roads,
Albany, Auckland, New Zealand

Penguin Books (South Africa) (Pty) Ltd, 24 Sturdee Avenue,
Rosebank 2196, South Africa

Penguin Books Ltd, Registered Offices: 80 Strand, London WC2R 0RL, England

www.penguin.com

First published 2003

1

Set in 12/14.75 pt Monotype Dante
Typeset by Rowland Phototypesetting Ltd, Bury St Edmunds, Suffolk
Printed in England by Clays Ltd, St Ives plc

A CIP catalogue record for this book is available from the British Library

ISBN 0-718-14496-1

To loved ones and good friends who went far before their time: my father: Sidney Ivor Matthews, Arnie Levie, Roy Murray, Lillian Kerr, Norma Fernandes-Lall, Richard Evans, John Le Breton and Vincent Kilgallon.

Acknowledgements

My thanks go to the many researchers and doctors in France, the UK and America who helped with invaluable information on recent research with AIDS, cancer and genetics, at the following: Pasteur Institute, Paris; MIT, Massachusetts; Mayo Clinic, Minneapolis; the Hammersmith and Royal Marsden Hospitals in London; the Sanger Institute, Cambridge; the Terence Higgins Trust; London zoos (primate veterinary advisers); and most especially to the Curie Institute, Paris and Oxted, Surrey.

I

André Lemoine took a deep breath as he surveyed the panorama before him: a thick carpet of dark green tree-top foliage spreading for miles, faint mist drifting up as the heat of the rising sun burnt off last night's torrential rain.

From his vantage point, a rocky outcrop with few trees, he could catch glimpses of some of his team in the first ten yards, then they were swallowed under the dense green blanket: the tree tops stretched flat for almost ten miles, until the first foothills of the Dorsale Camerounaise, the long ridge of mountains that ran along Cameroon's north-west border. But any clear definition of the mountains was robbed by the film of mist above the tree tops; they were like the hazy backdrop in a Chinese landscape painting.

There was a suspended stillness to that time of morning: only a faint unified trilling from the crickets and cicadas and the occasional bird call, as if they were waiting, along with the myriad of other jungle animals, for the sun to rise higher before their main crescendo of sound; or better still, late at night when André's camp would be trying to sleep. André could hear the faint rustling and swish of sticks of his team through the undergrowth almost in time with the gentle insect thrum from the jungle.

'*Ega*! Here! Over here!'

Then suddenly everything was in motion, the stillness broken.

'*Lecu*! Quick! Five or six, maybe more.'

More voices rapidly joined the first, calling out in Yemba, the rustling changing to a wild thrashing as they started running. And above it all, the sudden excitable shrieking of monkeys calling out to each other, warning.

André scrambled down hastily from the rock ledge, jumping the last five feet. David Copell's sweat-streaked face greeted him as his feet hit the ground.

'They've found some! A group of five or six, maybe more.' David was excited, slightly breathless, having run back from their team of trackers to alert André.

They started running, David leading, flailing their way through the thick undergrowth and tree branches, trying frantically to catch up with the main body of trackers following the mounting shrieks of the fleeing monkeys.

Fronds and branches sprung back in André's face as they sped through, the voices ahead now closer, more animated, excited. As they burst through a last tangled clump of palm and bamboo, they could see the trackers standing in a ragged semi-circle in a clearing ahead. Two of them were pointing up.

'*Ege!* There! They've gone up this one.' The leader of the trackers, Kalume, looked back towards André and David with beaming excitement.

They could see the legs of one of Kalume's men just disappearing out of view as he shinned hurriedly up the tree. They moved closer and joined Kalume in looking up.

Darkness, made denser still by the contrast with the shafts of light that pierced through the tree canopy gaps and hit André's eyes as he squinted up. He couldn't make out much beyond the tracker reaching out his arm to help him up.

'You go now! You go now!' Kalume urged. 'I follow.'

'Yes. Right.' André gripped on to the hand and scrambled up into the first branches. They'd had a mix-up just the day before when they'd corralled a group of grey mangabeys, very similar to the silver-tailed mangabeys André sought. One of the monkeys' legs had been injured in disentangling it from the nets; this time they wanted André there to make identification sure before the final closing in of the nets.

André climbed up through two sets of branches with Kalume now following, and peered up. It was a tall tree, cavernous, the darkness within it almost impenetrable: a tangled mass of fig vines, epiphytes and moss around most of its branches; an ecosystem within an ecosystem. Still André couldn't make out anything clearly above: brief flashes of dull, indistinct shapes darting rapidly, the increasingly wild flurrying of branches, and pencil-thin shards of sunlight bursting intermittently through fleeting gaps. And the shrieking of the monkeys now filled the air, drowned out everything else. Five or six, David had said, but it sounded like a dozen or more.

André knew that two or three of Kalume's helpers would be near the top of the tree by the nets. With the three of them now moving up, the mangabeys would be trapped in between.

They grappled their way steadily up the branches, and as André looked up he thought he caught a silvery glint in the last few inches of the tail of a monkey above. Then it was gone as it darted through the higher branches; it might easily have been just a reflection from some sunlight filtering through. The small silver tail marking was all that differentiated it from the grey mangabey; that and the elusive R gene which had brought André and David three thousand miles to track it down. They needed to get closer to make sure.

André was sweating heavily from the exertion and stifling heat as they clambered their way up, his attention alternating between his hand and footholds and the activity above: he didn't notice the snake at his side until almost a third of it had appeared from around the thick branch he was on. It had been nestled between some fig vine and the branch; obviously his movement had disturbed it.

André froze, not daring to move, watching transfixed as it slithered out only inches from his waist. Red with green diamond patches, it appeared to be around four feet long, its tongue gently probing the air as it moved. Then, as it sensed him, it coiled back, ready to strike.

André held his breath, tried to control his trembling by gripping tighter to the branch. André's eyes were bleary and stinging with the sweat running into them, and he watched as two droplets slowly fell from his forehead on to the branch.

'Don't move!' Kalume's voice came sharply, redundantly, from below. Then, as Kalume angled himself for a better look: 'No, no. It's OK. I think it's only a garter snake.'

Think? André kept his breath held as he watched the snake slither over the back of one calf and ankle, and then – seeming like a lifetime – slowly away. It wasn't until it was a full yard away and slithering on to another branch that he finally breathed out.

'It's OK. It's gone now,' Kalume said.

But André stayed transfixed, clinging to the branch, something else suddenly assaulting his senses as he watched the snake slither away: how high up they were!

He watched as a sweat droplet cleared the branch and sailed downward, the yawning chasm of the forty-foot drop hitting his synapses; he felt suddenly dizzy, unsteady, as if he might fall despite his tight grip on the branch.

Voices now from above, the screeching of the monkeys even more frantic, deafening.

André clung tight, closing his eyes, trying to shut out all the noise and activity and the drop below as he felt everything start to sway and spin around him, as if the whole tree was suddenly tilting.

'Look! They've got one!' Kalume called out excitedly. 'You can see it clearly now, see the silver marking.'

But still André clung on, afraid to move. Three thousand miles to try and save mankind, and now he couldn't lift his head a few inches to see if the prize was within his grasp or not.

'Look! They're holding one now for you to look at!' Kalume called out louder, perplexed that André hadn't looked up; or perhaps thinking that he hadn't heard the first time above the cacophony of shrieking from the monkeys.

André was unable to move. He opened his eyes for a second, but the ground appeared to sway and tilt sickeningly below him. He closed them quickly again. He was trembling hard, his sweat feeling suddenly cold against his skin, and still everything seemed to sway and spin around him in his self-imposed darkness.

Oh God. One way in which he wished he were more like his brother, Eric. Eric would have had no problem, would have laughed in the face of a drop four times as high; it was what much of his career had depended on.

Eric Lemoine levered himself up the last few inches on to the narrow ledge and, as he straightened, took his bearings for a moment. One more floor up and he'd edge back along the way he'd come twenty minutes ago; a short hop to the adjoining roof, then he'd scamper across and shin down the drainpipe on the far side.

It was harder returning, his backpack was now full. His breath vapours were heavy on the night air. Through a gap in the buildings opposite, the Pont Neuf and part of the floodlit flank of the Louvre were visible; and, to the left, above the buildings, the top half of the Eiffel Tower. But Eric paid little attention to the night-time vista; it was a view he'd seen many times before, from many different angles, as he'd plundered the wealthier inhabitants of the city over the years.

He started edging his way along the narrow ledge. Two more yards to the window balcony and its rail to be able to clamber up. He paused for a second as he heard a distant police siren, trying to gauge its direction. It sounded as if it was speeding along the embankment or maybe along St Germain, heading his way. But he'd been careful to bypass the alarm, and he was sure that there were none he'd overlooked that might connect directly to the police or a security firm. As he heard the siren pass and fade into the distance again, he relaxed and continued his way along.

On taller buildings or more difficult climbs, he'd have come equipped with ropes and grapples and a safety harness. But this was a cakewalk. Six-storey, turn-of-the-century building, target on the third floor, approach from the roof: variations on a theme he'd enacted so many times before, on many similar buildings, that he could have practically done it blindfolded.

The only small problem was that the light was now on in the room behind the balcony. It had come on shortly after he'd stepped from the balcony rails on his way down, and for a moment he'd worried that his movement had made a small sound to alert the people inside. But as he froze with his face pressed against the building, the shutters hadn't opened, and they were still shut. Yet with the light now on – one of only two visible in the building at this hour, 2.48 a.m. – the people in the room were probably awake and therefore could more easily pick up any movement outside.

He edged more cautiously as he got closer to the balcony, only a couple of inches at a time, careful not to make any sound. After a second he could discern faint orchestral music from inside, violins building to a crescendo; then as they faded and louder voices superimposed, he realized that it was a television film. It would help mask any smaller movements, but still he'd have to be careful.

He reached out for the railings, levered deftly up and crouched on top of them. Listening again for any movement inside the room – *nothing* – he raised slowly until he was standing.

The next part was going to be trickier. The ledge above was three inches beyond his grasp. Dropping down had been easy, and making the jump up wasn't too much of a feat: the question was, could he do it without making any noise?

He crouched down again, ready to spring. He'd have to get a solid grip with both hands on the ledge to be sure of holding his weight. What Eric didn't notice – his attention was fixed on the ledge – was that one of the wall screws securing the railings was missing and the other was loose and hanging by its last bit of thread. He waited expectantly a second more, breath held – still the sound of the television, nobody approaching or moving around inside the room – then leapt up.

As the full thrust of his jump hit the rail, the screw ripped loose from the wall and the railings jolted away. The railings didn't break off completely and fall, they hung at a forty-five degree angle away from the balcony. But the effect on Eric's jump was disastrous; its impetus was killed and he was only able to get a few fingers' grip with one hand on the ledge.

Eric felt the strain in his arm instantly, tearing at the tendons. He couldn't keep hold much longer; he'd have to swing up and grip on to the ledge with his other hand. But his body was angled away from his free hand, and the building was old, the plaster loose where he clutched on. As he started to swing, he could feel it crumbling beneath his fingers, white flakes and dust falling on to his face and shoulders. And now footsteps from inside the room. Heading towards the balcony.

The pain from his stretched tendons was excruciating, a searing white-heat screaming down and through his shoulder blade. He couldn't hang on longer. Footsteps now closer, the balcony windows being opened behind the shutters. With one last desperate lunge, Eric swung again and reached out with his free hand. But only an inch from making contact the plaster crumbled and gave way beneath his other hand, and he fell.

Only a short fall – he connected with the loose railings a few feet beneath and splayed them flat, level with the balcony floor. But he was winded and in shock; it took him a second to realize where he was. Sound of the shutters' latch opening, the right shutter swinging slowly towards him. And something else in that second that froze his heart: the concrete mushrooming up suddenly around the last stanchion holding the railings. He scrambled desperately forward to get his weight off and for a moment he thought he'd made it. He managed to get one hand and forearm on the balcony floor just before the stanchion gave way.

The base rail jolted his arm away as abruptly as it had made contact, then both he and the railings were sailing free into the night air. He caught a quick glimpse of a small brick wall and some dustbins four floors below, and had instinctively started to curl into a ball before he hit them and everything went black.

2

The rain pattered against the roof of André's tent. Single, heavy droplets at first, a full second's gap between each one; and then, with only a faint crack of thunder in the distance as warning, suddenly there was a deluge.

The monkeys in their cages started shrieking louder. André waved towards them and David Copell, then put his hand over one ear. He raised his voice on the mobile he was speaking into.

'Yes, yes. That's right. Four of them. Two of them got away before we could net them.' On the other end of the line was Marc Goffinet in Paris.

'Marielle's here with me,' Marc commented. At his end he repeated a précis of what André had told him. 'She's smiling and jumping up and down.'

'But she always does that. Isn't she excited?' André heard his own chuckle echoed at the other end. Equally, he could have chosen to speak first to Marielle Barbier, his other main assistant at the ISG, Institut de St Germain; but he knew that to Goffinet, now HIV positive for the past three years, the news would have more poignant significance.

The ice-packed samples they'd been working on for the past two months had provided them with the first glimmer of a breakthrough. But they desperately needed to have live samples to go to the next stage. André glanced across at David Copell trying unsuccessfully to calm the shrieking monkeys as the thunderstorm rumbled. It was either them or chimpanzees – the only other primate to carry SIV, the monkey form of HIV, with the same R gene present as in humans. But then SIV was found in monkeys in the wild, not in Paris primate houses, and chimpanzees in the wild were a protected species. Also, André had noticed something else about the mangabeys' immunity.

'When will you be back?' Marc asked.

'A couple of days, I suppose, by the time we've arranged the paperwork and transport.' From the sound of the torrent outside, the mud track back to Yoko would no doubt be a quagmire by morning, the going heavy. It would probably take them five hours just to make that leg.

'Maybe we'll be able to do something now for Eban,' Marc said.

'Let's hope so.' André swallowed back the lump in his throat. They could get carried away with thoughts about healing mankind, but that suddenly brought things down to earth, sharpened focus. Eban, the young Rwandan boy with AIDS they'd been treating, who, having lost his entire family to the disease, André had taken in as part of his own. That had been one of the main catalysts for this rush trip now: André knew that Eban probably didn't have much time left.

They were silent for a second. The thunderstorm was intensifying, a couple of heavy lightning cracks, suddenly sounding close, added portent to what they might be on the edge of: life or death for Eban and countless millions more.

David was trying to calm the monkeys by offering them nuts through the wire of the cage as André signed off. 'I'll phone you again just before we catch our flight.'

André went over to David. Only one of the monkeys seemed to be tempted; the other three looked on suspiciously from the back of the cage, still shrieking.

'I wonder if those are the three females,' David commented. 'Sometimes I have that effect on women.'

André smiled limply. 'We'll have to give them names and pick out some identifying markings to know which is which.'

'Well, that one's got a silver bit at the end of its tail. And that one, and . . .' David's voice trailed off and he straightened up, giving up the ghost on trying to feed them. 'Have you phoned Charlotte yet?'

'Only the once, when we first arrived.' A subconscious prompt for David, the sound of shrieking female monkeys? André's wife's erratic behaviour was hardly a secret back at their Paris lab, and their separation sixteen months ago had done little to stem the flow of Charlotte's frequent panic calls, to his home or work. Whenever there were problems, invariably storms-in-teacups or imagined, she phoned. 'But I was planning to speak later to Joël and Eban, so I'll speak to her again then. Tell her we're on our way back.'

Their seven-year-old son, Joël, stayed with Charlotte for most of the week. Eban, two years older, stayed with André, except for a couple of hours after school and when he was away. Their fourteen-year-old daughter, Veruschka, spent her time equally between them.

André picked up a couple of nuts from the table to see if he'd have more luck in tempting them. The same monkey came forward to take one and started nibbling, but the other three stayed obstinately at the back of the cage, looking at him curiously for a second before resuming their screeching.

'Hard to believe that finally we could be so close,' David commented, studying the monkeys.

'Yes, I suppose it is.' It had taken two years of intense research before the breakthrough with the first mangabey samples, but probably months' more work still lay ahead. And right now, with them having trouble getting the monkeys to even take food from them, the prospects seemed somehow all the more distant.

André was sweating profusely, the hairs damp on his arm as he held out the nuts by the cage. The humidity had risen probably twenty per cent just in the last ten minutes of thunderstorm. Or perhaps it was residual nerves from his ordeal in the tree; it had taken Kalume and two of his men to prise him from the branch and help him down. Or maybe the daunting challenge that now lay ahead of him: the time pressure to try and save Eban and the wider implications for legions of AIDS sufferers.

His arm reaching out became slightly blurred by sweat running into one eye, and he pictured it suddenly as the bridge he recalled from his childhood, the tombstones below it spreading into the distance. *Standing on the hillside in northern Rwanda, looking over the wasted remnants of Eban's old village, tears seared dry with the heat as he watched the few surviving elders and their children hobbling pitifully on stick-thin limbs*. And each time he'd had the same memory, usually in fragmented dreams that would wake him abruptly in the night, sweating heavily like now, the line of tombstones stretching into the distance was longer, melting into misty white infinity. *No, no . . . too many, too many! I can't save them all.* And sometimes he'd awaken to hear those words echoing from the dark corners of the room and he'd wonder whether he'd shouted them out loud or if they were just echoing in his mind.

He shook off a faint shiver. David was right. It seemed unreal that finally a cure might be so close within their grasp.

'Can you hear me? . . . We've called for an ambulance.'

'It should be here soon . . . but meanwhile you shouldn't try and move. Can you hear us?'

Two different voices, a man and a woman. The mumble of some fainter voices in the background.

Everything slowly swam into focus for Eric: an elderly couple leaning over him, their expressions concerned, and a group of three people behind them.

Eric's eyes darted from one face to another, as if ensuring that they were real, before realization fully dawned: he was still alive!

Then a wave of pain hit him a second later, took the edge off his elation. An ache in his right thigh as if he'd been dead-legged, but a far stronger, searing pain higher in his right hip and the soft flesh just above: it felt as if he'd been stabbed with a jagged knife. He reached down with his right hand, but he couldn't feel anything there except dampness from his own blood. He peered down – his vision blurring for a second as he verged dangerously close to blackout again – but as it cleared he could make out the spreading pool of blood tapering into a trickle by his right ankle, and two yards away the dustbin on its side with a heavy gout splattered around its rim.

'Looks like he's conscious, at least,' the woman said.

The old man at her side scratched at his sparse grey beard. He leant closer to Eric. 'The ambulance should be here soon. Just try and stay calm and don't move.'

Eric smiled weakly at the slightly hazy face of the old man. As if moving was even an option. Then suddenly what they were saying hit him like a thunderbolt: *ambulance!* Registration, his ID number taken, blood tests, questions about how he fell, did he live in the building? Someone might even look in his backpack. Even if he was lucky enough to get through all that without raising any alarm bells, how long before the people he'd just robbed woke up to that fact and contacted the police? He'd probably hear two sets of sirens approaching, the police car following only seconds behind the ambulance.

'I . . . I've got to go.' He propped up on one elbow, struggling to raise the rest of his body.

'No, no . . . you shouldn't move.' Unease now in the old man's voice.

'I . . . I must . . . I'm OK now.' He managed to scramble up on to one leg, but the pain from even that small movement was excruciating. He took a tentative step, and a lance of pain shot from his hip to his skull. He had to get clear of here, and fast. Yet it felt as if he'd struggle to make even five yards.

The old man put one hand on his shoulder; not holding him back, but not helping him along either. 'You shouldn't . . . you could hurt yourself worse.'

Eric hobbled another step and forced a smile beyond the pain. 'My brother's a doctor, he'll . . . he'll see to me.' The old man's hand left his shoulder, but still his face was grave with worry. Another step, another pained smile. 'Afraid of hospitals, you see. Just can't face them.'

The sound of a siren now in the distance, moving closer.

'Are you sure?' The old man held out the same hand imploringly. 'It sounds like the ambulance is here now.'

Eric just nodded, biting back against the pain as he shuffled away a few more steps, trying to pick up pace. He had to get away! Only one siren, but even if the police arrived hours later it wouldn't take them long to piece it all together. They'd probably walk in the hospital while he was still in the emergency room.

The siren was moving nearer, fast. Faster, it seemed, than he was able to shuffle away. In his jolting vision his eyes fixed desperately on the next street corner where he could turn and get out of view.

Slightly raised voices from behind, the woman now berating the old man, presumably her husband, for letting him go.

Eric tried to shuffle faster. Forty yards still till the nearest turning before he could disappear from the view of the people behind. The siren was moving closer, sounded as if it was only a couple of streets away.

He gritted his teeth hard against the pain as he hobbled. The numbness of his right leg helped him pick up pace, but each step felt like a white-hot knife thrust in his right hip and abdomen; and there was a strange liquid sensation in his stomach, as if his guts were drifting looser as he walked.

As everything swam in his vision, blurring and distorting for a second, he feared that he was going to black out before he even reached the turn-off. He'd collapse in a heap ten or twenty yards short of it for the people behind to point to.

The siren was now deafeningly loud as it cut through the stillness of the night. Eric looked hastily over his shoulder, saw it turning into the road. He hobbled faster, fifteen yards, *ten*, the siren spinning in his head and the buildings around tilting as he fought to straighten himself, shaking off another blackout.

But just before the turning, he saw something else that froze his heart: a man rushing out of the building and talking frantically to the group of people outside. Two of them raised their hands and pointed in his direction.

Eric darted into the turning, his heart in his throat as he shuffled hurriedly along, listening out for running footsteps from the street behind. It was difficult to pick up anything beyond the deafening wailing of the siren, which suddenly became static: the ambulance had probably pulled up in front of the building. But would they too come after him?

The siren stayed where it was, but after a second he could pick out the rapid patter of someone running. His eyes darted frantically. He had to find somewhere to hide. The street was long: he'd still be plainly in view as the man cleared the corner! It was then that he noticed the small street on the right just ahead. He shuffled hurriedly across and into it.

But still his eyes shifted from side to side in search of a hiding place. A sweet, acrid smell hit his nose, stabbed his brain like raw ammonia. The buildings around started to tilt again, but this time everything was grey.

He staggered and held one arm out blindly, felt his hand connect roughly with the wall to one side as he half toppled. He leant his shoulder against the wall and took deep breaths, trying to claw back from getting dragged completely under. The sudden, urgent patter of footsteps in the street behind snapped him awake again. And something else now in the distance: the sound of another two sirens. The man had probably called the police before bolting downstairs from his apartment.

His eyes scanned desperately for a quick hiding place, and came to rest on a large street-bin eight yards along on the other side of the road, half of it tucked in where the building recessed back two feet, the other half sticking out into the pavement. It wasn't ideal, but it was all there was.

Eric shuffled across, the footsteps in the street behind pressing ever nearer, the sound of the sirens growing. He lunged the last few feet to get behind it, not sure if he'd completely gone from view before the man came level with the street.

He heard the feet shuffle to a stop, the man pausing, looking down the street. Eric held his breath. Seven full seconds with the man stood there – though for Eric it felt far longer – then he ran on. Eric's breath fell unevenly from exertion and panic as he eased it out again. He knew that his relief could be short lived. How long before the man realized that he hadn't run on and headed back? And the police sirens were close now, very little separated their sound from that of the ambulance. They'd be able to scour all the neighbouring streets with ease. His own car was four blocks away, he'd never be able to make it that far without being caught.

Eric watched a small trickle of his blood run under the rubbish bin as he crouched, and his stomach sank. He wasn't going to get away. He'd be stuck there for the man or the police to find – if he didn't die meanwhile.

Then he noticed the wooden door inset in a large garage door further along the street. He scrambled towards it. The police sirens were now static, seemed to be falling almost in unison with the ambulance siren. Obviously they'd already arrived at the building, were probably right now being told in which direction he'd run. He yanked off his backpack as he drew level with the door, fumbling in one of its side pockets for his lock picks.

Like André's building and so many others in Paris, the garage door probably led into a parking courtyard for the neighbouring buildings. At this time in the morning it should be quiet, nobody around.

Eric's hand trembled on the picks as he probed the door lock. The police sirens were moving again, heading his way. He'd always prided himself on being able to pick almost any lock, and this should be a simple tumbler variety – but could he do it with his focus swimming and the sound of sirens filling the night, drowning out the delicate clicking of the tumblers he needed to listen for? Or before those sirens closed in on him? Or the man running, he reminded himself, as he heard the patter of rapid footsteps returning. Probably he'd reached the end of the street and decided to head back. One of the cars, from the sound of its siren, had turned into the adjoining road, was almost upon him.

He felt the last couple of tumblers slip back, and with one last frantic turn of the pick he opened the door and leapt inside just as the police car passed. He prayed that they hadn't seen him, but then a few yards past the turning they stopped. Either they had, or they'd met up with the man running back. Eric counted off the wait almost in time with his heavy, ponderous heartbeat and his laboured breathing against the back of the door – then came the sound of the car reversing and turning into the street.

His heartbeat pounded heavier as the car approached. As it came to within a few yards, he held his breath, every nerve on a tripwire as he listened out for it slowing or stopping.

But it slowly, very slowly, drifted past – though he didn't let out his breath again until it was almost at the end of the street.

Oh God. He closed his eyes as he leant back against the wall behind. At thirty-seven, he was getting too old for this: scurrying around the streets like a hunted rat, the night air filled with sirens. And he'd still need help to get clear: they'd probably trawl the neighbourhood for a good hour or more before giving up.

He took out his mobile and dialled André's number. It went into a recorded message:

'I'm away now until the twenty-sixth. Leave a message after the tone, or if you wish contact my secretary on –'

Eric dialled straight out to Hervé, his eldest brother. It answered after the fourth ring.

'Oui? Hello?' Hervé's voice was tentative, groggy.

'Hervé! It's Eric. I'm . . . I'm in a spot of trouble.' He kept his voice hushed but urgent. Even then it seemed to echo slightly in the confines of the small courtyard. He glanced anxiously along the short driveway to the ring of parked cars and the buildings behind. He should be safe here for a little while – unless somebody heard him.

'What sort of trouble?' More alert now.

No *Zut alors!* or expletives for the late hour he was calling, just instant, unreserved concern. But then that, his profession aside, was so often Hervé's nature.

'Well, it's . . . it's a long story.' Eric glanced down at the blood dripping rapidly from his thigh. 'I . . . I've had an accident. A bad accident . . . and I can't drive. I need someone to pick me up.' Eric pressed his other hand into his stomach; his guts felt loose and awash, as though if he moved the hand they might fall away.

'Yes . . . OK. But shouldn't you be calling for an ambulance and seeing a doctor?'

Eric smiled to himself at the thought of trying to explain that he'd spent the last frantic minutes avoiding an ambulance. 'That's another long story. I really need someone I know and can trust to pick me up. That's why I've called you, Hervé.'

'Yes, yes . . . of course. Where are you?'

Eric's nerves bristled. He could hear one of the sirens moving towards him. The second police car, or the first heading back for a second look?

'Ah . . .' Eric only remembered the street where he'd done the robbery. 'A block over from Rue Linoille on the Left Bank.'

The sound of paper rustling at Hervé's end as he wrote. 'OK.'

The siren was getting closer, practically at the end of the street. But suddenly everything was tilting again, the grey film behind his eyes washing in. The siren echoed and spun in his head and the sweet ammonia smell stung his sinuses, making his eyes water.

'Phone my mobile when you get to Rue Linoille. And hurry, Hervé, I'm losing blood quickly. I . . . I don't know how much –'

But at that moment the grey verged to black and the floor rushed up to meet him.

Hervé shouted 'Hello!' a couple of times into the silent phone before jumping up for his clothes.

He was going to throw on just jeans and a sweater, but then he reached for his priest's robes. He had a feeling they might come in useful on this journey.

3

They'd had to stop twice on their way back to Douala. The first stop was just to shift a small tree that had fallen over the narrow mud road and they lost little time. But on the second stop the last in their convoy of four Land Rovers got stuck in a foot-deep mud quagmire, and the more they revved its engine and spun its wheels, the deeper entrenched it became. This time they found themselves putting small branches and loose twigs back on the road, packing the mud to be able to get some traction on the Land Rover's wheels, and they lost almost forty minutes.

The sun was quite strong by the time they got clear of the jungle, most of the rising mist vapours had burnt off, and the panorama beyond – Cameroon Highlands scrub with a random patchwork of farm fields – seemed to stretch endlessly. But just before 7 p.m. that night, there was another heavy thunderstorm. It rattled and banged in the background while André was on the phone at Douala airport to Charlotte, and at one point he had to repeat himself.

'I said . . . did they both get off to school OK?'

'Yes, yes . . . of course. Why?'

'Well, when we spoke earlier, you were in a bit of a rush.' André avoided the first word that came to mind: panic. 'You were worried whether you'd get them ready on time. And you said you'd also had a bit of trouble with the car the other day.'

'Oh, yes . . . yes. It started OK in the end. On the button.'

He had been worried about leaving Eban with her when often she had trouble coping just with Joël – but there was no point in voicing it, adding pressure. And though she had Veruschka to help, that often created problems of its own. She and her mother saw eye to eye much less as the years progressed. He lowered his voice a note. 'How has Eban been?'

'Didn't you speak to him earlier?'

'Yes, but only briefly. He said he's been OK. But how has he *really* been?'

'Well . . .' She mulled the question over for a second. 'He picked at his meal a couple of nights ago, didn't really eat that much, and he looked tired. But he's been OK since, has eaten better and been more lively.' She let out a tired breath. 'Sometimes it's hard to believe that he's so ill.'

'I know. I know. He's very brave.'

'Sometimes *I* probably seem a lot sicker.' She forced a weak chuckle.

André made sure not to respond to that. He glanced over towards David at the far end of the room, whose voice had risen as he jabbed one finger at some papers and stressed a point with a couple of customs officials. They thought they'd get all the paperwork sorted out with hours to spare before their flight – now he was beginning to wonder. 'Looks like David needs my help. I'll phone you again as soon as we've landed in Paris: early tomorrow morning, your time – as long as it's not delayed.'

He signed off, and they managed to get the paperwork concluded just twelve minutes before their flight, by which time André was exhausted. Though it was over an hour into the flight before André's nerves finally wound down from all the rush and panic and he managed to sleep.

In the last forty minutes of André sorting out the papers, David had gone across to tend to the mangabeys. He pointed to one of them and looked worried as André joined him by their cage.

'Little Anouk is still not taking food.'

They'd decided to name them after sixties film stars – Brigitte, Catherine, Anouk and Alain. Anouk was the smallest and youngest female, probably only two or three years old. Another two had started to take some nuts and fruit during the last leg of their drive to Douala, but Anouk had stayed obstinately at the back of the cage. All of them had got past the frantic, shrieking stage, had started to accept their cage and their surroundings. Though still they looked on with suspicion and caution, even more so when they took food, except for Anouk; she avoided anything but brief eye contact, and looked sullen, morose, her eyes weary.

André started to fear for her health with no food or liquid taken for so many hours, and so they decided to give her a liquid glucose feed through a pipette.

It was difficult to get her to take it, and she fired a few weak shrieks before André finally got the pipette in her mouth. She looked up at André with weak, pleading eyes as she started to suckle, and at one point she reached up and grabbed at André's ponytail.

'I told you to get rid of that thing,' David remarked with a smile.

'Just when do I ever get a chance to go to the hairdresser's?'

Seven years ago when he'd first adopted the style, it was considered chic and stylish; but now, in his forties, with the first tinges of grey in his light-brown hair, he risked looking like an ageing hippie. He could have added: when do I get a chance to buy new clothes? Or get a builder in to see to all the small things that had been wrong with his new apartment since he'd moved in sixteen months ago? Or devote some time to try and bridge the widening gap between him and Charlotte? Outside of his research and Eban, Joël and Veruschka, he had little time for anything or anyone else, least of all himself. But the rest of it, unsaid, just hung in the silence between them as Anouk continued suckling on the pipette.

He was still worried about Anouk as they rushed for their flight – he'd have liked her to have taken more glucose feed before such a long journey – and part of that replayed in his dream as he slept on the plane: her large, pleading eyes staring up at him as she suckled and tugged at his ponytail. Then it became Eban reaching out to him: *'Help me . . . help me! Please don't let me die.'* A sudden flash of lightning and a shriek and the image was yanked back to the monkey, now screaming in terror, its eyes wide as the thunderstorm flashed and rumbled around them.

André pleaded with it, *'Please take the food . . . please take it.'* But the monkey kept its head turned obstinately from the pipette, its eyes seeming to grow wider in terror as they fixed on something to his side. It shrieked excitedly and yanked harder on his ponytail.

André turned to his side to see the snake, but this time it held its raised striking position, staring transfixed at him and the monkey. The monkey's shrieking became wilder, its teeth and gums bared in a rictus, ghostly in the next lightning flash. But with the monkey's incessant yanking on his ponytail, André became suddenly afraid of losing his grip on the branch, and his vision was drawn to the drop below. It tilted and swayed sickeningly below him, and he pleaded with the monkey to stop pulling. *'Please . . . please stop! Otherwise I'll fall.'*

But it continued to pull, so hard now that he could feel the hair starting to tear from his scalp, its shrieking deafening: a kaleidoscope blur of the monkey, the snake and the drop below lit starkly by lightning, spun in his head. He struggled to cling on to the branch, but with one final yank and shriek he felt the last of his grip wrenched free, and he was falling . . . *falling* . . .

He woke up with a jolt just before he hit the ground, his mouth dry as he swallowed. He rubbed at his eyes and saw distant lightning as he looked out of the plane's window.

'Storm over the Atlas Mountains,' David at his side commented. 'We should be through it in about ten minutes, the pilot said.'

André just nodded, his throat too tight and parched to speak. The jumbo pitched and yawed as he took a few gulps from the bottled water he'd tucked in the seat-back.

He thought the dream was merely a product of the madness and rush of the last few days. But when he landed in Paris and Charlotte told him about Hervé's frantic call in the middle of the night and he phoned Hervé and heard the full horror of the story, he began to wonder.

The New York conference hall was packed to capacity. As the presenter finished his introductory speech and stepped aside with one arm held out, the large screen behind him came to life.

Warren Gifford's image filled it. A trim figure in his mid-fifties with close-cropped stone grey hair and blue-grey eyes twinkling out of a lean and angular tanned face. He was sat by an ornate white wrought-iron table with a pool and tabled lawn as a backdrop, Roman statues and topiary hedges flanking a path that ran through it into the distance.

It was like one of those live Hollywood telecasts from an actor who unfortunately couldn't be at the Oscar or Tony awards that night; someone who regularly played tennis and had a private fitness instructor in order to remain lean and trim in their advancing years. Except that when the camera moved in close, the faint grey-yellow tinge to the whites of Gifford's eyes could be picked up and his skin appeared slightly loose and creased, his leanness the result of muscle waste and rapid weight loss. And everyone in the conference hall knew that Warren Gifford had died some eight months before, this speech recorded probably only weeks before his death. The image and voice on screen were from the grave.

'I'm glad you could all make it. But then, as I know all too well, money can be a powerful draw.' A well-timed glance to one side, an expression of regret. He must have gone over this speech a hundred times before finally putting it on video. 'Though as I was soon to discover, it couldn't buy everything. It couldn't buy what was most important to me: my life. Not even, in the end, a bit more time.' He looked back directly at the camera. 'God wouldn't be bargained with.'

Even in death, Gifford was a consummate audience player, had the hushed auditorium hanging on his every word. But then, awaiting the announcement of the largest medical awards ever known, Gifford had expected no less.

He talked about his long fight against cancer. Two years, three years maximum he'd been given; in the end he'd lasted nine years. He talked about the skilled team of doctors who'd fought bravely to try and save him, and acknowledged them now by lifting one hand. '. . . Particularly Larry Bernstein, Jeff Warrell and Vicky Kramer.'

Two-thirds of the way back and to the right, Larry Bernstein tamely lifted one hand in response while Warrell and Kramer just smiled as a number of heads in the audience turned towards them, a light murmur rising.

Two rows from the front, Dr Julius Chisholm turned to his

colleagues, Murray Kalpenski, Russ Hebbard and Danielle Stolk, with a wry smile. 'He certainly knows how to play us all, the old dog.'

On screen, uncannily, Gifford's gaze went directly to where Bernstein waved back at him. The seat positions and camera angles had obviously been set up in advance.

The seating was arranged more or less in order of importance, with the leading cancer research institutes taking up the front rows. As much as Bernstein and his team had been important personally to Gifford, they were cancer treatment specialists and surgeons – the last back-stop in trying to halt the disease's progress.

As treasurer and one of five main board members of the Spheros Institute in Philadelphia, a trailblazer in cancer research for the past decade, Dr Julius Chisholm had earned his place among the front rows. Murray Kalpenski had headed up the Spheros's cancer research division for the past three years, and Hebbard and Stolk were two of his leading protégés.

At thirty-six, Stolk was the youngest of the group, with two years on Hebbard, eighteen on Kalpenski and twenty on Chisholm. Attractive, vivacious even in their normally dull lab environment, she had dark hair and bright, charcoal-brown eyes, though her features were somewhat angular, pinched: the only warning of the harsher, sterner mettle that Chisholm knew lurked beneath. Hebbard too, with tight-knit brown curls and a ruddy face as if he was permanently angry or excited, had been earmarked by Chisholm as showing strong ambition and promise, though in a different way. They probably thought they'd been asked along today purely because they were Kalpenski's rising stars. But Chisholm had requested their presence because he had plans for them; plans that went far beyond the tight confines of Kalpenski's purely academic grasp. Particularly given how he expected everything to rapidly change after Gifford's announcement. What he hadn't decided yet was which one of them he was going to put in the frame: Stolk or Hebbard?

The murmur of the auditorium died as Gifford's voice came over again.

'You will probably all remember the press interviews years ago when I first discovered I had cancer, and I vowed that I was going to "beat it".'

If indeed anyone in the auditorium had forgotten, that bold statement had been revived and rammed posthumously down Gifford's throat in the press before his body was barely cold: *Cancer finally beats Gifford . . . One battle Gifford couldn't win.*

A second-generation oil magnate and for almost two decades America's richest man before the new wave of computer and Internet billionaires dropped his ranking to third, Gifford's death – as had much of his life – dominated the news.

A sly smile crossed Gifford's face. 'Never one to openly lie or mislead, or to be proven wrong – what I didn't say is whether or not I'd beat it within my own lifetime.' A pause for effect as Gifford's expression became serious again, his jaw jutting determinedly. 'But beat it, I will – that you can be sure of. Whether it takes ten years, or twenty, or a hundred!' Gifford fixed his gaze unflinchingly towards the camera, but his eyes held a slightly distant look, as if they were focused on something beyond his audience's grasp. 'Which brings us all together now. More cancer specialists in one room than probably at any time before, all wondering what the future of cancer research might hold.'

As Gifford came to the meat of what his audience had been waiting for, a muted rustling ran through the auditorium: a slight shifting of nervous expectancy, or perhaps the medical journalists starting to take notes.

'. . . The first will be the Gifford Associate Researcher Award, given annually in the amount of three million dollars. To be adjusted for inflation every four years by a nominated accounting firm.' Gifford's eyes did a slow pan of the audience and his mouth curled into an enigmatic smile, clearly relishing these purposeful pauses, the thrall of expectancy in which he knew he held his audience at that moment. 'And the main prize, granted every four years, will be the Gifford Founding Researcher Award . . .' Another slight pause as he gently moistened his lips. 'In the amount of twelve million dollars – once again inflation adjusted every four years. I know . . . I know.' Gifford held up one hand, as if anticipating the hubbub that arose around the auditorium. 'But that's not all. In addition, the winner will also receive ongoing research funding of another one million dollars a year for the following seven years.'

The audience became more excitable, the clamour rising as the first ripples of applause broke out.

'Much larger than we expected,' Kalpenski commented.

'Yes, much larger,' Chisholm agreed. The medical community had speculated between three and six million dollars, but nothing on this scale.

But looking into Gifford's keen eyes on screen, now twinkling with a slight moistness as he kept the same hand raised in acknowledgement of the rising applause, a Pontiff calming his throng, Chisholm was sure that Gifford knew the game all too well: that at this level of cancer research, it was as much about big money and power-jostling as it was about bright, inventive minds. And that his money would be just the tip of the iceberg. Twenty times larger than any Nobel award, other investment funding would follow like mice to the piper, as would no doubt a flood of stock investments. The winner of the Gifford would sweep the board on all fronts, and the rest of the research establishment would be left swimming in its wake.

And Gifford had probably drawn a strange delight from all the wrangling that he knew would ensue, Chisholm surmised. Having spent the last nine years with his life in the hands of doctors and specialists probing and testing and pumping him with one drug after another while his body and self-esteem withered to a wrinkled shell, Gifford had no doubt relished that reversal of manipulation. Turning the tables on those who had the power over life or death by now making them dance to his tune: from now on, the future of every cancer researcher worth his salt rested in Gifford's hands. In death, he'd been able to do what he'd ultimately discovered he'd been unable to in life: play God.

'One thing's for sure,' Chisholm commented as he joined in with the applause of the auditorium audience, many of whom were now standing up. 'The future of cancer research is never going to be the same again.'

David Copell read the news about the Gifford Awards on page four of the *International Herald Tribune* as their cab headed into the city from Orly airport.

'Just the sort of funding boost we could do with for AIDS research,' he commented to André.

'Yes . . . yes, it is.' André was slightly lost in his own thoughts, staring blankly out of the side window as they turned off of the Périphérique.

'It made page seven in *Le Monde*,' David added, trying to spark some interest from André.

André glanced back briefly at the newspaper laid between them in the back of the taxi. 'Sorry . . . yes. I'll read it later. Lot on my mind right now. Already planning ahead so that everything runs smoothly when the mangabeys arrive, and I'm concerned also about how little Anouk might have fared with the long journey.'

'And about Eban?'

'Yes, that too. That too.' André went back to staring out through the taxi window, his expression taut. The lie that he'd told David just after signing off from Charlotte and hearing about Hervé's call: *'Eban's apparently not very well. Got a high fever. Hopefully it's just Charlotte panicking more than she should.'* He'd then excused himself, saying he had to go to the washroom for a moment, then made the return call to Hervé from a payphone as soon as he was out of sight of David.

David picked up *Le Monde* and studied the article again, his eyes rapidly scanning. 'Lot of column inches, at least.' Two years now he'd been in Paris from his native Baltimore with his wife, Pamela, and two children; his spoken French was passable, but he was still some way from being able to follow lengthy written passages.

André knew that even with the preoccupations he'd voiced to David, he still should have shown more interest in the article. It had been one of his pet beefs for so long: AIDS put way down the list when it came to research funding.

First there'd been the homophobes and moral purists who said that it only affected sexual deviants and drug addicts, so there wasn't much to worry about for 'normal' people; then came the religious zealots who claimed that it was a disease cast down from God to rid the earth of the sodomites and the impure. It wasn't until AIDS started to spread to the heterosexual community and college girls contracted it from visits to their dentist and infants from blood transfusions, that the public at large and politicians finally sat up and took notice and research funding was raised above its previous pathetic trickle.

Those sectors worst affected – the arts, fashion and music – had rallied round strongly, raising funds through benefit concerts and dinners and showing documentaries about how the disease had ravaged countless millions across Africa. But it was still a case of, 'It's over there – not here.' If people were dropping like flies in downtown Chicago, London or Paris, it might have been different. But as things stood, mainstream funding for AIDS research paled in comparison to cancer research, and now, with the Gifford Awards, that gap was even wider.

But it was difficult to focus on the broader picture when he was besieged by so many crises close to home: Eban, Charlotte, a famished infant mangabey called Anouk, and now Eric.

He'd planned to have an evening in with Eban and Veruschka and had promised to have Joël over too: a respite for Charlotte, plus she had some fashion dinner planned. A chance to hug them all and then a quiet moment alone with Eban, smiling encouragingly as he ruffled the boy's hair and told him that now, finally, there was some hope in sight. A successful gene-therapy treatment was still probably some six to eight months away – depending how their lab work went – but it was something at least to help ease the shadows from the boy's eyes.

'Please hurry! I've bandaged Eric as best I can – but he's lost a lot of blood. I don't know how much longer he can last.' The urgency of the words was bad enough, but it was the undertone in the voice and thinking about Hervé's usual nature that now sent a shiver of unease up his spine. Hervé was usually the calming voice of the family, the one to soothe and play down the panics and gloom.

André had protested that he wasn't that kind of doctor, and besides, from the sound of it, Eric urgently needed to be in a hospital, and Hervé had thrown at him Eric's fear that the police would have alerted hospitals because they knew he was injured. *'I argued exactly the same with him, but he said that he'd rather run the risk than face prison. You know what he's like – he can be very obstinate.'*

A horn blared ahead and their taxi lurched to a halt as it hit a tailback of cars on Avenue Wagram. André glanced at his watch.

'Six o'clock they said for the mangabeys arriving. I'll see how I go with Eban when I get him back to my place. But if he's as bad as Charlotte makes out and I can't get away later – can you sort everything out?' The second part of his cover-up lie: Eban being ill allowed him to steal some time away. 'Maybe get Marc or Marielle to go out there with you?'

'Sure, sure – no problem.'

'And if I can't make it, keep a special eye on Anouk for me, will you? If she still won't take food, perhaps put her on a drip back at the lab.'

'Yeah, will do.' David folded the two newspapers back on the seat between them. 'Maybe more glucose, too, as soon as she's out of the crate. We might be a while with Customs.'

André nodded and lightly clasped David's arm in thanks. He knew already that he wouldn't make it back in time. He'd pick up his car and head straight out to see Hervé and Eric in Nemours, the small town forty miles south of Paris where their mother still lived and Hervé had been priest for the last four years. The town where André had spent most of his childhood and which held so many memories; and now perhaps a few more dark memories to add to the pile, André thought.

He felt his hand start to tremble as he lifted it from David's arm. Despite having slept on the flight, he still felt tired, his nerves frayed. He wasn't sure he was ready to face whatever horrors awaited him at Nemours.

4

André followed the beam from Hervé's torch as Hervé led the way along the arched passage. The ceiling height at the apex was a good foot above their heads, but it tapered down quickly at each side with the curve of the arch.

As they'd headed down towards the passage, André had asked Hervé if going to these lengths wasn't a bit extreme, and Hervé had said that it wasn't so much keeping Eric hidden, it was the bloodstains. It had taken him over an hour to clean up everything upstairs from bandaging Eric in the kitchen.

'There's too many people calling in and out upstairs – the church caretaker, the cleaners. I was afraid they might see the bloodstains, become alerted. And if the police did call round at short notice, I just wouldn't have been able to clean up in time.'

Bloodstains. André could see the splatters at regular intervals in the stark torch beam as they made their way along. Despite Hervé's bandaging, Eric was obviously still losing blood heavily.

At the end of the passage, André could see a pile of discarded furniture with a glimpse of the church catacombs beyond above a large mahogany wardrobe. The passage ran under the small road separating the church from Hervé's house, the first in a row of village houses built at the same time as the church in the mid-1800s. It had always been the priest's house, the passage so that he could magically appear for services without having to mix with the congregation. But modern-day priesthood was very much hands-on and Hervé considered himself at the hub of community life in Nemours. He'd always felt at home there, probably why he'd finally asked for the transfer from Paris. Hervé never used the passage to get to the church and it had increasingly become a repository for discarded and broken furniture from the church and his house. They edged by a pew as Hervé shone the torch on a door to their left.

'I put him in here.'

Hervé swung the door open. A light was on inside the small room, no more than eleven foot square. Hervé kept his torch on to point the way, its beam flickering past some more broken pews and old chairs before coming to rest on Eric's legs dangling over the side of a desk, the rest of his body obscured by a tall grey metal cabinet. He was laid flat on his back, a heavy blood patch spreading across the desktop and running in tentacle strands down its side like some ghoulish scene from a medieval torture chamber.

Eric registered André's presence with a guttural groan and brief eye contact as André came in close and examined the bandaging on the left side of his abdomen. Then Eric's eyes drifted slightly away again.

'He's been in and out of consciousness practically since I picked him up,' Hervé said. 'But in the last few hours there's been hardly any lucid, conscious moments.'

André traced one finger lightly around the bandaged area. 'What did you clean the wound with, if anything?'

'Water, then brandy and some mercurochrome. But I had very little mercurochrome left.' Hervé pointed to an empty plastic bottle on the shelf behind.

'And to ease his pain, if anything?'

'More brandy.' Hervé smiled weakly. 'I had plenty of that – but I stopped after he'd had a tumblerful. I wasn't sure how it might react with whatever you wanted to give him.'

'When did he have that?'

'Two-thirds of a tumbler in the first hour or so of us getting here at four this morning. Then the last bit just a few hours ago.'

André went through the rest of his check-list – any other liquid taken? Any food? Time the accident happened? – as he took Eric's temperature and blood pressure, timed his pulse and checked his mouth and throat for signs of blood: 101.5. 86 over 49. Pulse weak. But at least it looked like there were no lung ruptures. André was sweating from the flurry of activity and mounting worry. Blood loss so heavy that operating without a transfusion would be an enormous risk, and acute dehydration. A saline drip would ease the dehydration, but would it also expand blood volume enough until he could get fresh blood? That had been one of his first main worries: Eric's blood type. He looked around the grimy cellar.

'We're going to have to move him back upstairs,' he said. 'I can turn your kitchen into a makeshift operating room. *Just*. But not here. I'm going to need fresh running water, boiling water and disinfectant. And electricity plugs and better light.'

'But what if somebody calls by and . . .' Hervé's objection trailed off as he met André's penetrating gaze. André had already moved around behind Eric and had his hands under his shoulders. 'I . . . I suppose if there's no other way.' Hervé took Eric's legs and they lifted.

André explained his worry about Eric's rare blood type – vel, only a 1 in 4,000 occurrence – as they took Eric upstairs, laid him flat on the kitchen table and André made preparations. 'I put a call out for some before I headed here. But it might be hard to find at such short notice.'

Hervé nodded as he helped André set up the drip; he recalled that Eric's blood type was rare. 'But I thought that when he had his appendix out – what, twelve years back now – they simply gave him O-type blood. That it was a sort of common denominator.'

'Yes, that's so. But that's exactly what has caused the problem now.' André attached the intravenous feed and started the drip. 'You can give universal O blood to a vel recipient only once. After that, antibodies develop and it can't be repeated: the only blood that will be accepted is the same type, vel. Let's see how they're going with tracking some down.' He peeled off his surgical gloves and took his mobile from his jacket slung over a chair-back. His speech rapidly became a series of sporadic, staccato confirmations. '*Oui*, Jacques. *Oui*. I see. When? Well, if that's the best that could be done. Thanks. Good work.' He rang off.

André looked anxiously at his watch. His contact at the blood bank that supplied ISG, who in turn were part of a network of blood banks around Paris, had struck gold on the fifth one phoned. But with the added time for the courier to get out to Nemours, they'd have to wait almost another hour for the vel to arrive.

Fifteen minutes was killed with André setting up a small unit to monitor Eric's pulse rate and blood pressure and to lay out his instruments. He turned to Hervé. 'You're going to have to help me. Be my assistant.'

Hervé looked uncertainly between the instruments and the monitor. 'I . . . I'm not sure how much use I'll –'

'It's either that or in a while you can do what you *are* more used to,' André cut in. 'Give our brother the last rites.' Seeing the crestfallen, hurt look on Hervé's face, André quickly added, 'Sorry, that was uncalled for. I'm annoyed with him, not you. Putting us through having to do this when he should be in a hospital.'

Whatever Eric's chances were, the long delay and operating under these circumstances severely reduced them. And once he removed Eric's bandages, he'd be confronted with the sort of hands-on cut-and-stitch work he hadn't done since medical school. All of it went against the grain of the perfectionism honed during his years in research: painstaking planning and getting the odds as high as possible in their favour, and still so often they faced failure. Yet this time failure didn't just mean heading back to the lab bench to re-work everything for a few more weeks or months, it meant his brother's life.

André felt the pressure of it weigh heavily on him. He fought to control the tremor in his hands as he gave Eric a local anaesthetic and then a general one of Ropivacaine, reducing dosage because of the brandy Eric had drunk. Then he waited for them to take effect. An anxious twenty minutes watching the monitors as Eric's breathing became even and shallow, with whatever small talk could be struck up between him and Hervé – how was Mother? How had his trip to Cameroon gone? – made all the more trivial by Eric clinging to life beside them.

André started unwrapping the bandages twenty minutes before the vel was due to arrive. Eric was still losing some blood despite the bandages, but he was unprepared for the copious fresh flow once they were removed – and a frantic couple of minutes ensued before he was able to see the rupture in the lining of Eric's spleen. In that position, André knew that it had to be either the liver or the spleen, but the blood loss was too heavy for it to be the liver. He'd have to be careful; one suture put in too strongly could pierce the spleen's membrane and septicaemia set in.

Staccato, urgent calls to Hervé for each fresh instrument required, not daring to look up for a second as he probed and stitched, the activity – their working so closely in harmony with what was at stake – strangely, uneasily, bonding them.

But without the proper vacuum-sucker to clean the constant flow of blood from the area, it was hard to see clearly. André put the third suture in place, but blood seepage still seemed as strong.

Sweat beads massed on his forehead and ran into one eye, blurring his vision, and for a moment he felt dizzy, as if he was falling again. Hervé dabbed at his brow with a cloth. They were closer than they had been for years – but then so often the best and worst had brought them together. *The worst.* André felt as if a heavy, cold cloak had suddenly been laid over his shoulders, a chill coursing through him as if in warning that this moment was somehow different, far darker than any that had brought them together before. When Eric's blood pressure dipped sharply to 43, the chill turned to an icy stab. He began to fear that he'd seriously miscalculated.

He looked anxiously at Hervé's kitchen clock: still ten minutes to the vel arriving, yet he needed to transfuse right now. Eric had lost far too much blood. A steady trickle ran over the side of the kitchen table and the tile floor was slippery and sticky with it beneath their feet. 41 . . . 40.

André shouted to Hervé to tighten the arterial clamp. But with the fourth suture in place and Eric's blood loss still heavy and his blood pressure dipping sharply again to 37 in only seconds, André felt the last hopes slipping away. They were rapidly losing Eric and there was little left he could do to save him.

★

'What time would that have been?'

Inspector Donnet hovered over the desk as his assistant, Lieutenant Martot, one of his team working the Rue Linoille burglary, took details over the phone. The second breakthrough they'd had in tracking down requests for vel type blood over the past fourteen hours. Martot had waved urgently towards Donnet as soon as he realized he'd hit gold.

'Six thirty-four this morning. Hôpital Ste-Anne, you say.' Martot repeated the highlights for Donnet's benefit as he took notes. 'Male, twenty-eight years old. A car accident. Are they sure about that?' Martot's raised eyebrow knitted into a slight frown as he scribbled another line. 'I see. Yes, right.'

'Were there any witnesses to the accident?' Donnet asked.

Martot put one hand over the mouthpiece as he looked up. 'They say the man was brought in by an emergency team who attended the accident and actually cut him free from his car. So it looks pretty conclusive.'

'Yes, it does. It does.' Donnet grimaced tautly. 'Thank them and keep trying.' He turned and headed back to his office. Strike two.

This was the seventh such robbery with a similar MO in the last two years since Donnet had transferred to the 14th Arrondissement: jewellery and portable antiques and art – anything that could be put easily in a knapsack – with a value in excess of 2 million francs; difficult to near-impossible access, alarms easily bypassed, no trace left of fingerprints or fibres.

The 14th Arrondissement saw scores of robberies annually owing to its residents' wealth and its historical cachet, but most fell well under the 500,000-franc mark. High-value robberies were thankfully rare. But because of the size of such robberies and because on occasion the victims were famous, they attracted a disproportionate degree of media and police attention. Only seven such robberies in two years, but that was seventy-five per cent more than the figure notched up by any other Paris arrondissement, and with each one Donnet had become increasingly determined to nail them. No forensic evidence whatsoever – until now.

The perpetrator had graciously left a few litres of his blood at the scene. Still he reminded himself not to get too excited: unless they hit gold with a DNA profile already on computer, they'd still need a suspect in hand to be able to run a match.

But with the news from forensics two hours ago, his hopes had swiftly risen: rare blood group with sufficient lost to warrant urgent transfusion. 'Not many requests for vel will have come in over the past twelve hours, and with any luck your man could be among the recipients. Unless it's a first transfusion, in which case O-type blood could be used.'

He'd put three of his team immediately on phone canvassing of city blood banks. Strike one had come in after only forty minutes: a woman in her late fifties with complications after a hysterectomy. Now strike two.

When strike three came in twenty minutes later – a medical lab, ISG, supplied to further their retro-virus and AIDS research – and the next hour passed with no fresh leads and there were only two blood banks left on their list to check, Donnet's hopes began to fade again.

It had obviously been the thief's first transfusion. They weren't going to strike lucky this time either.

The neon of city lights struck in more frequent bursts across Hervé's profile – turned intermittently towards André in the back seat hunched over Eric – as they hit the outskirts of Paris.

Hervé looked worn and harrowed. The eldest of the brothers by seven years and still handsome at fifty-one despite his fast-receding, greying hair, his energy and bright-eyed alertness made him seem ten years younger. His warm, deeply hooded brown eyes somehow made you feel you were the only focus in a room when they settled on you. André and Eric often teased that if it wasn't for his chosen vocation, he could have had a wild, debauched time in Nemours. They were sure that he got more than his fair share of female confessions just so that lonely widows – and a few married and not so lonely – could feel those eyes settle on them and melt with compassion at their stories.

But with the panic of Eric, André had seen the years piled

suddenly back on, the compassion in Hervé's eyes giving way to raw fear with each scream for a fresh instrument as the chances of saving Eric slipped rapidly away.

'Hurry, Hervé. Hurry! I don't know how much longer he'll hold out.' Again now, three hours later, he was back to shouting again, pleading for Eric's life.

'I know.' Hervé nodded solemnly as he picked up speed, his shoulders sagging slightly, as if he could hardly bear the weight of any more worries or years being piled back on.

They'd saved Eric with probably only minutes to spare, and André was all too keenly aware that it had been more by dint of good luck than planning: he'd managed finally to stem the blood flow and the courier with the vel had arrived five minutes earlier than anticipated. But he knew that hoping for a second break was pushing his luck.

Eric's colour worried André the most: a yellow-grey pallor to his skin that had set in over the last ten minutes. He was worried about septicaemia or kidney or liver failure, or internal bleeding, or any combination in between without the instruments to check. All he could do until he got Eric hooked up at the lab was to feel his pulse, check his blood pressure and pupil dilation.

He'd spent the last two hours juggling the desperate need to get Eric to the lab to check his condition more thoroughly with the necessity for some rest and stabilization before he could be moved. When his blood pressure finally levelled at 108 over 62 and his breathing and pulse were steadier, André decided to take the risk and move him. But just twenty minutes into the drive, his blood pressure and pulse weakened and the yellow-grey tinge came to his skin.

There was an awkwardness between himself and Hervé that went beyond the fact that Eric might be dying. André had always been close to Hervé, but their exchanges were invariably stilted, as if their absorption with their respective professions kept them from fully opening up. And while they both on occasion sermoned and tried to steer Eric from the life he'd chosen, Eric was the wild card, the spark of fun and life that gelled everything between them.

When Eric joined them, the smiles and laughter would start, the hand gestures and body language would become easier, the stories and reminiscences would flow. It was as if when Eric had chosen his path of crime, he'd lost all of his inhibitions and André and Hervé were still left with theirs.

Now the thought of losing him made them face the terrible void that would be left, all the fun and sparkle and unpredictability suddenly gone from their lives, and they'd be reminded of Eric's death each time they struggled to find that level of ease that would probably never be there again without him.

It had started drizzling and Hervé switched on the wipers. That impending void, that terrible sense of emptiness, settled heavier in André's stomach with each sweep of the wipers, with each beat of Eric's ever-weakening pulse, as Hervé sped through the Paris night. And now the worry on top that David Copell might still be at the lab when they got there.

André had phoned the lab just minutes after they'd left Nemours to make sure the coast was clear, the ringing tone falling almost in time with Eric's pulse held in his left hand; and he was about to hang up when on the fifth ring David answered. Anouk had taken a turn for the worse and so he'd decided to stay on. When they'd last spoken, shortly after Eric's operation, Anouk had taken some glucose and had perked up after her flight, so David had been planning to leave any minute.

'I was hoping she'd continue to improve, when suddenly she slipped back. Worse practically than when you last saw her at Douala airport.'

'But I'm leaving any minute.' André spoke as if he was still at home with Eban. 'Twenty minutes or so and I'll be there to take care of her. You should leave now, David. You sound tired. I'll take over.'

'I . . . I'd rather wait until you get here. I wouldn't like to leave her like this. She's back on the drip – doesn't look good.'

'Leave now, David. You've done enough. It's –' André checked his watch '– nearly midnight. You've been on your feet non-stop since sun-up after an eight-hour flight, and your wife hasn't seen you since you left over a week ago. She'll start to think you're married to that monkey, not her.'

'I know. But Delatois has apparently already leaked to the press about our little triumph. Probably hoping to steal a bit of glory from the Giffords hogging all the headlines. It wouldn't look good if one of the monkeys died.'

'Nothing's going to happen to her in the next twenty minutes. Even if you hung on and by some freak it did, it would look even worse coming on the end of you having had no sleep for twenty-four hours. Medical ethics would have a field day. I mean it. *Now*, David!'

'OK . . . OK. I hear you. I'll . . . I'll just run some checks on her one more time, then head off. But only twenty minutes, you're sure?'

'Yeah, yeah. Half hour, tops.'

But the hesitancy in David's voice as they signed off made André worry that he might still hang on until they got there. André looked up expectantly at the side of the ISG building as Hervé turned into Rue St-Jacques. But his angle of vision was quickly obscured by some trees – he wasn't able to see if there was a light on in their second-floor labs. Hervé swung into the barriered entrance and they were confronted by the guard, a smiling Moroccan named Ahmel who took his job seriously and scowled at anyone he didn't recognize.

Ahmel's scowl softened to bemusement at the sight of a priest, and André quickly wound down the back window and held out his pass. Ahmel squinted more at André than the pass for recognition – André thought for one horrible moment he was focusing past his shoulder to Eric prone in the back seat – then Ahmel's trademark smile quickly rose with the faint glint of a single gold tooth and he lifted the barrier and waved them through.

André eased out a slow breath, but as they pulled clear of the gatehouse he could see a light on at the back on the second floor. His heart sank.

'He's still there.' He sighed heavily. 'I just need a couple of minutes to get rid of him.' But looking back at Eric as he got out of the car, he wondered if he could spare even that long.

★

Claude Donnet sat in his favourite café on Rue des Carmes and sipped at a large café au lait with cognac chaser.

Approaching midnight, but it was still busy, mostly with students from the nearby Sorbonne. Lectures had finished long ago, but the fact that it was a popular daytime meeting place for them seemed to carry through to the evening.

Donnet wasn't sure if he liked it for its changing throng of young, pretty girls, or because it was a reminder of his own, happier student days fifteen years ago. Or, with their final lead on vel recipients crashing almost four hours ago, because right now he craved being surrounded by brighter minds.

The vacant looks, head-scratching and, 'Merci néanmoins', each time the phone was put down on yet another non-starter lead had begun to wear on his nerves.

When the last Paris-based vel recipient had come in as a fifty-six-year-old heart bypass patient, they'd spread the net in desperation to Rouen: there, only one person had been supplied with vel in the last twenty-four hours, a seven-year-old girl.

Donnet flicked out wide his copy of Le Soir in disgust. He'd already scanned the headlines, but the only item he'd read in any detail inside was the report on the robbery, tucked away at the bottom of page fourteen.

He browsed and read at random, sipping at his coffee and cognac as he went, glancing up only occasionally at nearby activity or when a fresh group walked in.

He read the article at the bottom of page five mechanically at first, without much of it really registering, about a doctor returning from Cameroon with some monkeys that were one of the key links in the fight against AIDS: the 'Darwin man', as he was becoming known. The article had caught Donnet's eye purely because most of the AIDS and cancer research institutes were only a block away, wedged between the Luxembourg Gardens and the Sorbonne, and came under his precinct.

He moved quickly on, was halfway through reading an article about an Iranian ex-cabinet minister shot dead at his Créteil apartment, when he was suddenly drawn back to the AIDS article.

Institut de St Germain? That was one of the names that had come up in their vel enquiries. Supplies for research?

Donnet started to wonder about the coincidence of the timing. And why only vel on its own? Probably they had ample supplies of more common blood groups – but if they were running tests on rare blood groups, why not a few more at the same time? There surely must be other blood groups as rare as vel.

He looked back at the name: Lemoine. André Lemoine? Something about it struck a chord, but he couldn't pinpoint why. Perhaps he'd seen it in earlier articles.

He hastily knocked back the rest of his coffee, paid, and as soon as he was back in the squad room he asked Martot to phone the blood bank that had supplied the ISG and find out if they'd supplied other blood types to them recently, particularly rare ones.

The last delivery had been two weeks ago for types O and AB. Then ten days before that for types B and A negative. The last rare blood types delivered had been six weeks ago.

Prompted by Donnet, Martot asked, 'Are there many rare blood types? As rare, for example, as vel?'

'Yes. A dozen or more. Some are far rarer, such as Pk – one in a hundred thousand occurrence rather than just one in four thousand.'

Martot thanked him, but just as he was about to sign off – prompted no doubt by Martot fishing for irregularities – the man added, 'Oh, there was one other thing that was unusual this time. We were asked to deliver to an address out in Nemours rather than to the ISG laboratories directly.'

'Really?' Martot raised an eyebrow up at Donnet as he started making notes. 'And which one of the doctors there made this request?'

As Martot mumbled it out loud as he wrote, Donnet suddenly remembered where he'd come across the name Lemoine before. He held one hand up towards Martot and headed towards his computer to check.

5

Julius Chisholm scrolled down through the information on his computer screen as he talked on the phone.

'Interesting reading, interesting reading.' A hushed, slightly breathless timbre, as if he was worried his secretary and the other Spheros staff beyond his closed office door might hear.

At the other end of the line was Frank Ralston, the private detective he'd contacted to dig into Danielle Stolk's background. Ralston had e-mailed through his report just twenty minutes ago with a note that Chisholm should phone if he had any questions.

'And so that's how she ended up with the house?' Chisholm confirmed.

'Yeah. Her ex's old man had a tiling supply company. Did a lot of cash business with builders. So he made a private mortgage with his son. And because it was his son and he was hiding from the tax man, there was little or no paperwork. All she had to do was deny the existence of the private mortgage and she was home and dry.'

'Right.' That had been Chisholm's first puzzler: how a divorcee single mum, on a meagre intern's salary at the time, could afford a house in Chestnut Hill, one of Philadelphia's most exclusive residential areas. Only in the last two years had Stolk's salary dramatically risen. 'You say that she claimed the original house was a "wedding gift".'

'That's right. Her husband and family said that only the deposit was a wedding gift and the rest was on private mortgage. She claimed that it was the whole thing. With no paperwork to support their mortgage claim, she won the day. The house, a seven-bedroom pile in Chestnut Hill, was sold, she grabbed a bit more from her ex's earnings due to what she claimed she lost in their six years of marriage by giving up her career in medicine – and so she managed to keep a toe-hold in the same area. Four bedrooms, no mortgage.'

With the financial strain, her ex had to move to Lexington. Cute, huh?'

'You could say, I suppose,' Chisholm agreed begrudgingly. Wily, cunning, Machiavellian, perhaps. 'Cute' wasn't in Chisholm's dictionary.

'She was generous though with his visitation rights with their daughter, who was only four at the time. She let him have her every weekend and one week-night every week, then just a year later she let him have custody and that situation was reversed. She used that as a boast with friends as to how good she was to him over the divorce – but it looks like that was all part of her plan from the outset. She'd already set her cap on going back into medical research, so that arrangement suited her down to the ground. She's a dab hand at making out she's goody two-shoes with no end of favours done for others – but let me tell you, this girl don't do nothing unless it suits her own ends.'

'When's the court case with her mother?'

'They haven't fixed a date yet. Could still be anything from four to eight months away, especially with your girl's lawyers delaying at every turn.'

Chisholm's attention had first been drawn to Danielle Stolk by her rapid rise up the research rungs. From a Grade 1 assistant to Associate Researcher in only four years. There had been a couple of departmental complaints about her being overtly ambitious, 'not a team player', but he and Kalpenski had put that down mostly to peer jealousy due to her fast rise. But Chisholm had decided to dig deeper on departmental scuttlebutt. 'She's aggressively ambitious in her home life too; how do you think she ended up with a house in Chestnut Hill? She's trying to make up for the years she felt she lost in research while married. She blames her husband for that, so it's an anti-man thing too.' It was true that Stolk's rivals in Kalpenski's section were mostly male, so Chisholm had to carefully assess the comments, make sure they weren't just inspired by male ego-denting because a woman was grabbing the limelight. Then Chisholm heard about Stolk's court case with her mother, but he had no idea that such a momentous iceberg labelled Ambition and Greed lurked beneath.

'You know, this thing with her mother.' Ralston paused and swallowed, as if he'd suddenly encountered a bad taste or was having trouble wrapping his tongue around the words. 'In my business, I come across some pretty low types. Guys who'd waste you without losing a night's sleep, would suck your eyeball for a grape while your body's still warm. But as rotten to the core as they might be, when it comes to their own families, nobody could be more protective. Would lay down their lives and all that shit.' Ralston swallowed again. 'What I'm trying to say is, well . . . with the husband is one thing. Greedy divorcees are almost par for the course these days. But pulling something like this with your own mother takes some doing. A heart of stone for starters.'

'I know. I know. Bad business all round. Where's the mother living now?'

'In some nursing home out in Byberry. Word is that's why dear Dani's lawyers are throwing in every possible delay: they're hoping the old girl dies meanwhile and then there's no case.'

'Bad business,' Chisholm repeated, easing out his breath as he leant back in his swivel chair. Ahead through his office window, the Schuylkill River was a silver snail's trail through the early morning September light, and beyond that the old spires and campus playing fields of University City; behind him, the Penn Center and hustle-bustle of Philadelphia's downtown. The position mirrored how the Spheros Institute corporately saw itself: ideally placed between academia and commerce. But Chisholm knew from long and bitter experience that a privileged position was by no means a continuing birthright, as some of the Spheros's older, more staid board members might wish to ignore. And now with the Gifford Awards, there was more change in store than they could ever imagine. Someone had to draw up advance battle plans. 'Let me know when you find out the court date.'

'Yeah, sure.' A heavy pause from Ralston's end, another swallow. Something else was on his mind. Finally: 'Is that why you asked me to check on her, Doc? She's due for promotion or something and this case with her mother could look bad? You know – the need for good ethics being what they are in your profession.'

'Yes, well, that's pretty much it. But as you can appreciate, I can't say too much.'

'Yeah, I understand.'

Chisholm couldn't resist smiling as he hung up. Exactly the opposite: that volatile mix of relentless ambition and lack of ethics was, in fact, what made Stolk the ideal candidate for what he wanted. *Heart of stone.* She was looking better by the day. A couple more simple tests and he'd know for sure.

'You should leave now, David.'

'Just a quick look-see at this last saliva swab, then I'm gone.'

'And what happened with Michel?' André asked. Michel was the ISG vet who'd been tending to the mangabeys in the animal house. Now, through the adjoining glass screen André could see Anouk in the Laferge section where they normally monitored patients on clinical trial.

'He'd already left when Anouk took a turn for the worse,' David said without looking up.

'But I'm here now. *I* can do that,' André protested. He tried to keep the edge and panic from his voice, but David's look as he finally glanced up from the microscope was slightly withering. He was starting to suspect something was wrong.

'Look – I waited on to do this until you arrived, because I didn't want to leave her alone. Not even for a minute. You can see how bad she is. And you can't do both: see to her *and* run tests. I'll only be a few minutes.' David went back to looking through the microscope.

A few minutes? Eric was fast slipping away as they spoke. André could feel himself still trembling from the breakneck drive to the lab. He glanced out the window towards the car, but from that angle it was shielded by the conservatory at the lab's entrance. A soft rain trickled down its roof, the palms beneath slightly obscured by mist and condensation on the glass.

44

Suddenly he was back in the jungle again, trembling as he gripped tight to the branch, the snake probing the air with its tongue, sensing his fear.

'Are you OK?' David raised a quizzical eyebrow as he glanced up at him. 'Got a girl outside you're trying to sneak in? Or are you running secret tests here I don't know about?' David's mouth curled slightly in a smile, but his attention was fixed back quickly on the microscope; he didn't look up for André's reaction.

'I . . . I'm just concerned about you. You haven't had a break since we got back.' He glanced agitatedly between the window and David, grasping for inspiration as to how to get rid of him quickly.

'Damn. I can see some sickle cells.' David was hardly listening, was wrapped up in the cocooned world of what he saw through his microscope. 'I'd better add some albumin, see how it reacts. Maybe take another mouth swab.'

'No, *no* . . . I . . .' André reached a hand out. The edge to his voice subsided quickly into panic.

'What?' David looked at him curiously as he opened the cabinet for the albumin.

André kept the same hand held out, a pleading gesture, his lips sticking and trapping any words, even if he could have thought of something worthwhile. At this rate, David was going to be at least ten minutes. He just couldn't afford to leave Eric for that time. And with Anouk in such a bad way, how was he going to cope with both? If Anouk died while in his care, he could hardly tell David in the morning, *'Oh, that was because of a little emergency I had with Eric that I couldn't tell you about.'*

Finally, as all other options slipped away, he let down the arm with a deflated sigh. 'There's something I haven't told you. It's Eric . . . he's had a bad accident.'

For the first minute of explaining, André found it hard to meet David's penetrating, incredulous gaze, his eyes shifting between the bench where David had been working and the window. He didn't mention the robbery, just said that he'd had a bad fall. It was bad enough that he had to involve David, so he wanted to limit any possible complicity.

45

'I saw to him as best I could, then headed here. Eban's OK. I just needed some time to sort out this problem with Eric and –'

David held one hand up at that point, cutting in; a strained, almost disbelieving tone as he confirmed that Eric was here with him now. And with André's mute nod, his eyes finally lifting to meet David's, they were suddenly galvanized into action, rushing down to get Eric from the car.

Claude Donnet breathed deeply of the night air at Nemours as the church warden hustled towards him from his house four doors along, shrugging the last shoulder into his jacket as he went. A burly man in his early sixties with thinning hair and bushy grey eyebrows, the warden held a bunch of keys in his right hand. He fished one to the front as he came close.

'I hope he's OK.' The eyebrows knitted in concentration as he inserted the key and turned.

'Let's hope so.'

Donnet kept close in the warden's shadow as he entered Hervé Lemoine's house with Martot and his other assistant, Perlaud, who'd alerted the warden, following.

It had taken him only minutes on the computer, scrolling through old case files, to discover why the name Lemoine rang a bell: Eric Lemoine, a key suspect investigated two years ago for a similar robbery, the name supplied by a fence facing charges and trying to do a deal. But in the end they didn't have sufficient evidence to charge Lemoine, the case file didn't even make it to an examining magistrate's desk.

They'd originally rung Lemoine's door four times with no answer. A curtain had parted at a window across the road and an old woman peered out, alerted no doubt by their flashing car beacon. She came out and told them about the warden four doors along. Martot had meanwhile been looking through a gap in the net curtains of Lemoine's house, and while he could pick out some spots and smears on the kitchen floor, it was difficult to tell for sure if it was blood with what little street light filtered in through the kitchen window.

But they used that to effect when alerting the warden, saying they had concerns about Hervé Lemoine's safety. If Donnet had spilt the full story, the warden might have balked at letting them in, and Donnet didn't want to lose time with having to get a warrant.

As the warden flicked on the kitchen light, Donnet could clearly see bloodstains in its stark glare. Somebody had made an attempt to clean up, but it was hasty: watery smears of blood could still be made out on the tile floor with a few spots around the edges that they'd missed. Two or three of the most prominent spots were only a few feet to the right of where they entered.

Donnet took a step back and peered down the hallway. He thought he could see a couple more spots a few yards down where a patterned carpet took over after the tiled entrance hall. It was hard to pick up the bloodstains among the carpet's pattern, and Donnet had to stoop over slightly as he examined. As he picked out the first spots, he saw what he thought were two more a couple of feet away, then another. He followed their trail.

They led him towards a small door to the right at the end of the corridor, then down some rough stone steps to the cellar. The bloodstains were easier to pick out on the steps, and easier still on the pale flagstone floor of the arched cellar that stretched for twelve yards before a jumble of furniture at its end.

Donnet led the way with his two assistants and the warden following, their footsteps echoing ominously against the stone walls. The blood spots were heavier and more frequent as they led towards a half-open door to their left.

'*Mon Dieu*,' the warden said in a hushed breath. 'He's been butchered. Look at all this.'

'We don't know that yet. It was in fact a problem with his brother that brought us here. Then we started to become concerned about Hervé Lemoine as well.' Donnet thought that he'd better sow the seeds; he didn't want it later argued that he'd gained evidence through obtaining false entry.

As Donnet swung the door to the small room wide open and flicked on the light, the full horror of what had taken place there hit them: a large blood patch almost completely covering a waist-high table, strands of blood running off of its side to a heavy gout on the floor, then a trail of large blood spots between the door and the table.

'*Mon Dieu*,' the warden said again, breathless with shock.

No attempt had been made to clear up here, thought Donnet. Either they'd left in a rush or were only worried about cleaning up where callers-by to the house might see.

He instructed Martot to takes some samples from the closest bloodstains. 'Keep to the outer edge. Avoid stepping near the heavier stains and the table.'

He could make out two or three footprints in the blood from which they could hopefully get a clean lift. He took out his mobile and headed upstairs to call forensics. He needed some fresh air, plus he wasn't sure he'd get a reception from the cellar.

Forensics said they'd send someone within ten minutes. The dead of night, 1.14 a.m., the journey shouldn't take them more than half an hour.

Donnet tucked his mobile back in his jacket and looked over to the old woman still by their squad car. She'd stayed there looking on at the house.

He eased out a tired breath, winding down from the scene inside, and asked her, 'Did you see anyone turn up earlier? Two or three hours ago, maybe more?'

'No, I didn't see anyone arrive. But when I looked out later, I noticed a car outside I recognized. Green Peugeot, his brother's, the doctor.' The old lady held Donnet's expectant gaze for a second. 'And I saw them leave.'

Donnet nodded keenly. 'I see. Did you notice someone else with them when they left, or anything unusual?'

'I could only see the two of them. The car doors closing is what alerted me. By the time I looked out they were already in the car. And nothing unusual, except . . .' She looked aslant at the police car for a second, as if prompting herself as to what she'd seen. 'I . . . I noticed that the brother was leaning over, seemed preoccupied with something alongside him in the back seat.'

'And which way did they go?'

The old lady pointed towards the main road junction fifty yards away.

Didn't really tell Donnet much. Right headed towards the town centre, left towards the A6 to Paris and all points south. They could have gone anywhere. Donnet inhaled deeply of the night air, smelling fresh grass and pine trees and a damp-leaf bonfire burning near by – the sort of smells you didn't get in central Paris – overlaying the petrol and diesel fumes from the nearby A-road. Nemours was one of those small Paris satellite towns that few people stopped at; little more than a roadside sign that they sped past en route to somewhere else.

'They could have headed to their mother's, I suppose,' she added after a moment, joining Donnet in looking thoughtfully towards the junction. 'She lives on the north edge of town. Or she might at least have more idea where they've gone.'

They worked as a team.

Eric's pulse was weak and his blood pressure dangerously low by the time they got him hooked up, and a quick scan showed heavy internal bleeding.

André opened him up immediately and saw that he hadn't managed to completely seal the wound on the spleen with sutures – the difficulty of trying to operate clearly with only swabs to clean up. With the air-sucker on and following as he went, he was able to make sure it was fully sealed this time.

'86 over 48,' David Copell called out.

André dabbed at his brow with the back of one hand as he looked up at the clock: systolic rate up four points since the last call two minutes before. The first sign of hope since they'd lifted Eric in, but still some way to go before they could start hoping that he might be stable long term.

Hervé meanwhile took care of Anouk and tried unsuccessfully to get her to take some glucose through a pipette. There was a moment when she perked up and looked like she might take some, her eyes brightening as they fixed keenly on his face and she reached one hand out limply towards his chin. But then she quickly slipped back into her previous dull-eyed stupor and the hand fell away, as if she didn't have the strength to hold it there.

When David had finished assisting André and it looked like Eric was out of immediate danger, he took over from Hervé, put Anouk on a saline drip and continued with his mouth-swab analysis.

For the first time in the nightmare night, André felt his tightrope nerves ease a fraction. David had been right, he'd never have been able to manage with just himself and Hervé. They'd have lost Eric or Anouk, or both. But it could take another two hours for Eric to stabilize; he was uneasy about keeping Eric at the lab for that length of time.

Eighteen minutes into eagle-eyeing Eric's progress, André's mobile started ringing in his jacket slung over a nearby workbench. He removed it from his jacket pocket: his mother's number in Nemours. If it had been Charlotte, he probably wouldn't have bothered to answer. Countless times she'd called him in the dead of night with some panic that had ended up as nothing. But his mother had never called him at such a late hour. Something was wrong.

He answered and felt his whole body go rigid as she told him breathlessly about the police calling on her, having just visited Hervé's house.

'What's happening, André? What's going on?'

'When did the police leave your place?'

'*What?* Uh . . . about five or six minutes ago. They were looking for Eric and said that they had reason to believe he might have been injured. *Please* . . . what's going on, André?'

André exhaled heavily. 'Yes, it is Eric. He has been injured – but he's OK now.'

'Are you sure he's OK?' Again that breathless timbre. She was heavy with doubt, wanting desperately to believe him.

'Yes, yes, I'm sure, *Maman*. You can rest easy. He's out of danger now.'

'But what about the police? Why are they looking for him?'

'It's a long story. I don't have time now to explain.' André's mind was reeling: five or six minutes? It would take them half an hour or more to get back from Nemours, but if they decided to radio through to a local precinct, they could have a squad car there any minute. How had they tracked them so quickly? 'I'll phone you tomorrow and tell you everything.'

'But, André . . . I don't understand, why –'

'Tomorrow, *Maman. Please*, tomorrow!' His voice was raised, almost shouting as the wave of panic washed fully through him. He hung up abruptly and turned to David. 'We've got to get out of here. Now!'

'What is it you haven't told me, André?'

'I'm sorry, I don't have time to explain now . . . *later.*'

'That's a lot of explaining that you're going to have to do later or tomorrow.' David looked at André levelly, his anger transparent. 'I'd like to know now.'

André shook his head. 'I can't . . .' He glanced anxiously towards the window. No fresh cars yet at the guard barrier, but it probably wouldn't be long. 'Then you'd be implicated. That's why I wanted to get rid of you earlier. Eric is in trouble . . . shouldn't be here.'

David turned to Hervé. 'Can *you* tell me?'

'I'm sorry. Priest's discretion and all that.' Hervé forced an awkward smile. Being cutely obstructive didn't come naturally to him and his face reddened with the effort.

David looked back at André. 'So the police are looking for Eric?' *Police.* The main word to have alarmed him from André's conversation with his mother.

'Yes . . . yes.' André let the air from his body like a deflating tyre, and felt the last strand of futility of trying to argue the toss with David go with it. 'So now you know why I shouldn't have brought him here, and why I didn't mention that. I don't mind putting my own neck on the line for him – he's my brother. But not yours as well. So nobody ever told you about him being sought by the police. You didn't know that. *Right?*'

David blinked slowly as he assimilated it all, then finally shook his head. 'We can't move him in this condition.'

'We've moved him here, and he's far more stable now. And

51

we've got the gurney and attachments for blood pressure and respiration and . . .' As he watched David start shaking his head again, heavy with misgivings, he moved a step closer and gripped David's arm tight. 'This isn't just anyone, David – it's my brother. So I'd be the last to want to risk his life. But I probably alerted the police myself through my request for his blood.' He wasn't completely sure of that, it could have just been through a Usual Suspects check. But now that the police had been to Nemours and seen the blood at Hervé's house, they must be close to piecing it all together. 'So how do you think he's going to feel waking up to find the police standing over him, knowing that he's facing ten years. He'd probably say that he wished I'd let him die.'

David's eyes shifted uneasily between Eric, Hervé and Anouk.

André pressed: 'All you have to do is help us down with Eric, then you can return to take care of Anouk.'

Finally, David closed his eyes for a second in defeated acceptance and nodded. 'OK. OK.'

André looked anxiously towards the window again as he heard a sound outside; a car had pulled up to the entrance barrier. But after a second he recognized it as Burquold's, one of the lab assistants, probably on graveyard shift this week. Burquold worked in section 4 by the library; he wouldn't be coming their way.

'All clear now,' André said with urgency. 'Let's go!'

It took them only four minutes to get Eric attached and on the gurney, and in that time André checked the window again almost a dozen times – still no worrisome cars approaching. Then they set off along the length of the lab and the corridor towards the lift, and André wouldn't have sight of the entrance for a short while. As they started almost running along, breathless, adrenalin pumping, André felt all the madness and rush of the past forty-eight hours pile back in on him – racing through the Cameroon jungle, Anouk shrieking in his dream as their flight hit the storm, driving like a madman out to Nemours, battling to save Eric's life – 'I'm not that kind of doctor . . .'

And as they hit the ground-floor corridor that led to the conservatory entrance, a fluorescent light that was having trouble firing-up pumped the images in flicker-form through his mind – the jungle lightning and the snake in the tree, flashes of sunlight through the jungle foliage on the drive to Douala, following the trail of Eric's blood spots along the torch-lit cellar, the intermittent strobe of orange streetlights hitting Eric's body as Hervé sped through the Paris night – but as they came to the end of the corridor, André was disorientated.

The fluorescent light was fully on, had stopped faltering, and André shook his head to clear the last flickering images from his mind; but still there remained a stark flashing light, spreading across the conservatory roof, opaque and distorted with the condensation on the glass.

André couldn't see the police car for the mass of plants and the misted glass, but he knew already that it must be at the gate barrier from its flashing blue light.

6

The first bomb went off at GETOPE, a genetic research laboratory four miles outside of Phoenix, Arizona.

No casualties. Nobody in fact was inside the building when the bomb went off at 2.17 a.m., except for two security guards by the ground-floor entrance. But there was considerable property and collateral damage: the bomb almost completely gutted the third floor, where most of the more sensitive, cutting-edge research work took place.

At first, the Phoenix District police thought it might have been purely an accidental blast from a faulty Bunsen burner gas tap, but when the forensics report came in ten days later, they knew that a bomb had been planted. This caused a renewed flurry of activity with the police, some fresh page 4 and 5 stories in the local press and some minor sidebars in medical journals, but it never made the major or national newspapers; and with no casualties and no leads, the case quickly lost steam with the Phoenix police and was all but forgotten within a month.

'*Ça va*, Monsieur Lemoine? Not a bad day, no?'

'*Ça va*, Madame Chercule.' André glanced up at the sky as he unchained his bike. The morning air was cool, but it was dry and bright, few clouds. '*Oui.* Looks good . . . looks good.'

Madame Chercule. Touching seventy, in a floral print dress as bright and confused as the array of plants and flowers in pots and tubs she was busily watering, she was the only other person to have used her courtyard space as a small garden. Everyone else in their small block wrapped around the courtyard had used their space for parking, and the two of them called their greetings over the tops of a Citroën ZX and a BMW 5-series parked in-between their last bastions of greenery amongst the cobblestones, cement and shining metal.

The estate agent had pushed it as a plus point when André had first viewed the apartment: being on the ground floor, he could actually park right in front and keep an eye on his car. He could think of nothing worse than the flat's main aspect being taken up by a trophy BMW or Mercedes, as most of the building had chosen to do. It was less than three kilometres to work, so he'd bought a ten-speed bike and found a discreet corner of the wall to chain it to, parked his eight-year-old Peugeot on the street outside, marked the perimeter of his parking oblong with potted palms and dwarf conifers, and put a table, umbrella and four chairs at its centre. Practically the only work he'd had done upon moving in, but it had been important for the kids: their own little oasis from the rush of the surrounding city, rather than them just looking on to a car park.

'Children with you this week?' Madame Chercule commented as she watched the three of them come out, Veruschka leading the way.

'Yes, most of it.' He didn't feel inclined to explain the usual roster and the fact that for the last two weeks he'd had the children an extra day because the problems with Eric and the police had thrown Charlotte into another mini-breakdown. Once again she'd stolen the dramatic spotlight, completely missing or ignoring the point that, given that it was his brother, perhaps his grievance should have come first.

'Oh, I forgot my L'Oncle Hansi book,' Joël called out, turning back inside.

'Come on, come on!' Veruschka perched one hand on her hip, staring testily at his departing back. 'Always the same. You're always forgetting something.'

Eban just smiled and sniggered, looking down at his feet.

The only time that Veruschka came close to acting adult was when she was given charge of them. Her little bit of power and control in life, her chance to treat them like she felt her parents treated her, payback, and sometimes she overdid it; though more with Joël than Eban. Perhaps because with Eban she felt she only had half the right.

André joined Eban in smiling and shook his head as he wheeled his bike towards the courtyard door and waved a hand in the general direction of everyone behind him. ''Bye.'

Joël and Eban got on famously, like two long-lost friends, hardly a bad word between them in the two years since Eban had become part of their family. For most of the first year Joël had been in awe as he asked questions about Africa and Eban told him about his life there, his hands wide as he described the size of the fish at market, the monkeys and antelopes, snakes and crocodiles, a rhinoceros he'd once seen. The arms grew wider apart with each story and Joël's eyes would widen too, mesmerized by a dark and mysterious Africa that he'd seen only in books and nature documentaries.

But the Africa Eban described was a far cry from the failed crops and starving, disease-decimated villages that had been Eban's last years in Rwanda. Probably he couldn't bring himself to talk about that which had robbed him of most of his family. And so only a glamorous, story-book Africa remained in his mind. The wild wonder and happier days he recalled from his early childhood.

Eban had seemed better, perkier, the past few days, but that's how it went with him: a few good days, sometimes a week or more, then a few bad ones. But it was the regimen of drugs that he had to take that made him weak and feel ill as much as his T4 cell count dropping.

As André got on his bike and started off, he heard the rapid foot-patter of the children the other side of the courtyard door. They always left at more or less the same time. He'd cycle the 2.8 kms, most of it along Boulevard du Montparnasse, the children would catch the 35 bus which followed the same route and take seats at its back and, as it passed André, Eban and Joël would wave at him excitedly through its back window. Veruschka would wave more calmly: it wasn't cool to be seen as so gleeful and enthusiastic when you were fourteen.

Veruschka would see that Eban and Joël got safely off the bus halfway along Rue Guynemer, then she'd continue on the same bus to her school in Rambuteau.

Routine. The same routine every morning.

Joël and Eban's journey was easier when they stayed with Charlotte, less than a kilometre in the opposite direction in St-Michel. André would have stayed in the same area, but the only way he'd been able to afford three bedrooms for the kids had been to move further out to the Gare Montparnasse area.

André clicked up to sixth gear as he started to hit his stride along Boulevard du Montparnasse. But it was a pleasant enough journey, the wide avenue still dotted with cafés from its more bohemian past. Behind him was the restaurant where George Orwell used to wash dishes, ahead the café where Hemingway had done much of his writing overlooking the Luxembourg Gardens, where, in turn, Jean-Paul Sartre had played as a child – presumably not all at the same time.

André glanced over his shoulder. He couldn't see their bus yet, obviously it was running late this morning. He checked his watch: 8.42 a.m.

David had reminded him to get in on time. After two weeks of deliberation, Delatois had finally called a meeting to discuss their fateful night with Eric at the ISG. Two weeks? What had he been waiting for? Time for more details to filter through from the police? Or to see how those details might fit in with his and David's account? Or, more likely, as David had suggested, time to see if their research with the silver-tailed mangabeys was shaping up as hoped. Delatois wouldn't want to make a rash move with two researchers on the verge of the most significant breakthrough the ISG had seen in years.

André grimaced as he rose up from the saddle, levering more impetus into his pedalling. Then, as he heard the familiar whoosh of the 35 bus, he eased a ready smile as he watched it go by.

Through the back window, Joël and Eban waved enthusiastically and Veruschka followed suit more tamely.

Routine. The one thing left that helped push away how much the rest of his life – his adopted son dying, his wife teetering on the edge of madness, and now his brother facing prison – was falling apart.

★

'And you say that you didn't know that your brother was being pursued by the police until he was already here?'

'Yes. I didn't know until my mother phoned,' said André, 'and she told me that the police had called on her.'

Delatois turned to David Copell. 'And I suppose that was the first moment that you knew also?'

'Yes, yes . . . that's right,' David said hastily, nodding.

Delatois had already asked a half-dozen questions, but this was obviously the key point and also the one that he was most unsettled about. The rest had been just setting the scene: What time did you arrive? Where did you first treat your brother before bringing him here? Who first alerted you to his injuries? And David Copell was already in the lab, you'd spoken to him earlier on the phone?

Eugène Delatois was a tall man, six-foot-three plus, the antithesis of his two small, mousier and timid Chef du bureau predecessors. The only touch of timidity was in his movements: slow, deliberate arm actions as he articulated questions and then made a note of their answers, as if he'd long become used to slow movement because of his size, so as not to trip up over obstacles or bash his head on a low beam he hadn't at first seen, or startle anyone with a sudden gesticulation. His size and his slightly bulbous, penetrating blue eyes were intimidation enough.

Eugène Delatois didn't look settled with what they'd told him, as if he didn't quite believe them.

His assistant, Pierre Salquiere – who could continue the tradition of the smaller, mousier and bifocalled when Delatois retired – was at his side and made few notes, while the third in the line across the conference table facing André and David, Jacqueline Roest, Delatois' PA, made notes constantly. It was difficult to tell what Salquiere was thinking owing to the thickness of his glasses, and Roest hardly ever looked up from her notepad.

Delatois' eyes were cold, cod-like, and stared straight through them, also giving little away. Within minutes of being in the room answering questions, André felt his pulse beating rapidly at the back of his very dry throat.

'And so you gleaned most of what was in fact the real situation from this short conversation with your mother?' Delatois said.

'No. She just mentioned the police, then my other brother Hervé filled in the rest of the details.'

'The priest?' At André's nod, Delatois looked down briefly at his notes. 'The same one who first alerted you to your younger brother's injuries?' Another nod and 'yes' from André and Delatois took a fresh breath. 'And what reasons did he initially give for those injuries?'

'He said he'd been the victim of a hit-and-run driver.'

'He didn't see the car, get a number?'

'No. He said that he'd blacked out immediately he was hit, didn't come to until minutes later.'

'And why not take him to a hospital?'

'Hervé said that Eric asked not to be taken to hospital, he has a fear of them – and this much I can vouch for as true – from a small operation that went wrong years ago. He asked specifically that I tend to him.'

Delatois flicked back a page in his notes, checking something. 'Now, when you'd spoken to your mother and your brother filled in the details, is that why you suddenly tried to rush away? To get away from the police because you knew they were coming?'

'No. It was because I suddenly realized, given the circumstances, that I should never have brought Eric here in the first place.'

'I see.' Delatois looked at David. 'And why were you still here so late? It all seems a bit convenient, pre-arranged.'

David shook his head. 'It was because of a problem with one of the mangabeys from Cameroon. We couldn't get her to take any food and she'd become quite ill.'

'No other reason? No call from Dr Lemoine to say that he needed help?'

'No. When he called me earlier to say he was on his way in, I was already here.' David knew – one of the first potential obstacles he and André had tussled with – that the police had a record of all their phone calls made; on this one point, though, it could actually work in their favour.

59

Another deep breath from Delatois at the end of the quick-fire exchange.

They'd faced a similar chain of questions from Inspector Donnet and a colleague the day after Eric's arrest. Huddled in a ground-floor store room at the back of the conservatory as the police approached and took the lift up to their lab, they'd hastily thrashed out the bones of a story in case they were hauled in immediately. After a couple of suggestions from André that it quickly became evident were flawed and unworkable, Hervé offered to take the blame. 'It's the only way of keeping you two clear of any problems. If only I knew what was going on.' Within two minutes, with the police already heading back down towards them, they had eighty per cent of their plan mapped out.

Although the fourteen-hour delay before questioning – to let them get some sleep and, no doubt more importantly, for the police to put their own fact-sequencing in some order – had allowed them to fill in the texture and nuances of that final twenty per cent, the questioning had still been a nerve-wracking experience: himself and Hervé were in for over an hour each, David for thirty-five minutes. Meanwhile, Eric was under house arrest at St-Louis hospital, a policeman outside his door. It was five full days before he was well enough to answer questions for Donnet, but Hervé had visited him every day to say prayers at his bedside and on one of the first moments he'd been awake and lucid, forty-eight hours before his questioning, Hervé had whispered, 'You told me you were hit by a car. A hit and run. OK?' With Eric unconscious virtually throughout André tending to him, there was no way of him knowing what was said between Hervé and André and spoiling their story.

But as terrifying as Donnet's questioning had been, in a way this now was far worse: even if Donnet decided finally to press charges for aiding and abetting Eric, it was a long process, ten months to a year of *instructions* before the final jury trial; a sense of distance and a lot of chances on the way to escape any ultimate fate. Whereas Delatois could decide right now, with another deep breath and a quick flick of his wrist as he made a closing note on his pad, that their careers were over.

Delatois' bulbous eyes stared straight through him, and he could tell from the taut, enigmatic smile at the corner of his mouth that Delatois didn't believe them. André felt his stomach sink.

He should never have helped Eric, should have insisted on him going to a hospital. To risk everything like this, everything he'd worked for and the chance to help Eban – as he'd told himself countlessly in the two long weeks he'd had time to dwell on it more rationally – had been suicidal. But then, what choice had he been given? It had been either help Eric or let him die. Because that was what he did: he was André the healer, the helper, and so everyone made demands on him. And maybe this time he should have put his foot down, said no; but somehow all of those demands, constantly helping other people, had a numbing effect, and so he said he'd help automatically, because that's what he did, and he'd long ago lost the ability to think what he wanted for himself.

But then surely Delatois wouldn't throw everything away when they might be on the verge of such an important breakthrough. Why, only a few days ago, Delatois had stopped him in the corridor and asked him how their research was progressing, and he'd played it up well, he thought.

Delatois moistened his top lip to speak. Everything hung in the balance.

The e-mail was there, along with two other messages, when Danielle Stolk turned on her computer that morning:

> Are you going to just sit back and let Russ Hebbard take the lead, be Kalpenski's golden boy? Surely you've worked and battled too hard to let that happen?

She wheeled around, eyes darting, as she took in the room around her. A couple of lab assistants by John Page on the far side, Mithil Senadhira a few yards along from them, three secretaries, a clerk and a techy spread in-between in the open-plan room – but nobody seemed to be looking in her direction, paying her any attention. Nobody was watching expectantly for her to open her e-mail to gauge her reaction.

But apart from Page and Senadhira, the other three Associate Researchers – Kirsten Bremner, Andy Luttman and the subject of the e-mail, Russ Hebbard – weren't in sight. And surely it had to be one of the other ARs who'd sent this message. Who else had any interest in the rivalry between them? Leaning slightly to one side, she caught a glimpse of Bremner with an assistant in one of the five sealed bio-hazard rooms flanking one side, but could see only lab assistants, no ARs in the others. Though nobody seemed to be peering out of the glass door-panes to see her reaction. Everybody was busy with their own work.

She looked back at the e-mail address it had come from: phil46 @cybriv.com. It wasn't one of their internal addresses, all of those ended with sperophil.com. Nor was it from another lab or company they regularly worked with or any other addresses she recognized.

She felt uneasy, restless, and noticed that her hands were starting to shake. This was an unfamiliar role for her. Normally she was the one planning, positioning, playing with others. Now, suddenly, she was the target; somebody was playing with her. If that was what lay behind it, payback, it was probably Kirsten Bremner. Bremner hadn't forgiven her for taking the credit with that P53 project last fall, and now had hatched some plan to get back at her. It seemed about right: almost a year for Bremner's feeble, scientifically myopic mind to finally wrap itself around how to get her own back.

As she noticed one of the secretaries looking over at her, she realized that she was lost in thought, staring vacantly. She snapped out of it and abruptly got up. She chose one of the empty bio-hazard rooms, and as soon as the door clicked shut behind her, let out a deep breath. She took a block of agarose and put it in the microwave, then went over to the window and looked out as it gently hummed behind her.

Six ARs in oncology, but she'd fought harder to get where she was than any of them. They'd all had the easy route of med-school to get their PhDs She had only eighteen months of med-school followed by a six-year hiatus – the death-knell to many an academic career – that had been her disastrous marriage. She'd had to scramble her PhD while struggling through her divorce, then finish it off on night courses in the first two years as a lab assistant at the Spheros. She was so mentally exhausted at the end of it that when suddenly she had no more night courses, she crashed out as soon as she got in from work, slept for thirteen hours solid every night for almost a month. It had ended with her having to give up her daughter in the divorce battle, and now she was facing another court case, this time with her own mother. They had no idea what she'd been through. No idea.

Battled too hard. Except for one person, the writer of that e-mail. Would Kirsten Bremner have phrased it like that? She would probably begrudge giving her any credit, even if it might serve a wider cause. She wasn't Machiavellian-sharp enough for that.

But if not Bremner, then who? Behind her the microwave dinged to let her know the agarose was ready, the block had turned to liquid. But her thoughts still needed longer. A lot longer.

In the end, Eugène Delatois did what André and David should have realized somebody like him would do: he sat on the fence, gave himself the luxury of what to do with them when *he* chose, in his own time. And in doing so, he tortured them with uncertainty, which seemed to add the final gratifying piquancy to Delatois' sense of control over them. Their lives and future rested in his hands, and over the coming weeks Delatois relished in playing on that, stretching that simple tune into an opera.

At first he said that he didn't want to make a decision until he'd had a few days to think on what they'd said and go over his notes; then he said that he wanted to wait until he'd spoken again with the police and compared their statements with the accounts they'd given him, and also knew whether or not the police would be pressing charges; then, when the main Sword of Damocles was lifted three weeks later and the police announced that they wouldn't be pursuing charges against them, Delatois raised the spectre of possible press leaks: 'For now, the Institute's position is also not to take any action. But if anything untoward should appear in the press that could be potentially awkward or embarrassing, that situation of course could change. Inspector Donnet has assured me he has a tight rein on leaks from his own department, so nothing should come from there. But with the *instruction* hearing coming up at which you and David Copell will have to testify, there's nothing to stop an inquisitive court reporter going along. Then there's the possibility of leaks from any of the functionary offices in between the police and the examining magistrate – the various court clerks, paralegals and secretaries. Who knows where the press might have their contacts?'

André groaned and felt sick to his stomach when he received the court papers with the date for their appearance: over two months away! Already they'd been on Delatois' tightrope for five weeks, and felt they could hardly bear it a second longer.

And on top, Anouk was ill again and Charlotte, after her first weeks of head-cradling and histrionics over Eric's arrest, in the last ten days had suddenly had a change of mood, been in high spirits. Now, out of the blue, she wanted a meeting. It was urgent. The sudden change of mood combined with the summoned meeting made him uneasy, one anxiety he didn't need on top of all else. In a way he wished she'd just continued head-cradling; at least that was familiar territory.

'Don't worry. It will probably never happen.'

'*What?* Sorry.' André looked up to see Marielle Barbier smiling tightly at him.

She nudged back the pink hair-grip at the side of her head with the back of one hand, then it rejoined the other manipulating samples inside the glass-fronted hood. Half Italian-Venezuelan from her father, French from her mother, her long black hair hung in a wavy cascade the other side. She used to wear her hair tied back in a bun until Marc Goffinet told her it looked too severe. Goffinet, friend, confidant, lover of women, if never *in love* with them, had a keen eye for what made them look good and when it came to Marielle his expectations were high. He saw her in the Loren class. Since then she'd always worn a hair-grip, different colours nearly every day and only on one side, facing the portion of the room she wanted a clear view of. Her smile, even subdued, held genuine warmth.

'How's it going?' André asked.

'The last slot it shows up in is one to a million.' Marielle pointed to the fifth in the row of eight round slots, each iodinated to leave the germinated virus showing in white dots against blue. The number of dots reduced through slots one to five and by the sixth had disappeared. 'By here, one in ten million, it's completely washed out. No trace left.'

'So, the T-cell count has either dropped again, or at best it's static.'

'Or it might have gone up slightly. We won't know for sure until I've done another tray graded between a millionth and ten millionths to see exactly where it falls.'

'Unlikely, though, after starting to go down last week. It would just give us another variable we can't explain.'

The concern in André's voice was heavy, verging on panic. Of all the things he'd had to worry about, this had become paramount. In their original experiments run with test-tube samples from eight mangabeys four months ago, they'd sampled eleven HIV patients ex-vivo (outside of the body) with T-cell counts ranging from 38 to 424. From each of the eight mangabey samples the T-cell counts – the patients' HIV resistance – had risen, except from one. It rose steadily like the others for almost six weeks, then suddenly started dropping. They ran a series of tests, but it remained an inexplicable phenomenon; and, with only test-tube samples, one that they were unlikely to be able to explain. Thus the need for live samples and the trip to Cameroon.

But now it had happened again, this time out of only four samples, and the T-cell immunity downturn had kicked in ten days earlier than before. Now it was no longer what they'd originally hoped, a fluke or a rarity, but a possible serious obstruction. And if they lost Anouk, more worrying still: one in three failure and less chance for cross-comparisons.

André rubbed his brow with the back of one hand. 'Are you doing the PCR and computer rundowns on the samples as well?'

'No. Marc is doing those.'

Marc Goffinet was at the far end of the room, three work places along on the same lab bench as David Copell, peering into a microscope and periodically lifting up to tap details into a computer.

But what panicked André the most, set his pulse pounding, was the way in which he'd played everything up with Delatois. As Delatois became entrenched in his waiting game, every so often in passing André in the corridor or on one of his infrequent visits to their lab unit, he'd ask how everything was going and André would say fine, fine. Everything's going well. Right on track. The truth was far removed. He was behind in practically every test target he'd set originally, and now the disaster of the T-cell count dropping again in one of the samples.

Yet André had played it up every time because he had the uneasy feeling that it was all part of Delatois' waiting game: he was measuring and balancing how their experiments were going against the problems possibly lurking in the background with the investigation. And if it suddenly looked as if things weren't going well, Delatois might decide to cut his losses early, make a pre-emptive strike by ousting him and David immediately. So each time André eagerly nodded, yes, good, fine. Better than expected. In the hope that later he'd be able to catch up and make good on his promises. But now his promises and the reality were moving even further apart, practically out of reach of each other.

And what had now compounded everything, added that final nightmare shot to the whole problem cocktail, was that, buoyed up by his progress reports, Delatois had chosen tonight's regular three-monthly open forum for visiting doctors and researchers to announce how well their mangabey-AIDS programme was going.

André felt the intense pressure of it all clutching like an iron claw in his chest as he crossed the room.

David Copell saw him first and half swivelled on his chair, but Goffinet, more heavily absorbed in whatever was at the end of his microscope, didn't look up until he was only two paces away.

'How long before you've run the new samples through the PCR and computer?' His voice was taut and wavered with his uneven breath. 'Marielle's just finished her first stage of flushing through.'

'Four or five hours.' Marc shrugged. 'Three if it needs a push.'

'It needs a push.' André looked towards David. 'Anything yet on viruses or infections that might have led to Brigitte's immunity depleting?'

'Nothing significant showed up so far. Just the normal monkey mild infections – RSV, B-virus, shigella. But a couple of the others have those also.'

André checked his watch. Already 4.20 p.m. Six-thirty for Dela-tois' reception, then, straight after, the meeting with Charlotte – he'd tried to put it off until tomorrow, but she was busy then and it just *couldn't* wait for two days. It was turning out to be one of those days.

He'd hoped to have news before Delatois' reception, but at least he'd know that evening – halfway through if he asked Goffinet to slip in with a note as soon as he had the results – just how far the bold claims he'd fed Delatois were from reality, how much ground he had to make up. Or whether it could be made up at all.

7

The second e-mail appeared on Dani Stolk's computer five days later:

> So, what are you going to do? I know you. It's not like you to just sit back and do nothing. Or to be stuck for what to do. But if you need some suggestions – just ask.

It was true, she had done nothing. But it had occupied her thoughts every other minute of the past days, and in that respect she'd in fact done quite a lot. Sorted a fair few mental drawers and files. Andy Luttman: too meek and scientifically introspective, not ambitious or concerned enough with rivalry to make a play; John Page ditto, except that he carried a flame for Kirsten and so that might have pushed him over the edge into action; Mithil Senadhira, too nice and too new – still trying hard to ingratiate himself and be everyone's friend to risk getting involved with departmental politics; Russ Hebbard himself, a strong possibility – he was certainly sharp and ambitious enough, and a crafty double-play like this might appeal to him; Kirsten Bremner, the other main suspect, except for the phraseology of that first e-mail. Now this one too was distinctly complimentary.

The only slight difference this time was the sender name, phil19 instead of phil46, but the address was the same: @cybriv.com.

She'd done most of her mental sorting within hours of the first e-mail arriving, and her first instinct had been to answer it, draw the sender out; maybe in a second note they'd say something that would give them away. But then she thought: that's what the sender would expect her to do. So she decided to play things up, grab a little bit of control by frustrating them with no answer. Meanwhile she roamed and made contact more than she did normally, looking for small signals that might give them away. An anxious 'Are you OK? Everything all right?' Or even just a sharp or challenging look. Eyes lingering on her a second longer than they should, measuring. *Anything*. But there was nothing. She'd even spread her wings to cellular biology and virology on the two floors below – she visited them three times in as many days when normally they'd be lucky to see her once a week – before deciding that none of the eight ARs there were interested or involved enough in oncology inter-wrangling to make a play.

By day four she was at her wits' end, felt that perhaps she'd used the wrong tactic and should have answered within the first twenty-four hours. What if they never sent a follow-up message? She'd be left for ever wondering. So when another message did finally arrive, she answered it straight away:

You're right. I do need some help with this one. What do you suggest I do?

The reply was on her screen first thing the next morning:

Why not try the same ruse you played with Kirsten Bremner? After all, it would only mean going back and changing a couple of lines in your file notes.

She read the reply three times over, her mouth poised mid-bite on her early morning Danish, her heart beating wildly. Whoever it was knew what had happened with Bremner. Kalpenski urged them all to regularly transfer computer file notes to each other, then every two weeks send them to him so that he had a complete electronic record of work in progress. Last fall, Kalpenski had set them the task of discovering how P53 – one of the body's main natural tumour suppressants – responded to various anti-cancer drugs. Their most significant find was that only two types, wtP53 and quasi-wtP53, proliferated significantly across a range of drugs tested. She and Kirsten Bremner discovered this more or less at the same time, but Dani didn't feel like sharing the glory. So she went back into her file notes of the night before and altered two lines to make reference to this in order to gain precedence. While Bremner might not have even read her file notes of the night before or, even if she had, could easily have missed the two lines – Dani had always harboured the uneasy feeling that Bremner suspected what she'd done. 'I mentioned it in my file notes of yesterday. Remember?'

Bremner had looked slightly perplexed, then just nodded numbly, red-faced, as she checked her computer a moment later.

But this was different. Her last file note to Russ Hebbard was six days ago. Hebbard had mentioned his breakthrough with Quinazoline to Kalpenski four days ago when Kalpenski phoned from Geneva; and Hebbard's file note to Kalpenski, as with the rest of them, would have been made two days ago. It just wasn't workable in the same way.

Besides, looking at the message now, she was becoming more convinced that it was Bremner, Page or Hebbard setting a trap, especially since the more obvious responses would immediately incriminate her. And so this time she answered simply, guardedly:

Ruse played with Bremner? I don't know what you're talking about.

The answer was waiting for her the next morning:

Yes, you do. And if you don't already know Hebbard's password, it's hld48573 and Kalpenski's is lpdk7639. Don't forget, you haven't got much time left. Kalpenski returns from Geneva the day after tomorrow.

She felt her whole body turn cold. It felt like the person was speaking to her directly, knew her every move and thought – but who? *Who?* – then had taken it a step further, thought of a couple of things she'd missed: Kalpenski had been away on a round trip visiting research faculties and drug companies in Switzerland and Germany. All the file notes were still sitting on his computer, unseen. If she could get to his computer before . . . but it was just too risky without first knowing who was sending the messages. *Who?* It still smelt too much like a trap.

Her eyes darted wildly around the office. She needed help with this. Senadhira seemed the only likely candidate. He was the only one she was remotely friendly with – perhaps because, like her, he'd fought to get where he was, had bus-boyed and hospital portered while doing his PhD. But she remembered Senadhira telling her that it had been a toss-up between medicine and software programming and that one of his brothers was a big fish in the computer industry. She beckoned him over.

'Mithil. Do you recognize this e-mail address?' She wrote down the address from the first message sent: phil46@cybriv.com. 'Or have any idea where it might have originated?'

'No, I'm afraid not.'

'Oh, I see.' Her hopes sank.

He ran one hand through his wavy dark hair, and smiled. 'But I think I might be able to track it down for you. I've got the most wonderful e-mail address finder.' He went back to his computer two desks away and started tapping, his eyebrows knitting for a moment in consternation before lifting again. 'Not an exact address, I'm afraid – but a general location. The cybriv tag belongs to a chain of Internet cafés: Cyberling Rivalry. Quite a large chain, they've got a fair few branches all over.'

Her hopes sank again. A chain of faceless Internet cafés. She'd never track down the sender.

'They've in fact got one downtown, on Arch Street,' Senadhira said. 'A marvellously inventive name too, don't you think? Almost as catchy as that West Coast chain, Easy.com, easy.go. My brother thought at one time of –'

She held one hand up. She usually had more time for Senadhira's jovial, if often aimless, banter, but not now. The second that he'd mentioned that there was a Cyberling Rivalry café on Arch Street she'd punched out the number, and Bell Enquiries answered after the first ring. She got the number and dialled out immediately again.

'Cyberling. Greg speaking.'

'I've been receiving e-mails from a branch of Cyberling Rivalry, and I wondered if it might be yours?'

'Each branch ends in the same cybriv-dot-com. What's the sender name?'

'Oh, uh, phil46 one time, phil19 another.'

'Yeah, that's us. Philadelphia, computers 46 and 19. We've got seventy-eight altogether here.'

'But I've been sending return messages. How would they get those?'

'They all go to a central server. Everything's time-slotted and we ask the user if they want return messages held or not. They then go into their computer number and time slot for when they next come in.'

But when Dani gave the times and computer numbers and asked who might have sent the messages, she drew a blank. They didn't hold that sort of information and, even if they did, wouldn't divulge it.

'Anonymity's part of the service here. Most people pay cash, and when they come in to pick up their messages they're just Mr or Mrs X, computer 20, time slot 11, day 14. We don't know any more beyond that, and don't wanna know.'

'Right. Thanks anyway.' She clutched lightly at one side of her hair as she hung up. Senadhira fired her a tight-lipped smile of sympathy.

She looked again at the times of the messages: the earliest was sent at 7.12 p.m., the latest at 7.43 p.m. The only way she was going to find out was by sending a reply and then staking out Cyberling Rivalry between 7.00 p.m. and 8.00 p.m. to see who picked it up.

'. . . This year has seen notable advancements in drug treatment research at the Institute. The development of more sophisticated protease inhibitors, for example, but – perhaps more importantly – how these may be combined with other drugs, most notably nucleoside analogues, to provide effective AIDS treatment. Out of clinical test samples run with eighteen patients . . .'

André faded out Delatois' voice coming over the PA system and looked around. A forty-foot square reception area, it was two-thirds full with doctors, researchers – only half of whom were from the ISG – and the main people Delatois' quarterly round-up speech was aimed at: ISG stockholders and a sprinkling of scientific journalists. The room was a half-basement with a cathedral-height ceiling, so that it was overlooked by the building's main entrance foyer and two floors above in gallery style. The room's guests, in turn, could see where much of the ISG's recent wealth had been poured: on the first floor Europe's most complete virology library; going up, second floor, more records, many of them now microfiched for space 'and a computer database second to none'. More than once André had been caught behind visiting notables being given the guided tour. He dabbed at his brow with the back of one hand as his gaze settled again on the entrance foyer. Where was David? He promised that he'd come in as soon as Goffinet had the final test results, hopefully before Delatois started his speech.

'. . . seen significant advancements also in our gene therapy programmes incepted last year: antigen-specific CTLs and neo-resistance genes. And our key programme from the previous year, anti-HIV ribozymes, was entered into phase two clinical trials just last month . . .'

Delatois was well into his stride. André had stayed as long as he could with David and Goffinet waiting on a result, then had raced at the last minute to the reception, putting on a tie as he ran across the main courtyard of the ISG compound. He was already in a sweat with the rush as he walked in, and now, again, he could feel his skin hot and prickling. He stopped dabbing at his brow as he noticed Dr Valmy, one of their main research rivals at the Censier Faculté de Médecine, looking over at him through the crowd.

Valmy, an eccentric looking character with a handlebar moustache and an unruly mop of curly brown hair, who always wore bright bow ties to occasions like this, started edging his way through the crowd and milling waiters with hors d'oeuvres trays, towards him. André averted his gaze, tried to appear to be concentrating on what Delatois was saying, but it was already too late. Valmy jostled through the last few yards and then leant in close so that his voice didn't carry.

'Well, well, not a bad year. If the venerable Dr Delatois is to be taken at his word.'

'Seems so.' André fired Valmy only a brief courteous smile before turning his attention back to Delatois on the small rostrum at the end of the room.

'. . . Significant progress too in our AAVs and gene-targeting programmes, much of it aided by the new equipment installed earlier this year.' Delatois referred to his notes as he gave technical details of the equipment.

'This gene therapy, I don't know.' Valmy shook his head. 'Four years in and I ask you – just how far ahead are we?'

'It's early days yet.' André could have added that with the gene identification programme still not even completed, what did Valmy expect? Or elaborate on a few cases – aside from how far progressed he might or might not be with the mangabeys – to support the contention that breakthroughs were probably closer at hand than Valmy might appreciate. But he reminded himself to be on guard with Valmy – keep his answers short and non-committal. The eccentric, absent-minded-professor look had caught many un-awares. Valmy was a past master at sharp, often combative comment to draw out his rivals, and the next thing they'd see would be their comments ridiculed in a rebuff in some scientific journal. Maybe that was that Valmy was trying to do, draw him out about progress with the mangabeys? André risked a quick glance back towards the entrance foyer. Where *was* David?

'When you look at the tremendous progress made with drugs and combination therapies – it hardly warrants comparison,' Valmy said.

André met Valmy's trite smile evenly. A predictable statement, he supposed, given that Valmy had largely ignored gene therapy and had focused all of his work on combination drugs treatment. But recalling Eban's reaction to the drastic regimen of drugs, so debilitated at times that he couldn't walk, lift his schoolbag or even eat a single mouthful, this time André couldn't resist a comment.

'Yes, I suppose we have come a long way from the dark days of AZT, which gave half the patients incurable cancer within three years, when their life expectancy with HIV was probably ten years or more. Now all they have to put up with is ten years of muscle cramps and vomiting and *wishing* they were dead.'

'At least we're keeping them alive. We've already extended life expectancy by four or five years. In a couple of years' time it could be six or seven, or even indefinitely.'

'Yes, but it's hardly a . . . a long-term solution.' André avoided the word 'cure'; the first lesson of virology was that a virus could never be cured, it was merely diminished to a state where the body could co-exist and cope with it, like flu. 'The admission is right there, "keeping them alive" – because that's *all* you're doing. At least with gene therapy there's some real hope of kick-starting the body's immune system to fight and eventually defeat HIV. No more ten-year drug debilitation programmes.'

'But unlike me, my friend, nothing you've done as yet has actively helped a *single* AIDS sufferer. It's all just theory.' Valmy's smug smile was quick to re-surface. 'And now all of this monkey business.' Valmy's tone was undisguisedly derogatory as he looked towards Delatois.

'. . . When earlier this year Dr Lemoine identified SIV in the mangabeys similar to human HIV, but this time with the all-important R gene, the most elusive factor in primate SIV studies . . .'

André's heart sank. Delatois had already hit the topic, and still no sign of David. But then, what was he going to do? Hold his hand up and stop Delatois mid-speech, say that there'd been some complications?

'In a few thousand years I suppose our immune defences to HIV might have evolved to catch up with theirs,' Valmy muttered under his breath. 'But hoping to leap-frog that now?'

'. . . Dr Lemoine has recently returned from Cameroon with four mangabeys to provide live samples, and both in-vitro and ex-vivo tests have shown marked improvements in T-cell counts. No treatment so far known has shown this potential, and it has significant implications for gene therapy and future AIDS vaccines. Possibly the most significant AIDS breakthrough of this decade.'

A faint ripple of applause broke out and André nodded in acknowledgement, his face flushing slightly as a number of heads turned towards him. *Or perhaps suggest that claims shouldn't be made too boldly, given that their research still had some way to go?* Too late for that now. Delatois was eagerly firing up a PR express train, possibly headed for derailment before it had hardly started. The applause and Delatois' voice over the PA seemed to echo in his head, and he felt suddenly dizzy, nauseous, increasingly awkward with each approving smile turned his way; and as he glanced away for a second he saw David approaching the foyer gallery rails.

David stood there uncertainly as he surveyed the scene below and made no move his way; perhaps because so much attention was on him at that moment, or because Valmy was so close. He needed to get away from Valmy to hear the results from David.

'You don't seem as excited by Delatois' announcement as you should be.' Valmy raised one eyebrow acutely. 'Something troubling you?'

'Perhaps because unlike you I don't wallow in these sort of glory announcements. And you shouldn't be so hard on monkeys. Most of us just share gene similarities with them; in your case it goes some way beyond that. Excuse me.'

But only two steps away from Valmy, judging from David's taut expression, he'd already guessed what the results said.

Dani Stolk laid out her plans – Cyberling Rivalry was fifty yards from the 9th Street junction with Arch Street, so she should leave no later than 6.30 p.m. to get there for 7 p.m. – before sending her reply just after lunch:

What do you want out of all of this? Why do you want to help me?

Her hand hovered over the keyboard for a second as she pondered whether to add – *Who are you?* – before deciding against it. They

76

weren't going to tell her. They'd either say nothing or lie, but worst of all it would alert them that she was eager to know, they'd be more likely to be defensive, perhaps lay diversionary tactics to foil her tracking them.

The second she'd sent the message, the hustle and bustle of the office crashed back in. Kalpenski's secretary, Tara Adams, down from his sixteenth-floor office to talk to John Page about something; Senadhira calling out to one of the lab assistants about some tyrosine kinase results; Andy Luttman looking up at her briefly before putting his head back down to some files before him; Kristen Bremner studying her computer screen, not paying her any attention; Hebbard in the fourth bio-hazard unit along.

She felt claustrophobic, trapped, couldn't bear it, this feeling that one of them was playing her, silently observing her every move, her every action. Like just another cell or microbe under the microscope. She needed to be alone for a while with her thoughts. She grabbed a file and headed towards the Flow Cytometry room, but at the last second noticed a lab assistant inside. She moved two along to the CELL-ULA room.

CELL-ULA had the most stringent safeguards of all the bio-hazard rooms – not because of the danger of what was handled there, but because of possible movement disturbing its sensors. Dani had to put on specially cushioned boots as well as a lab coat, and display a time for the length of experiment – which she set at seventy-five minutes – so that she wasn't disturbed.

CELL-ULA, Ultramicrometer Linkage and Analysis – the name moulded in the Spheros boardroom to create that catchy tag that would hopefully go down well with investors and the stock market. Everything they did now had one eye on the markets, even more so after the Gifford Awards. One of only six of its type worldwide, in layman's terms the CELL-ULA counted, measured and cross-compared cell progressions. From a few simple parameters fed in, it provided projected results that could take months or years to discover through conventional lab testing. With the optimum word being *projected*: they still needed to run conventional tests to prove its findings. But it was an invaluable tool in indicating where or where not to head and the likely end results. And they'd discovered that it was uncannily accurate: 93.7 per cent hit rate, up from 92.4 per cent a year ago. As they fed it more data, it became more 'intelligent'.

Dani slid out a tray of uterine samples she'd been working on a few days ago, fed them into the CELL-ULA, then started keying in data from her files. The main cell-reading unit was rubber- and air-cushioned, but still its keyboard and screen were positioned on a workbench ten clear feet away to cut down on the risk of vibrations transferring. It was said that even a cough or a sneeze could throw off its delicate micro-millionth counting process.

Dani stayed very still, tried not to move, shuffle her feet or even swallow too hard. A couple of people passed and glimpsed through the door screen, but nobody disturbed her; times posted were always strictly observed. Just the sort of peace and stillness she wanted, like solitary confinement. And as she sank deeper into it, watching the white lines of codes and numbers appear on the blue screen, she became more conscious of the sounds of her own body: her shallow breathing, her heart pounding. Faster than it should. Who? *Who?*

Maybe there was a return message waiting on her computer already. What if they didn't reply tonight? The chance to do anything before Kalpenski returned would then be gone anyway.

By the end of the seventy-five minutes, the small room too had become claustrophobic, stifling. She didn't trouble to check the data from the CELL-ULA, couldn't concentrate on anything else at that moment, couldn't wait to see if there was a return message for her.

She stripped off the white gown and boots, strode across the office, signed on and checked. Nothing. Only a reply from a Chicago lab she'd sent an enquiry to yesterday. She breathed a sigh of relief: if there had been one, she'd have lost the opportunity of tracking them that night, would have had to . . .

'What?' She jumped as she noticed Russ Hebbard hanging over her shoulder.

'I said, nothing new from me the last few days.' That weak, smug smile that so irritated her. 'But I hope to be sending out some update notes on Quinazoline in a couple of days' time.'

'Right. Thanks. I'll look out for it.' She met his gaze and mirrored his smile just as weakly. Was Hebbard baiting her, trying to read behind her eyes how fazed she was, or was this just his normal smug oafishness, thinking that they all had little better to do than regularly check their computers for his next golden morsel on Quinazoline?

She clock-watched for much of the rest of the afternoon, shuffled papers, gazed blankly at items on her computer, didn't pay attention to much, and left sharply at 6.20 p.m.

But the rush hour hadn't trailed off yet, and it was slow going, eating into the extra minutes she'd given herself. And when a car ahead paused and then stopped on amber at the 13th Street junction, she beeped and banged her fist on the steering wheel in frustration. The 9th Street junction was where the city's downtown skyscrapers gave way to Chinatown on one side and the Old City on the other, and parking was difficult. The closest she could get was a block up on Cherry Street, and she practically ran from her car, glancing at her watch as she went: 7.04 p.m.

Breathless, she stood twenty yards along on the opposite side from Cyberling Rivalry, and observed. Hopefully she hadn't already missed them and wasn't too obvious. She'd positioned herself by a news-stand and a tree so that she was partially obscured and could turn and appear to be browsing newspapers if someone looked her way.

Nothing for the first twenty minutes, nobody she recognized. Though by then she'd attracted the attention of a tramp on the corner, who sized her up for a moment before approaching. She gave him a dollar to get rid of him quickly, though when she looked again towards the entrance she noticed a couple of people that she'd missed, now obscured by a larger group behind.

Then a city bus stuck in a tail-back of traffic obscured her view of the entrance for another minute or so. Maybe five or six people now she'd missed going in. And when eight minutes later the tramp on the corner was joined by a friend – now also looking her way, probably wondering whether she was good for another dollar, and a truck pulled in blocking her view again – she decided to head across.

She paused for a car passing on her side, the truck started moving, and, as she gained a clear view of the entrance again, she saw the profile of a figure she recognized: stone grey hair, dark serge overcoat.

She halted mid-step and turned a hundred and eighty degrees as the figure started to look towards her. Had he seen her? Her heart beat wildly, her throat dry, as she paced briskly back the way she'd come. Now *who* had been replaced with a more perplexing *why*? It made little sense. She couldn't grasp any immediate rationale.

Her stride picked up with each step so that soon she was almost at a run, her breath ragged by the time she reached the car, started up and pulled out.

Why? *Why?* The question bounced around in her mind with few tangible answers as she sped back to the lab. She'd let her mind roam freely through work colleagues for culprits, but it had never even considered anyone above: Kalpenski or his counterparts in virology and cellular biology. Let alone the echelon above that, the rarefied sanctums of the Spheros boardroom. Why on earth would someone in Julius Chisholm's position be interested in the petty wrangling among Kalpenski's minions?

She flashed her pass at the guard, rode up the fifteen floors, darted across to her computer, booted up and signed on. There was a message there. Her hand trembled on the mouse as she double-clicked and opened it up:

Because I believe you have an edge which the others don't possess. A drive to succeed <u>at all costs</u>. What you decide to do about Hebbard will either confirm or deny that. One way or the other.

She checked the time it had been sent: 7.41 p.m., four minutes after she'd seen Chisholm go into Cyberling Rivalry. There was little doubt remaining that it was him. She re-read the short message three times over, but still it provided few clues as to *why*.

8

'. . . Gérard. Gérard Lacroix. You remember, I mentioned he had quite a successful show at the Villepinte exhibition a few months ago.'

André had trouble focusing on what Charlotte was saying, his thoughts were still spinning with calculations: average T-cell count drop of eleven in just eight days. How long before they returned to their base-line test readings? Five weeks, six? 'I'm not sure,' he said, narrowing his eyes slightly as he sipped at his coffee, as if he was applying thought to trying to recall rather than to his own problems. The name didn't seem to ring a bell.

'After that show we decided to collaborate on a few designs together, so he'd come over to my workshop for a couple of hours usually on a Tuesday and, if we were on a tight deadline to finish something, on a Friday as well. I think you saw him a couple of times when you picked up Joël and Eban. Quite tall, wavy black hair.'

'Oh yes, yes. I remember now.' He remembered a man in his late thirties looking at him with sullen curiosity before being introduced briefly, and then him just as quickly forgetting the name. Was the rate of T-cell decline increasing? It was certainly more rapid at the outset than last time, but by how much?

Charlotte drew hard on her cigarette and looked thoughtfully at the back of a man in a bright check jacket and lilac trilby hat who'd brushed close by their table. It was 9.11 p.m., and the streets of St-Michel were humming with life. André said that he'd snacked at the reception, she'd had a small bite before leaving and so could manage only a pastry, so they'd headed to Café Monteaucon, where she'd ordered an apple tart and mineral water and he just a coffee. Gas heaters under the canvas awnings fought back the chill of the

October night, and the terrace was almost full. One of Charlotte's perfectly manicured crimson nails tapped at the table-top.

'Then, five or six weeks ago, we started to do more work together. It wasn't particularly planned, it was just that some things from our respective collections seemed to complement each other well, and so it was an avenue we both wanted to explore more. Our first big success was at a show in Orléans a couple of weeks back . . .'

André lost her at that point, his thoughts drifting again. Average T-cell drop of sixty-seven over nine weeks last time, but there'd been a curve to the progression, the fall rate decreasing in the last few weeks. If the same happened this time, perhaps in the end there wouldn't be much difference between the two results. The case histories of the test patients could also be a vital factor. He couldn't even start coming up with answers until he'd run detailed week-by-week, case-by-case, comparisons. Suddenly, all he could think about was heading back to the lab to start on them. 'Sorry . . . what happened?' He focused back on what Charlotte was saying. She seemed to be anxious, eyes darting, as she waited for his response.

'It just *happened* between us, you know . . . like these things do.' Her finger tapped faster at the table-top and she took a long, hard draw of her cigarette. 'My God, it's not easy for me, you know, asking you here and telling you like this. The least you could do is pay attention.'

'I'm sorry. It's just some panic that's come up with some test results, and I don't have much time to sort it out.'

She shook her head and smiled tightly. 'Never any different. There was always some panic or problem with your work, André. And meanwhile everything else was forgotten.' This time she blew out her smoke in an elaborate billow, as if it somehow contained all the cobwebs of their life together. 'Which is why we are where we are now.'

Charlotte was uncomfortably right, there was little André could say in his own defence, and he should have realized that Charlotte asking for this meeting now, urgently, wouldn't be just to discuss the recent tribulations of her fashion business. They'd agreed at the outset that they could have separate relationships – in part because Charlotte's affair which had led to the split continued for some months after – so why the need for any announcement now? Perhaps because so long had passed since that last affair, or purely out of politeness, deference. André felt a sudden stab of alarm.

'You don't want a divorce, do you?' That was the final step they'd agreed not to take until Joël was a few years older and could hopefully understand. Meanwhile they could all live in hope of a reconciliation.

'No, no. I just thought you should know before you found out somewhere else. From the children, for example.'

'They don't know, do they?' Rule two of their separation. Any relationships should be discreet, kept from the children.

'No. I've been careful. I only go out with Gérard on the nights you have them. But sometimes he's there and we're working together when you drop them off and, you know, often children are much more intuitive than we give them credit for.' Another carefully blown smoke plume. 'Sometimes they pick up on these things.'

'Oh, right.' All the other signals gelled in that instant: on the last few visits her asking him to be more precise about the time he was arriving with the children; her sudden lift in mood two weeks ago, no doubt about the time she and Gérard started getting serious. And as usual he'd been too absorbed with his work to notice. For a while now he'd stopped thinking about Charlotte romantically or about what he wanted for himself from the wreckage of their relationship; how she was faring and coping had become the only concern, and so he was actually glad that this Gérard had made her feel more confident again, had eased some of her worry lines and put the trace of a smile on her lips. But reminding himself now of what Gérard looked like, he couldn't help thinking of the possible downside as well. Charlotte's nerves couldn't take another disastrous break-up like the one with Pierre. 'He looks quite young. How old is he?'

'Mid-thirties. Why? What difference would that make?'

'Umm.' It was like walking on egg-shells. So many of Charlotte's problems, both emotionally and in business, stemmed from her trying to recapture the eighties glory days of her fashion business. *Everything was brighter and better then? One of the best periods both for your marriage and your business?* Yes, the eighties was the most successful period for my business, and Veruschka was born then. *And so it's natural that you would try and re-create that. But others can also see that need in you and try and take advantage of it.* At least the fiasco with Pierre and the subsequent psychiatric sessions had brought it to the fore, got her to finally face what those close to her had seen for years. 'Just that after Pierre,' André said, 'I'd have thought younger men would have been well worth avoiding.'

'Oh, don't be ridiculous.' She waved one hand away dismissively. 'The age difference this time is only six years. It's nothing. Pierre was only twenty-eight, so that time I admit I was reaching for it.' She pulled hard on her cigarette and puffed it out. 'Being silly.'

André looked at her. Her blonde hair was piled up high and she was still swan-necked and slim and always immaculately presented; and, when she was relaxed and confident like now, she could pass for five years younger than her forty-two years. But as he well knew, the other side of her, the tension and neurosis, was just a beat away, could change in the flicker of an eye with the wrong thing said; and then the taut lines would show and slim would quickly become gaunt and she'd look drawn, a tense wire of a woman on the edge, and those five years and more would suddenly pile back on. And from what he'd seen, Gérard was a smooth and good-looking mid-thirties, could easily attract a woman five or ten years younger rather than older, and so he only hoped that Gérard saw the Charlotte he was looking at now, that she was careful not to let the mask down with him. One other thing suddenly concerned him about Gérard.

'And he hasn't asked you for money?' he enquired.

'No, no. Of course not. He has his own successful business. Why on earth would he?' But there was a flicker for a moment in her eyes that André read as uncertainty. Then, as her expression became tense and she brusquely flicked the ash from her cigarette on to the ground, perhaps it was simply because she was stung by the comment. 'And, quite frankly, I find that suggestion offensive: that you think the only thing a younger man might want me for is money.'

'No, it's not that.' He closed his eyes for a second in submission and shook his head. 'I suppose after your problems with Pierre, it's just not wanting a repeat. Probably I'm being too protective. Something I lost the right to be a while ago without realizing.'

She looked ahead, her eyes fixing on nothing in particular in the bustling street, and her expression was slow in relaxing back. André felt the heat of one of the gas burners against the back of his neck in strong contrast to the cool wind that whipped around their table. Across the street a fishmonger picked out some prawns for a client from the brightly lit display that made up the frontispiece for the restaurant and oyster bar behind.

Too protective? At least in that way he still cared for her, didn't want to see her hurt again. Was that all that was left of their relationship, their years together? He was now little more than an emotional counsellor, a secondary psychiatrist? And, as they started talking lightly about other topics *du jour* – Eban and the aftermath of Eric's arrest – he felt a strange resentment slowly building within him. For it struck him that with his work he'd become conditioned to think of others, the greater cause, and now so much else in his life had become an extension of that; he'd long ago lost sight of what he wanted for himself from anything. Since returning from Cameroon, what with Anouk's illness and the problems with Eric, and now struggling to fend off Delatois to keep his job, he'd hardly had a chance to draw breath; and if anyone had the right to be paranoid, neurotic, it was him. Yet Charlotte had robbed him even of that; that was her domain and there couldn't be two of them falling apart at the same time, and so they'd slipped into the familiar roles of her panicking and him consoling that everything was going to be all right. And this time he resented her for it, for denying him an emotion – anxiety or panic or whatever – that was more rightly his at that moment than hers.

'So you're not saying that you think I can no longer attract a younger man?' she quizzed, looking at him aslant.

'No, no. Of course not.' He reminded himself that despite Gérard buoying her spirits, her shell was still frail.

'I mean, I've only been to your place a few times, and I've seen the way that that Marielle looks at you.'

'Don't be ridiculous. I'm seventeen years older than her.' As he met Charlotte's steady gaze, she merely gave a teasing half smile and raised one eyebrow. He sipped at his coffee and shrugged. 'She gives that look to Goffinet too, and he's gay. It's her normal look. She has a naturally seductive smile.'

'Oh, is that it?' Charlotte held the smile as she looked straight ahead.

'Besides, she's got a boyfriend.'

'I thought he used to beat her.'

'That was the last one. She got rid of him. She's got a new one now – he's OK.'

'Oh, right.'

Finally they seemed to have circled around enough to return to the main topic. She held her pout for a second after blowing out her cigarette smoke, her expression becoming pensive. She reached out one hand and laid it lightly across his. 'I'm sure everything will work out OK with Gérard. But I thought I should tell you.'

'Yes, yes. Probably best I knew, if nothing else because of the children.' He closed his eyes for a second in acceptance and patted her hand back. 'And I'm sure you're right, I'm worrying for nothing.' But he wondered whether, despite his concerns, he was trying to convince himself because for the time being Gérard had eased her trademark neurosis; and with everything else he had on his plate at that moment, it was one less thing to cope with. At least in that respect, for once, he probably was being selfish.

Because I believe you have an edge which the others don't possess. A drive to succeed at all costs. What you decide to do about Hebbard will either confirm or deny that. One way or the other.

Dani Stolk finally lifted her head from staring at the message, picking apart every word and possible hidden meaning. The last remaining secretary on her floor had just switched off her computer and was starting to clear away papers, and John Page was in the CELL-ULA room showing a finish time of 8.15 p.m., twelve more minutes. She should be alone after that.

What to do? *What to do?* It could be a trap, as she'd first thought. But why would Chisholm bother to come down from his lofty boardroom to get involved with the inter-wrangling of ARs? And especially not to go to these lengths. Surely he'd have just summoned her to his office and confronted her. Maybe he had high principles about things like that, wanted to see justice done whatever it took; but again it seemed out of step with the Machiavellian way he'd gone about everything. High principles and Machiavelli didn't sit well together.

Machiavelli and low principles: now that was a possibility. But what grand plans could Chisholm possibly have for her to make it worth his while going to all of this trouble? Her thoughts went around in circles, ricocheting off possibilities, until they were back again at the likelihood that it was a trap. Then shifted again, probably not, and back.

Her mind was in turmoil, her body flushing hot and cold, her hands still shaking from the rush to Cyberling Rivalry. She panned through what she could recall from the few times she'd been in Julius Chisholm's company for small clues: a nervous tic, a frown or smile, an admiring or disapproving glance, something maybe that he'd said; *anything*.

The only thing that struck a chord was the way he'd looked at her briefly during the announcement of the Gifford Awards: a hint of tease, challenge in his eyes. It could have been the excitement with the size of the prizes, or what he was expecting from them as a team in order to win one. But then she hadn't noticed him share that look as well with Kalpenski or Hebbard; it was as if Chisholm had singled her out.

But what if she was wrong? What if he was just flirting with her? Or he was just more comfortable sharing his exuberance with women, an extension of his regular role-play with his wife or girlfriend. That was another question: was he married, single, gay? She knew absolutely nothing about him; he was a total dark horse. Whereas he no doubt knew practically everything about her. The thought made her uneasy, once again feeling like something under the microscope.

She jolted as a door shut at the end of the room. John Page said, 'Hi', with a small wave, went to his desk and leafed through some papers. After a moment he looked up and asked, 'Anything I can help with?' Perhaps he'd glanced out of the CELL-ULA room and noticed that she seemed perplexed, troubled.

'No, no. It's OK. Some formulas I'm having problems with, but in a half-hour or so I'll have cracked them. Get home to the cat.'

He pushed a strained smile as if he was almost relieved she didn't take him up on the offer. He stayed another ten minutes leafing through papers and checking something on his computer, then packed up and left. 'See you tomorrow.'

'Yes, see you. Or maybe I'll still be here and my cat will have starved.' She fired back an equally meaningless smile. She was on her own.

She closed her eyes and shuddered. *Oh God*. Perhaps she should do nothing: there were just too many parameters she couldn't see, couldn't take stock of. If it were a trap, her career would be ruined. She'd be fired from the Spheros and wouldn't have a hope of finding a job anywhere else in research, unless it was cleaning Petri dishes.

At least if she did nothing, everything would carry on as it was: safe. She'd continue as an AR. Hebbard would get the glory over Quinazoline, so she'd probably stay in his shadow for a while. A long while, since he already had the advantage over her of longer experience. Then no doubt Hebbard would take over when Kalpenski retired, and she'd be stuck as an AR for another five or ten years – by which time she'd be an old maid! She clenched a fist tight on the desktop.

Damn Chisholm, he certainly knew how to play her. That was the decision right there: make her move now or for ever stay as an

AR in Hebbard's shadow. Risk her whole career – glory one side, ruin the other – on one toss of the coin. Make or break right now. She looked across at the clock accusingly, its second hand ticking down almost in time with the dull ache of the pulse at her temples. By tomorrow, Kalpenski would be back and it would be too late. Now or never.

Wouldn't last long. Just an expression, until you put shade and texture to it. In Eban's case, with his T-cell count already dangerously low at 261, that meant anything from eight to eighteen months. In Goffinet's case, with a T-Cell count of 426, he probably had a good four or five years left. But combination drug therapy could easily stretch that expectancy by another two or three years, and so much else could happen in the meantime with AIDS therapies and possible cures – not least his own endeavours – that it was hardly worth thinking about.

Everything always started in André's mind with Eban; Goffinet and everyone else became merely an extension of that singular focus. If he could cure Eban, then he could cure the rest.

André looked up from his notes and eased out a long breath. Except that now for the first time since the breakthrough with the silver-tailed mangabeys, he wasn't sure if he would make it in time; if at all.

He'd taken the minimum eight months Eban had left, then worked everything back from there. He reckoned it would take him six months to run all the necessary side reaction tests, purifications and selection of the ideal vector for administering the therapy, before getting to the phase one testing stage – therefore leaving two months' leeway. But this current problem could easily eat up that two months and more. Particularly because it was no longer a straightforward problem, now they were dealing with a variable. The sample this time was decreasing more rapidly, would be back at the base line it started at in seven weeks rather than nine. Even if they found out the common denominator linking the two, they'd still have to answer why it declined faster the second time; they wouldn't be near getting phase one test approval until they had done so. He'd known variables like that often hold up research for years rather than just months.

And he'd also in part left that two months' leeway because there was a point where Eban's T-cell count would have dropped so low that his body wouldn't be able to respond to the therapy; he'd be so weak that the treatment itself could kill him. So, if Eban's final stages – a combination of his rate of T-cell decline and what opportunistic illnesses might strike in the meantime – hit early rather than late, there really was no leeway. No margin left.

He ran one hand brusquely through his hair. After seeing Charlotte, he felt that he just couldn't get his thoughts clear, wouldn't be able to sleep until he'd compared David's results with past file results to see exactly where he was. And so he'd phoned Veruschka to check if everything was OK with Joël and Eban, and said that he'd be delayed a bit, wouldn't be back for an hour or so.

He hoped that the bicycle ride home might clear his thoughts. But he felt his eyes stinging and rapidly watering; not sure if it was the sudden wave of despair, of hopelessness gripping him over Eban, or from the cool wind-rush. He quickly shook it off, rose up in the saddle and pedalled faster.

He blew Eban and Joël a kiss through the half-open bedroom door on his way to bed; then lingered there for a moment, looking at Eban's sleeping profile in the faint light spilling in from the hallway.

He'd focused everything on Eban, because the thought of trying to find a cure for millions was just too daunting, and somehow felt out of reach, unreal. Even the possible glory that went with it was a driving force more for the likes of Delatois than him. And so by focusing just on a cure for Eban it all suddenly became more tangible, real; and then by extension he could think of the thousands and millions of Ebans. Only then would it hit him; the weight in his chest would become leaden, the emotions at times so overwhelming that his whole body would tremble as if in fever, and he'd awake screaming in the dead of night, 'No, too many. I can't save them all,' as again in his nightmare he crossed the bridge over the ever-expanding lines of tombstones.

He started to slowly close the door, watching the stream of light narrow until it left just Eban's face. So much easier to focus all of his grand aims on just one person, he thought; yet so much harder when those aims started to slip away, look out of reach.

Dani was shaking almost uncontrollably as she made the changes on Kalpenski's computer, she could hardly keep her hands steady on the keyboard.

It had been bad enough making the changes on Hebbard's computer, but at least she'd been only yards away from her own desk. Here, she was on totally foreign ground, she hardly ever went up to Kalpenski's office unless summoned. When she'd heard George, the building's security guard, approaching while she was on Hebbard's computer, she'd quickly made her way back to her own desk. She knew that, upon seeing lights on, he might come along and check. As he'd looked through the glass doors and smiled at her, he'd noticed nothing unusual. From his angle he couldn't see that Hebbard's computer screen was on and, even if he had, he probably couldn't remember whose computer was whose.

But this was different. He'd be surprised to find her in Kalpenski's office; so, three minutes after hearing him go down again in the lift, she'd put the light on in the CELL-ULA room, turned the dial to forty minutes' time, and headed up to Kalpenski's office without switching on any lights. If George passed by again, he'd assume she was in the CELL-ULA room. He couldn't see the far sides of the room unless he got close to the small glass pane in its door. Unlikely: he'd see the 'Don't disturb until' time posted from a distance.

And so she worked on Kalpenski's computer in near darkness: the only light was from the glow of the screen and spilling in from the corridor, where lights were left on throughout the night.

Carefully match the number of word bytes to the original document and save the whole thing as a new document to match the old document name. Then go into Norton Delete and cover her tracks, matching the last Save times to when the document was originally received by Kalpenski. Almost exactly the same procedure she'd gone through on Hebbard's computer. Then back to Windows and . . .

She froze. The sound of the lift rising again. Stopping. The doors opening on her floor, footsteps coming out on to the corridor.

She ducked down below the desk and held her breath. Who was it? George again, or perhaps Kalpenski back early from his trip? Or Tara, his secretary, returning because she'd forgotten something? She heard the footsteps shuffle hesitantly: probably George. Kalpenski or Tara would have just headed straight her way. But was he going through his normal check routine or pausing because he thought he could make out a faint glow from Kalpenski's office beyond the light from the corridor?

At that moment the screen went into Saver, became a spinning spirograph that merged to form the Spheros logo; then a second later exploded back again into a spirograph. She broke into a sweat. The faint changes in light glow might draw his attention even more. She couldn't switch off the computer, she'd lose all her changes; but she could unplug the monitor. She reached out and after a few seconds fumbling, found the wire. She started tracing her hand up, but at that second the footsteps shuffled again, turned, then there was the sound of lift doors opening and closing. The lift started heading down again.

Dani eased out a long breath. Never again. In the end she'd gone ahead based on the brief look Chisholm had fired her at the Gifford Awards; a look that told her it was more likely he had a plan in store for her than a trap. Her whole career gambled on a four-second glance. She must be mad. She waited a couple of minutes to get her breath and her nerve back, then went down, turned off the lights and left.

She was still shaking as she drove home. She'd convinced herself that she was doing the right thing mostly due to her not wishing to face the prospect of years in the AR doldrums under Hebbard. But the nightmare of actually going through with it had sapped her spirit and nerve, and with it came a sinking despondency: she'd done the wrong thing. It had been a trap; that had been the most likely explanation all along. And now she'd just thrown her entire career down the toilet. As soon as she got home, she headed for the bathroom and was sick.

9

The second bomb went off in the Roswell district of Atlanta. This time, though, there were casualties from the blast: a thirty-one-year-old lab assistant, Stuart Greer, was killed outright, and a guard lost part of a leg and two fingers and suffered severe skin lacerations from flying debris and glass.

The case was first of all handled by Atlanta PD. But then two days later, computer searching brought up a bombing with a similar MO in Phoenix, Arizona, two months before. The FBI were called in and it became a joint operation.

The files ended up on the desk of agent Todd Wenner, simply because he was the only one in the Atlanta field office with any medical knowledge, having spent a year at medical college before dropping out and going to Quantico. He claimed that he'd realized too late that he felt queasy slicing through skin with a scalpel, but the truth was that even the smell of hospitals brought back the last year of visiting his mother before she died. He knew that with each patient he lost, the pain of that memory would resurface; he wouldn't be able to face it.

Thirty-seven, married with two children, both girls, eight and five, his shiny-bald head and his passion for smoking strong cigarettes, Mahawats or dark Virginia slims, had earned him the nickname Kojak – though he never wore a hat or sucked a lollipop. He did, in fact, have some hair remaining, but it was so sparse and blond that he'd decided it looked pathetic; it was better to stay permanently shaved.

'So this was the centre of the explosion?' Wenner crouched down beside a five-foot wide blue-painted circle. At the middle of the circle was a carbon-stained crater eight inches deep in the concrete floor.

'Yeah. Pound of C4, taped under or in one of the drawers of the

94

desk that was here. Damn near blew a hole clean through to the floor below.' Lieutenant Lewis Eldridge, heading the Atlanta PD investigation, dabbed at his forehead with the back of one hand. It was a close, clammy day, and the electricity and air-conditioning for four floors had been knocked out by the explosion. Eldridge, a 300-pound ebony mountain of a man, seemed to be suffering with it.

Wenner paced to the far end of the room and the chalked body marking. 'And the fatality was found here.' It was a statement more than a question and Eldridge just nodded. Wenner's eyes measured a path back towards the blue circle: a good forty-eight, fifty feet by the look of it. 'And the animals before they were let out – where would they have been?'

'Those two units at the end there.' Eldridge pointed to the last two in a row of eight bio-hazard rooms.

Wenner could see the glass screens blown out in all but one room, and the doors were shattered and off their hinges on three of those. 'Any idea how long before the bomb going off, the animals were set free?'

Eldridge shrugged. 'Not an exact time – but probably about fifteen, twenty minutes before. Enough time for one of the monkeys to make his way down to the lobby and the lab assistant, Stuart Greer, to get here. Greer wasn't meant to be here, but when the security guard, John Dehan, found himself facing a grinning monkey and more mice running around than a Pied Pipers' convention, he had a number to ring and Greer lives only four minutes away. Greer had just got the monkey back up here . . . and booooom! Dehan was looking on from the corridor, which was why he wasn't caught so badly. Eldridge took another couple of dabs at his forehead. 'Did they let the animals free in the last bombing?'

'No. No, they didn't.' But then that might have been because the animals were in an adjoining sealed annexe that wasn't reached by the explosion.

'Any ideas yet who's behind it?'

'Too early.' Wenner pushed a tight smile. 'But we should know more soon.'

★

Onion salad? Peppers? Hot salsa?

Eban said '*oui*' to each, nodding eagerly as Madame Ahlnaj, who ran the kebab and falafel bar fifty yards from their apartment building, piled up high his falafel in Arab bread.

When the mountain was finished, she smoothed it out, rolled it in the bread and wrapped it in paper with just the roll-end showing almost in one motion. She handed it to Eban with a smile. 'Now the little one. Joël, have you made your mind up yet?' She perched one hand on her hip challengingly, as if she'd been waiting half the day rather than the half minute that had led her to serve Eban first while André and Joël looked on.

'I'll have the chicken kebab, please.' Joël's voice was squeaky and high and his head was only just above the counter viewing Madame Ahlnaj's display. He said yes to peppers, but no to onions and hot salsa.

'*Lâche*! Sissy,' Eban chimed in. 'Stomach not strong enough?'

Joël looked hurt. 'No, I just don't like them, that's all. They give me wind.'

Eban burst out laughing. André smiled and playfully ruffled Joël's hair, which raised a latent smile on Joël's face as if he'd only just realized he'd been funny.

'I'm not having any of the hot stuff either,' André said, patting his stomach. 'Don't want to end up with an ulcer. But since you have to share a room together, nice to know you're being so thoughtful.' One last hair ruffle and then André pointed out what he wanted as Madame Ahlnaj picked and piled with her lightning tongs.

He'd bit his tongue to avoid adding that perhaps Eban shouldn't have anything hot either; it could upset his stomach, already raw from the drugs he was taking. At times they needed these respites, these escapes from the overpowering shadow of Eban's illness. When André saw him like this, going about his day-to-day activities as if he was just another normal little boy, it was easy to forget the dark shadow moving rapidly across the horizon towards them.

Two weeks until Christmas. André had set a tentative deadline of then to find the link between the T-cell abnormalities on the two samples, and tried to tell himself not to panic in the meantime. Worrying seemed to have a cloying effect, not leave his mind open for the chink of light that he hoped would suddenly shine through the mountain of data they'd waded through, burning the oil late at the lab most nights.

Madame Ahlnaj's, or the café five doors along that did takeaway pizza with a choice of fifteen toppings and lasagne, or the corner bar that did burger or chicken with pommes frites, had become the mainstay of the children's diets the past five weeks. André had rarely been home early, and when he was, like now, he didn't have the energy to cook. He'd normally send the children out for takeaway at most twice a week.

But despite his mental conditioning, André felt seeds of panic setting in again. Though that might have been in part because Eric's *instruction* hearing at which he, Hervé and David had to testify was now only three days away. André was dreading it. There'd been two huddled, back-of-café meetings – one in Paris, one in Nemours – between the three of them in the last ten days to get their final stories straight. They'd avoided using phones, were worried the police might be tapping them. They were acting like some Mafia clique rather than two doctors and a priest.

And he was fast running out of excuses with Delatois. He'd finally admitted, two weeks ago, that they'd had a small setback with the T-cell rate decreasing on one of the samples. He'd pushed it very much as a minor glitch, one that he expected would be sorted out very quickly. But Delatois had enquired about progress three times since, and on the last one two days ago he couldn't help noticing that Delatois' nods in response to his assurances were slightly weary, the first trace of scepticism creeping in.

Perhaps Delatois had had his doubts for a while, but was just biding his time until the *instruction*. If a reporter picked up on the story, no doubt he and David would be out on their ears double-quick. Whether or not they discovered a link between the two samples by Christmas would be immaterial; it could all be over in a few days, the mangabey project dead in the water before it had hardly started. And any chances of saving Eban would die with it.

André swallowed hard and brought his attention back to Madame Ahlnaj as she confirmed a couple of final items he wanted in the kebab to take back for Veruschka. She wrapped it up and he paid.

Maybe he too needed this sort of evening, takeaway kebabs and watching TV with the children, to escape from all the madness, try and convince himself that everything in his own life was normal. But his step felt heavy as they crossed the road back to the apartment. And as he looked at Eban, smiling and joking with Joël as they walked ahead, he was reminded that that was one of the joys of being a child: it took so little to lift their spirits, make them forget. Sometimes he envied that simplicity.

'Did you include something about Quinazoline in the file notes you sent me last week, two days after I left on my trip?' Kalpenski had one eyebrow slightly raised, as if he held doubt or concern.

'Yes. Yes, I did.' She gave back the most level, calm look she could muster, but her stomach was doing somersaults. 'You got it OK? No problems with it, is there?'

He contemplated her a second longer, the eyebrow slowly deflating, before answering. 'No, I got it OK, and no particular problems with its contents.' He forced a taut, deferential smile. 'It's just something else I'm trying to clear up.' He nodded curtly. 'Thank you.'

Hebbard, who no doubt had watched the exchange keenly from his desk, looked away quickly as she glanced round. He studied a file he had open on his desktop for a couple of seconds, then jumped up sharply and caught up with Kalpenski in the corridor. She watched a heated exchange between them through the glass, with Hebbard doing most of the talking and Kalpenski nodding at intervals and finally laying a calming hand on Hebbard's shoulder.

Hebbard returned to his desk and buried his head back in his file; and it soon became painfully obvious that he was avoiding all eye contact with her. Ten minutes later, Kalpenski's PA, Tara, came down and approached him and, after a few words, they left together. No doubt summoned to Kalpenski's office to flesh out his full account of events.

Dani's stomach sank. It was all going wrong, terribly wrong. She'd tried in the last eighteen hours to claw back some calm, tell herself that everything was going to be OK, but her first assumption had been right: it was a trap, a set-up. Now they were just going through the final motions with Hebbard to ensure they had their fact and evidence file complete before canning her.

A few minutes later, Tara returned with one of the techies and they went to Hebbard's computer. The techie played around with it for a while, then printed out two pages and handed them to Tara. More evidence.

There was a longer gap this time, nine or ten minutes – though to Dani it felt like a lifetime – then Tara came down again and summoned her up to Kalpenski's office. She didn't say anything in response or question why, just numbly nodded. Everything was no doubt going to their pre-arranged plan. Despite having resigned herself to her fate, still her mouth was dry, her step leaden as she followed Tara upstairs. Her stomach was a writhing mass of butterfly contortions.

A short preamble by Kalpenski, perhaps a chance for her to put across her case while he nodded with tired understanding; a last effort to retain the decorum and civility that he thought their profession demanded before, regretfully – 'Believe me, nobody here wants to see you go. Least of all me. But under the circumstances there remains no choice' – his effort at understanding stretched to the limit, his face contorting with awkwardness as he finally plunged home the knife. 'I'm sorry. So sorry.'

Heading along the corridor upstairs, they passed Hebbard on his way down. He studiously averted his gaze as he approached, then, at just two paces away, he fixed her with a searing stare. A 'You wait!' look. Then, as quickly, he looked away again.

Dani caught her breath as she walked into Kalpenski's office. Julius Chisholm was sitting alongside him.

Perhaps Kalpenski wanted another, more heavyweight, witness to her dismissal; he was worried that Tara on her own might not be enough. Or it was a two-man show: Kalpenski would deliver the preamble, then Chisholm would take over for condolences and how sorry they were to see her leave the Spheros. Or, because Kalpenski had just returned from his trip, he wasn't sufficiently up to speed on the final stages of Chisholm's sting operation. Chisholm needed to be there to run through that.

Kalpenski spoke first. 'You know that earlier I asked if you'd sent details of Quinazoline in your last file report to me?'

'Yes.' She tried to stay calm, but she could hear her voice quavering with just that one word.

'Well, Dr Hebbard has disputed that,' Chisholm said. 'He says that that message would have come before he'd in fact first discovered the anomalies with Quinazoline, which he subsequently shared with the whole department. He's claiming precedence on that discovery.'

She just knitted her eyebrows quizzically. Her tongue stuck to the roof of her mouth, too dry to slide out any words, even if she could have thought of anything sensible.

'And as well as sending a file note to me,' Kalpenski pressed, 'did you also send one to Dr Hebbard a few days beforehand that included a reference to Quinazoline?'

'Yes. Yes, I did.' Her quavering was more acute, made her voice almost crack. She didn't sound convincing. But they probably needed that admission, that final lie for their file.

'Four days, in fact, before Dr Hebbard claimed he had his breakthrough with it?'

'Yes.' She nodded numbly, feeling her face redden. *Oh God*, this was unbearable. She felt as if her head was going to explode.

'Of course, you realize that we have to take claims like this seriously,' Chisholm said, his expression heavy, grave. 'Very seriously.'

She just kept nodding numbly, the blood pounding through her head so hard that her temples were aching. Why didn't they just get it over with? But they probably needed this: the perfectly orchestrated finale after all the trouble they'd gone to in setting her up, discovering her duplicity.

'Particularly because this is not the first time something like this has come up,' Chisholm emphasized. 'Though last time it was just a tame query, not a direct confrontational disclaim like the one made now by Dr Hebbard . . .'

Their moment of glory, the unravelling of how clever they'd been to catch her: their suspicions with her and Bremner, and then the perfect set-up with Hebbard. Researchers to the end: it wasn't enough for them to simply announce a conclusion, they had to painstakingly account how they'd arrived at it. They couldn't resist riding it home, wallowing in how smart they'd been. Smarter than her.

'And so we set about investigating, getting to the bottom of what had happened . . .'

But if she was going to get canned anyway, she could at least rob them of this final gratification. Cut short the agony of their tedious build-up and the tightening pounding at her temples; save herself some grief.

She shook her head. 'I know that what I did was wrong. I was very foolish . . .'

'Yes, you *were* foolish,' Chisholm cut in sharply. 'You should have shared your findings openly with others in the department, not just in file notes to Dr Hebbard. Because that's exactly what he did to try and claim precedence in the discovery.'

The turn-around caught her breath. She looked down quickly to give herself a second to re-group her churning thoughts, get back some composure.

'Hebbard claimed that you sent him nothing about Quinazoline. But when we sent someone down to check his computer, it was right there.'

Suddenly all the pieces fell into place: the techy with Tara checking Hebbard's computer. Hebbard had been stupid enough to voice his claim before checking back through his file notes. That's why the glare as he'd passed her: if he knew he'd triumphed, he'd have been wearing his normal smug smile. The wave of elation, of relief, was intense. She made an effort to conceal it as she looked up again; after all, she hadn't done anything wrong. She shouldn't look either relieved or surprised. 'I see.' Her best dead-pan.

'Not a pleasant business,' Chisholm said, pursing his lips tightly. Kalpenski nodded his concurrence.

And as Chisholm contemplated her, for a second she thought she saw that same challenging gleam in his eyes as at the Gifford Awards.

She resisted meeting it head on, was afraid she might give away that she knew it was him sending the messages. She looked down again coyly. For now, she'd keep that secret; it would be her ace card in case whatever he had planned for her later went wrong or he had second thoughts. Meanwhile she should try and find out more about the illustrious Dr Julius Chisholm, to get some clue as to what those plans might be.

'What time did you arrive at your brother's house in Nemours?'

'Early evening. Six or seven o'clock, I don't remember exactly.' André shrugged. 'All I remember is that it was almost dark by the time I got there.'

A pause. A long pause. Only the sound of the examining magistrate's pen scratching on paper as he made notes. Faint key taps from the male court clerk that had ushered André in, the only other person in the six-yards square room.

'And what time was it that you arrived back at your place of work with your two brothers?'

'Quite late. Nearly midnight.'

'Now, your colleague . . . David Copell, is it?' Nod and a 'Yes' from André as the magistrate, Marcel Houle, looked up. '. . . He was still there, I understand. Why was it that he was still there so late?'

'Because we had just received a shipment of some monkeys for research from Cameroon, and one of them was ill. David was staying late to tend to it.'

Another, longer pause; this time Houle's notes seemed to extend to two or three lines. At least, as Eric's lawyer, Guy Saumier, had assured him before he went into the session, unlike Inspector Donnet's, Houle's questioning very likely wouldn't be angled. 'It's his job just to set down the details of the case, not try and bend them to any particular direction to suit.' Donnet had fired a chain of awkward questions just around that one point: *'Isn't that unusual, him working so late? It all seems a bit convenient, pre-arranged: "My brother's badly injured, I need help." Indeed, would you have been able to cope without Copell's help?'*

But despite the difference in style, no punchy quick-fire bombardment or angles, André found himself no less tense. The style was slower and more deliberate even than with Delatois, and André began to realize that the tension hung in the silences, the pauses; time to dwell on what Houle might be making of his account, how it might tie in with what others had said or would say, and how it all might end.

And as Houle took him step by step through Eric's injuries of that night and how he'd tended to him both out at Nemours and at the ISG, the images came back; too vividly, too painfully: *following the blood-spot trail along Hervé's cellar, spider blood strands spreading down a table leg to the floor, streetlights flashing like a strobe across Eric's broken body as Hervé sped through the night*. With Donnet he'd been too busy frantically batting and defending to think of anything else. But now with each laboured pause, the images had free rein, ran riot.

How it all might end? At least that, according to Saumier, was clear: five- or six-year prison term. Three eye-witnesses. Exact match blood and DNA found at the scene. Cut-and-dried case. Nothing any of them said at the *instruction* could possibly alter that outcome. So all of this tension now was mainly because of how it might affect him and David. Delatois' words still rang in his ears: 'We'll wait until the *instruction* to decide finally what to do. Just pray that some court reporter doesn't pick up on the story.'

He'd been alert for any unfamiliar faces waiting on the benches outside the courtroom. He accounted for each one – court clerk, bailiff, Saumier's assistant – except for a man in his late twenties who turned up just after him and appeared to be on his own. But at the last minute, Inspector Donnet appeared and came up and talked to the man. Donnet's eyes were somewhat challenging as they'd met his just as he was summoned to give evidence, a faint smug smile appearing at the corner of Donnet's mouth, as if there was some surprise in store of which André was unaware.

His nervousness mounted steadily with each methodical, deliberate question from Houle, his answering voice at times so shaky and uncertain that it hardly sounded true, even when he was just stating fact and wasn't embellishing to save his and David's necks. At the end of the one-hour, thirty-eight-minute ordeal, he rushed straight out to the washrooms down the corridor, past the pleading eyes and obvious questions from Hervé and David, and looked in the mirror long and hard, gripping tight to the washbasin to quell his body's trembling.

'I'm sorry, Eric, so sorry,' he uttered under a heavy exhalation. 'We should be here to help you, not ourselves.' Maybe he had a streak of selfishness after all. A wry smile struggled to lift his taut expression as he splashed some water on his face to freshen up.

As he stepped back into the corridor, he was reminded that his fears about his career were driven mainly by him wanting to see through his mangabey research, not just for the healing it could bring to so many, but more poignantly, more immediately – the days were fast ticking down and still no breakthrough in sight – for Eban. Yet again he had trouble identifying anything in his life he did just for himself.

10

Three days before Christmas, the last working day for many of the businesses around, and by 6 p.m. Jacques Borchaud's Bar Soupçon was already starting to get crowded. By 8 p.m. it was heaving, but André, David, Marielle and Marc managed to grab some space at the bar. Their last late session before the Christmas break, surrounded by alcohol rather than agarose.

At the end of the bar near the door, Borchaud had placed an enormous wicker tray piled with straw on which he'd arranged his finest rare vintages. An imbiber's nativity scene: Where Jesus should have been, a '73 Dom Pérignon magnum; Joseph and Mary, a '76 Rayne Vigneau and '49 Dupeyron; frankincense, a '67 Chambolle-Musigny.

In case any doubt remained that it was a Christmas display, Borchaud had trailed silver tinsel and mistletoe sprigs between the bottles. The fact that the tinsel somehow devalued the esteem of the vintages was no doubt lost on Borchaud, in the same way that the red Santa Claus hat he wore completely destroyed whatever coolness he aimed for with the black suit and slim black tie that had been his habitual bar maître's uniform ever since *Reservoir Dogs*; or was it *The Blues Brothers*? Borchaud had owned and run the Soupçon for longer than André dared remember.

Towards the end of the second glass of champagne André felt his body mellowing, but disengaging his thoughts was more difficult. Nothing in the newspapers as yet, but then just two days ago, Delatois had asked him for a full up-to-date report on the mangabey project by 20 January so that it could be included in Delatois' 31 January annual round-up. It was as if with one pressure appearing safely out of the way, Delatois felt he needed another to keep André on the tightrope. If they didn't hit a breakthrough by then, Delatois would know that he'd been bluffing all along; that it was far more than just a minor 'glitch'.

David Copell had his hand covering his glass more than the others; his flight back to Baltimore for the Christmas break left early in the morning, and he was telling André that he had mixed emotions about the trip.

'It'll be nice to see my mom, and my sister and her kids. But my dad hasn't been the same since that stroke fifteen months back. He's no better at all, according to Mom, and I'll probably have the same feeling I had last year when I visited: that this might be the last Christmas that I'll see him.'

'I know,' André put a comforting hand on David's shoulder. 'It probably won't be easy. I went through the same with my uncle.' Then as the thought sank home, *last Christmas*, he looked away.

David realized the nerve he'd unconsciously hit. André's uncle had become like a replacement father ever since André's father died when he was a young teenager, but four years had now passed since his uncle's death. Whereas André's worries about Eban since their recent setback had consumed their every working hour these past weeks. 'It's only nine days I'm away. We'll get stuck in again as soon as I'm back. I'm sure it won't take long for us to crack it.'

'I suppose you're right. Shouldn't take too long.' André forced a weak smile. 'I just hope we're not too late.'

The noise of the bar crashed back in and Marc Goffinet, a yard behind them talking to Marielle, raised his voice above it.

'Let's get you two in on this. Marielle's problem with her current boyfriend. Should she leave him or not?'

'What's the problem with *this* one?' David perched one hand on his hip, feigning an impatient mother's voice. Marielle had only had two problem boyfriends in the two and a half years she'd worked at the ISG, but David made it sound as if there'd been a constant chain.

'Too controlling,' Goffinet said. 'Plans everything – her life along with his – to the last detail. She feels like she can't breathe.'

'Oh, they're the worst,' David mocked in the same voice. 'You're better off with the ones that hit you. At least with them the message is clear. You know where you stand.'

Marielle punched David's arm playfully as André and Marc chuckled.

'No, seriously,' David said. 'The more control you allow him, the more he'll want. He'll just get worse. So, either you leave him, or, if you don't want to go that far, then state your case here and now. Tell him you need more space and all the other overused expressions that go with that speech.'

'That's what I tried.' Marielle's voice carried a twinge of desperation. 'He had everything mapped out for Christmas. Us seeing this one, that one; but all of it revolving around *his* friends and relatives. When I said that I wanted to see my parents and a few friends, he begrudgingly allotted a few hours the day after Christmas. But only up until two o'clock – he had everything planned again after that.' She shook her head. 'We ended up arguing, as you can imagine.'

'Well, at least he's probably made the decision easier for you.' David waved his champagne glass in a semi-circle. 'If he's going to be that unreasonable about you seeing your own family at Christmas, he's not going to get better in a hurry. Probably you are better off leaving him.'

Marielle chewed lightly at her bottom lip, as if there was something else troubling her or she felt uneasy making that ultimate move so quickly. 'Maybe it's something in me. Maybe I just always pick the wrong guys. Like Marc, I'm attracted by strength, but for me it somehow always goes wrong, backfires.'

André noticed Marc flinch; obviously he'd hoped that was something Marielle would have forgotten, or at least wouldn't repeat. Marielle had been tearful after the split with her last boyfriend when he'd beaten her for the third time, and André and Marc had taken her to the Soupçon after work to console her. She'd knocked back the drinks quickly and become maudlin, started to tease and flirt with them: why couldn't she find men like them? So understanding, *so* . . . she gripped Goffinet's forearm at that point. He was short but stocky, built more like a rugby player than the stereotypical effete image of gays. *'Have you never loved a woman, Marc? Could you ever love someone like me? Treat me like I should be treated?'* She had tears in her eyes as she said it, and with her drunk and emotionally weighed down the question didn't seem, as it might at many other times, ridiculous or out of place. And tears came to Marc's eyes as he leant into her and kissed her on one cheek and said that he did love her, but not in that way; that he'd tried, tried hard to love women, but it had never worked. He'd in fact slept with four or five women before realizing it. 'It felt wrong. I felt I didn't have the strength to protect them and I suddenly felt vulnerable; as if there were two of us that needed protecting, but nobody to do it. In the same way that you feel attracted by a man's strength to protect you, I feel that way too. We've both got the same problem.'

But André could sense that Marc was stung now by the reference. He hadn't wanted it repeated. 'Perhaps because you're confusing bluster with strength,' André said to Marielle, breaking the tense blip in the conversation. 'The physicality is nothing without the emotional strength to go with it. If in that way these men are lacking, then they'll bluster, show a bit of muscle – physically or mentally – to try and compensate.'

'Thanks,' she said. Her eyes were moist and glassy. 'So spot on.' She leant across and kissed André on one cheek, but it was uncomfortably close to his mouth and for a second he was caught up in the warmth and perfume of her.

'That's OK.' He smiled wanly, more to himself than to her. So spot on, with everyone else's relationships. Already he'd had three strained conversations with Charlotte allocating the children's time over Christmas: one day for you, one for me. This Christmas, like last, was shaping up to be an ordeal.

'You know, if you feel uneasy about splitting with him,' Marc offered, 'if you feel it might be too rash a move – then make a list of his good and bad points; and if you feel you just can't live with what's wrong with him, then . . .'

'I think that what *isn't* wrong with him would probably be the easier list. A lot shorter. But thanks.' Marielle raised her glass, took a sip, and smiled above it. 'Who needs psychiatrists and counsellors with you three around?' It was difficult to tell if she really meant it, since part of David's advice had been pure vaudeville. But it was a clear signal that the serious talk was finished.

'I hear that Valmy comes in here now and then.' David winked over André's shoulder at Marc. 'And Christmas is apparently one of his favourite times.'

'I didn't know that.' André furrowed one eyebrow questioningly.

'Yeah. He has a special bow tie with flashing lights for the occasion.' David chuckled as André's expression eased into a smile. 'Or is it one that spins? I forget now.'

The jokes and banter increased as the drinks flowed, Marc at one point making fun of Delatois' stature and swinging his arms like a gorilla. 'The colossus of the ISG, the ass-kissers term him – more like the King Kong. That's what most of us call him behind his back: the gorilla. You want monkeys for research, André, start with him.'

'No, wouldn't do,' David cut in. 'No fucking heart, and you'd probably find he's the result of countless generations of inbreeding.'

André grimaced. 'And, I know, he's got a snake's circulatory system rather than a mammal's.'

'He's got big hands.' Marielle smiled slyly as she sipped at her drink.

'Yeah, but because of that reptilian blood,' Marc retorted, 'there's no pressure there to get anything up.'

André was a beat late joining in with the laughter, half of his thoughts were still elsewhere. In all the years that André had been in medicine, it had never been any different. As if, more than in most professions, they needed the escape valve of humour to get away from what they faced daily: the pregnant mother with breast cancer so advanced that they might have to cut the baby from her on her deathbed; the infant with untreatable raboid cancer who wouldn't make it to their third birthday; *a twelve-year-old boy, Eban's cousin, his body stick-thin and wasted by AIDS, reaching out and taking André's hand; one of only twenty-nine remaining from Eban's originally 140-strong Rwandan village.* André closed his eyes as the noise of the bar swam around him. *Oh God*, he only wanted to save one from all of that. Only one. Was that too much to ask?

'So. Tell us, what would you like us to do with him?'

The question was posed by Chisholm towards the end of their meeting. What would *you* like us to do . . . ? Dani felt her head swimming with the sudden reversal in fortunes, the unfamiliar sense of power.

'Because, certainly now that Hebbard has challenged you openly like this, it would be too awkward for you both to be working in the same department.' Chisholm opened out his palms on the desktop. 'The options are that we shift him to virology or molecular biology, where you'd still see him, but infrequently. Or we remove him completely.'

'I . . . I'm not sure. It's quite an important decision . . . I'd like a few days to think on it, if I may. All of this has caught me by surprise.'

'Yes, of course.' Chisholm inclined his head slightly in understanding. 'If he had to leave, he'd be given the option of resigning, none of this would be made public and he'd be given good references for wherever he decided to go. So don't be too tough on yourself if, in the end, you felt that would be the only option. That you'd feel too awkward facing him again, at any time. In the end it's completely up to you.'

The sense of power, of control, consumed Dani for much of the day – her step felt unusually light as she went around; no sign of Hebbard, perhaps he'd been given the rest of the day off – and the feeling was still with her as she pulled into her driveway at home. Though she hadn't yet decided what to do. Maybe she should pick a daisy from the garden. Get rid of him, get rid of him not.

The only damper was that the house was empty, nobody to share her elation with. Allison spent weekdays with her father, wouldn't be visiting till the weekend. Dani poured herself a large glass of red wine, turned up the stereo, sank down into the sofa with a heavy exhalation and after a few heavy slugs, halfway through Bruce Springsteen's 'Born to Run', she let out a loud, banshee yelp of excitement.

She hadn't felt this good since . . . since she'd shafted her ex over the divorce property settlement. She took another heavy slug, and smiled, nursing the glass as if it contained an elixir. Her body felt warm, glowing, and suddenly she remembered who she could share this with: Leona Bertok. They'd both got divorced about the same time and they'd spent many happy hours on the phone comparing notes, and afterwards, settlements, while character-assassinating their ex's: mine's worse than yours; no mine, he used to . . .

Leona answered almost immediately. 'Dani! Long time no hear. How's everything going?'

'Fine, couldn't be better.' Dani nestled up with her glass by the phone for a long session. 'You know that jumped-up asshole in my section I mentioned a while ago . . . Russ Hebbard? Well, you'll never guess what happened today . . .'

Dani told a selectively edited version that didn't mention Chisholm or her own complicity, that painted Hebbard as a sinner and her – as with all her stories by the time she'd re-vamped them – as a saint. She'd become so expert at it by now that she hardly had to think about it; just slot in Hebbard instead of her ex or the many others over the years that apparently had put her down, or more accurately *tried* to put her down – she invariably turned the tables on them before the final chapter – and the stories came out that way almost of their own accord. Made her look good.

And halfway through her conversation with Leona Bertok, she decided what to do with Hebbard. For them to stay around each other would be more difficult and painful for him than for her; he'd probably leave of his own volition at some stage. At least she wouldn't get the blame. Some extra saintly points gained among work colleagues. If she was on her way up, their future co-operation could be important. She might need them on her side.

Charlotte was on the phone within minutes of André arriving home, in the middle of Veruschka telling him that both Joël and

Eban had eaten well, but Joël had gone to bed early complaining of a cough.

'I tried earlier, but you weren't in. Working late again?'

'No, Christmas drink with the department staff. That's it now for the holidays.'

'That's good. You need the rest. You looked a bit worn down when I last saw you.'

That might be because between your incessant calls with your petty dramas, I've been trying to save the life of our adopted son, he thought. But then she was usually at her most tactless when she was feeling more confident; there'd been hardly any drama calls since their meeting two months ago. No doubt the 'Gérard effect'. 'Nothing wrong, is there?'

'No, no. Just that with the children coming over to my place the day after Christmas, the thing is . . . well, Gérard is going to come by later for a drink, after lunch. And I wondered if . . . if you could make a point with Veruschka that she should try and make a bit more effort with her dress.'

'Oh, I see.' An old contentious issue that André thought had been long forgotten. He remembered much hair-tearing and screaming from Charlotte over Veruschka's dress sense, and him defending that it was practically a uniform for all of them at that age: tracksuit or jeans, trainers, baseball cap turned the wrong way. The girls looked much the same as the boys. Far removed from the image of her namesake, the sixties fashion icon Veruschka, and probably why Charlotte had chosen the name. Yet another way in which her glossy mind-bubble image of the future had been disappointed by reality. 'It's a holiday for her, too – she'll want to relax. If she's trussed up like a Barbie doll, she'll just feel awkward. Besides, you know she'd never agree to it.'

'Not like a Barbie doll, but . . . but a bit of an effort. The same old tracksuit is bad enough, but last time she came over it had some stains down the front.' Charlotte huffed disdainfully. 'Food or something.'

'Sorry, that's my fault. When I come back late at night from trying to save the world, with hardly the energy left to eat my dinner – I should put the washing machine on. I can watch it spinning round while I pick at my food.'

'My God, you're impossible at times. I can see now why we live apart.'

André stayed silent. He knew that the sarcastic outburst was uncharacteristic. Eric's trial, the setback with the mangabey research and Eban, the pressure from Delatois, had all taken their toll on him. His nerves were worn, jaded, and he didn't know how he was going to detach his mind from it for nine whole days to even start enjoying Christmas.

'Just an effort.' Charlotte exhaled heavily. 'A small effort, is that too much to ask? I know she wouldn't wear a dress. So, jeans, OK. And then a blouse or nice shirt. Something colourful. That's all I'm asking.'

'OK. Jeans and a blouse or shirt.' André sighed. Veruschka, still hovering to one side, had picked up what the conversation was about. She was shaking her head, mouthing a silent 'no'. André looked down at his feet. 'That shouldn't be too difficult.'

'Thanks, André. It's not so much for me, you understand, but Gérard. I wouldn't want him to think we're slobs.'

'I understand. And I promise – no food stains.'

There was a second of silence and then Charlotte hung up. Gérard might have brought more stability to her life, but she still wasn't ready for irony or sly humour, he reminded himself.

II

Eban was dying. André had known that from the start. Yet it had always somehow seemed at arm's length; at least enough for him to be able to meanwhile find a cure. But now the recent setbacks and time fast ticking down without any light in sight brought an immediacy to it that made him want to shake those around him by the shoulders. 'Eban's dying! *Dying!*'

Though, as usual, quietly reserved, he'd kept everything bottled up, kept his emotions to himself and just nodded and smiled as he went through the motions of Christmas. More chestnut purée? Cranberry?

He even told Charlotte – when he'd brought over the children the day after Christmas and she'd grabbed him aside for a moment to ask how everything was with Eban – that all was progressing well. Gérard had definitely buoyed her spirits; it was the first time too that he'd got a chance to talk to Gérard directly, and over Gérard's shoulder Charlotte hung on every other word, beaming. But she probably still wasn't strong enough to know the truth; that his hopes were fast diminishing and for the first time he had grave doubts about being able to save Eban.

They'd explored every possibility for differences between the two renegade mangabey samples and the others: nothing. Continuing efforts would merely follow much the same ground. But then he was reminded of the many times in the past when a research path had seemed equally hopeless, and then a breakthrough would suddenly come out of the blue; sometimes through obscure, seemingly unconnected factors. Things that he couldn't possibly have taken into account. He shouldn't close his mind to those possibilities.

And so in this way his thoughts bounced through Christmas: hope, hopeless; or he'd sift through his memory in every moment he had free – between the children excitedly opening their presents and smiling and kissing him in thanks; the cracker he'd pulled with Veruschka that almost knocked the candles from the table and sent the boys into fits of laughter; Eban's attempt at singing 'Noël' that was so raucous and out of tune that a neighbour started banging on the wall, Joël by now convulsed with laughter which ended in a heavy coughing fit – searching for something, *anything*, that he might have missed. Something that might make a difference: a few cells out of shape or with abnormal acid or alkaline readings among millions. Those infinitesimal but vital clues that so often in his work was all that divided life and death.

Life and death. As Eban kissed him on the cheek and thanked him for his present, he'd turned away, not wanting the boy to see the moistness in his eyes or feel his body trembling as he struggled not to break down completely.

And he was reminded of the promise he'd made; the promise that had started everything with Eban.

The small village was in the north of Rwanda, eight miles south of Ruhengeri. André held the hand of a twelve-year-old boy, Nsoro, stick-thin from the ravages of AIDS, as his father looked on.

'Can you save him?' the father asked.

'I don't know. It . . . it would be difficult.'

André had dealt with the boy's father, Mpundu, more than any other person in the last five days of their visit. One of the village elders and elected as its main spokesman, it had been Mpundu who'd patiently explained the history of how their small village had been laid waste by AIDS and war.

Long before civil war finally broke out, there'd been raids on Tetsi villages. On one of them, most of their cattle had been stolen, their main source of revenue, and the men of the village were forced to seek work in the tin ore mines in the south. Prostitution was rife near the mining camps, and the men brought AIDS back to the village. Within no time their wives contracted it and it was then passed on to their unborn children.

The average HIV infection rate in Rwanda was twelve per cent of the population, but here in this small village sixty-eight per cent of its people were infected. That's why André had chosen it to study the disease's progression. In a small community of originally only 140, it was easy to trace how the disease had been passed from husband to wife and then on to the next unborn generation. Listening to Mpundu relate the village's tragic history, it had been easy for André to still look upon it as a detached exercise, just another experiment. But having to tell Mpundu that his son was going to die, that there was no hope of being able to save him, made the personal tragedy tangible, immediate; it could be felt in the withered skin of Nsoro's arm, in the desperation on Mpundu's face as he looked on.

'Please ... *Please* help him. He's my only remaining son.' Mpundu's eyes watered. 'I lost my other son just last year.'

'I ... I don't know.' André found it hard to look at Mpundu directly. With a T-cell count of only 82 – André knew the T-cell counts of all remaining twenty-nine villagers – Nsoro had little time left. The first ailment to come along would finish him, he'd be lucky to last the three months it would take to get the paperwork through. Even if he did, he'd be far too weak to survive the rigours of drug therapy back in Paris, let alone last the wait for more enduring cures. But seeing the desperation in Mpundu's face, André was tempted to bluff, keep his hopes up, say that something could be done. A message sent from Paris months later would be a lot easier than meeting those clinging eyes here and now and telling him that there was no hope left, his son was going to die. It would keep it all at arm's length, as it had been so far: a detached experiment. But Mpundu had been honest and forthright with him over these last days of relating the village's painful history; he couldn't mislead him. Mpundu's shoulders slumped as André spelt out the dismal odds; he was slow in looking up again.

'But I could save you,' André said hopefully.

'Me? *Me?*' Mpundu's eyes twinkled with amusement. He shook his head. 'I've had my life, such as it has been.'

André looked at Mpundu. Just turned fifty, and with a T-cell count of 194, he still looked reasonably healthy, vital. In the first or second world, he'd be considered to have many years still left; but here in third-world Africa, where infant mortality was common and average life expectancy was only 38, he was an old man. Particularly in this village, where seventy per cent of its people had been lost to AIDS or the civil war. Perhaps Mpundu felt uncomfortable being one of its oldest surviving members, or guilt because he was one of the men who'd brought AIDS to the village from the mining camps.

Mpundu's eyes settled on André steadfastly. 'Are you saying you can save me for sure? Or just maybe?' And for a moment André thought that Mpundu was thinking seriously about whether he could be saved.

André shrugged. 'Somewhere in between.' 194? Ten months, a year, possibly even fifteen months before Mpundu's immune system became too weak to respond to treatment. André would have liked longer – his hopes of a breakthrough were at that stage no more than that, nothing tangible – but Mpundu was a stronger bet than Nsoro. 'It would be touch and go, but at least there'd be some hope.'

Mpundu looked down thoughtfully. When he looked up again, it was towards the village, his eyes fixing on a young boy playing football among a group of five.

'Then, if not me, you can save Eban. Save him for sure, no?'

André looked towards the young boy as Mpundu pointed him out. Eban, T-cell count of 389; and as Mpundu remarked that it was his young nephew, his brother's son, suddenly it made sense why Mpundu, one day in going through the list of villagers and respective T-cell counts, had beamed when he'd come to Eban's entry. 'That's good, no?'

'Yes, I . . . I probably could.' 389. Two and a half years, maybe more. A lot of leeway for hope.

Mpundu shook his head, as if André hadn't quite grasped his meaning. 'I don't mean probably, doctor. I mean for sure. Sure, *sure*. It's important to me.'

'Yes, I . . . I'm sure.' André, flustered by Mpundu's sudden insistence, hastily offered his assurance. Then, seeing Mpundu's rising smile, he tempered his enthusiasm. 'But it couldn't be done here. It would mean Eban going to Paris – you probably wouldn't see him again.' The harsh realities of AIDS treatment in Africa. Combination drug therapy for one person for a year cost $20,000. In the West, doctors readily signed off treatments, regardless of age, but in Africa mothers with AIDS-infected infants were simply told to take them home and let them die. Funding of that size just wasn't available; even if it had been, such an amount could feed four or five whole families for a year: it couldn't be squandered on one person. And if they tried to send either money or drugs directly, it evaporated in a chain of bureaucratic paperwork, or was stolen to pay for AK-47s for the civil war or the next dictator's air-conditioned limousine. But besides that dilemma – the divide between AIDS treatment in the West and in Africa – he'd need Eban with him in Paris for regular tests.

'It doesn't matter. Just as long as you can save him.' Mpundu looked back wistfully towards Eban. 'My brother died two years ago and his wife soon after. Nsoro, Eban and me are all that's left out of our family. If you can't save me or Nsoro, then Eban's the only one left. The *only* hope for the future. You see now why it's so important to me that you save him.'

'Yes . . . I see now.' André joined Mpundu in looking towards the boy; so young and seemingly carefree as he played football under the relentless African sun. Eban. Suddenly a symbol not just of the last hope in the generation-chain of Mpundu's family, but of this disease- and war-torn village, and of Africa as a whole. Those wide and dusty plains and dark jungle expanses beyond the field of his and Mpundu's vision. That first wave of feeling for André that if he could save this young boy, then maybe he could save the rest.

And from that initial seed of hope, as they bonded closer and Eban became part of André's family, it wasn't long before Eban became the main symbol and focus in André's mind for all AIDS patients.

'You'll save him?'

'Yes . . . I'll save him.'

'For sure?' Mpundu reached out and gripped André's hand tight at that moment. 'Sure, *sure?*'

'Yes. Sure, sure.' André closed his eyes solemnly and gripped Mpundu's hands back in reassurance.

Nsoro died after only two months, and fifteen months later they received a telegram telling them that Mpundu had died. Eban cried for days; after his parents' death, Mpundu had raised and cared for him single-handedly.

Eban was the only one left; the only survivor from generations of Mpundus.

At times André felt the pressure of it all was too much, too stifling. But at others, it was probably just what he needed: the incentive to work those extra research hours and hunt down every possible angle; the frantic drive and push that had finally led to the breakthrough with the mangabeys.

But now over these past weeks, as doubt crept in and his hope with Eban began to dwindle, his final promise to Mpundu came back to haunt him, at moments the echoes of his own pleas waking him in the middle of a sweating nightmare.

I tried. *I tried.* But I can't save them all. *I can't save them all* . . . André woke up with the sound of Joël's repeated coughing from the put-up bed a few feet away. Or was it Eban coughing next door?

Eban was dying.

Joël's cough had steadily got worse through Christmas. He'd separated the boys almost immediately, put Joël in his room to sleep on Christmas Eve. That was the worst thing that could happen at this stage: a bad cough or flu could deplete Eban's T-cell count by 80 or more. In the final stages of AIDS, it was the most common ailment to kill people, their T-cell count so low it couldn't even fight off simple flu.

But it was impossible to keep Joël and Eban completely apart. They'd sat opposite each other at Christmas lunches both at his place and Charlotte's, then on the 27th had to be in the same car – the only separation he'd been able to achieve was Eban in the front and Joël in the back with Veruschka – when he'd driven out to

Nemours to have lunch and swap presents with his mother and Hervé.

It was the second time he'd seen Hervé over the holidays. The first had been visiting Eric in La Santé prison the day after Christmas when the children were with Charlotte. Their mother had refused to come, she was still in shock over the imprisonment as well as upset with Eric for his actions; either way, actually seeing him behind bars would have been too painful a reminder.

But Eric's absence at the lunch, when normally every year he'd be there as well, underlined the fate that had befallen him almost as painfully. Clinking glasses and wishing each other well somehow had an empty ring to it.

André was quiet for most of the drive back from Nemours, and as they hit the outskirts of Paris, Eban started to cough. Only a few times at first, not as frequent as Joël's coughing, and later that night it was still sparse, just a few coughs here and there. But in the middle of the night Eban woke up with a fever – André gave him cough syrup, Amantadine and an extra dose of his regular Invirase – but by morning his coughing was heavy, and by the following night some of his coughing fits were so incessant that he had trouble getting his breath back.

André felt each cough like a hammer blow, imagining Eban's T-cell resistance being relentlessly battered and weakened. Already he'd lost the two months' leeway he'd allowed himself with the current research setback, now this illness was evaporating any further margin he might have hoped for; the last straw he'd clung to was that Eban's T-cell decline wouldn't be too rapid.

Eban was dying.

By the third day it had developed into fully fledged flu and André was in a blind panic. By how much would Eban's T-cell rate have fallen already? 30, 40 points? 50? He knew that it was pointless testing until the flu had run its course; three full days afterwards, in fact. By then the body would have rallied back any T-cells it was going to – the recovery usually weaker each time with HIV sufferers – and the overall impact to the immune system could be measured accurately.

André held his head in his hands when six days later he looked at the results: 61-point drop since Eban's last test three weeks ago. David, back from Baltimore just two days before, tried to lift his spirits.

'OK, we've lost some time and initiative. We'll just have to make it up. We'll get there, don't worry.'

'But we've gone over practically every possibility.'

'Then we'll just have to go over them again. We've obviously missed something.'

They worked around the clock. On nights when the children weren't with him, often he worked until eleven or midnight, crawling straight into bed after a quick snack. And on the nights they were, a succession of frantic last-minute calls to Charlotte to ask if he could pick them up half an hour or an hour later, then they'd grab takeaways on the way back home. André couldn't remember the last time he'd cooked for them.

By the end of January when they still hadn't found anything, André's despondency set in again, with a vengeance. Exhausted from overwork and his nerves ragged over Eban's fast-worsening condition, he felt suddenly as if he had no energy or reserves left to fight with. In addition, he still had to contend with the tightrope game he'd been playing with Delatois. He'd had no choice but to come clean in his mid-January report to Delatois about the extent of the recent setback: 'But we expect a breakthrough any day now.' With each passing day, André felt his stomach tightening. Each day with Eban's T-cell count steadily decreasing; at times André felt it counting down almost in rhythm with his pounding pulse.

Eban was dying. Eban was dying.

André was practically in a daze when the thought struck. His mind crushed by overwork and worry, it was a miracle anything of any clarity seeped through.

They were in the nearby pizza takeaway and Eban was hesitating over what to have on his. Normally, Joël would be the one to be undecided, but of late the frailty of Eban's health had become painfully evident. André had increased his dose of Invirase, and in response the number of foodstuffs that seemed to upset him had also increased. He'd pick at most of his meals, often complained of stomach and general muscle cramps, and at times his shaking was so bad that he could hardly hold a glass steadily. He'd lost six kilos over the past two months and in the last few weeks his eyes looked slightly glazed, with one of them becoming increasingly bloodshot.

Eban hesitatingly asked Pascal, the pizza-shop owner, if he had sweetcorn and maybe tuna instead of anchovies, and as Pascal pointed to the wide array of bowls in a glass display below his countertop and commented that it was more a question of what he *didn't* have, it triggered in André's mind one of Marielle's comments at Christmas: 'I think that what *isn't* wrong with him would probably be the easier list. A lot shorter.' And a moment later the thought hit.

André's breath caught slightly in his throat with excitement as he hastily paid and they headed out. He phoned David at home as soon as he was in the door.

'We've been looking in the wrong places. We've been looking for what those two samples *had* which the others didn't have – when we should have been looking the other way round.'

'Whoa, whoa! Back up a bit.' David had also obviously just arrived home and it took him a moment to catch up.

'We should have been looking for what they *didn't* have – viruses, traces of past ailments, whatever – which *has* affected the others.'

It took them five weeks to find it. Longer than André would have hoped for, but the cross-referencing and elimination process was voluminous. Out of the twelve mangabey samples – the eight previous samples and the four current – they'd discover something in three or four, but then not in the others. At one point they found shigella in eight and thought they'd hit it – before finally finding a virus in all ten bar the two with regressive results: hepatitis B.

'Didn't we find some anomalies with hepatitis B before?' David quizzed. 'Those hookers from West Africa . . . Sierra Leone, was it?'

'No, Côte d'Ivoire,' André corrected. 'Ivory Coast.'

A number of prostitutes with long-term AIDS immunity, eight in total, had been discovered between three Abidjan brothels. Their single common factor was that they'd all previously had hepatitis B. In fact there had been numerous cases where prior hepatitis sufferers had stronger resistance to AIDS, to the extent that at one stage it was reported, incorrectly, that they carried immunity. But it was certainly true that they had more resistance, their T-cell decline was slower, possibly owing to some similarities between the hepatitis and HIV viruses.

'What was the name of that one we arranged to come over?' David enquired. 'Dou something?'

'Dhoumil.' The most startling case out of the eight with hardly any T-cell decline that they'd brought over for further tests.

'Whatever happened to her?'

'For the first two tests she came in with no problem, right on time. For the third she was almost two months late . . . and after that we didn't see her again. I phoned the last number I had for her, and someone else answered.' André shrugged. 'She didn't leave a forwarding address and they didn't know where she'd gone.'

They were filled with elation at finally making the discovery, and André immediately rushed with the news to Delatois, so at least he was off that tightrope. But the tightrope with Eban was still very much with him. André was seriously worried that the breakthrough had come too late. In the last five weeks that it had taken them to identify it, Eban's T-cell count had dropped another 28 points . . . ticking steadily down towards the doomsday 100 points.

Eban was dying.

André didn't know why the point of no return, the point at which HIV suddenly became AIDS, had been set at a T-cell count of 200; it could just as easily have been set at 220 or 250 or 175.

But the various medical bodies had decided in their infinite wisdom on 200; this was the point at which they deemed the body to have insufficient remaining T-cells to combat infections. From that point on, a count of 200 or below, any infection – flu, chicken pox, dysentery, bronchitis – could kill a patient. There just wouldn't be sufficient T-cells left to fight them.

This often planted in the public's mind that it was two separate diseases: one day someone had HIV, then suddenly it had become AIDS. But they were in fact one and the same, the T-cell clock gradually ticking down from one to the other. However, that process could take an extremely long time: eight to ten years from initial contraction of HIV before it became AIDS. Initially it was believed that there was a dormant period, but it was later realized that the HIV virus was incubating, day by day, year by year – a silent army recruiting for its onslaught on the body's T-cells. Almost as if it knew that if it attempted its attack early, it would be defeated and knocked out. Only by biding its time would it be able to have an impact, be sure of steadily depleting T-cells until it won.

A normal healthy individual had a T-cell count of 700–1,000. For the first three to five years in an HIV carrier, depending on the subject, little happened. Then battle would commence, though the number of T-cells killed in those early skirmishes would often be so few that there would be little visible effect. But with each battle, as the HIV gained dominance, the T-cell losses would be heavier; the clock started to count down ever faster.

The body still responded well to new treatment far beyond the 200-point barrier, so André had set the ideal minimum for treating Eban at 140 points, with an *absolute* minimum of 100 points. Below that the immune system was too weak to respond and any new treatment far too risky.

So now with Eban, André started to measure everything by events and Eban's T-cell count rather than time: 374 when he'd first returned from Rwanda; 257 before Christmas; 196 after Eban's flu; 181 when the flash thought hit him in the pizzeria; 149 now.

André could clearly see the precipice of 100 looming ahead; and he felt suddenly as if he and Eban were on a fast-increasing downhill run without brakes.

They'd found the breakthrough. But there was a mountain of other things to do – testing, refining, side-reaction monitoring, deciding on the ideal vector – before they even got near being allowed phase one clinical trials.

Eban was dying. André had always lived with that, but suddenly it was inescapable. For the first time André knew with certainty that unless there was some sort of miracle, they weren't going to make it in time.

12

Dani spun it out for six days before finally informing Kalpenski and Chisholm that she thought Hebbard should stay.

'I think it would be unfair for him to have to leave the Spheros over this – he's got so much time invested here.' She looked down coyly at that point, chewing at her bottom lip. 'However awkwardly I might feel about what has happened, I think I should in this instance give my feelings second place. He should be given another chance.'

'That's very gracious of you – but are you sure?' Kalpenski confirmed.

She just nodded hastily, only looking up for a second, as if she was too troubled over the whole matter to talk about it further. Chisholm, too, contemplated her with a mixture of concern and approval of the graciousness of her gesture, but she couldn't help catching again that fleeting wry smile and gleam in his eye. Chisholm *knew* it was an act, and approved.

She'd revelled in the six-day wait, enjoying watching Hebbard squirm in the knowledge that his entire career hung by a thread on whatever she decided. *Get rid of him, get rid of him not.* She couldn't help glancing at him thoughtfully at times with just the hint of a quizzical smile. Now, what am I going to do with you? Hebbard would invariably look quickly away, red-faced and flustered. No doubt panicking that if he gave her the wrong look – his past trademark smugness, defiant challenge or superiority – his fate would be sealed. Oh, the feeling of power was joyous, made her feel positively giddy. She didn't want to get rid of that feeling in a hurry. Much better to keep Hebbard around. That way she could keep him dancing on her strings for months or even years more.

She was also starting to get her first taste of what Chisholm might have planned for her, and it felt good. If this is what it felt like with power over just one person, then what was it going to be like with a whole department? She'd be walking on air, feet clear of the ground above everyone else, omnipotent, all-powerful, nothing could stop her then, she'd . . .

Hebbard was transferred to virology two days later – no point in prolonging her agony, the management obviously thought. Little did they realize – except perhaps Chisholm – that it was more Hebbard's agony. On the day of his move, he looked visibly relieved, as if a heavy weight had been lifted. But during his first month there, she found excuses to visit the department far more regularly than normal. She wanted him to know that he wasn't getting off that easy; it was *her* turn to challenge and taunt, and she was going to be in his face for some time to come. A constant reminder of his fall from grace. Probably after a few months – or maybe he'd last as long as a year or so – he'd get sick of it and hand in his notice. But meanwhile she'd milk it for everything it was worth.

And at the same time she'd gained the accolade of her peers for being gracious and letting Hebbard stay. That added deception – getting pats on the back over Hebbard when actually she was steadily grinding the last of his pride into the ground – was the final icing on the cake.

Basking in such gloried light from her colleagues, and no doubt from Chisholm too, she wondered if it could possibly get better than this. She checked her e-mail every day for fresh messages from Chisholm as to what the next stage in the game plan might be. The other thing she regularly checked for were messages from the private investigator she'd hired to unveil Chisholm's background. That was the one thing that still made her feel uncomfortable about the entire scenario: as much as she was pulling everyone else's strings – Hebbard and now the rest of the department – she knew that in turn she was being played. She desperately needed something to even the stakes.

A miracle. For the first few weeks, it looked as if André's wish might just be granted. Not through anything dramatic – working through all the stages towards a final green light on a clinical trial was going to take a minimum of five months, nothing they could do to alter that – but because Eban's rate of T-cell decline slowed. His count reduced by only 9 points over a three-week period. Suddenly there was renewed hope that he might actually last out.

André had reduced the absolute minimum T-count watershed in his mind from 100 to 80. Below that André knew it would be hopeless; the rigours of the treatment itself would kill Eban, as certainly as any flu or everyday virus would at that stage.

André did a quick calculation: 140 T-cell count now, 9 points lost in three weeks: 90–95 by the time of a clinical trial. Not ideal, far less than he'd have liked, but at least it was above his new target minimum of 80.

Then suddenly Anouk fell ill again, and everything changed once more. The symptoms were similar to before: fever, trembling, not eating her food, eyes bleary and bloodshot. Michel, the ISG vet, was called in and diagnosed bacterial pneumonia.

'The shock of capture no doubt brought about the first infection. But I think she's also responding worse to continued captivity than the others, and that has probably been the main cause of the infection now coming back.'

But after two days of tests, he discovered a far more serious fungal pneumonia; possibly derived from the first infection, or even something that had been there all along. 'Perhaps there was a trace on her lungs when she was ill before, but too small for us to detect. And now it has mushroomed.'

Michel administered heavy doses of amoxycillin, but Anouk's decline was more rapid and dramatic than last time. And in the midst of them battling to save her, with her by then in the Laferge room in an incubator being fed intravenously, Charlotte phoned.

'Oh, you're still there. I phoned your place and Veruschka sounded quite concerned. Thought you'd be back over an hour ago.'

'A panic came up here. I'm still caught up in the middle of it, so –'

'Nothing changes, it seems.' She exhaled heavily. 'Look, I wouldn't have troubled you at work, but it *is* important. I've got involved with a little investment with Gérard, and I wanted to get your advice.'

'I thought you said that he hadn't asked you for money. That after Pierre, you wouldn't get involved with anyone like that again.'

'No, no – he hasn't asked me. This is a business arrangement, he's put in money too. We've both gone into it with our eyes fully open, as equal partners. He risks losing the same as me.'

'Losing?'

As Charlotte explained that sales of a collection they'd jointly invested in weren't going as hoped, he wondered why she was phoning him. Surely this was something she'd be better off discussing directly with Gérard. Halfway through he interrupted and voiced that thought, adding, 'And, I mean, if you really thought my opinion was worthwhile – surely the best time to ask would have been at the outset?'

'I know. But since things started going wrong with the investment, it's been difficult to talk to Gérard about it. I've only spoken to him once in the last week, and then he said he was just too busy to discuss it.'

André smiled wryly at the fact that he was merely an afterthought. She'd only thought of him once she was no longer getting feedback from Gérard – but suddenly it was world-crushingly urgent and he was meant to drop everything. Typically selfish Charlotte action – but then maybe she'd become conditioned to the world revolving around her panics. Or was it more a cry for help, her afraid of losing another man because of this business arrangement gone haywire? Either way – at the other end of the room, David and Michel were in the midst of a flurry of activity with Anouk, David intermittently looking up anxiously to see when he'd be finished on the phone – this wasn't the time for business or emotional counselling, even if there was anything of use he could have offered.

'Look, Charlotte. What I know about fashion investments you could fit on the back of a postage stamp. And you've caught me in the middle of the most terrible panic. If we could talk about this another time?'

'Yes, yes, another time,' she echoed blandly, as if she'd suddenly been distracted by something else or her thoughts had drifted.

Across the room, David was frantically beckoning him over.

'Got to go! I'll phone you in a couple of days, and we'll –'

'Yes, of course. A couple of days,' she cut in. The same bland echo. 'Maybe by then it might have sorted itself out.' She hung up abruptly.

There was something that worried him in her voice, a tremulous undertone that hinted of deeper concerns that she was reluctant to discuss, and for a moment he felt guilty about brushing her off. But he had no time to dwell on it, he was quickly sucked back into the nightmare with Anouk: 82 over 39; respiration 13 p.m; pulse rate 78 p.m; temperature 103.4.

Michel had given her more amoxycillin together with a shot of adrenalin two hours ago, but they were still losing her. Rapidly.

'Her temperature's dangerously high with fever,' Michel commented. 'We've reduced the temperature in the incubator to try and control it. Let's see how that goes.'

They watched anxiously as over the next fifteen minutes it rose to a peak of 103.6 before slipping slowly back and settling finally at 102.1. Pulse rate by then was also lower at 49 p.m, which Michel commented he'd have expected with the lower incubator temperature. When all indicators had been more or less stable for almost forty minutes, André took the opportunity to head home to see to his kids.

He grabbed a takeaway Chinese on his way and just over an hour later, after instructions to Veruschka as to what time Joël and Eban should be in bed, he headed back to the lab.

'What's wrong with her?' Joël asked as he was on his way out of the door. Joël had overheard him comment to Veruschka that the reason he was working so late was because of problems with one of the mangabeys, Anouk.

'She's very ill. Pneumonia.'

'She's going to be OK, isn't she?' Joël asked, his little voice heavy with concern.

'Well, we . . . we don't know yet.' André looked down, found it hard to meet Joël's eyes directly. 'It's just too early to say.'

Eban, a couple of yards behind Joël, looked down almost in

unison with him. Eban hadn't said anything, but he looked equally concerned about Anouk's plight. Possibly because Anouk was the only one of the monkeys the children had actually seen, when one night he'd stopped by the lab briefly on his way back home after picking them up from Charlotte's.

When he got back to the lab, he walked in on the middle of another crisis. Anouk's temperature had risen so high that Michel and David had taken her out of the incubator and covered her body with ice packs. The ice packs worked in lowering her temperature, but her pulse rate and respiration were correspondingly weakened and twelve minutes later her heart stopped. Michel frantically massaged while André and David prepared the electric shock pads. After two jolts, her heart started again, and immediately afterwards they gave her another adrenalin shot. The following four hours were a desperate juggling of Anouk's temperature, pulse and respiration, and more amoxycillin and adrenalin shots – but when her second heart attack hit, it was a battle they finally lost. After the fifth electric pad jolt and still a flatline and no response, with the three of them by then physically and emotionally exhausted, they switched off.

The fall-out from Anouk's death was devastating. Press headlines appeared such as 'Monkey Mishap' and 'Blow to AIDS cure', with one article questioning how we could possibly hold faith in a cure for AIDS deriving from a species of monkey that had itself just died from simple pneumonia, something humans had long ago developed reasonable immunity to. The negative media coverage combined with the fact that they'd lost a vital live sample for cross-referencing – something that could seriously hamper them in the final clinches of getting a phase one clinical trial clearance – once again had Delatois having second thoughts. André had to be at his most persuasive to convince him not to stop the project.

'We've had the main breakthrough, and we're almost there in putting everything together to back it up. Just a month or two more and we'll have the press singing a different tune.'

Of all his past lies and truth-bending to Delatois, this was the most audacious. He knew already that he needed a minimum of four months. But by far the most worrying impact of Anouk's death was to Eban. In the week after, Eban's T-cell count dropped a startling 11 points, then another 15 points in the two weeks after that. Perhaps because he'd formed an unconscious bond with Anouk: something from his part of the world that might lead to him being cured. That somehow seemed fitting. But now with her death, a large part of that symbol of hope in Eban's mind was gone; it was also perhaps a portent of what lay ahead for him. Everyone he'd ever been close to in Africa went the same way: Nsoro, Mpundu, now Anouk. André couldn't help feeling that with Anouk's death, Eban mentally let loose the last strand of hope he'd been clinging to.

Perhaps that too was why André had lied to Delatois. For so long he'd linked the cure for AIDS with Eban in his mind that he found it impossible to separate the two. And subconsciously he knew that was all the time they probably now had left: one or two months. Whatever hope had appeared briefly a few weeks ago had been yanked cruelly away, *now you see it, now you don't*. There was little or nothing that could be done to save Eban within that time.

13

There was nothing for almost two months, no messages, and Dani felt a certain tension building with the silence. As if she and her conspirator had formed a bond and she was lost and adrift without his guiding hand.

Perhaps there was nothing to say. Hebbard had been suitably humbled and she was now Kalpenski's top protégée, nothing to stand in her way. Everything was heading in the direction that Chisholm had no doubt hoped. But then perhaps, more worryingly, the silence was because Chisholm had found out that she'd put a private investigator on to him.

His name was Ken Meikle and she'd asked him to be discreet: paperwork and file digging and, if he had to make any phone calls, subtle and low-key so that they couldn't be traced back or in any way alert Chisholm. And no trailing or phone-tapping: she wanted to know purely about Chisholm's background, not about his current love-life or movements.

Meikle's report arrived after three weeks. Much of the early parts of it were readily available surface information: fifty-six, twice-divorced (last marriage ended seven years ago). Two daughters from his first marriage, now aged eighteen and fifteen. A son from his second marriage, now ten and living with his mother in Aarau, Switzerland (second wife is Swiss and they married there twelve years ago while Chisholm was with FILSA). Harvard graduate, first in medicine, second in economics, with a post-graduate PhD in economics.

Dani skimmed quickly through the next two pages detailing Chisholm's work career in the ten years after leaving university. A variety of minor posts mostly in the finance and marketing departments of pharmaceutical or medical research establishments – though one was a chemical supply company and another a technical publisher (two medical journals among its fourteen titles).

It wasn't until Chisholm was in his mid-thirties that he started seriously climbing the career ladder. Three assistant finance directorships at pharmaceutical companies and assistant treasurer at two hospitals (one of which was Chisholm's closest posting, Delaware County) took up the next ten years before Chisholm's move to FILSA in Switzerland, his first finance directorship. Chisholm also stayed with FILSA longer than any other company so far, six years in total. A brief posting of only ten months followed with a Boston research company, Votex, then two years with a Palo Alto genetic research establishment, GRC, before Chisholm finally joined the Spheros as treasurer four years ago.

The only possibly troublesome notes were Chisholm leaving Votex prematurely under a cloud, reportedly because of his undisclosed financial involvement with GRC, at that stage in early start-up (Chisholm in fact still maintains a stake-holding in GRC but, unlike last time, *with* Spheros's knowledge and approval); and his acrimonious divorce and custody battle with his Swiss wife (apparently, part of Chisholm's motive for investing in GRC was to salt as much money as possible out of reach of his ex-wife, in retaliation for her playing hard-ball over custody).

Dani looked up from the report and out of the window as a rising wind ruffled the tree branches outside. For a moment she sucked in the silence of the house around and felt it settle heavy in her stomach. One thing she and Chisholm had in common: a child sacrificed on the altar of their careers. Though in Chisholm's case it sounded more forced than chosen, and at least she had the benefit of still seeing Allison at the weekends.

Dani felt a sudden chill run through her, though it was little to do with the cold wind outside and thoughts of lost children; it was because of the sudden reminder that Chisholm had probably dug into her background. He certainly knew everything about her past run-in with Bremner. Which probably meant he also knew about her giving up custody of Allison in order to advance her career *and* about her current legal battle with her mother. She'd made sure to keep that secret from work colleagues; it would be impossible for them to view with anything but abhorrence, however much she bent the truth or tried to give it a favourable spin.

She let out a long, slow breath and closed her eyes. The fact that Chisholm probably knew about that and yet had still earmarked her as his golden girl said a lot about him. Probably far more than Meikle had put in his five-page report.

Twelve days later, by which time her nerves were ragged as she became convinced that the long silence was because Chisholm had found out about her digging into his background, there was an e-mail message waiting for her when she arrived at work:

> Now you need to take care of Kalpenski. He's the only remaining obstacle in the way of you heading the department. No clues this time as to how and when – you're going to have to work that out for yourself, use your own initiative. That in itself will tell me if you've got what it takes to fill his shoes.

The Métro station faded into the blur of the passing tunnel walls as the train sped up again. Blanche, the first station after their change at Place de Clichy. André glanced up at the map above the window: two more stations to go before they got off at Barbès Rochechouart.

Marielle forced an encouraging smile at him from her flip-down seat opposite, but then his vision was blocked by a group of three people preparing to get off at the next station. André went back to staring vacantly at the tunnel wall speeding past – the monotony and his gaunt reflection broken only by brief electrical flashes – before finally closing his eyes. The past few weeks had become little more than that: a blur.

Working late in the lab almost every night, hastily grabbed pizzas and kebabs on his way home or, if the children were with Charlotte, sending Marielle or Marc out to grab a roll or sandwich which he'd nibble at between spells hunched over a microscope or spread of agarose trays; or sometimes because of his absorption with work he'd forget to eat completely. Then home for another fitful night's sleep – though thankfully he'd only had the same dream once over those weeks. His sleep was so sparse that when he did finally succumb he was probably sleeping too deeply to dream. And all the time, Eban's T-cell count was steadily ticking down. A blur, and with the same feeling as now: hurtling through a dark tunnel with little hope at its end.

Dhoumil? André wondered whether she really could be Eban's salvation.

Steadily ticking down. At least Eban's T-cell decline had been just that for most of the past few weeks: *steady*, dropping by no more than 3 to 4 points each week. Until four days ago. Eban got another cold which quickly turned to flu – probably because by now his immunity was so weak it was susceptible to even the faintest germ strain – and his T-cell count dropped 12 points in two days. Then another 4 points the next day, 3 points the next . . . *Eban was dying*. But now, suddenly, it was being measured in days and weeks rather than months. André began to fear that he might not even last through this current bout of flu; or, if he did, he would simply be too weak to respond to any treatment.

They were still months away from a clinical trial – most of which would be taken up running prior-infected hepatitis-B models with transengenic mice and ex-vivo human samples – and Eban no longer had that sort of time left. It was then that David suggested Dhoumil.

'She's the best case example we've had of someone resistant to developing AIDS who's also previously had hepatitis. If we can see where her T-cell count is now and how it responds ex-vivo to the mangabey serum – it could put us months ahead, knocking at the door of a clinical trial almost in one leap.'

André immediately saw the sense in it. Dhoumil's T-cell count had slowly declined from 712 to 518 before rising again to a plateau of 585–620, where it had been holding steady last time they'd tested her a year ago. Whether it had since dropped or was still holding, any rise now in response to the mangabey serum could provide the vital final proof and, in conjunction with their earlier tests, provide them with a pertinent body of data that could take them months to achieve through other means. The only problem was that Dhoumil had moved from her last address, and when they'd phoned the new tenants said that they didn't know where she was. She hadn't left a forwarding address or telephone number.

They decided to try their luck again with the new tenants. Marielle offered to make the call; they might have to plead their case and a woman had a better chance of hitting the right compassionate note and drawing them out more. At first Marielle got the same blank 'we don't know where she's gone' as last time. But then she laid it on thick and said that Dhoumil was seriously ill and needed urgent medical treatment. 'What she has is also highly contagious. So she's not just in danger herself, she's also a threat to others.'

After some worried conferring with a couple of voices in the background, the woman at the other end said that they didn't know exactly where Dhoumil had gone, but her brother had seen Dhoumil just a few blocks away on Rue Myrha a couple of months ago. 'Perhaps she's living somewhere around there now.'

It made sense that Dhoumil was still in the area, no doubt lying low from social services and immigration. With its predominance of immigrants from North and West Africa and the Caribbean, few areas could offer Dhoumil the same combination of anonymity and low-rent housing as the Goutte d'Or. Their only option would be to head to Rue Myrha and start knocking on some doors.

Security was suddenly an issue. The Goutte d'Or was a known haven of drug-dealers, thieves and Algerian GIA terrorists. Even the police thought twice before venturing into the area. Marc offered to go instead of Marielle, but, while appreciating the gesture, Marielle insisted that a soft touch would still be essential. 'Two men on the doorstep will just ensure more doors closing in our faces, or them not even opening in the first place.'

But then while Marielle was digging out Dhoumil's file with her photo, Charlotte phoned. More whining about Gérard. After two weeks of giving her the runaround, Gérard had finally presented her with the accounts of their failed joint enterprise, claiming that he'd felt too awkward and embarrassed to show them to her earlier. But André was suspicious and, through a company search man recommended by Marc, discovered that it was a shell company with Gérard Lacroix very much behind it; also, it wasn't the first time he'd done it. It was another two weeks before André summoned up the courage and found the right cushioning words to break the news to Charlotte, and this was now the third 'woe is me' call from her since. What am I going to do? Why didn't I see it earlier? Is that all that men want me for these days: my money? He'd listened patiently throughout each call, bitten his lip and was careful not to say or even hint 'I told you so.' But now with the panic with Eban, her wheedling tone was beginning to grate. He glanced at his watch as Marielle finally lifted a file from the cabinet and looked over at him hopefully.

At the end of last week, Hervé had phoned to remind him that Eric's trial was in just six days' time. 'Of course I'll be there,' André had assured. As always, everyone making demands on him, pulling and pushing him in every direction. And he suddenly had the feeling that if anything happened to Eban, that could be partly to blame: his attention dragged away at a key moment and him missing vital clues that might help save Eban in time. *I can't save them all . . .*

'I'm sorry . . . I don't have time for this now,' he cut in halfway through Charlotte's whining. She was covering much the same ground as last time and he'd switched off minutes ago. Across the room Marielle waved the file and raised one eyebrow, silently mouthing, *'Come on.'*

'Busy as usual, I suppose. Like all the other men in my life, no time for me now. I would have thought that knowing the state I'm in, you might at least spare a few –'

'Eban is dying!' he blurted out, suddenly sick of her whining; not just now, but over the past months and years. The exclamation felt strangely gratifying, a dam-burst release of frustration; all the times he'd bit his lip and patiently listened suddenly let loose.

A short gasp as she took in the news, or perhaps it was partly the surprise value that others apart from her also had dramas and problems. Then, seconds later, a more relaxed exhalation. 'But we've known that right from the start. And you always said that it was years away and that you'd probably hit a breakthrough before anything might happen to him.'

'That's the problem – it's not years away any more. It's weeks or perhaps only days. The breakthrough I was hoping for is close, very close. But Eban's in such a bad way with this recent flu that I'm not sure I'm going to make it in time. That's why I'm rushing.'

'I see. I'm sorry. I didn't know.' Her voice was suddenly subdued, heavy. She cleared her throat and struggled for a more hopeful tone. 'But surely there's still hope?'

'Yes, of course. We're trying for something right now that might give us the short cut we need. I'd just got some fresh news in as you phoned.'

'I . . . I see.' A forced, muted chuckle, her voice on the edge of cracking. 'I seem to have the knack of always phoning at the wrong time.'

'No, no . . . it's OK. I was going to tell you earlier. But you already had so much on your plate.'

'. . . Always a bit slow on catching on when people don't want to hear from me any more,' she continued distractedly as if he hadn't said anything. 'Not just you . . . but *everyone*. I think Sylvana had the right idea. No trouble to anyone any more. I . . . I'm sorry.' He could hear the tremble in her voice become more pronounced with every word, as if it was taking every ounce of her effort to keep from breaking down. He wished now he hadn't said anything. 'I should let you go now . . . shouldn't trouble you any more.' She hung up abruptly.

Bang! André's nerves jumped with the sudden thud to one side. As the man sat next to him got up, his flip-down seat sprung back with a bang. Marielle was looking at him expectantly as she also got to her feet.

'It's our stop. We get off here.'

The sudden stream of lights to one side burnt his eyes. And as the train slowed, the repetitive sign markings became clear: Barbès Rochechouart. Minutes later they were swallowed up among the shadowy warrens of the Goutte d'Or.

Dani answered her phone on the second ring.

'Hi. Merrison calling. We've got it! We've got the adjournment.'

'I see.' Dani looked around. Everybody on the lab floor was busy with their work; nobody seemed to be paying her any attention. But still she felt anxious, hesitant. She kept her voice muted. 'You know, you shouldn't really call me here.' The thought of whether Chisholm, or indeed anyone at the Spheros, knew about the case with her mother had preoccupied her increasingly over the past few weeks.

'Sorry. But I thought you'd want to know this straight away. Especially given that last time we spoke, your mother wasn't very well. What we discussed then might actually now be a possibility.'

'Right. Well, I . . .' Dani faltered. Andy Luttman was looking up from his computer towards her. He got up and started heading her way. She felt a sudden rush of blood to her face. 'I . . . I'm not with you. However misguided I think she might be in this action, you know I could never have such an unkind thought about her.' She hung up abruptly before Luttman got close.

At his end, Silas Merrison held the receiver a foot away and stared at it curiously. A strange fish, this Dani Stolk. When he'd told her two months ago that the chances of winning with her mother were no better than 50/50, she'd begged and pleaded with him to get an adjournment, delay as much as possible. Her mother had been ill recently. 'With any luck, the old hag might not even make it that long.' Now she was the complete opposite, playing the morally sainted.

Two hours later, just after he'd returned from lunch, she called back.

'Sorry about that. Someone came by my desk.' He could hear traffic sounds drifting from the background. She was obviously calling from a street booth. 'How long a delay might that mean?'

'Four months minimum. But if I'm creative with my diary and make things awkward, date-wise, because of other trial commitments – we could stretch that to six months, a year, maybe longer. How's your mother's health now?'

'She's OK right now. It was flu last time. A pretty bad one. Developed into pneumonia and dragged her under for more than a month. But then when she's like she is now, it seems like she might soldier on indefinitely. Just my luck.' She forced an uncomfortable laugh. 'You know, she had a big operation a couple of years back before any of this started. And I silently prayed then that she wouldn't make it, because even then I could see all of this coming down the line in the future.' A fresh breath. 'But hey, at least now we've got more chance of that happening. She can't last for ever. Right?'

'Right.'

As Dani thanked him and signed off, for the second time that day Silas Merrison stared at the receiver curiously just before hanging up. But at least the Dani Stolk he'd come to know over the past year was back. He knew exactly where he stood and what he was dealing with.

Charlotte lit the last of the night-lights and carefully placed it on the wide tiled bath surround as steam rose from the bath water.

The bath soaps and oils, creams, scents and strategically placed decorative pebbles, were all pushed back to make room for the night-lights, eleven in all. Eleven: new beginnings. Except that she could no longer see anything new or hopeful in the future, and she felt too tired, too defeated to try and reinvent herself and her fashion line yet again. But she just couldn't think of a new number to suit how she felt now, so she'd stuck with an old faithful. A reminder of good and more hopeful times past.

Eban was dying. She'd felt the news like a stomach blow, totally taking the wind out of her. But perhaps she shouldn't have felt so shocked. For a while she'd had the feeling that something was wrong, but nobody had the forthrightness to tell her, let her in on the secret. That's all it was these days, her diet from hereon in: whispers behind closed doors and cupped hands. 'Don't let her know. She's too delicate, too frail . . . *too old.*'

She caught the reflection of her naked figure for a moment in the long mirror opposite and slowly shook her head. She slowly averted her eyes downwards, as if in shame, and finally closed them. No wonder that Pierre and Gérard just wanted her for her money. What else was there to want? The best had long gone. Her figure, the sparkle in her personality. All that was left was a sad and sour middle-aged woman, a shadow of her former self. A cauldron of self-doubt and neurosis to whom none of the men in her life ever told the truth. Pierre, Gérard, now André. His lies were meant to be more noble and well-meaning because they weren't led by the need for money, but out of pity. But in a way that was worse. It told her in no uncertain terms that was the most she could now expect from men: *Pity.*

She turned off the bath taps as the water came near the top. The rising steam started to obscure her reflection in the mirror. *A shadow of her former self.* But much better like this, she thought: the mist obscured where the years had taken their toll. Much better that that was the last image she'd take with her.

She took the bowl from one side and sprinkled the red petals on top of the water. The image in the bath too was now almost perfect, how she remembered it to be. How long ago was that now? Fourteen years, fifteen? Her business was at its height and they'd just moved in to the St-Michel apartment. André bought champagne to celebrate, and she'd surrounded the bath with night-lights and sprinkled petals on the water and they'd both sat in the bath and drunk the champagne and then made love half the night. It was the last time she could remember feeling truly happy, whole. She'd tried many times since to recapture and relive perfect moments from the past, but they always remained somehow elusive. Perhaps this was the only way: one perfect moment, one perfect image, forever frozen in time.

Eban was dying. She couldn't take it any more. Every year everything got worse, slipped further away from the perfect images she'd fixed in her mind. A song lyric about time rewriting all the lines, from one of hers and André's favourites when they'd first met, came briefly to mind. She wiped away a tear that had trickled down and felt suddenly cool on one cheek. She was kidding herself that things were ever going to get better, let alone anywhere near perfect again.

One day she'd told Sylvana about those old baths she'd prepare, and from then on Sylvana admitted doing the same when she had a special lover. Then she'd done it for that final day and made the newspapers. Maybe she would, too; another bit of the past recaptured. It had been a while since they'd written about her, she'd been long forgotten.

She picked up the open razor and put it within reach at the side of the bath as she stepped in, the warm water soothing and comforting as she slid slowly down. She rested for a moment with her eyes closed, breathing steadily in and out in an attempt to settle her nerves. But still her heart beat wildly, almost double time to her breathing. When her nerves had calmed as much as she thought they would, she opened her eyes and picked up the razor. But still her shaking hand as she brought it close to her left wrist betrayed her nervousness. She wanted to be calm, at peace in her final moment; not the frantic, neurotic bag of nerves she'd been these past months and years. Only then would it be perfect.

She took deep, steady breaths again and after a moment managed to stay the shaking. She moved the razor closer to her wrist and, as she felt the cool of the blade touch her skin, closed her eyes. She'd never been able to watch people being cut in films – remembered shrieking and curling up close to André with her eyes closed at that moment in the Buñuel film with the razor – let alone able to watch herself being cut.

She drew the blade slowly across. She was surprised it didn't hurt more. After a moment she felt brave enough to open her eyes and look. A lazy stream of crimson swirled into the water, almost matching the colour of the petals. Another touch of perfection.

But suddenly she started to get bombarded by conflicting thoughts. What time would the children arrive? She didn't want them to be first to find her. It had to be the police: that first snapshot catching her perfectly arranged scenario for posterity. Especially if, like Sylvana, she hit the press. *Eighties fashion designer dies . . .*

She sat forward and turned on the taps again, a slow trickle. The bath would overflow, and as blood-tinged water seeped through the floor, the man below would call the police.

She leant back, her breathing heavier with the fresh steam rising from the hot water trickling in. The only remaining problems were that she didn't think she had the guts to just lie there and watch herself slowly bleed to death, she'd need some pills to knock herself out. And what if she bled so slowly that she was discovered before she died?

Was that what all this was about? Subconsciously, she didn't really want to die – she simply wanted to make a cry for help. She was still trying to fathom out that final nagging question as she stood up and reached towards the bathroom cabinet and the pills.

A curtain to their side flipped back, startling them; then just as quickly it was pulled shut again. The third such overt stare they'd received during their short time in the Goutte d'Or, not counting the two Algerian or Moroccan twenty-somethings on the corner in their Hilfiger bomber jackets and kaffirs, who, having measured them with a searing gaze as they'd passed, kept glancing at them warily every other minute – particularly when they'd knocked on doors to ask questions. It was as if the two were on look-out, but they could have simply been waiting for somebody and cagey and surly were all that was in their street-stance repertoire.

Across the road, two adjoining derelict buildings appeared to have been taken over by squatters. At one time there'd obviously been some development planned because the builders had concealed the ground floor of each property behind plywood board, on which there was now a myriad of graffiti and the announcement JOUR 90, 150, 210, 270 . . . each 60-day marker in white crossed through with a bold red line all the way up to 570, the only number not crossed through. Presumably the number of days the squatters had managed to hold out against the developers and the local council. At the centre of the plywood expanse a rough hole had been cut and a heavily soiled, bright-striped blanket had been draped over it. A pathetic reminder of Bedouin tents or African kraal huts among the city sprawl.

The blanket was pulled aside as they approached and a plump black woman in a long floral African dress, trainers and anorak looked out. It was as if her dress, along with perhaps much of her spirit and thoughts, had only made part of the transition to urban

Europe. Her gaze their way was only fleeting, it was more of a general survey up and down the street.

'Let's try her,' Marielle said, leading the way across the street.

'Looks promising,' André agreed. Just the sort of squat that might suit Dhoumil. Probably as many as thirty or forty occupied the two buildings.

The woman, who at the last second realized that they intended to speak to her, made as if to duck back hastily behind the blanket before deciding that the gesture would be too obvious. As Marielle started speaking, she nodded in acknowledgement with the blanket half pulled across her lower body. She paid a bit more attention to the photo Marielle produced than the three people so far canvassed, squinting at it briefly, but the end result was the same.

'No. I'm sorry. Don't know her.'

'Are you sure?' Marielle pressed. 'If not in this building, then maybe in the street? We were told that she might be in this street.'

The woman squinted at the photo again for a second before shaking her head. 'No, no. Very sorry.' She gave an attempt at a courteous smile. But as she went to pull the blanket back, Marielle reached out and lightly gripped her shoulder.

'It's very important that we find her. She's very ill. Very ill indeed. And also her condition is highly contagious. She could infect many others in the same house and in the general neighbourhood.' Only the first part held any truth and Marielle had used the tactic previously, when she thought a dreadlocked teenager was being evasive and possibly hiding something. But this time it was probably more out of frustration, desperation.

The African woman held Marielle's gaze steadily without glancing again at the photo. 'I hear what you're saying very clearly. But I have not seen this woman. This I am sure of. I'm sorry.' She lowered her eyes and gave a curt nod, but just before she pulled the blanket across Marielle handed her their department's business card.

'If the situation changes or you later remember anything, please phone us. It's important.' The same routine on every call so far, just in case somebody later had a stab of conscience or recall.

The woman reminded André of a surlier version of Bernice, the Martiniquean ex-nurse André had brought in a week ago to take care of Eban. As Eban's condition worsened, he had to be taken out of school and André didn't have the time to take care of him round the clock. He couldn't hunt down the cure for him *and* nurse him. It was one or the other. And he couldn't ask Charlotte, otherwise she'd have known how ill Eban was, even if she was in a fit state with all her other problems right now. So in the end the only option was a recommended nurse who used to work at Necker Enfants hospital.

He needn't have worried about bringing in somebody new. Bernice and Eban got on like a house on fire. He'd phone a couple of times a day to find out how Eban was, to be greeted by Bernice chuckling. 'That Eban – he so funny. He's got some stories and a half, I can tell you.' All Bernice and Eban seemed to do all day was swap funny stories and anecdotes about Africa and the Caribbean.

He should have brought Bernice in earlier, though knew why he hadn't. A constant nurse might have been a painful reminder to Eban of just how ill he was. But now if anything was helping Eban's T-cell count remain stable while they were out hunting down Dhoumil, it was Bernice.

The next three houses went much the same as the first, but when on the last Marielle used the same tactic of pushing harder – possibly because the woman's eyes above the mouth-cover of her djellaba kept shifting to something or someone slightly behind her – everything started to go horribly wrong.

An unshaven man in his early thirties suddenly burst from the shadows behind her.

'Who are you? Coming around asking questions like this.' He gesticulated wildly, the back of one hand almost slapping against Marielle's shoulder as his eyes darted between the two of them. His left eye had a slightly milky cloud and it was more difficult to tell where it was focused. 'The police? Social services?'

'No. We're medical research workers,' Marielle offered. But the sudden quaver in her voice made it a weak claim, as if she was uncertain of her ground. Or lying.

'Medical research?' The man raised one eyebrow incredulously. 'What business could you possibly have here, in the Goutte d'Or?'

'As I . . . as I said before. We're looking for this woman, because she's very ill.' Marielle held up the photo of Dhoumil still clutched in her hand, which was now visibly shaking. He gave it only a passing glance. 'And what she has is highly contagious.'

'Contagious . . . *contagious*,' the man mimicked with a sly smile. 'What would the authorities or anyone outside care if all of us here in the Goutte d'Or perished? In fact that would probably suit them . . . all of their problems gone in one!' His eyes glared, and this time as he made a sweeping arm motion, the back of his right hand lightly connected with Marielle's shoulder. 'They look upon us as no better than vermin here. It would only concern them if they thought it might spread outside. If their own might be affected . . .'

But in the middle of the man's tirade, the thought suddenly hit André: *Sylvana!* Oh no! *Oh God, no!*

He stepped forward and took his mobile out in the same motion. 'We don't have time for this now!'

'Time? Time?' The man suddenly turned on André. Now, dealing with a man, he felt he no longer had to hold back on physical contact. He prodded André's chest hard with two fingers. 'That's more like it. What we're more used to hearing. You don't have *time* for us here.' The two-fingered prod very quickly became a solid flat-handed push.

André stumbled back. But all he could think about was Charlotte. '*Sylvana had the right idea.*' He was half switched off, numbed to the possible danger of the situation he was in. He straightened and brought his mobile up again, starting to tap out Charlotte's number. His whole body was shaking, his finger struggling to hit the numbers square-on. He just prayed he was wrong. 'Really, there's something else I've . . .'

But the man was on him quickly, pushing hard again with his hand. André stumbled back and his mobile flew from his grip before he'd tapped out the last few numbers. He went to pick it up, but the man kept coming forward, hovering over him and gloating as he crouched down.

André's arms and torso were probably too weak to fend the man off, but his legs were like steel cords from his daily cycle ride. He grabbed his mobile and looked up uncertainly, still slightly winded from being pushed – but then the sudden reminder that the children would soon be arriving from school at Charlotte's gave him the final adrenalin rush he needed. He sprung up without warning, hitting the man solidly in his chest with his right shoulder. The man exhaled with a burst of surprise, his eyes wide as he stumbled back. He back-pedalled frantically for balance and looked as if he was about to fall when he thudded into the house wall behind, a second burst of air spewing from his mouth.

The man was at a difficult angle, his feet almost a yard ahead of his chest pinned back against the wall. But André kept up the pressure, pushing his forearm up under the man's chin.

'I said – we don't have time for this now.' A hoarse, threatening whisper, his face so close that he could feel the warmth and sour-spice odour of the man's breath.

The man's eyes held his defiantly for a moment and his body tensed as if he was about to struggle back. The woman in the djellaba started to shriek and pound André's shoulder and the two men on the corner were again looking on curiously. It was all starting to slip away; André didn't think he could hold the man pinned back much longer. He shrugged the woman off and gave one last desperate push with all his strength, feeling his thigh muscles lock as he squeezed the last air from the man and jammed his forearm tighter into his neck.

'OK . . . *OK*,' the man said finally, gaspingly.

André waited a second for the last of the fight to go from the man's body and his eyes look down in final acquiescence, then with one last push he stepped back and started heading away. Marielle quickly fell in step beside him.

He took out his mobile and dialled Charlotte's number again, giving one last look back in case the man once more summoned bravado and decided to come after him. But he was too busy waving his arms at the woman, reassuring her that he was OK.

'That was brave,' Marielle commented, one eyebrow raised. 'And more than a little foolish.'

Looking at Marielle, it was difficult to tell which had won the day: brave or foolish. But she certainly looked surprised. Charlotte's number started ringing. 'I had to do something. He wasn't going to let us be.'

'True.'

The number kept ringing. And ringing. André finally gave up on the seventh ring, by which time they were halfway back down the street. André felt his fears turn to real panic, his stomach tightening. Unconsciously, he broke from his brisk stride into a light jog.

'What's wrong?' Marielle asked. 'Something you remembered about Eban?'

'No. Something Charlotte mentioned on the phone this morning about Sylvana, a model she used to know.' Between breaths as they ran, André explained. Originally from Czechoslovakia, Sylvana, after initially falling in love with Paris and a dazzling first two years on the circuit, became beset by problems: boyfriend wrangles, drink and drugs, finally eating disorders and anorexia and resultantly fewer modelling assignments. 'Not too different to the problems that hit many a model, I suppose. Except that in Sylvana's case one day she decided to opt out by emptying a bottle of pills down her throat and cutting her wrists.' André sighed heavily. 'When I spoke to Charlotte this morning, she said that she thought Sylvana had the right idea.'

Marielle remained slightly quizzical. 'Why should that suddenly come up now?'

'Well, she's also been having relationship problems recently. And then just this morning I told her about Eban, how seriously ill he was. I'd kept it from her until now.'

'Oh.'

They were silent for the rest of the block and a half run to Barbès Rochechouart station. As they went down the escalator André tried Veruschka's number. She should be on the bus home from school now and about to pick up Joël. But it was engaged.

On the platform there were already groups of schoolchildren, some Joël's age and younger, their laughter and screeching voices filling the air. Suddenly he wasn't so sure what he wanted most if and when he got hold of Veruschka: to get to Charlotte before she did anything rash or, if, as he feared, she might already have done something, to make sure Joël didn't see her like that. He tried Veruschka's number again. Still engaged. The screeches of the children echoed in the tiled concourse, and he felt suddenly dizzy and faint. He braced one hand against the nearest wall and let out a slow breath, fighting to calm his pounding nerves. Who else could he try? The police? But then what if he was wrong and she wasn't answering simply because she was with a customer or in the back room checking stock?

Marielle looked at him with concern and lightly gripped one arm. 'Don't worry,' she said.

She leant forward and for a second he thought she was going to kiss him, but she simply touched one cheek gently, pressing home her message with her eyes before lifting the hand away.

For a moment he was caught up in the warmth and perfume of her, the compassion in her suntan-brown eyes, and a part of him wanted to sink deeper into that, push away the world outside and his problems with Eban and now Charlotte; while another part of him felt it was totally the wrong emotion to have at that moment with what might be happening with Charlotte.

Their train hurtling into the station broke the spell.

Suddenly, André remembered another option: the man who ran the antique bookshop adjoining Charlotte's shop and below her apartment, Henri Porce . . . something. He'd know whether or not she was there or what she might be doing. Porcern? Porcenet? *Porcelet!*

As their train started gathering speed and the lights of Barbès Rochechouart station gave way to the darkness of the tunnel, André dialled directory enquiries.

14

Henri Porcelet climbed up the ladder to reach the top shelves.

He had a collector arriving late that afternoon from Tours and he already had two of the books requested – Dorgelès' *Le Reveil des morts* and Vallotton's *Les Rassemblements* – on his desk. The third book on the collector's list was far rarer and so Porcelet had put it on a high shelf. It collected more dust there, but saved the wear and tear from day-to-day handling, the countless customers who'd pick it up out of curiosity, 'Ah, Eluard's *Doubles d'ombre*,' and leaf through before deciding it was too expensive. The high shelves were usually for serious collectors only, and Porcelet often informed casual browsers scanning the top shelves, 'The prices go up as you go higher. If it's out of reach of your hand, it might well also be out of reach of your pocket.'

Occasionally, he'd hook a casual buyer with that line, their ego dented that anything was beyond their pocket, and they'd leave with a handful of books costing a king's ransom, when all they'd originally walked in for was a few leather-bound tomes as decoration for their newly put-up library shelves, which they'd never read but would give dinner guests the impression that they were intellectual.

Porcelet handled the book with due veneration and blew off its light cover of dust. He gently stroked its red leather cover as if he was caressing a new-born baby or a lover. It was then that Porcelet noticed something: a damp patch on the white plaster wall where he'd removed the book. He quickly removed two more to judge the spread of the patch, and it appeared to get slightly larger as Porcelet looked on. Water was coming in from above! But it had a slightly pink tinge. Pink champagne?

He'd spoken to Charlotte, the woman who owned the adjoining fashion shop and apartment above, a few times, but they were far from close acquaintances, despite the many warm smiles he gave her as he caught her eye walking in and out of her shop, to make it clear that he wouldn't mind knowing her better. Always busy, slightly frantic and living on her nerves, she was attractive in an almost classical way – how he imagined the Princess of Cleves and some of the other heroines in the books lining his shelves – and she was always immaculately turned out and elegant; something that was sadly fading these days, even on the Left Bank.

She looked the sort that might drink pink champagne, but it would have to be a cascade to run through like this. One of those champagne-glass waterfalls. He decided in the end that it was probably bubble bath or rust from the pipes providing the pink tinge. The patch seemed to have spread almost another inch in the time he'd been looking at it. He was going to have to remove a fair few more books to protect them, and fast! Then he'd go up and knock on her door to see what was happening. Strangely enough, he'd noticed that her shop had been closed the last hour or so and he hadn't seen her about.

Porcelet started removing the books six and eight at a time, and on his third trip up the ladder, halfway through piling up a fresh stack of books, the phone started ringing. He looked at it accusingly for a moment, wondering whether to put the books back and answer it, before deciding against. He had to get the books clear of the damp – he could easily lose three or four to water damage just while he was talking. He'd let it go into the answerphone.

'. . . Claire will be there, Thérèse too. No, no. Don't see much of Angel these days. Not since she started going out with Maurice.'

Veruschka was on her mobile to her best friend, Claudette, as the 35 bus pulled up at the stop by Joël's school. A light rain had started to fall and a faint mist had formed on the bus window. She rubbed a clear patch and spotted Joël among a group of three boys, beckoning with the same hand and lifting her eyes only briefly in acknowledgement. She gazed into mid-space as she brought her attention back to her call.

'I know . . . I know. She said that Simon had her bra off and was fondling her last time that they went to the cinema. No more than that, she says. But you never know with that Angel. They might have done more, but she'd never let on. Too afraid that it would get back to her parents.'

Joël slumped down on the seat next to her with a half-puff, half-sigh, fired a faint smile which Veruschka barely acknowledged – she was too engrossed in her phone conversation – and took a Gameboy out of his school bag.

'Makes you wonder. I think she told me about the bra because she wants to make like something exciting is happening . . . but not *too* exciting, too shocking. Something that would send her parents into orbit, *if* it got back to them. Yeah . . . yeah. I should be there in about eight minutes. The bus is just coming onto Raspail now.'

Joël only then became aware that she was arranging something. He looked up from his Gameboy. 'Are you going somewhere?'

'Yes. Café Mantellan.' Confronted with Joël's pensive expression, she added: 'It's OK. I'll walk to the corner and wait until I see you go inside, like before.'

Joël still didn't look happy. 'Can't you come in with me for the first fifteen minutes – then go to the Mantellan?'

'No, I can't.' She looked at him with incredulity and disdain, as if he'd suggested something remarkably loathsome. 'I'm meeting Claudette. And Claire and Thérèse. The arrangements are already made.'

Joël dived back into his Gameboy. If Veruschka had come in with him, she'd have got the brunt of their mother's standard ten-minute inquisition upon walking in the door. Now he'd have to shoulder that alone. *You're late. You're all wet. How did school go? I told your father that you shouldn't wear that shirt . . . it's far too tight.* Plus on top now he'd get: *Where's Veruschka? Why didn't she come in with you? Who is she seeing? What time will she be back?* He sighed deeply. It was difficult being eight years old. But whatever else he might say, it didn't look like Veruschka was going to budge.

As the bus turned on to Rue de Sèvres, it looked for a moment as if the phone conversation was ending, but then obviously Claudette brought up something new.

'I know. I thought exactly the same – a dream. But dangerous
. . . *dangereeeuuuux*. If he was taking off your bra, you couldn't
imagine him just fumbling with his hands. It would have to be with
a knife, or maybe ripped off with his teeth.'

Confusing, Joël thought ruefully. The two women around him
were so different: one hardly noticed him, acted as if he wasn't
there; the other paid him far too much attention, continually fussed.
He wished Eban were with him. At least then there would have
been two of them to handle his mother's questions, and with Eban
being ill she would probably have gone easy. He felt a sudden pang
reminding himself about that. When he'd asked a few days ago if
Eban was going to be OK, his father had answered quickly that
he'd be fine. But there'd been an uncertainty in his father's eyes
that worried him. Eban and his father were the only ones in the
family that he felt he could truly talk to, but his father was always
so busy. So in the end there was really only Eban.

As the bus slowed approaching their stop, Joël put his Gameboy away and hitched his schoolbag back over his shoulder.
But Veruschka was still on her mobile as they got off and turned
the corner into Boulevard St-Germain towards their mother's
apartment.

Engaged. Engaged. Engaged.

André tried Veruschka's number every other minute as the
tunnel lights flashed by. Still engaged. He decided to try Porcelet's
number again. *Beep, beep. Beep, beep.* Damn! That was engaged now
as well. Last time it had rung four times and then gone into a
recorded message. Unconsciously his other hand had balled tight
and was beating a rapid tattoo on his thigh as the RER train hurtled
along.

He tried Charlotte's number again, letting it ring seven times
before he finally gave up. Still no answer.

'Don't worry. Everything's probably OK,' Marielle offered.
'People say the strangest things when they're upset. She's probably
just nipped out to the shops or is busy with a customer and can't
come to the phone.'

André nodded, chewing at his bottom lip. Maybe she was right. But looking into Marielle's eyes, he could see that she was only half convinced by her own assurances. Heavy doubt and worry lay there too.

What would Charlotte do? Take pills and cut her wrists, like Sylvana? Or maybe she wasn't answering because right now she was wandering around looking for a bridge to jump off. He stared pensively into the darkness of the tunnel rushing by his window. The sudden burst of light stung his eyes.

'It's our station,' Marielle announced.

And as soon as the doors were open, they sprinted along the platform and took the escalator steps two at a time. As they neared the top, André's mobile started ringing; he was heavily out of breath as he answered. It was Henri Porcelet.

'You left a message. Something about your wife . . . you were worried about her. I tried you back a moment ago, but you were engaged.'

'Yes . . . yes. Thanks for calling back.' André struggled for breath as he fed in his ticket and went through the barrier behind Marielle. 'Have you seen my wife this afternoon? Has she been in the shop?'

'No, I haven't. I saw her this morning and at lunchtime. But for the last couple of hours I haven't seen her, and the shop is closed now. And I . . . I was starting to wonder about her, in fact, because of water coming through from her apartment above – when your call came through.'

'Water?'

'Well, I . . . I think it's water. It has a pinkish tinge, and for a moment I thought it might be pink champagne.' Porcelet forced an awkward laugh. 'But it's probably just rust from the pipes.'

Pinkish tinge. André's stomach sank. She'd chosen exactly the same way as Sylvana. Cut her wrists and let the bath overflow. Eleven night-lights spread around – André forgot the symbolism of the number – and a mass of petals on the water. The picture had made page seven in *Le Soir.* Her last shot at fame.

'Can you please . . . *please* check on her? Go up and ring her door. I'm desperately worried something might have happened to her.'

Marielle frantically flagged down a taxi, and a dark blue Peugeot pulled in.

'Yes . . . yes, of course,' Porcelet said. 'I can do that for you.'

Marielle shouted 'Rue de l'Eperon' to the taxi driver, and they jumped into the back. 'Number fifty-seven.'

'I should be with you in about four or five minutes,' André said. 'We've just got in a taxi at Les Halles. But it's urgent that she's checked on immediately. Every minute could count.'

'I understand. I'll . . . I'll go up right now.' Porcelet's voice quavered; he was obviously uncomfortable with this errand, starting to worry about what might confront him.

'Thanks.' André rang off and dialled straight out again to Veruschka. Now at least he knew what he wanted from the children: to stop them getting to the apartment and seeing the nightmare scene he feared awaited there. The images of Sylvana in her blood-soaked bath swam inside his head, made him dizzy. Or was it the movement of the taxi fishtailing as it sped through the traffic?

Two rings. Three. André began to panic again when finally it answered at the start of the fourth ring.

'*Veruschka!* I've been trying to get hold of you. Where are you now?'

'At the corner of l'Eperon. Why?'

'Thank God I got hold of you in time. It's important that you and Joël don't go up to see your mother right now.'

'Why?' Veruschka looked anxiously towards Joël thirty yards ahead pacing determinedly towards their mother's. Hopefully he'd glance back, as he usually did when she stayed on the corner and let him go on alone, and she'd wave and hold him back. 'What's wrong?'

'It's just something I'm worried might have happened with your mother. I might be . . .' The taxi swerved wildly and a horn blared from behind. 'Look – just don't go up there right now, that's all.'

'But Joël's walking ahead of me.' She broke off and shouted out, 'Joël! Joël!' But a large truck passing drowned out her voice and blocked her vision for a second. When she had sight of him again, he hadn't turned round and was still pacing steadily away. He hadn't heard.

She shouted again, but, combined with the traffic noise, he was now too far away to hear. Veruschka started running after him.

'Why aren't you with him?' André snapped. 'We told you to always –'

'I don't have time for that now,' Veruschka said breathlessly. 'I'm trying to catch him.'

She shouted 'Joël!' again, but the same truck was only twenty yards ahead and revving heavily, caught in a jam behind a few cars as someone parked. Joël didn't turn round.

'Have you caught up with him yet?' André pressed, but no answer came. Only Veruschka's rapid breathing and her pounding footsteps almost in time with his own pulse; background traffic sounds for a moment were hard to distinguish from those around him, a car behind beeping twice as their taxi cut sharply in front of it. Another swerve and fishtail to get in the outer lane, then their driver floored it approaching the Pont Neuf.

André felt suddenly dizzy with it all: the swaying of the taxi, Veruschka's pounding footsteps, his own adrenalin rush and rapid pulse. *Bridge*. And as they hit the bridge and he saw the water, he closed his eyes. But suddenly it was no longer water there, but the rows of tombstones stretching into the distance. *I can't save them all, I can't* . . . Lights hit his eyes in a flaring burst, a slowly expanding arc as Charlotte's apartment door swung open, and he saw clearly the horror and trauma reflected on young Joël's face – but he couldn't make out what Joël saw in that moment beyond the door, the searing light whited everything out . . .

He opened his eyes to see a car coming directly towards them, its lights flashing frantically. Their taxi swung back in again and the car's blaring horn Dopplered quickly past.

'Have you caught up with him?' André repeated.

'No. But don't worry, I will.' Joël was only five yards from the entrance. She felt sure that he'd look back just before going inside, as he did every day.

'We're just crossing the Pont Neuf. I should be with you in only two minutes.'

'OK.' Joël was only a yard away from the entrance. She moved the mobile away from her mouth and shouted 'Joël!' one last time.

Joël's shoulders seemed to flinch slightly, as if her shout had hit him there and caused a moment's indecision; but then he continued on without altering pace or looking back.

15

'Madame Lemoine. Madame Lemoine!' Porcelet waited a moment and then knocked a couple of times sharply, the third time he'd done so. And waited. No response. He rang the bell again; his fourth ring, he'd rung twice before he started to knock and call out. And as the echoes of the last ring died, Porcelet became aware of footsteps at the bottom of the stairs. He turned towards them.

He'd seen the boy before, coming in and out of the building past his door, and he remembered one day seeing Madame Lemoine ruffle the boy's hair and kiss his forehead as she packed him off somewhere. As the boy's eyes settled on him quizzically, as if questioning what he was doing there, little doubt remained which door he was headed for.

'I'm calling on your mother,' Porcelet said. 'He glanced down momentarily at the thin stream of water running out under the door. 'It appears she might have left a tap on.'

Joël paused only for a second in his progress up the stairs, still looking slightly perplexed. From where he was standing, he couldn't see the water and didn't know what Porcelet was looking at.

As Joël neared the top, Porcelet again rapped sharply on the door and called out; then, falling almost as an echo, Veruschka's sharp voice came from the bottom of the stairs.

'Joël! Joël! Don't go up there!'

Joël paused after a step, the three of them for a moment forming a hesitant triangle.

Porcelet, as Veruschka's gaze shifted towards him questioningly, offered, 'Your father phoned and asked me to call on your mother. He was concerned about her.' A couple of other things struck Porcelet in that instant. 'Obviously your father has phoned you as well. Do you have a key?' Porcelet shrugged as he saw continuing uncertainty in Veruschka's face. 'It's just that it's better than my breaking the door down. Or calling the police to do it.'

'Yes, I . . . I do.' Veruschka took a couple of tentative steps as she fished in her pocket. 'But we . . . we're not meant to go up there.'

Porcelet nodded with a grimace and moved to the top of the stairs a yard from Joël. 'Perhaps if you just hand it to me here, then go back down to the bottom with your brother.'

'Yes . . . OK.' After the first few steps, Veruschka moved with more urgency up the stairs, but her body language was still taut, constrained, screamed uncertainty and worry.

Porcelet went down a couple of steps almost level with Joël and reached out a hand, so that she wouldn't have to come all the way up. And as she passed across the key, he felt all of that worry and uncertainty in the gentle trembling of her fingers and saw it in the taut lines of her face. A faint flicker in her eyes as she glanced to one side, and the worry quickly transformed to fear. She'd seen the water running out from beneath the door. Porcelet had also noticed the spider strands of red diffusing through the water, and realized now why André Lemoine had caught his breath when he'd first mentioned that the water had a pink tinge. He found his hand shaking too as he took the key from Veruschka.

'If . . . if you go back down and wait at the bottom. I'll come down to you after I've been inside.'

He waited until they were halfway back down, then wrenched himself away from their fearful, expectant eyes and turned towards the door.

As soon as they turned into Rue de l'Eperon, André saw the jam twenty yards ahead. Their driver slowed and beeped his horn.

It didn't shift, and as the taxi braked and came to a halt, André said, 'I'm getting out here.' It would be quicker running the remaining forty yards. He hastily peeled a 100-franc note from his wallet. 'You settle up.' He opened the taxi door in the same motion, and the instant Marielle took the note he was out.

A quick matador-style feint as a moped suddenly cut up the inside and almost hit him, and then he was running headlong. His mounting pulse during the train and taxi journeys pumped the blood so furiously through his head that again he started to feel dizzy. Everything slipped sideways for a second as he stumbled – the road and traffic around shifting and blurring, a car horn blaring close by becoming a continuous echo. He quickly righted himself, shaking his head for more clarity as he hurtled on.

Eighteen more jolting strides and he slammed against Charlotte's apartment building door, bursting through without hardly altering pace. Veruschka's startled face halfway up the stairs turned towards him. 'What's wrong, *Papa*? What's happening?' And him patting her hair as he rushed past. 'It's OK. It's *OK*. Go back down to the bottom and wait. Or better still – the café across the road.' And from her look and what she saw reflected in his face, her knowing instantly that everything was far from OK. 'Just go. *Go!*' Joël just beyond her, equally startled and now frightened and, at the top of the stairs, waving the apartment key as if it were a rare prize, Henri Porcelet. 'Do you want me to come in with you, or would you rather be alone?' He'd rather not go in if he could be spared the duty was what he really meant. But André realized he might need help. 'No, no. I'll need you with me.'

Striding feverishly towards the door, the hall light went off just before he reached it. André was suddenly aware how much water there was as his feet sloshed through it. The light burst back on as he opened the door, Porcelet quickly rejoining him and walking in hesitantly behind him. And now André could see clearly the pale red hue of the water, suddenly a river again as his throbbing pulse spun him crazily into it, a raging torrent swilling between the gravestones underneath the bridge. '*Papa, are we there yet? Is this the Seine?*' Up to his waist as he waded through and hardly making any progress. *I can't save them all . . . I can't save them . . .* A bright light ahead that he forged towards, and after a second everything focused again and he could see that it was coming from the bathroom, flickering candlelight, and his feet were moving freely through the water, running now, his breath rasping, Veruschka's frightened voice from the bottom of the stairs, though it seemed miles away: '*Papa? Papa!* Is everything OK?'

Suddenly, startlingly clear – the glare from the night-lights around the bath, the blood red of the water, the few petals that remained on top and hadn't spilled on to the bathroom floor almost matching its colour, the pale outline of Charlotte's body a few inches below the water's surface – and as the full horror of the scene gripped André, he wished that it had stayed mercifully blurred.

André lunged in and grabbed her under the armpits and lifted the top half of her body clear, realizing he'd have difficulty lifting the whole of her as his left hand slipped on her wet skin and she fell back a few inches.

'Help me! Help me!'

Porcelet gripped her legs and they lifted Charlotte from the water, Porcelet following André's lead as he backed hastily out of the bathroom and laid her down on the nearest rug a couple of yards away in the lounge. Porcelet looked heavily distressed and as much as possible kept his eyes averted from her body.

André felt for her pulse. Nothing.

Porcelet's eyes lifted to the side as Marielle appeared at the open door.

André informed Marielle that there was no pulse, but that Charlotte's body was still warm. 'Though that could be from the heat of the bath water.' He nodded back towards the bathroom and then threw himself into a rapid, pumping heart massage. 'Can you do her stomach and diaphragm?'

Marielle, kneeling, started a steady, rhythmic pressing against Charlotte's stomach while Porcelet went back into the bathroom and turned off the taps. They'd been left running and the blood-red water still swilled around them. After the fourth press: 'Anything yet?'

André felt for her neck pulse with his left hand while still pumping with the right. 'No.' He was becoming frantic, sweat beads massing on his forehead and his breath still ragged from running and the effort of lifting Charlotte from the bath. How long since her heart had stopped? Anything longer than two minutes – just when their taxi was turning into her street – and they were wasting their time. He pumped harder. 'Come on. *Come on!*'

What had got her? Drowning or loss of blood? Or maybe pills – André had noticed some scattered on the floor by the bath as they'd lifted her. The bloodied water slid and squelched beneath his hands as he pumped.

Charlotte's skin was drawn and wrinkled from the bath water and ghostly white from blood loss, her mouth jarred in a rictus and her eyes rolled back high in their sockets, and André had a sudden pang for the lost years and what could have brought her to this. Closing his eyes for a moment on the horror and recalling the hot, torrid touch of her skin on their first nights of passion rather than the cold, clammy feel of it now. Her sly smile and the tease in her eyes as she'd lifted her wedding veil and he'd kissed her. 'For God's sake, Charlotte. *Come on!*' Remembering it as the many times he'd called out when she was late getting ready rather than his scream now as he frantically pumped.

'No, Charlotte, please! Not like this.' And as he opened his eyes again, tears were streaming down his face.

Marielle wanted to reach out and wipe them away, and her eyes too were moist as she soulfully held his gaze and cocked her head to one side as if to say she was sorry. *So sorry.* But then a sudden steeliness came into her eyes.

'We can't give up yet!' She scrambled around and gave a few sharp puffs of mouth-to-mouth, then slammed the flat of her hand hard in the centre of Charlotte's chest. 'We can't!'

André tried to massage more vigorously, but his arms felt suddenly tired and weak and his tears made everything blurred – the merciful haze he'd wished for earlier – and somehow more distant, the blood-red water swilling around them seeming to pull at him and draw him away. And as André felt that there was still no pulse, he felt the last hopes slip away, the water rising and pulling at him harder, becoming an irrepressible torrent as it ebbed towards the distant tombstones.

The third bomb went off at 3.14 a.m. at Caldyne Biotech, a spreading green-fields research establishment six miles south of Lancaster, Ohio. Eight hours were lost with notes and files passed between the Columbus PD, the local field office and FBI central in Virginia, and finally a message was passed to Todd Wenner in Atlanta late that same morning.

Wenner immediately dived into a flurry of phone calls before and during lunch to get more background and set up interviews, and finished off the last few bites of a take-out deli sandwich as he put on his coat and rushed out to catch a 2.40 p.m. flight to Columbus.

The first breath came in a long, agonized gasp on the back of a gout of water spewed out. Three more shallow breaths followed in quick succession with more water coming out before the next heavy vortex sucking-in of breath, and then a strangled coughing and gargling.

'She's choking,' André said. 'We need to get her on her side.' André glanced up and Porcelet got the signal and came over and helped them.

André pressed against her back and lungs while Marielle continued with her stomach, but it was almost another full minute with a chain of gagging coughs and more water expelled before it appeared that Charlotte's lungs were finally clear and her eyes started to flicker and focus on what was happening around her.

'We lost you for a minute,' André said. Then, as her eyes still seemed to have trouble focusing on him: 'Can you hear me? Can you breathe OK now?'

She simply nodded and closed her eyes in acquiescence, as if unsure she'd have the strength to answer. After another moment of looking around and taking her bearings: 'I . . . I don't know what happened.'

'*Papa!* Is everything OK?' Veruschka's voice strained up through the open door. Obviously she'd stayed with Joël at the bottom of the stairs and had heard the frantic shouts and coughs and spluttering, and now more voices. 'What's happening?'

'Everything's OK now,' André shouted out. He turned his attention back to Charlotte, lowering his voice. 'I think that you tried to take your own life and thankfully we got here just in time. That's what happened.' A flat, sober tone.

'No . . . no.' Charlotte shook her head. 'I didn't want to go ahead with it in the end.'

A fresh trickle of blood appeared at Charlotte's wrist and Marielle went to the kitchen and grabbed a couple of tea towels to wrap and tie it.

'Then I suppose we're imagining all of this.' André held one arm out towards the bloodied water. 'And the pills on the bathroom floor.'

'Can we come up yet?' Veruschka's voice again.

'No, *no*! Not yet!' André shouted back. They'd come so close to the children finding Charlotte first; the image of young Joël seeing his mother's body in the blood-filled bath was still with him, made him shudder. Seeing her like this was only one stage better. He took a 50-franc note from his wallet and handed it to Porcelet. 'Could you take my children across the road for coffee and Coke or something while we clean up here? Tell them we'll be about fifteen, twenty minutes. But, please, nothing about what's happened here or what we're doing.'

'No, of course not.' Porcelet nodded and headed out, looking relieved to be set free from the scene of carnage. He'd studiously kept his eyes from settling on Charlotte's bloodied body throughout.

Charlotte slowly, falteringly, sat up, and Marielle grabbed a robe and wrapped it around her.

Pills. Suddenly it all started coming back to Charlotte. She'd just grabbed the pills and was straightening up when the bathroom suddenly slipped sideways and everything went black. 'I . . . I didn't take any of the pills. I'd decided not to. I must have . . .' She looked around as she pieced it all together in her mind '. . . must have slipped and hit my head on the bath.'

'Decided *not to*?' André shook his head in wonderment. 'So is that what all of this was about? Just a cry for attention?'

'No! I wanted to kill myself at first, believe me.' She reached out and gripped his wrist with a slippery, bloody hand. 'But then I had a change of heart.'

For years, by far the strongest emotion he'd had for her had been pity, but now he felt nothing but contempt. She was fickle about so much, but now she couldn't even be sure whether or not she wanted to kill herself. 'You know how ill Eban is.'

'I know. It was when I heard that – '

'And Marielle and I were trying to track down someone that could help save him when we had to break off to come and see to you.'

'No, no . . . *please*. Don't lay that on me.' Her grip on his arm tightened, but her eyes drifted, as if she was again having trouble making sense of anything. 'Anyway, how did you know to – '

André cut her short again. 'And Veruschka and Joël coming home from school. Do you know how close we came with stopping them getting here? Joël could have been the first to find you.' He stared the message home into her darting, uncertain eyes, and the reminder made all the tension and mounting adrenalin from the rush to get to her spill over into white-hot anger. 'Do you know that? Did you even bother to think about that?' He found himself gripping her shoulders, pushing harder with each exclamation. Charlotte started shaking her head and mumbling, 'No, no,' and he was aware of Marielle's eyes on him imploringly, telling him that it was enough. With Charlotte still in pieces, just dragged back from the edge of death, it probably wasn't the best time to berate her. But he'd suppressed it for so long that now he found it impossible to hold back. 'Or is it always about you? *You!* You always have to be the centre of attention and drama.'

'No, no, no . . . *No!*' Charlotte's mumbled mantra steadily rose until it became a scream, her head shaking stronger with each denial. There was silence for a moment, the echoes of her shouts bouncing off the walls and settling. Then, her voice shaky and more subdued: 'It was thinking about the children that made me change my mind. Not just them finding me first, but the effect my death would have on them. How they'd cope with me gone.'

André took a fresh breath, as if to clear the air. 'Well, one salvation at least – you finally came to your senses before it was too late.' She nodded and smiled thinly for the first time since they'd entered the room, but she had trouble meeting his gaze. And somehow it seemed too easy, letting her off the hook just because at the last instant she'd seen the light and done the right thing. 'What you put us through just now was unforgivable, Charlotte. And you've got to face it at some time. You make too many demands on everyone, me especially. I can't wet-nurse you when I'm trying to save lives. Busy with people with real problems, real ailments. I can't save everyone.'

He saw her flinch, and, suddenly saying out loud that he couldn't be everyone's saviour, rather than it just plaguing his thoughts, sent a faint shudder through him as well. In the end he hadn't just pressed home the nightmare she'd put them through, but voiced a deep-seated emotion, something that had been building up and should have been said long ago. And he wondered what that said about him, that only now, when she was emotionally naked, confused and barely clinging to life, was he bold enough to speak his mind. He felt suddenly ashamed that he hadn't been stronger and said something earlier, hiding as he always did from confrontation in his work; the silent, non-arguing movement of cell structures at the end of his microscope. If he had, perhaps things would never have come to this. He was as much to blame.

16

After a brief consultation with a Columbus PD sergeant, Wenner's main interview was with a Dr Tom Jennings, who'd stayed on late to meet him.

'Do you have many experiments with animals?' Wenner enquired. 'Not just mice, but larger animals such as monkeys?'

'Less now than a few years ago. The controls are more stringent these days, even with the "house" monkeys. With mice we get less problems and quicker response times.'

'Right.' Wenner had his notepad out, pen poised, but he didn't bother to write anything. After the first incident, the bombed lab had received a cryptic newspaper-letter pasted note: NO MORE ANIMAL EXPERIMENTS. STOP THE MONKEY BUSINESS. It pointed to animal rights activists, but would they feel so strongly about experiments involving only mice? Nothing was received after the second bombing, but perhaps that was because there was someone killed. They weren't so keen to hold their hands up to that one.

Wenner ran through a chain of questions, some of it covering ground he already half knew: no people injured. No animals killed, unless you counted the half-dozen mice in that section for various tests. But extensive file and data damage.

'It could take us several months to recover,' Jennings commented. 'It's not particularly going to help us with our bid for a Gifford Award.'

Gifford. It didn't strike a chord until halfway through Wenner's flight back to Atlanta. He remembered from press clippings that the first establishment bombed had been a contender for a Gifford. He checked the second upon his return, but found nothing. Still, two out of three – it was worth watching. At this early stage he was grateful for anything that could help narrow focus.

He sat back after the first sip of a freshly poured coffee and wrote on his notepad: *Animal activists. Monkeys. Gifford Award.*

Five days later, Caldyne Biotech received a cut-out-letter pasted note – ANIMAL AND HUMAN GENES DON'T MIX. GENESIS 24 – and he had two more to add: *Religious links. Genetics.* They had a mountain of information on religious fanatics from abortion-clinic bombings, but genetics was another matter. Four-teen months of medical school didn't even start to scratch the surface. He might have some reading to do.

Charlotte was admitted to a clinic for four days, after which she'd undergo a fresh bout of therapy, the first for two years, so at least that was one less thing for André to worry about immediately. But within twenty minutes of him arriving at the lab the next morning, Hervé was on the phone reminding him that already two days had gone of Eric's trial. Which day did he plan to put in an appearance?

'I'm sorry.' He cradled his forehead. 'But what with everything with Eban and then Charlotte yesterday, it completely slipped my mind.'

'I know. I understand,' Hervé said. A voice heavy with com-passion, but somehow too quick, trite; André could imagine the same delivered at countless confessionals. 'That's why I didn't say anything last night when you told me.' Hervé's tone suddenly became sharper, more pressing. 'But you know how much this means to Eric. How important it is to him. And the trial might not last more than another four or five days. So now that Charlotte's going to be in a clinic for a while – when?'

Everyone pushing and pulling at him, making demands. André rubbed at his temples, trying to force some clarity into the mush of his mind. The night before, he'd headed back to the Goutte d'Or to continue searching. This time Marc accompanied him; he was on late shift rather than Marielle, and while a girl might get more doors opened, after their earlier experience, a man was far better for back-up if things turned sour. The evening became a blur of *Non, pardons*, head-shaking and hastily closed doors – those that had opened in the first place. Dhoumil's picture didn't seem to strike a chord with anyone.

'Late tomorrow morning or early afternoon,' he said finally. By tonight they'd have exhausted all the door calls worth doing, Eban for the moment was holding stable, and he'd probably need no more than the morning in the lab to catch up and make sure the fort held until he got back.

'OK. Thanks.' Hervé eased a relieved breath. 'Eric needs our support more than ever right now.'

But then the next morning after another fruitless night of door canvassing in the Goutte d'Or with Marc, as he was clearing his desk of papers and about to order a taxi to the courtroom, Bernice phoned.

'It's Eban. He's bad, taken a turn for the worse. I'm real worried about 'im.'

It was a voice he hadn't heard before from Bernice. Dark and heavy, no chuckle or even a hint of humour. He didn't need to ask how bad.

'I'll be there in under an hour.'

Kalpenski? Dani didn't have the first clue how to get rid of him. Shafting Hebbard had been one thing; they'd worked and interacted together daily, there were a lot of lines where their paths crossed for her to be able to trip him up. But Kalpenski was a totally different ball game.

He was on the lower of the two floors above carrying the boardroom gods like Chisholm, and she was a mere minion below along with all the other research assistants and lab workers. Her chances of getting to him – let alone doing something deeply wounding where her word would be accepted over his by the boardroom – were nil. Yet if she did nothing, her career would be stuck on hold indefinitely. Already it had been three weeks since the last e-mail, and as things stood now it didn't look like she was going to be answering any time soon. The only coup had been discovering that it was Chisholm, then finding out some of his background.

Chisholm obviously had big plans for her, but it looked like they were all going to turn to dust. She just couldn't see them progressing any further. It had been fun while it lasted; she'd found the knife-edge tension of the e-mails and then finally winning the day with Hebbard quite exhilarating. She hadn't felt so alive for a long while, not since . . .

Then one morning she noticed the way that Kalpenski looked at her and began to amend her thoughts. It was only a two-second glimpse at her legs on one of the rare days that she wore sheer black stockings to work, but enough to at least give her the first seeds of an idea.

When André got to Eban his temperature was 102.8 and he had trouble breathing, his chest rattling with fluid with each slow, tortured breath.

'I put an ice pack on him and gave him some ibuprofen two hours ago,' Bernice said. 'But his temperature came back up within the hour.' Her face was taut with worry and the dark orbs of her eyes settled back quickly on Eban.

'And when did you last give him his Invirase?'

'About half an hour after the ibuprofen.'

Another two, two and a half hours before he could be given more of each, André calculated. But in-between, with Eban's temperature so alarmingly high, could be a long and potentially dangerous haul. Eban's face was shiny with sweat, his mouth dry, some sores evident at the corners of his lips and on his chin. André swallowed hard as he lifted his head towards the window. Drifting through from the courtyard outside came the diesel engine rattle of the taxi he'd asked to wait for him.

'I think I'd better get him back to the lab,' he said. Maybe meanwhile he could give some acetaminophen; that wouldn't react with the ibuprofen. And some relenza for his breathing.

Eban had been dozing, his eyes half-open and bleary throughout André talking to Bernice. Only as they started moving him did his eyes fully open and then settle on André. They took a few seconds to fully focus.

'*Papa* André. You're here.' *Papa* André. *Papa* Nwaro. *Papa* Mpundu. The way that Eban termed all of his fathers/guardians; as if, if he didn't attach the names, he'd get confused between them. Three fathers in his short life to date; it was enough to confuse anyone. Or perhaps he didn't just use *Papa* because it somehow faded and diminished the memory of his real father. 'Where are we going?'

'To the lab. We can get you better there.'

Eban's eyes stayed open, gently flickering, as they got his things, wrapped him in a blanket and headed out towards the taxi, as if he was still orientating himself and making sense of what André had said. But as soon as they got him in the back, his eyes closed again and he drifted off. Bernice insisted that she stay with Eban for a while to help out, and got in alongside him. André got in the front by the driver.

Eban opened his eyes only once, about six minutes into their drive, as if he'd suddenly remembered something. 'Will Anouk be there?'

And André realized immediately just how delirious he was, his mind clouded. He'd forgotten that Anouk had died a few weeks ago, and André didn't have the heart to remind him now.

'Maybe. Maybe she's in the animal house. As soon as you're better we'll try and find her.'

It was a foolish lie, one that Eban would find out as soon as he recovered – but for the moment he seemed to accept it, a look of contentment, almost serenity, settling on his face as his eyes closed again.

And as André remained looking at him for a moment – the weak sunlight playing across Eban's face as their taxi sped along, Bernice touching some water she'd brought in a cup gently to his dry lips – his heart broke. Everything had shifted and turned against them so quickly. Just before Christmas they'd been talking about months, then weeks; and now if they couldn't get Eban over the mountain of his current illness, hours or days. Yet still they had to track down Dhoumil to have any chance of saving him and all hope there was fast fading. André knew then that perhaps that was why he'd lied, because a small part of him sensed that this time Eban wouldn't make it.

The argument with David Copell started almost immediately they came out of the Laferge section and Eban was out of earshot.

'You know that we can't keep him here long,' David said.

'I know that.' André was still sweating and agitated from the panicked flurry of activity with Eban as he peeled off his surgical gloves. Forty-eight hours was the normal maximum stay time in the annexe, emergencies only; after that, clearance would have to be gained from Delatois. 'It's just to get Eban over this current crisis, then I can get him back home.'

'But what if he doesn't get over this one? What then?'

'Of course he'll get over this. Don't be –' But as André turned and met David's penetrating gaze, he stopped himself. David had seen the truth in the shaking of his hands and the haunted look in his eyes as they'd fought furiously to bring down Eban's temperature over the past two hours and, like him, he'd seen his T-cell count: 76. Down 21 in only two days. They both knew that Eban might not make it out of this one, might not even last the night, and he went back with David far too long to start lying to him now. But with the Charlotte nightmare and everything with Eban catching up with him so quickly, he hadn't yet formed a clear idea of what he was going to do. And still he was meant to head to the Palais de Justice at some stage to see Eric. 'I . . . I'm not sure. I haven't even stopped for a second to think in those terms.' He closed his eyes fleetingly and rubbed his forehead. 'It's just for a day or two to try and get Eban over the brink, then I can get my head clear on what to do next.'

'I understand that.' David nodded with compassion, but his eyes stayed keenly on André. 'But as soon as you call in a duty nurse for the night, Delatois will be on your back, asking questions.'

'I know. If one of us can hold the fort till midnight, I was hoping to use Bernice for overnight.' He looked back towards Bernice. She'd hovered outside the Laferge annexe looking anxiously through the glass for much of the time they'd been tending to Eban.

Now she was inside at his bedside, holding his hand. 'She made the offer on the way over.'

David eased out a tired breath. 'And you're still looking for this Dhoumil?'

'Yes, of course.' André knitted his brow. 'She's the only hope left of possibly being able to save Eban in time.'

Another tired sigh. 'But you appreciate that even if you find Dhoumil quickly and we're able to put together the final pieces of the data for treatment, to process that and get a green light back on a clinical trial will take at least three weeks – even if we fast-track it. And first it's got to be passed by Delatois for his approval.'

André met David's sober stare squarely for the first time since they'd exited the annexe. So, finally David had got around to what was really troubling him: David feared that if he tracked down Dhoumil and Eban only had days left to live, he might be tempted to cut corners and risk all. And as he faced that possible choice head-on for the first time – saving Eban or observing ethics and protocol – he thought he knew which he'd choose, and David as he looked at him knew it too. Suddenly uncomfortable, he flickered his eyes down and away. 'As I said before, I . . . I just haven't thought of things in those terms.'

David gripped his shoulder. 'Well maybe you're going to have to. I mean, look at Eban.'

But André didn't look up, knowing what David would see there: confirmation of his fears. 'Maybe I just can't think of that. I'm pushing it away because I just can't face it – have you ever considered that?' André angrily shook off the grip. 'Maybe thinking in terms of Eban lasting weeks or months or more is all that's keeping me going.'

Marielle and Marc were looking across from the far end of the lab as their voices rose.

David shook his head, lowering his voice to almost a whisper. 'I know how difficult it will be for you, André, but if it comes down to that, I'm begging you – don't do it. Don't throw everything away.'

André felt himself start trembling, all the tension of the past forty-eight hours suddenly bubbling back up. It was a dilemma that he knew was looming, but hoped that he'd never have to finally face – the choice between raw emotions and ethics, what his heart told him or his head – and David was making him confront it now. The only saving grace was that with Dhoumil still eluding them, he could keep it at arm's length.

'Since we haven't found Dhoumil yet, it's immaterial. What's the point in even discussing it?' And as he said it, a small part of him perversely wished that she wouldn't be found so that the dilemma wouldn't be back squarely in his lap, and he felt a twinge of shame. As with Charlotte and so much else in his life, always looking for the easy way out to avoid confrontation.

David was shaking his head. 'André. André. Stop pushing it away.' He gestured towards Eban. 'The problem's right here. Now!'

André continued as if he hadn't heard. 'Besides, if we can get Eban over this current crisis, we'll need Dhoumil's sample more than ever. And we'll have the time then to process everything and clear it with Delatois.'

'I understand that.' David's sigh was more out of exasperation this time. 'But you've got to look at the downside as well, rather than just let it rise up and strike you in the face at the last moment, catch you by surprise.'

Like it did with Charlotte, André thought. He flinched and turned away. 'I . . . I don't have time for this now. I was meant to go to the courtroom to see Eric hours ago.' He moved towards his desk and started tidying away papers and files. 'If I don't leave soon, I'll miss the afternoon session as well.' Yet another family commitment tugging at him when already he was spread too thin; or was he just using it now as one more safe-option boulder to hide behind, keep him from facing the inevitable with Eban?

David gave up on him at that point and headed towards his own desk. But just before he was ready to leave for the courtroom, David's eyes were back on him keenly as Marielle frantically beckoned him over to a call she'd just taken.

'It's about Dhoumil,' she said. 'One of those people I left my card with the other day. They think they know where we can find her.'

★

There was no other choice but for him to head to the Goutte d'Or alone. Marc had a prior dinner engagement that evening, Bernice had to head home at 4 p.m. in order to be able to return at midnight, and Marielle had to stay with David to help out with Eban.

'You'll be OK with him until I get back?'

'Yes, yes. Go, go!' Marielle urged.

'I'll phone in later and let you know how things go. And you've got my mobile number if anything comes up meanwhile.'

He made all the last-minute arrangements with Marielle, with David offering only mild acquiescent nods in the background. He didn't want to risk another confrontation with David. But David's searing eyes hardly left him as he rushed from the lab, and he could still feel their message being pressed home now as the Métro train rattled along. *Eban's going to die. Eban's going to die.* And this quest now with Dhoumil was all going to be a waste of time because they simply wouldn't be able to process the data and get it rubber-stamped in time. *Protocol.* Eban just one more to add to the mountain of African children who died each year because protocol couldn't be observed. The drugs were too expensive. Or the aid money or the paperwork or the convoy didn't arrive on time. Or it did, but it had been pilfered and sold off by an unscrupulous dictator to pay for a new palace or his next shopping jaunt to London or Paris with his four wives.

Protocol. André shook his head. David knew him so well; knew that breaking down established barriers and protocol as he broke new ground had become almost a trademark of his career. And faced with that dilemma – his career and observing protocol on one side, breaking it and saving Eban on the other – David knew the decision he'd make, and a part of him felt strangely empty inside at the realization, as the train rattled and lurched along, that he could be on a collision course with dooming his career. The end of the line. He could save Eban, but not any others. After a moment he gently shook his head again and closed his eyes. Standing by and coldly watching Eban die just to save his own neck, that was as much against the grain as his trademark railing against protocol. But again for a fleeting second the unworthy thought passed through his mind that if finally Dhoumil couldn't be found, he wouldn't even be faced with that dilemma.

As he opened his eyes again, he noticed a couple of people on the seat opposite looking at him curiously before quickly averting their gaze, and he suddenly realized that his whole body was gently shaking, his hands gripped tight on his thighs as the conflicts tore away inside him, the film of sweat on his face and neck from the panic rush to catch the train suddenly feeling cold against his skin. And he felt tired, oh so tired. The mounting urgency of Eban's condition and their frantic searches through the Goutte d'Or of the past two days, then the nightmare with Charlotte, now his confrontation with David – all of it seemed to have drained him so that now he felt he had hardly anything left to give.

It was approaching rush hour and the train progressively filled at each station. He gave up his seat to a woman carrying an infant at Château d'Eau and stood the rest of the way to Barbès Rochechouart. The trembling in his body felt more pronounced and his legs felt weak within a short while of him standing, and he clung heavily to the central pole, muttering a silent prayer under his breath. Oh God, please help me. *Please help me.* Unsure for a moment whether he was pleading for Eban or his own inner strength to be able to carry on. But at least with the crowds nobody was any longer staring at him. He was just one more face lost among the throng of city commuters. Rushing to save a young boy that everyone had long since given up caring about, just one more African AIDS casualty lost in a sea of statistics and protocol.

'You'll save him?'

'Yes . . . I'll save him.'

'For sure? Sure, *sure?*'

André could almost still feel Mpundu's grip on his arm and the deep, soulful plea of those eyes locked on him as he'd offered his final assurance. 'Yes. Sure, sure.'

The memory of his promise to Mpundu was the main thing driving him, putting some spring back in his step as for the fourth time in three days he headed back into the shadowy warrens of the Goutte d'Or. Except that this time he was alone, and it was dark.

He'd hoped to get there with some daylight to spare, but he'd misjudged how quickly the light faded. As he'd come out of the station, the last dusk light was dying, and now only a couple of streets away it was almost pitch black.

The only significant light on the street was from a corner grocery and spice store where the owner had strung a line of bare bulbs beneath a canvas canopy to spotlight his outside display of cassavas, melons and mangoes. The pungent spice aromas had hit André as he'd passed, but now were distant, as was the light. In the rest of the street ahead the only light came from widely spaced street lamps and the occasional muted grey light straining through curtains on some of the houses. But so many houses were unoccupied or derelict, or squats with no electricity, that those lights were few.

The gaps in between were dark, foreboding. André started to feel more unsettled as he walked deeper into the street. Still, he reassured himself, unlike the other three visits he wouldn't be staying long. Straight to the house in question, then on to see Dhoumil. From what Marielle had passed on, apparently Dhoumil was staying at a house quite close to the caller. If Dhoumil was there when he called, he could be heading back out again with her within fifteen minutes.

As he turned into the street he was looking for, Rue Richomme, he checked the number he'd written on a scrap of paper: 68. About thirty houses up on the opposite side of the road. Rue Richomme was darker than the street he'd just come from. There was a small bar further up, but its front window was small with only a weak orange light; little shone through on to the street.

André's skin suddenly bristled as he heard a shuffling just behind him. He felt sure that someone had looked out from a doorway he'd just passed, but as he looked back they'd gone again, ducked back into the shadows. Or was he just imagining it? Perhaps it was the wind rustling through some leaves or rubbish or a cat scurrying past.

He walked on, his heartbeat now suddenly heavier; he could hardly even hear the fall of his own footsteps. Only twenty yards more now to the woman's door.

André imagined Mpundu's grip on his arm giving him strength, urging him on. His spirits were buoyed when the woman said that the house she thought she'd seen Dhoumil at was just across the road. She pointed. 'There! Only five doors down.' But then they sagged again when she added that she hadn't seen Dhoumil yet that day, or for that matter the night before. 'The last time I saw her was late yesterday morning.'

They both stood for a moment looking towards the house across the road, which looked like a squat. No lights showed downstairs, and only faint candle or torch-light filtered through from a first-floor window.

'I was hoping to catch up with her tonight,' André said. 'It's quite urgent, you see.'

'You're welcome to wait here. But with the children already home and my husband expected soon, it's a bit hectic.' The woman was in her early forties and dark complexioned, but probably Mediterranean rather than North African, André thought. She was well-dressed with quite a lot of make-up and jewellery, though André could imagine that if she wasn't expecting visitors she'd still be in a housecoat or tracksuit. 'There's bar not far down the road,' she offered more hopefully. 'You can still see the house from there. And maybe you'll want to check the house first, just in case I missed her coming in.' She shrugged. 'Or someone there might know what time she's expected.'

André thanked her and headed across the road, but her first assumption was right. The painfully thin black African man who finally came down in answer to his knock said that he hadn't seen Dhoumil since the day before.

'Maybe she come later, maybe not. Maybe not until tomorrow or the day after.'

André used the same ploy as before, stressing that it was urgent they contact Dhoumil because she was ill. 'Perhaps she isn't even aware just how ill. And what she has is highly contagious.'

One of the man's eyebrows arched fleetingly in surprise, but his headshake was firm and convincing. 'Sorry.' She wasn't there.

André headed down the road until the man went back inside the house, then he cut across to the bar. He ordered a coffee with Calvados chaser – he needed something to ease his jaded nerves – and took up a seat by the window. The Calvados helped at first, felt warm and soothing as it cut a passage to his stomach, but after fifteen minutes of waiting and no sign of Dhoumil his nervousness was back, his hand visibly shaking as it brought the coffee to his lips.

He felt restless, uneasy. He checked his watch: an hour and twenty minutes since he'd left the lab. He should see how things were going with Eban. David answered.

'His temperature is up point-four to 101.7, but otherwise he's stable. As for his T-count, we took the sample just minutes ago so we won't have the results for about ten minutes. Marielle's processing it now. I'll phone you straight back as soon as we've got it.' A brief awkward silence followed Andre's mumbled '*D'Accord*'. 'And André, I'm sorry about earlier. I had no right to –'

'No, no. You were right.' André ran one hand through his hair and sighed as he looked out into the gloom of the Goutte d'Or. A group of three people had just turned into the street, but were too distant to see clearly. 'It probably is too late and I'm wasting my time sitting here. Just going through the motions because I don't know what else to do.'

'You're selling yourself short, André, as you so often do. I think you know exactly what you're doing, and a lot of what I said earlier still stands. I'm worried which way you'll jump with this, and with very good reason.' David let out a long breath. 'It's just that I shouldn't have brought it up when I did. There was an assumption there that Eban wouldn't make it through this, and that was wrong.'

The group of three were now close enough to make out, two men and an elderly woman. Still no sign of Dhoumil.

'Thanks.' Typical David, André thought: an apology to get things straight between them plus reaffirming his earlier worries. He got it both ways. So now they were back to dancing around the problem: with Eban's immunity so low, his chances of making it through this current flu were no better than thirty per cent, but neither of them wanted to say it out loud. And when David phoned back ten minutes later and told him that Eban's T-count had dropped to 71, those odds were probably now only ten or fifteen per cent. A 5-point fall in just over an hour!

André felt suddenly desolate inside. He knocked back his Calvados and ordered another, but this time its warmth as it trickled down did little to ease the chill gripping him, or his nerves. He could feel them bubbling away like a volcano, though he felt so cold inside, the chill of the thin film of sweat on his skin suddenly making him shiver. Now the portent was directly in their faces, impossible to dance around any more: at that rate of T-count fall Eban would be lucky to last eighteen hours. He took another hasty sip of Calvados. His hand shook heavily on the glass, and he put both hands around to cradle it as he brought it slowly back down to the table.

The bar around was becoming noisier. Two teenagers had started to play at a fruit machine close by and a swarthy man in a leather jacket was repeatedly slapping the palm of one hand against the bar to add emphasis to his story shared with the barman. André felt like screaming out loud for them to shut up and let his thoughts run clear, but in the end he just shut his eyes and tried to close his mind to everything outside. In character even when his world was being ripped apart. Avoid confrontation.

Maybe that's why he felt so uneasy. A part of him sensed he wasn't going to find Dhoumil, at least not in time. David was right, he was wasting his time. Sitting in a bar full of strangers in the Goutte d'Or while halfway across the city Eban lay dying. He should be there with him, at his side. Battling away at the helm alongside David and Marielle. And for that he'd need a clear head, rather than trying to dull his nerves and drown his sorrows. He pushed the Calvados glass away at arm's length.

Maybe there was something he'd overlooked. Something in the pattern of the tests they already had. Or maybe he should be thinking obliquely for something new, even if it was enough just to buy Eban a few more weeks so that they could find Dhoumil and run their tests. Maybe . . .

He suddenly jolted as he registered the two figures approaching on the far side of the road, both black women in their twenties. One of them looked like Dhoumil, was the same shape and build, but with the poor streetlight it was impossible to be sure. But then as they came close to the squat across the road, they slowed and one of them fished in her coat pocket for something. They turned towards the building.

André jumped up, his chair grating back, and darted across the street. He caught up with them just as they had the door to the squat half open.

'Dhoumil!' he called out.

But as they turned to look at him, he could see that it wasn't Dhoumil. The same build and rounded face, but the eyes were slightly narrower and the nose broader.

'I'm sorry. I thought that you were someone I knew. Dhoumil.' He pointed to the building. 'She stays here too.'

Perhaps because of the disappointment on his face, she offered, 'I know Dhoumil.'

'It's urgent that I make contact with her,' André said, still breathless from the run. 'Do you know what time she'll be back?'

'Well, I think –'

'Difficult to say,' her friend cut in sharply. 'Sometimes she doesn't show up for two or three days.' She shot Dhoumil-lookalike a guarded sideways glance.

'Then do you know where I might find her tonight?' André pressed.

Again, the first girl looked tempted to say something, but after another glance from her friend decided against it.

'I'm sorry,' the friend said. 'We don't know anything more.' She pulled lightly at the first girl's arm. 'Come on, Yvette.'

André was sure that they were holding back, but with the second girl now controlling everything, what could he do? He felt as if he was at a sort of crossroads. Just nod and walk away, avoid confrontation as he'd done throughout his life, and Eban died for sure. Or fight back, push? And suddenly he felt all the tension and turmoil of the past days boil back up to the surface: Charlotte's blood-filled bath in the glow of the night-lights, the rush back and forth to the Goutte d'Or, his promise to Mpundu. *'I'll save him. For sure, sure.'* And all the while Eban's T-count was steadily ticking down like a time bomb. The Calvados provided him with that final burst of fire and courage. He gripped at Dhoumil-lookalike's other arm.

'Please! You've got to help me. It's my adopted son, you see. He's from Africa like you, and he's dying. And Dhoumil holds the key to the antidote than can save him.' André fished his ISG identity card from his pocket, in case they disbelieved him. 'If I don't find her tonight, it will be too late. He'll die. *Please!'* André gripped the girl's arm for a second.

Her eyes thawed slightly, but again it was her friend who spoke. 'I'm sorry to hear about your boy – but we've told you all we know.' She tugged more insistently at Yvette's arm. 'Come on.'

Yvette gave a last fleeting look back, a mixture of doubt and apology, as her friend hustled her into the house and shut the door quickly behind them.

André felt totally drained as he walked away. Perhaps it was because he was so unused to confrontation or laying bare his emotions – he left shouting those from the rooftops to the likes of Charlotte. Or perhaps it was just winding down from the nightmare dramas and rush of the past week. But he'd never felt so desolate. Eban was going to die and there was nothing left that he could do, nothing left for him to give. It was all over.

André's nerves leapt with the rapid patter of footsteps from behind. For a second he thought that someone was running up to mug him, but it was Yvette.

'I know where you can find her tonight. On Rue St-Denis.' She looked back anxiously towards the squat. 'But you didn't hear it from me, OK?'

'OK.' André reached out and gently clasped her hand. 'And thanks.'

She smiled tightly. 'Oh, and she's not known as Dhoumil there. All the other girls know her as Chloë.'

17

Dani wore the stockings for four days before Kalpenski really sat up and noticed them. Not consecutive days – that would have been too obvious, might have drawn attention from others – so in the end it was almost two weeks from hatching her plan to the point where she was confident it would work. She'd got him hooked.

They were from a Sansom Street lingerie shop and were shinier and sleeker than the pair she'd worn the day that Kalpenski first noticed her legs and, if you looked real close – close enough that your breath could be felt on her legs – they had a small heart pattern running through them. But it was probably her position when Kalpenski approached that day – stretched over the lab bench to make notes – that gave the final helping hand. Her lab coat rose up a few inches as she leant across, accentuating the length of her legs in the stockings.

This time Kalpenski's gaze was longer and more lingering than the first occasion, and she saw him swallow as she looked up. He turned hastily away, his face reddening slightly, as he started talking to John Page close by.

From then on she started teasing him, playing him, bit by bit hauling him in. On the days she wore the stockings, she noticed that he generally stayed longer in their department and would visit another two or three times through the day; when she didn't, they'd usually see him only once.

She became bolder, finding excuses to get him close to her, asking him over to consult on this problem or that, and making sure she'd visited the bathroom to spray perfume just before, so that its fragrance filled his head. Then the touching: a light touch to his arm or hand, a gentle clasp of thanks to one shoulder. And when one day she touched his hand and felt the raw tension there and caught the nervous gleam in his eye, she knew that he was ready. In under a month she'd got him fired up like a volcano, ready to burst. Poor Kalpenski; she could tell that he wasn't used to this, which should make it all the easier.

She smiled to herself as she sent her e-mail to Cyberling Rivalry. *Ready to make my play any day now. Watch this space.* She'd wallowed in the adrenalin rush and risk of the battle of wits with Hebbard, but a part of her also couldn't help relishing taking advantage of those that were easy prey. Perhaps that lay partly behind what she'd done to her mother, why so often she'd quietly sniggered, found it hard to keep from laughing out loud, after seeing her lawyer and finding out the next dark and devious stage of the game plan in store for dear Mater. Or perhaps it was because she'd had to fight and claw for everything else in life, so that when it was laid so easily on a plate she just couldn't resist it.

But she reminded herself to go easy with Kalpenski, not get over-confident. The risks were still high and there was a lot at stake, not least her career. And because Kalpenski was unused to being approached by women almost twenty years younger, that could, at the flip of a coin, also work against her: he might suddenly get warning signals and back off.

'You want sucky-sucky? Only two hundred francs.'

'Like what you see, Monsieur? Come closer, I won't bite.'

'Chloë, Chloë? What you want with her? Come with me, I'll show you real good time.'

André's head started to spin with it all as, for the third time that night, he made his way along Rue St-Denis looking for Dhoumil/Chloë. When he'd first arrived, there were only a couple of girls on the street and he was informed that most of the action didn't take place until later. And no, the girl he'd questioned hadn't seen Chloë yet, but there was a McDonald's and some cafés at the end of the street where some of the girls met up before work that he might want to check.

André breezed quickly in and out of the McDonald's and three nearby cafés – two groups that looked like hookers, but no Dhoumil – before deciding it was futile. She could be at any of countless nearby cafés or, for that matter, halfway across the city having dinner or drinks. He decided to sit it out at the last café, which had a partial view of Rue St-Denis. After over an hour and still no sign of Dhoumil, it looked like it was going to be a long night. André phoned the lab to check on Eban's progress and agreed to call them again every hour. On that first call, Eban's T-count was down to 67; on the second, 64; the third, 59, and his temperature was up again, 102.3. André had started off at the bar with Perrier to help clear his head, but by the last call felt that he needed another Calvados.

With his heavy intake of breath at the news, Marielle commented, 'Maybe David's right. Even if you do find Dhoumil, it might be too late for anything to be done. Eban could be too weak to respond.'

André wondered what David had said to her, but at least it was a shift in emphasis: no mention of protocol or paperwork, just that Eban might be too weak to respond to treatment, which had been his primary worry all along. But knowing Marielle, compassionate to a fault, she was probably saying it just so that he wouldn't feel too bad if in the end he didn't find Dhoumil.

67, 64, 59. André felt the descending T-count like a repetitive hammer blow driving him on, firing his pulse and his stride as he headed back down St-Denis. It was approaching midnight, and in the last half-hour the street had suddenly come alive with new girls and fresh activity.

André wished now that he hadn't had the Calvados. His nerves had steadily mounted again with the long wait, but instead of calming him, the drinks had raised them another notch.

By the time he passed the seventh or eighth girl – he'd lost count – inviting him for sucky, fucky and putting a finger to her brightly painted lips, he was ready to reach out and throttle her. *No, no. I don't. I'm here to try and save the life of a young boy. I'm not just another trick.* But instead he just kept repeating, like a mantra, 'I'm looking for Chloë. Do you know where I might find her? Is she here yet?'

Most of them were from Africa or the Caribbean, their make-up heavy and garish, many of them overweight with thighs that an American quarterback would have been proud of threatening to burst out of tight minis or hot-pants. André reminded himself that, like Eban, they too were victims; no doubt lacking work permits, their only choice was the raw fringes of city life. And probably Dhoumil wasn't the only one with HIV; with many of them fresh over from Africa the rate in the street could be as high as thirty per cent.

But almost everything about them began to grate on his nerves: their heavy perfume, their gaudy, beaming faces as they called out to him and pouted or licked their lips, their grip on his arm or occasionally his crotch, their fast-diminishing interest when they discovered that he was looking for Chloë and wasn't a trick, or at least not one that was going to put money in *their* pocket. And he felt like screaming at them that they didn't understand how important it was. Even if it were just the life of one young boy it was a hundred times more vital than what any of them was doing right then. *But there's the lives of legions at stake. And if I can't save him, I can't save any of you!*

The vacant, indifferent eyes of the girls simply stared back; the same look as the African dictators who lined their own pockets or bought arms with the money sent for AIDS victims, or the pharmaceutical giants whose profits were more important than bringing their drugs within reach of the millions who desperately needed them. And it struck André then that these girls had long ago given up caring – selling themselves like this for 200 francs a time couldn't be worse than any hell they might imagine they'd go to. And in that moment he felt terribly alone, as if he was the only one left who cared.

'Where is she?' André grabbed urgently at the arm of the girl who only a second ago he'd pulled away from. She'd been one too many touching and pulling at him, and as she came in close and breathed warmly in his ear – 'What you want with this Chloë? Come with me, I'll show you what a real woman's like' – her perfume and underlying musk swamped him and he felt physically sick. He wrenched himself away, so violently that for a second he lost his balance and took a couple of steps back into the road. An approaching car blared its horn as it swerved around him.

'Crazy man. *Crazy!*' the girl shouted. Then her eyes narrowed. 'Anyway, Chloë not available – she's busy with someone else right now. You'll have to wait for her to wipe her pussy dry from 'im.'

A couple of the girls nearby chuckled, but their smiles quickly faded as he leapt back and grabbed the girl's arm. 'What – she's here now? *Where is she?*'

She looked suddenly worried. 'I don't know. I . . .'

'Where?' He gripped her arm tighter. He was still slightly dizzy and off-balance. '*Where?*' This time it was a scream that made the hookers halfway along the street look towards them, and as she noticed his eyes fall on a girl leading her client into an alley forty yards down the street, it seemed futile staying quiet.

'Over there,' she said, yanking her arm brusquely from his grip and pointing. 'It's where most of us take our tricks – about six doors along, on the right. You'll know it from the man sitting in front.' And as he sprinted away, she repeated, 'Crazy man' and flicked her skirt with the back of one hand, as if ridding herself of his touch.

As André turned into the alley, the girl and her client were just entering the building. It looked derelict, its door long ago ripped off, and the man slouched in a chair by its gaping entrance sat up sharply as he approached, holding up one hand.

'To see Chloë. I arranged to meet her here,' André said breathlessly.

A wiry mulatto with a shaven head, he appraised André for a few seconds before finally nodding and waving him past.

André took the stairs two at a time and caught up with the girl and her client halfway towards the second floor. As he went past them, it suddenly struck him that he didn't know where to go. He turned and called back to the girl.

'Chloë? Where will I find her?'

'Fifth floor, two of the doors on the left.' Seeing that he was slightly nonplussed, she added, 'You'll know which rooms when you get up there, honey, from all the noise.'

André only then noticed how quiet the building was. *Like a graveyard.* He could hear his own footsteps and ragged breathing bouncing back at him from the stone steps and walls as he continued up. And it was becoming progressively darker, the only light from a stark bare bulb by the entrance shining up through the stairwell, and then the outside orange streetlight filtering through the windows – some broken, some with the frames completely ripped out – on each floor. The image of hell on earth for these girls was complete. André ascended deeper into the darkness.

Oh Jesus. Something rustled by his feet, a rat or perhaps some rubbish disturbed by his step – but as he shifted to one side and reached out to grip the railings he suddenly realized they weren't there. He was off balance, windmilling for a second, and it struck him for the first time how high up he was. He leant back from the sickening void of the stairwell and the stark light far below, stayed close to the wall as he edged up more cautiously.

But then as he looked ahead, his heart froze. There were no railings for the rest of the section or the first few feet of the fifth-floor landing, and four steps just before the landing had crumbled away at their edges. There was little more than a foot-wide strip of solid step remaining.

André stared at it in horror. But now from this angle he could also see faint cracks of light coming from two doors, and could hear the hubbub of voices beyond. And suddenly in his mind the gap became another crossroads: cross it and he reached Dhoumil and had a chance of saving Eban, turn back and . . . but maybe it was that final step into hell that he'd never make it back from.

He took a deep breath and closed his eyes for a second, trying to bring his hammering nerves under control. As he opened them again, he started edging gingerly forward, keeping his back pinned to the wall behind. In the end there was hardly any decision to make. He'd spent so much of his life devoted to others that his own welfare automatically took second place, so why worry about the fall, he told himself. Eban came first. *Blank it from your thoughts.*

But what he told his mind and what his body did were at odds. He was shaking uncontrollably, a pressure-cooker heat building in his head that made him feel dizzy again. He put his hands flat against the wall behind to steady himself; if he swayed or lost his balance at this juncture, he'd fall. With his next step, he watched some loose dust and plaster fall free from the steps and sail into the void. He closed his eyes before it hit bottom. He kept them closed as he edged up the next step, fearing that he might freeze, rooted to the spot as the terrifying void below swamped his senses.

He felt the step firm under his feet and levered his weight up – then as he opened his eyes again he noticed that there was only one step left, and he half-scrambled, half-leapt the remainder. His breath came out in a burst of relief as his feet hit the safety of the fifth-floor landing.

He straightened up, wondering which door to knock on, when the furthest door swung open and a group of three – two girls and a man – walked out. He asked them where he'd find Chloë.

'In dere,' the first girl said in a heavy African accent, pointing behind her. 'But she still in a back room right now – you might haf to wait a bit.'

André thanked her and went into the room. Two girls sat on a sofa with half the stuffing ripped out, passing some money between them which the recipient then tucked hastily into a plastic shopping bag along with some clothes. A third girl sat in an upright wooden chair opposite them, waving her arms emphatically and talking in an African dialect André didn't understand. They paid him scant attention, looking up only briefly as he walked in. But still he offered, 'To see Chloë,' in case they wondered. His eyes must have looked wild still from jumping the gap in the stairs and he felt awkward and tense just standing there as the seconds ticked by.

There were two doors at the back of the room. André could hear muffled voices beyond, but couldn't tell which room they were coming from. André tried to ease his nerves by taking slow, shallow breaths, and after almost two minutes of waiting, shifting his weight from one foot to the other and smiling tightly whenever the girls glanced his way, his pounding pulse finally started to abate. Then seconds later quickly rose again when another girl came in from the hallway who paid him more attention. Her eyes lingered on him increasingly as she talked to the girl in the wooden chair. She used the same African dialect, and her voice was becoming louder and her arm gesticulations more excitable – when at that instant Dhoumil came out of a back room with her client.

André's mouth was suddenly dry. He'd spun so many scenarios through his mind over the past days, but now he just felt tongue-tied. So much, *too much*, rested on what Dhoumil's reaction would be.

It took a second for her to fully focus on him in the poor light. She squinted in disbelief. 'Dr André? What are you doin' here?' She shooed her client away with one hand. 'You go now, I stay here for a while. You know your way down.'

Dr André. *Papa André. Please help me.* He swallowed hard as he started to explain. But in the end he blurted it all out too quickly and slightly out of sequence, jumbled, as if afraid of missing something that would make the difference between her saying yes or no.

Her eyes darted uncertainly as she took it all in, then she held one hand to her chest. 'What, me? I could help save this boy of yours?' Her voice was strained with incredulity.

'Yes, you,' André said simply, mundanely, belying the weight it carried.

For a moment she looked tempted to help. Something worth-while in her life for once, when so much of it so far had lacked worth or value. But then some darker shadows came into her eyes and dragged the thought away. 'No, no. I couldn't.' She shook her head. 'That's why I left the last time. All those needles and tests. I felt like a guinea pig.'

'But you needed to keep coming, Dhoumil. To keep up the tests. You're very ill.'

She cocked her head, looking at him aslant. 'But you said that I was immune. That I wouldn't die, right?'

'Right, but –'

'So in the end it wasn't for me, was it? To help others, maybe, like this little boy you tell me about now. But first of all you help yourselves.' She leant forward, rubbing one forefinger and thumb together. 'That's what it always comes down to, isn't it?'

She'd thrown so much across that he didn't know what to tackle first and, seeing his indecision, she huffed indignantly. 'Huh! Marcus was probably right. As soon as you were finished with me, I'd have been on the first plane back to Abidjan.'

Marcus? André should have realized that someone else was pulling her strings; she wouldn't have left the programme and come to this life of her own volition. 'And I suppose it was this Marcus's bright idea that you come here? You've got HIV, for God's sake, Dhoumil.' His voice raised to a near shout, then lowered again as he shook his head wearily. 'I know you might have given up caring about yourself – but knowingly giving it to others like this?'

An overweight fifty-something client had just come in with a new girl and, at the sound of André's raised voice, he turned back into the hallway and started a heated debate with the girl. This once again set off the girl who'd been eyeing him cautiously and the one on the sofa. They flew into another excitable exchange of African banter and arm waving.

'I use condoms. *Condoms!*' Dhoumil screamed above it all. She plucked a bright purple one from her purse and thrust it in front of his face.

'*Encoule ma grandmère!*' the girl in the hallway shouted after the departing footsteps of her client, then a second later she started heading back down herself.

'Anyway, it's what I do. What I know,' Dhoumil said, casting her eyes down for a second. 'How you expect me to survive on the peanuts from social security?'

André was getting desperate, could feel it all slipping rapidly away. 'But that was a condition of the social security, and of you staying here,' he stressed. The soft approach hadn't worked, so now try some pressure. But as soon as the words were out, he knew it was the wrong thing to say.

'Is that what you'd do? Report me to the social security?'

'No, no,' André appeased. 'But if they find you here, they'll kick you out. Marcus isn't going to give you any protection. And he probably hasn't even bothered to tell you the risk you run. You've got far more chance of being shipped back on the first plane to Africa from here than you ever would with me.'

Dhoumil shook her head, looking confused. 'I don't know. Everyone telling me different things.'

She was teetering again. He pressed home the advantage. 'As soon as things turn bad, he'll turn his back on you. Whereas I can keep you in the programme for years, Dhoumil.' He sensed that ninety per cent of the battle was a mental tug of war with Marcus; she'd probably long ago given up thinking what she wanted for herself. 'Even when it's finished, I can say you're needed for tests in another two years. Then another two. I can keep you here indefinitely, Dhoumil.' As he reached one hand towards her, he saw that it was trembling heavily. 'I wouldn't turn my back on you.'

He thought he had her then. For a moment all the confusion melted from her face and she looked settled. But then a second later the dark shadows were back in her eyes. Marcus was tugging at her again.

'No, no. This is my life now.' She shook her head resolutely. 'I can't go back to that again.' She kept her eyes averted from his as she brushed past him and went into the hallway. 'I must get on now.'

'Please,' he pleaded. All else had failed, nothing left but to beg. He followed her and lightly gripped her arm. 'You've no idea what I've been through to find you now.' *The fight with the man on that first day in the Goutte d'Or, banging his fist on Charlotte's bloodied chest as he screamed for her to start breathing again, racing back and forth on the train* – he could still see the lights flashing past his eyes now, making him sway and feel dizzy again. But then suddenly it was the bare bulb shining up at him from the bottom of the stairwell of only moments ago. 'Please,' he repeated, his eyes darting briefly to the hell-hole surroundings. 'You think I'd be here, would come to a place like this if there was any other way I thought I could save him? *Please* . . . you're my last chance.' He felt all of it, all the panic and frustration of the past days course through him like raw electricity, and he suddenly realized that he was holding her arm too tight, desperately afraid of letting this last chance slip from his grasp.

She pulled her arm away as he relaxed his grip, but something in her eyes seemed to have softened again. They glistened faintly in the dull light. 'You shouldn't be doing this to me, Dr André. Coming here and playing with my head. Getting me so I . . .' Then suddenly the shadows were back in her eyes, but this time slightly different: a mixture of surprise and fear as they fixed on something behind him. 'No . . . *No!*' she screamed.

André felt the blow to the side of his head before he registered any movement. He was sent reeling, staggering, lights spinning and swaying; and as everything fell into focus again he saw that it was the bare bulb below and he was slumped against the landing rails, looking down.

The man leapt in quickly and grabbed him by the lapels, pressing him back against the railings. 'You come here, trying to mess with my girls.' He spat the words into André's face from only inches away. 'I mess with you.'

At first André thought it was the guard from the downstairs entrance, but this man was burlier and a good few years older with a faint ring of cropped hair around his bald patch. He pressed André harder against the rails, and André felt them give slightly against his back.

'No, Marcus. *No!*' Dhoumil screamed.

Marcus smiled. 'None too strong these railings here. That's what happened to the last stretch.' He nodded to the missing railings to one side. 'Now – you going to keep away from my girls?' He gave André another shove against the railings.

'Yes . . . yes. I'll keep away,' André mumbled, frozen with fear.

'I don't hear you.' Marcus shoved again, harder.

André felt the railings give a little more against his back, and as he looked down he saw loose cement and plaster from their base drift down into the stairwell void. 'Yes, I'll stay away . . . I promise.' He closed his eyes. '*Please!*'

But looking down had been the wrong thing to do. Just before he'd closed his eyes, Marcus had seen his abject fear.

'You like the view down there, no?' He half-shoved, half-dragged

André along by the lapels, and André stumbled, his feet tangling as they went. 'So why don't we go where the view is clearer?'

André's eyes opened wide again with fear. Suddenly he couldn't feel the reassuring press of any railings as Marcus leant him back. Marcus had moved him along to where the railings had fallen away.

André made the mistake of looking down again, and suddenly he was back in the Cameroon jungle, paralysed with fear and clinging to a branch as the snake moved close, the monkeys' shrieking filling the air. Except that now the snake was Marcus and the shrieking was from Dhoumil and the other girls in the background.

'So you're a doctor, huh? Gives you a feeling of power, does it? Holding the lives of others in your hands?' Marcus grimaced. 'So now you know how it feels for them.'

'Marcus . . . no! *No! Enough!*' Dhoumil hit his shoulder repeatedly with the flat of one hand, and for a moment André feared that her pounding would send them both over the edge.

Marcus shrugged her off as if she were an errant fly. His grimace faded. 'You stay away from my Dhoumil, no? You don't come here again to see her. Don't trouble her no more!' With each burst of emphasis Marcus shoved André back, and on the last André feared that he'd been let go.

He struggled to clear the dizziness in his head, the sense that his body was swaying even when Marcus wasn't moving him. The light from below continued to tilt, the garish faces of Dhoumil and two girls looking on shifting from side to side for a moment more before falling back into focus.

'No . . . I promise. I won't come back to trouble her again. I'm sorry.' But as he let loose the last strand of hope with Dhoumil, in his mind he was saying sorry to Eban and Mpundu. They'd relied on him and he'd let them down. *Lives of others in your hands.* Yet in the end he'd let Eban fall free into the void – could almost hear his echoing scream as he sailed down, arms reaching pleadingly towards him . . . *Please help me* – just to save his own neck. He felt weak, tired and sick with fear, but most of all ashamed.

'Huh!' Marcus grunted disdainfully. He pulled André in and let go of his lapels, and André collapsed in a ball at Marcus's feet. 'You can go now.'

But as André looked ahead to the gap and the thin strip of stairs at its side, he didn't know whether he could. Unlike on his way up, there was nothing left to hope or aim for, nothing for which to summon up the bravery to help him across.

Today was the day. She'd got Kalpenski all fired up, then had starved him of the sight of her black stockings for a full week.

But she was wearing them today.

She'd spent the last few days planning where it should take place – somewhere hidden, obviously, but also somewhere that was accessed reasonably regularly – before deciding on the samples store room. But now she had to think of a good reason to get Kalpenski in there. It couldn't just be where's this or where's that? – any lab assistant could help her with that – it had to be something worthy of his position and gravitas.

Her nerves built steadily through the morning. He'd only been down to the general lab floor once so far, and there hadn't been a chance for her to get close and broach the subject without being too obvious. She didn't want anyone to overhear that she'd lured him to the sample room. Though she'd noticed his eyes fall to her stockings for a moment, a long moment. He'd be back.

But by 4.20 p.m., with still no sign of Kalpenski, her nerves were ragged, turning over this way and that in her mind what she was going to say and how it might go. It was going to be too late now today, she'd just have to start from scratch planning again tomorrow, for once wear black stockings two days in a –

'Oh,' she said, slightly startled as she looked up from her microscope. 'I didn't see you there.'

Kalpenski smiled warmly. 'I was just wondering how the Haynes tests were going.'

'Oh, OK.' She smiled back. A pet project Kalpenski had set her four days ago: measuring how the cell multiplication in a cancerous liver sample was affected by temperature. It had also given her the key to how she might trap him. She looked past his shoulder: nobody was within earshot. 'But there was something on the transit manifesto that concerns me. Something that could later raise the argument that the sample was corrupted.' She stood up, but waited for him to lead the way. The transit manifesto was in the sample store room.

The blood pounded hard and heavy inside her head as she followed Kalpenski along the corridor towards the sample room. But it was going well so far, she told herself: to anyone looking on it would seem like he'd approached her and asked her there.

Still she found her nerves impossible to control as they went inside the room. Now that they were there, she didn't think she could go through with it. Her hands were shaking uncontrollably as she picked up the manifesto attached to the Haynes sample.

'If you look at the time it arrived from Maryland General, it says 2.08. Yet they weren't logged in here until just after seven a.m. – no doubt because there wasn't anyone with sufficient responsibility on graveyard that night, or they were busy with something else.' She swallowed hard. 'But that five hours concerns me. Especially if in that time . . .'

'I know. I know. If it started thawing there could have been cellular activity before we even started testing. And I can see you're worried about that.' Kalpenski laid a calming hand on her shoulder. 'But they were ice-packed and Maryland General wouldn't have specifically known they were for here. They could easily have been for a lab in Colorado or Oregon – so that packing should have been good for twelve hours or more.' He gave her shoulder a couple of reassuring pats before taking his hand away.

'Yes, you're probably right,' she said, looking down coyly. Such a nice old man: a part of her felt guilty doing this. But the rest of her had built up such an irrepressible head of steam – the years in suburban exile during her marriage, the recent battle with Hebbard, the increasingly tense e-mail tennis with Chisholm – that she found it impossible to resist. It felt almost like destiny. Meant to be. Chisholm was right: she'd be living in Kalpenski's shadow for years, would probably never make the grade. *Now or never.*

'There is something else,' she said. She went towards the door and flicked the latch. As she turned back to Kalpenski, her face was hot and flushed. The blood boiled inside her head like a volcano. Now or never, while she could still pass her reaction off as passion: if Kalpenski read it as nerves or fear, he might get wary and back off. She leant in close before he had the time to think about it and kissed him on one cheek close to his mouth. Then she moved quickly across and kissed him fully on the lips and, as she felt him respond, snaked her tongue gently inside.

She brought one hand up to his left arm to brace him, keep him pulled in close, and felt him shaking heavily. She pulled back a fraction and saw that his eyes were flickering uncertainly.

'I . . . I'm not sure we should be doing this. Someone's bound to come in.'

She leant in again, smothering his objection with another kiss. 'I've locked the door,' she said in a low, sultry tone. Not true: she'd imperceptibly flipped the latch back in the same motion as locking it. 'I've seen you looking at my stockings,' she said, touching his lips with two more light kisses. 'And I can see that you like them.'

'I . . . It somehow doesn't feel right here.' His eyes darted anxiously towards the door and then around the small room.

She ignored it, drowning the words with another kiss. 'I'm wearing them again today, and you should feel how hot you've got me.' She swivelled him quickly round so that she was facing the door and perched her bottom up on the workbench. She raised her lab coat until the tops of her stockings were showing and parted her legs slightly. 'So hot . . . right here.' She pulled him in close and guided his hand to the few inches of bare flesh above her stockings. 'Sooo hot.' His body trembled wildly against her, and as his hand made contact with her skin he flinched and pulled away slightly.

'Couldn't . . . couldn't we do this one evening, perhaps?' he said breathlessly. 'Dinner and then going on somewhere.'

She studied him soberly: the milky blue eyes with their heavy bags, the rat face with thinning grey hair; there was more of it sprouting from his nostrils and ears. He was repulsive, and it would have been so easy just to say, 'Fine', and put it off indefinitely. But it was almost as if she'd gone too far, been through too much to stop now. *Now or never.*

'I'm an impulsive sort of person,' she said, stroking his left arm thoughtfully and then bringing the hand up to lightly touch his cheek. She smiled provocatively. 'Sometimes with me it's now or never. I'm just not sure how I might feel about things later.'

She watched the conflicting emotions jostling in his face. In the end her judgement was right: the thought that this might be his only chance with her was too much for him. She watched him crumble and melt before her, his eyes taking in her stockings and the bare tops of her legs. Chisholm would have been proud of her: risking all on the toss of a simple bluff. But still she'd have to take the last bit of initiative. She raised the lab coat a fraction higher to show an inch of panties and guided his hand in again. 'Sooo hot,' she said. She kissed him again and felt his last resistance ebb away. His hand started to move on the inside of her bare thigh, the back of one finger touching against her panties. Her eyes fixed on the door handle over his shoulder. If someone came in at any time now, her plan would work.

As she sank back into another kiss, she felt his tongue snake into her mouth, tangling with hers. *Repulsive.* But at least now seeing him in that cold grey light, the guilt had evaporated. If she saw this through and it worked, she'd feel she'd earned it. The old fool would have asked for it. 'And so wet,' she said, breaking off and breathing hotly in one ear. She felt his hand hesitate for a second before becoming bold enough to turn and touch two fingers against her crotch. She swallowed hard, her eyes fixing back on the door. Please, *oh God*, someone come in now. She wasn't sure how much more of this she could take.

She tried to keep her eyes on the door, but suddenly Kalpenski's rat face was before her with his eyes half-closed, tongue probing. This time as she went back into another kiss, she felt his nose-hairs tickling one cheek. She stifled an involuntary retch, turning it into a hot groan of passion against his neck as she pulled away again.

She felt Kalpenski's hand get bolder, one finger tracing up the edge of her panties and pulling them aside. *Please . . . Please!*

Someone come in and save me. Of course, he'd find that rather than wet she was dry as a bone with nerves and apprehension. She clamped her thighs together slightly. 'Oh, that's so . . . *soooo* sensitive there.'

She pulled him into another quick kiss and then, breathing hotly in his ear, fixed her eyes back on the door. Still no one. Come on. *Come on!*

Kalpenski's hand was probing again. At any second he'd know that she wasn't wet or excited, that her trembling was from nerves and fear rather than passion, and the game would be up. Or she'd be first to break off, unable to continue any more. Everything about him suddenly assaulted her senses: the grey hairs sprouting from the ear that she breathed into, the smell of lab spirits and agarose on his clothes, the pupils of his milky blue eyes like pin-pricks as they became lost in passion, his rat face screwed up and his breath starting to fall in shallow grunts as his excitement grew. She felt like beating her fists against his chest and screaming for him to get off. *Get off!* Then rush to the washroom to empty her stomach and swill her mouth out with a gallon of water. She must have been mad to think she could go through with this. There had to be a better way to . . .

She froze. Some voices and light shuffling came from the other side of the door. She moved her mouth closer to his ear to drown them out.

'Oh, yes . . . there. *There!*' She felt two of Kalpenski's fingers snake inside her panties. In turn she reached out and fondled his crotch.

But what if it was Hebbard or Bremner? They'd probably not report it, or would back up Kalpenski's version. It would all be for nothing. Or what if the voices outside the door just continued on down the corridor? She could still hear them in the same position.

She felt Kalpenski's finger tracing through her pubic hairs, and her entire body shuddered with revulsion. She gripped him tighter. 'Oh yes . . . *yes.*'

Please, oh God, help me. Help me! Please come in! And as she felt his fingers touch her, she was about to push him away, couldn't bear it a second longer, when the door handle started turning.

'Oh yes, *oh God*. There . . . *there!*' Her voice was barely a whisper only an inch from his ear. It wouldn't reach beyond the door, but it was enough to keep Kalpenski from hearing the handle turning.

There was a frozen moment between them as Kalpenski touched her. Perhaps trying to fathom why she was dry, the conflict with all her other bodily signals and what she'd said; or maybe he had heard the door handle turning or felt the sudden change in her body as she tensed for action.

As the door swung open, she started screaming and pushing him away. 'No . . . *no*! For God's sake! What are you doing?'

Kalpenski was slow to disentangle himself. It was Senadhira.

Red-faced, she brushed her lab coat back down. '*God!* What were you thinking of?' Her sense of revulsion gave her reaction the perfect timbre. Her voice was shaky and she was close to tears.

Senadhira looked embarrassed and started to close the door. 'Sorry.'

She reached out and flung the door wide open again, making it patently clear that the last thing she wanted was to be left in the room with Kalpenski. 'Jesus! How could you?'

Kalpenski was still catching up with the sudden turnaround. His pin-prick eyes struggled to fall back into focus. 'This isn't what it looks like,' he appealed to Senadhira.

'No, it's much worse,' she said, and stormed from the room.

18

They stopped checking Eban's T-cell count at 58. It was already more than 20 points below the minimum threshold André had set, and so further monitoring seemed immaterial. But more crucially, they were far too busy with the other readings – the second-by-second vital signs that told them whether or not they were winning in their battle to save Eban's life.

'102.7 and 42 b.p.m.'

'91 over 46. And . . . 23 p.m.'

Marielle was monitoring temperature and pulse, David blood pressure and respiration. Their voices barked out urgently one after the other as André looked on anxiously after giving Eban an adrenalin shot, his second of the night. Pulse and respiration had thankfully moved up a few notches – but they were both still dangerously low. André dabbed at his brow with the back of one hand. More acetaminophen and relenza in just over an hour and another double dose of Invirase in two hours. Anything he'd overlooked?

He felt strangely powerless looking at Eban. A mountain of the most incredible, cutting-edge viral research at his right hand – but, despairingly, just out of reach – and at a moment like this he was no more effective than an emergency-room intern.

He'd felt tempted to dive into his notes and his computer the minute he walked back into the lab, to desperately hunt through for something, *anything*, he might have overlooked – but then quickly realized the futility. It was too late. Unless they could get Eban over the hurdle of this current flu, now no doubt already turned to pneumonia, it was pointless trying anything else. There wasn't time and Eban was simply too weak.

In part that made him feel not quite so bad, not so despairingly empty and defeated, about failing to bring in Dhoumil. The same would probably have been true there. And after the nightmare night and the panic of these past days, he felt exhausted; perhaps all he could cope with now anyway was something mind-numbingly simple, straightforward. First-year intern's procedure.

But still it felt odd simply going through the motions, pitting blind hope against the ever-descending cloak of the inevitable, ticking down with each beat of Eban's pulse or respiration slowing. Eban's mouth was dry and cracked with some heavy sores at one corner, his eyes bleary and unfocused, and for much of the night he'd been delirious. André could hardly bear to look at him, could hear his promise to Mpundu echoing emptily with each vital-sign slide or urgent shout from David and Marielle.

Eban was dying.

Then at one moment late into the night – one of the few that Eban had been awake and anywhere near lucid – as André was double-checking Eban's pulse, Eban suddenly clutched André's hand.

'*Papa* André. I . . . I'm not afraid to die, you know.'

André shook his head resolutely. 'You're not going to die,' he said. A flat, emphatic tone. 'We'll get you over this.'

But, unlike an intern, his deeper knowledge had in that moment betrayed him, told him what they probably wouldn't have deduced: Eban's immune system had finally given up. He could have almost set his watch by it: 4.40 to 4.47 a.m. Eban's temperature stopped rising, yet his blood pressure, respiration and pulse continued to decline. André knew then that any last chance of a remission was gone.

And in that moment Eban had seen it too in his face; and as he tried to gloss things over, he could see that Eban wasn't taken in by the lie. They knew each other too well, had been through too much together to be lied to; especially at this moment of all moments.

'At least I'll see my father again. And Nsoro and Mpundu . . . be with them.' Eban's eyes drifted as his delirium again threatened to smother any clear thought. He struggled to focus back on André. 'Many times I think about them, and I . . . I miss them so.'

With the heavy lump in his throat, all André could manage was, 'I know. I'm sorry.' And as his eyes filled, he left the room before he broke down completely in front of everyone – the emotions and his exhaustion finally too much – and dived into the nearby washroom as the first sobs hit. Sorry! *Sorry!* He started banging his fist repeatedly against the cubicle door he shut himself behind. Sorry to Mpundu, sorry to Bernice who'd looked anxiously through the glass screen of the Laferge unit throughout the night's vigil; and to all those whom Eban had touched in his short life: Charlotte, Veruschka, Joël, Marielle and everyone at the lab, Madame Ahlnaj . . . *Oh God, Joël!* His heart broke for a second time at the thought of how young Joël would take the news. He and Eban were inseparable, like the brother Joël always wished he'd had.

And as it all became too much – the pain and the frustration and his sense of powerlessness – the portent of Eban's death rising as a mountainous burden that was too overwhelming for him to shoulder or accept, the 'Sorrys' became 'Noes'. No! No! *No! No! No!*

The repetitive banging of his fist against the cubicle door drowned out Marielle's knocking on the main washroom door and her voice the other side, so it took a moment for him to hear her.

He stopped abruptly, catching his breath and wiping his eyes with the back of one hand as he darted out. 'What was that?'

'I said – there's someone here to see you.'

And as he followed Marielle back into the main lab room and saw who it was, suddenly there was hope again.

Kalpenski didn't stand a chance.

Dani made her complaint that Kalpenski had sexually assaulted her first thing the following morning. Senadhira was asked up to the Spheros boardroom that same afternoon to give his account.

He didn't return to the general office until over forty minutes later, and although the tame, slightly embarrassed smile he fired Dani when she looked his way gave little away, she knew Senadhira well: ambitious and reluctant to ruffle departmental feathers, but he wouldn't lie to save Kalpenski's neck. That could too easily go the wrong way and be viewed in a dim light, harm his future prospects. He'd tell it exactly how he saw it.

She didn't see Kalpenski for the next few days. Either he was keeping his head low and was avoiding showing his face to anyone on the lab floor, especially her, or he just wasn't in at all. Nor did she have any idea what he might have said in his defence to the Spheros board, though undoubtedly he'd have been hauled in for an explanation almost immediately.

All became clear with the e-mail waiting on her computer the following morning:

Well done! Kalpenski was foolish enough to claim that he was lured, that it was all a setup. But looking at him and looking at you, who for a minute was going to believe that? Poor fool.

He was given two days' leave while the board deliberated, but now that the decision has been made, he'll be asked to resign, the whole matter quickly and quietly swept away. The alternative would be to face prosecution and the total destruction of his career and reputation, so no cigar for which he'll choose. In turn, you'll soon be asked a crucial question, and I'm sure I don't have to guide you as to how to answer.

Despite the prompt, still Dani felt her heart in her throat as the next day she was called up to the Spheros boardroom and asked, given that in respect of her complaint Dr Kalpenski had been asked to resign from the Spheros, did she intend to pursue the matter further?

'I . . . I'm not sure.' She felt her face flush, the blood rushing to her head. Chisholm was on the end of the line of five facing her, and she tried not to let her eyes settle too long on him for hidden signals – it might give away that she knew it was him sending the e-mails! But he was wrong: she did need some guidance. 'I . . . I suppose it would depend.'

'You see, we have to put the Spheros's reputation first and foremost,' offered Dr Warrell, Spheros Chairman at the centre of the five, sensing she was adrift. 'And if you did decide to take action, we'd unfortunately be forced to give you a leave of absence until the case was over – so that it didn't appear we were taking sides in any way. While internally – just between all of us here,' Warrell waved one hand along the line '– we can make it clear by our actions which side our favour lies, once matters are thrown open to the cold light of a trial and public and media scrutiny, we have to be more careful. We just wouldn't have that same luxury or latitude of movement.'

'Well, I . . . I wouldn't want to leave the Spheros, of course,' she said, possibly too quickly. 'And with Dr Kalpenski gone and therefore no further threat or cause for concern . . .' She kept her gaze evenly between the five, keenly gauging reaction as she laid assurances that given the new situation she didn't foresee taking any further action. They appeared to be settled with what she said, almost genuinely relieved – except for Chisholm. He raised a quizzical eyebrow.

'Is that all?'

Is that all? What was this, a set-up? The coup de grâce of all his e-mails heading somewhere she hadn't seen? She felt her cheeks burning, her blood pressure again at volcano point. They clearly didn't want her to pursue legal action. What else was there? The room fell excruciatingly quiet. 'I . . . I . . .' Suddenly she was in free-fall, clutching at air, her ears ringing and her pulse pounding at her temples. And in that moment, inadvertently, probably her eyes did settle on Chisholm a moment too long, pleading for help and guidance. 'I . . . I'm not sure . . . I . . .'

'I mean – you've done some good work for the Spheros these past years,' Chisholm said. 'And now you've very generously offered not to pursue the matter any further; mainly, it appears, in respect of the Spheros's welfare and honour. But what about your own continuing welfare, how do you see . . .'

Halfway through, the coin dropped. She'd been acquiescent too quickly. She should have been driving a harder bargain, or at least hinting at some sort of quid pro quo. 'The recognition of my work here has always been very important to me.' She swallowed hard, regaining her composure. 'But I don't really see it as my position to make a point to the board about any added worth my decision today might have.' She flicked her eyes down slightly, as if in modesty. 'I'm sure they're quite able to determine that and act accordingly. For my part, the good and strong continuing recognition of my work here would be more than enough.'

The poker faces returned, though not before she caught a fleeting glimmer of smiling accord, except from Chisholm: he remained poker-faced throughout. So she remained uncertain whether or not she'd said the right thing.

And when two days later she heard on the departmental grapevine that two outside names had been put forward alongside hers to take over Kalpenski's position – something that Chisholm had conveniently neglected to mention in his earlier e-mail – the spectre that it had been a set-up all along again rose strongly.

Chisholm wanted to get his golden boy in – some bright spark from Cornell or MIT – and she'd been used purely as the patsy to get rid of Kalpenski. And what could she do about it? If she showed her hand, she'd be out on her ear double-quick, plus would probably face lawsuits for compensation from both Hebbard and Kalpenski. And the e-mails sent from Cyberling Rivalry were completely anonymous – they couldn't for an instant be attached to Chisholm. Except her claim that she'd seen him there one day, which wouldn't even get to first base with convincing anyone. She couldn't back it up. Oh God, he'd played her well. So well.

Out on her ear? That's probably what he had planned for her anyway – as soon as his golden boy was in place. Get rid of all the evidence. And again there was nothing she could do about it and he knew it. *So well.*

But surely she couldn't have gone through all of this for it to end in nothing? Even though that would tie in with her first doubting thoughts as to why Chisholm would go to these lengths just to hand her glory. It made far more sense that he'd use her as a dupe to get rid of Kalpenski so that he could put his own golden boy from outside in the saddle.

Or maybe the delay, the terrible silence, was because he'd caught her look in the boardroom and was concerned that she knew it was him. He wanted to put some distance back between them. *For God's sake, say something*, she found herself silently screaming each morning she turned on the computer, her thoughts see-sawing wildly with the uncertainty.

But with each successive day and still no e-mail from Chisholm, the silence became increasingly ominous, bade the worst. It had been a set-up all along.

Dhoumil! André was surprised to see her, he'd completely given up on her; as was David as he caught his glance from the far side of the lab floor. Though perhaps it was more a look of concern.

Something he'd said a few hours ago had stuck in her mind, but she didn't elaborate. She said that she'd never forgive herself if she didn't at least *try* to help. He in turn agreed to keep Dhoumil on their books for four further tests at eighteen-month intervals. After that time, six years, she'd almost certainly get rubber-stamped to stay permanently. They set up the equipment and started their tests.

David didn't say anything right then, but André could feel his eyes on him questioningly, boring home their message: *It's too late, surely you know that? I thought we'd all already accepted that fact.* But, perhaps because of their earlier argument, David bit his tongue; or perhaps he harboured doubt that anything worthwhile would be found in the tests, or Eban's condition would have meanwhile worsened so as to leave no margin of doubt that they were too late – so any arguing in the interim was probably redundant. Or simply because by the time their tests were fully under way, the lab was busy and back in the full swing of its daily activity, and David didn't want to cause a scene in front of everyone.

But as soon as it became dark and the lab emptied out again, by which time there were encouraging results from Dhoumil's tests and Eban's condition had rallied a bit, David turned on André.

'You just can't do it, André. It's too risky.'

'But you've seen the results. They're better even than we could have possibly hoped for.' The T-cell rise with Dhoumil's serum was almost forty per cent higher than anything previously tested with the mangabey samples. Their assumption had been right: hepatitis B had been the final X-factor.

'Yes, but that's just with basic Ames Petri-dish tests and only two agarose wash-throughs. There's no way of knowing if those results will hold up in the long term. They could just slip back to the base line, like the others.'

'True. But we just don't have time for those tests – you know that.'

'I know that all too well.' David shook his head. 'That's why you can't do it, André. The chances are too slim, the odds too much against you. And if things go wrong – especially since you haven't done even a quarter of the prescribed tests – Delatois will crucify you. It'll be the end of your career.'

'My career? *My career?*' André gripped David's arm tight. 'So how do you think I'm going to feel, David, looking back in a year or two's time, knowing that my precious career is still intact only because I let him die?' André looked hauntingly towards Eban through the glass of the Laferge unit, and David's eyes dropped. 'If there was only a one or two per cent chance, I'd still have to take it. But I think the odds are far better than that – thirty or forty per cent or more.'

Most of the steam went out of David's argument at that point, and all that was left was a chain of sharp questions as he confirmed how André saw the procedure running.

David nodded at intervals, still obviously heavy with doubt and concern, but at least for the first time he appeared to be thinking it through in real terms.

'You know that using hepatitis B as the vector, with Eban's immunity so low, we might not even make it past that hurdle?' David cautioned.

'I know.'

David cradled his forehead and brusquely ruffled his hair. '*Oh God.* It would have been so much simpler if she hadn't showed at all.' Then, as he finally lifted his head. 'OK, let's go to it. The quicker we get on with it, the better.'

'*We?*' André berated that while he accepted putting his own career on the line because of his personal involvement, there was no need for David to risk going down in flames as well.

And David in turn threw back his own earlier defence. 'So, André, how am I going to feel later if you fail – knowing that a large part of that has been due to you trying to battle through unassisted?' David's raised eyebrow was smugly challenging and, meeting it, André was unsure whether David subscribed to his own argument, or felt that because of their friendship he simply couldn't leave André to battle through alone. Beneath the smug bravado he could sense David's uncertainty; he was as fearful as him of what they faced. They were breaking completely new ground and *everything* was at stake: Eban's life and now both of their careers. David sighed tiredly. 'With the procedure you've outlined, André, you'll need help. You can't do it on your own.'

They sent Marc and Marielle home, kept Bernice for extra comfort and brow-wiping with Eban purely because she didn't have a career to risk, and set to work.

Almost a month had gone by and still no e-mail from Chisholm. And now to add to the confusion, the departmental scuttlebutt was that there were *two* internal nominations for the post riding along with the two from outside. She was one of them – or was she, was she even certain of that? – but who was the other? The only thing she could think of was that one of the other section heads was earmarked to move across to oncology, or perhaps one of their shining stars. The only one she could think of that had nearly enough dazzle points was McAllister from molecular biology.

He'd also been a bit of a favourite of Kalpenski's. His name had often come up whenever they wanted input from MB. Perhaps that had been Kalpenski's parting payback shot. 'I'll go quietly, just as long as you give my position to someone who I think is worthy, such as McAllister. Certainly not to that avaricious black widow spider, Stolk.'

She was at her wit's end turning over the various possibilities in her mind. She'd found herself shouting and screaming at Allison over the smallest thing at the weekend just past, and had received a call from her ex, Bradley, the following day asking if she was OK. She'd defended that of course she was OK. 'Why?'

'Just that Allison said you were, well . . . a bit *tense*.'

She must be in a bad way, closer to the edge than she realized, for him to bother to voice his concern. Straight after the divorce and her shafting him over the property, he'd said to friends that he'd have happily taken her head off with a shotgun if it were legal.

Maybe that was it. Divine justice. After a lifetime of shafting the men in her life, finally in Chisholm she'd met her match and he was going to pay her back for all of the others.

She had to stay calm. *Calm*. She could sense some in her department starting to look at her curiously; though perhaps they put her unease down to shock and nerves after the assault from Kalpenski. The long wait might also be some sort of probation period during which the internal candidates were to be watched and monitored. And she wasn't going to fit the bill as a competent replacement for Kalpenski while she looked like a neurotic woman on the edge.

But as the days ticked by with still no news or e-mail, her thoughts swung round again to the overriding feeling that it had been a set-up by Chisholm to get his hand-picked boy from outside in place, or even McAllister; perhaps he too had been a favourite of Chisholm's.

So when finally there was an e-mail, she'd resigned herself to the fact that it was bad news.

The instant she saw the cybriv tag her hands started shaking. *Oh Jesus*, this was too much to bear. Her entire future either gone or confirmed in one simple double-click. She was conscious of Andy Luttman a couple of desks away looking over at her, perhaps picking up on her consternation.

'Some of these CELL-ULA calculations,' she said, shaking her head. 'This one is six pages long. Been driving me mad for a couple of days now.' She double-clicked and opened the e-mail.

You made it! Sorry about the delay, but there were a few bridges to cross on the way. The other internal candidate, Gerald

Thompson, virology section head, was reluctant to move across (which I knew from the outset), and one of the outside candidates fell by the wayside early. That left just you and one other outside candidate. Unfortunately, a skeleton jumped out of his cupboard at the last moment. (Oh dear, how did that happen?) But I think the clincher, what made them finally not want to look further either outside or internally, was your comment about *good* and *strong* continuing recognition of your work. The silent worry that you might kick up a fuss over Kalpenski if you felt you'd been sidelined. Plus the fact that it was pointed out to the board that having someone young and female (and dare I say glamorous) in such a high-profile job would certainly score some strong PR bonus points. The announcement will be made public in a day or so. Well done! There's nothing to stop you now.

She felt like jumping up and yelping and whooping with excitement, but she just eased out a satisfied breath and smiled, as though – to Luttman or others looking on – she'd simply had a breakthrough with the CELL-ULA calculations on screen.

But beneath her silent elation, as she felt the butterflies in her stomach finally start settling, she couldn't help dwelling on what Chisholm had put her through. Her life had been on an absolute knife-edge these past weeks, and his final e-mail could just as easily have gone the other way. Had there really been such a lengthy milling process? Surely he could have said *something* earlier? Was he punishing her for that fleeting look in the boardroom, or perhaps he just took a cruel pleasure in making her wait, knowing how much she'd be on tenterhooks? Whatever, he'd had complete control over her; something that nobody previously had held, and it made her distinctly uneasy. Perhaps she'd need far more than just knowing that it was Chisholm and some of his background to even the balance.

Though he was right about one thing. With him behind her, the last line of his e-mail held particular resonance, and she couldn't help re-reading it as she silently gloated: *There's nothing to stop you now . . . nothing to stop you now . . .*

★

André unchained his bike and wheeled it out through the courtyard.

Madame Chercule, straightening up from tending her plants, spotted his departing back as he was halfway across.

'Good day, Monsieur Lemoine. *Ça va?*'

André didn't respond. The traffic from the road ahead half drowned out her voice, and his thoughts were elsewhere.

He got on and wove through some slow-moving traffic at the end of his road, then quickly switched up through fourth, fifth and sixth gear as he turned on to Rue de Vaugirard. Finally seventh and eighth gear as he hit full speed. The wind rush felt good against his face. Refreshing, exhilarating.

At first, he and David thought they'd got over the initial hurdle of Eban's response to hepatitis B. Three hours after it had been administered as a vector and another two before giving him the mangabey serum – five hours they'd agreed was the optimum time between the two key stages – and Eban seemed to be holding out. His blood pressure, pulse and respiration had dropped only negligibly. Then, forty minutes later, the reaction they'd feared hit. Eban started sliding rapidly.

Vaugirard was busy with a steady stream of cars, as usual, but invariably one of its two lanes each way was clear or there was room for him to weave between traffic.

They administered the mangabey serum an hour early, and from then on it was a desperate race to see whether Eban's T-cell count would start picking up again before his blood-pressure, pulse and respiration sank too low. His systolic rate was the most vital.

'38 . . . 36 . . . 35.'

André felt the countdown strikes almost in rhythm with his pedalling. He turned into Boulevard du Montparnasse and raised up in the saddle to pedal faster, break it.

'13 p.m. . . . And 38 b.p.m.'

There was a moment when it appeared that Eban's immune system was rallying – his temperature rose for the first time in eighteen hours, up 0.4 to 101.7 – and his systolic rate held steady at 35, as if poised on a knife's edge: one way clawing back to possible recovery, the other . . . and he and David watched, breath held, to see which way it would jump.

A small jam of four or five cars loomed ahead. André checked over his shoulder and swung out, once again rising up to hit a stronger rhythm as he overtook.

But then it started falling again, sliding off of the cliff.

'34 . . . 33 . . . 32.'

André cut back in. It was clearer ahead, little traffic, and André hit a steady clip down Montparnasse. The first twinges of pain from exertion gripped his chest.

Pain. He'd almost felt the stab himself as he'd plunged home the syringe, pumping the adrenalin close to Eban's heart to hopefully kick-start his system again, lift his dangerously low blood pressure and pulse.

It lifted 4 points . . . 5, 6 . . . touching almost 40 at one stage, before it started falling again: 38 . . . 36 . . . 35 . . .

André's legs pumped hard, his breath starting to rasp.

34 . . . 32. The terrible rasping and rattling in Eban's throat as he struggled with his final breaths.

Another small jam ahead, this time in the outside lane behind a car turning left into Rue Stanislas. André quickly swung inside to avoid them.

Eban's heart stopped at a systolic rate of 30. They tried to get it going again with electric paddles – five times in all with heavy massage in-between – but it was no use. The flatline continued as an annoying monotone to his and David's ragged breathing as they slumped to one side, exhausted and defeated.

André's eyes watered heavily, but he wasn't sure if it was from the wind rush or tears. Surely he'd cried so much in the last forty-eight hours that there wasn't anything left. There was another clear stretch ahead and he switched up to tenth gear, pedalling harder. Pedal away the pain.

Delatois left only twenty-four hours' grace before hauling them into his office. He wouldn't fire them or make any public announcements, purely for the sake of the ISG's reputation. But he would expect their resignations on his desk by the next morning, to become effective immediately. André begged for leniency for Marielle and Marc, claiming that they hadn't in any way been involved, and Delatois reluctantly agreed to grant them a six-month stay of execution. 'After that time I'll expect their resignations as well.' André suspected that the concession was mainly down to more ISG face-saving; an entire department being disbanded at the same time might have raised too many eyebrows.

To his right was the Montparnasse cemetery. Not the cemetery recalled from his childhood that kept replaying in his dreams, that was in the north of the city on the way to Sacré Coeur. It wasn't until years later that he actually came across it again, when he'd first started working in Paris, and it appeared much smaller then. Was it just that everything seemed so much bigger when you were a child, or had it kept expanding each time in his dreams? . . . *Tombstones stretching into the misty reaches of the city, appearing never-ending*: His father Philip, who'd died from cancer when André was only fourteen, his beloved uncle who'd been like a surrogate father over the years since and had passed away only five years ago . . . *Nsoro, Mpundu . . . now Eban . . .*

The road ahead blurred heavily with his tears. He wiped at them with the back of one hand.

There had been a moment just before Dhoumil had shown up at the lab when his thoughts had turned again to Eric: at least now he'd have the chance to go to the courtroom. Then another day was swallowed up in trying to save Eban, and the thought didn't return until he phoned Hervé to tell him the tragic news. But the court hearing had already finished, Hervé informed him. A cut-and-dried case with little strong defence, they'd wrapped every- thing up late the day before. Eric was sentenced to five years. 'Yes – he was obviously upset that you didn't show, André. But this isn't the time to burden you with anything else.' In the end he'd let Eric down as well.

He'd let *everyone* down: Mpundu; Bernice; David and Marielle and Marc – their careers now in tatters; Joël and Veruschka; Charlotte, in therapy twice a week and barely clinging to sanity. And now Eric.

André blinked away the tears, pedalling hard and steady to try and pound away the pain. Trying to help everyone at the same time as trying to save the world – but in the end he'd spread himself too thin to help anyone. He'd failed on every front.

A bus whisked by. The same bus that Joël and Eban would catch to school each morning – and for a moment through his streaming tears he imagined them both at the back window of the bus waving at him, as they would every morning. But now it was just Joël on his own, and as young Joël realized that fact, his hand froze halfway up, all enthusiasm suddenly gone for a wave, then was quickly retracted. Joël stared out emptily from the back of the bus, a lonely and desolate figure.

Oh God. Joël. Mpundu . . . I'm sorry . . . so sorry. I tried . . . I tried.

The road ahead was a pastel blur through his tears, and he didn't realize that the bus ahead had stopped until a stream of blue washed up from the bottom of his vision.

He swerved to avoid it, and the scream of air brakes from the truck bearing down fast from behind filled his head, for a moment becoming his own screams of despair above Eban's flatline beep as they desperately tried the last jolt of electricity.

Then the truck hit him, a blow so solid that at first André thought the bike had been ploughed deep into him – except that as his body bounced off the side of the bus and finally came to a tumbled, tangled rest eight yards away, he could see his bike still skidding away from him, as if to tell him he wouldn't need it where he was going.

His pastel view suddenly had a grey tinge to it, as though someone had thrown a filter switch and it was instantly dark, and there was a sweet, acrid smell stinging his sinuses. He heard some car doors closing and excited voices, and as the first face loomed over him, he muttered, 'I'm sorry', just before the grey faded completely to black and dragged him under.

19

And Chisholm was right. There was nothing to stop her.

The official announcement was made two days after Chisholm's e-mail and a week later she took over Kalpenski's position when he left. There was some resentment at first, mostly from those with close allegiances to Kalpenski or from the Hebbard camp.

Most of it was along the lines of her being too young and inexperienced for the position and could be put down to standard professional jealousy. But some of it was more clandestine and worrying – particularly where Hebbard had been able to bend ears heavily – claiming that Kalpenski had probably been right, it had been a set-up all along.

None of it was overt or challenging, it was all silent whispers behind her back. The only outward signs were coolly appraising glances that might last a second too long when she was on the lab floor, one-word answers or mumbles of accord when she asked for something to be done, or eyes that would quickly avert when she looked up to meet those lingering glances.

She'd always held a slight distance, had never been fully part of the homogeneous work team – if there was such a thing. But now that gap was a veritable chasm. 'It's lonely at the top' suddenly had frightening resonance. But she wasn't so much worried about the sense of isolation, she could stomach that, in some ways she even relished it – she'd always considered herself as slightly aloof, better than anyone else, and this new distance merely confirmed that. She was concerned how it might affect her career: the blip in co-operation, the fact that they weren't gelling completely as a team, might harm future progress; and, if it was picked up on by the powers that be, they might fear that to be the case and seek her replacement.

She desperately needed some guidance, but that was the other problem about the isolation; with nobody on the lab floor she could confide in, her only remaining option was Chisholm. Besides, so far it had always been him angling and pushing for what he wanted. It was time she pushed back. She sent her e-mail to Cyberling Rivalry that evening after everyone had left.

Well, I'm here (presumably where you wanted me). I made it! But some guidance as to how you see everything panning out would also be appreciated. First and foremost, how to dampen this cold departmental blast of resentment? I'm concerned it might affect future project progress.

The answer returned two days later:

Be bold! We're going to have to be bold and adventurous in any case to have any chance of winning the Gifford Award. But my bet is that the detractors will raise the stakes, say that you're bound to fail. And in winning through you'll silence them in grand style and at the same time win stronger support from those who were part of that bolder strategy. Of course, as with everything, there's a risk, a downside: if you fail, you'll have proved the detractors right and the pressure could be even more insufferable . . .

Be bold. They had anything up to twenty ongoing projects at any one time, but only a handful enjoyed prime status and a concentrated body of researchers working on them – the rest were secondary projects with only one or two researchers allocated. Dani recalled one project in particular involving stem-cell research that had created initial excitement on the lab floor, but Kalpenski had proclaimed it as too bold and so it was instantly relegated to secondary status.

Genetic and stem-cell research had undoubtedly become the newest and most exciting research buzz words, but for that reason Kalpenski felt that every research institute worth its salt would be focused in those same areas and there wasn't much new that the

Spheros could bring to the table. Also, the core concept that early harvested stem cells might later prove more resilient to cancer was far from proven; lab tests to date in fact showed that they offered only negligible delay before becoming susceptible to an invasive cancer.

Dani wasn't sure how she might find any different, but she couldn't think of another area where 'be bold' might apply. And Chisholm was at least right about one thing: if they did find a breakthrough, it was the sort of sexy new area that would make the Gifford Award committee sit up and take notice.

She put Senadhira on alongside John Page, allocated two more lab assistants and gave at least thirty per cent of her own time to the project. But as the weeks went by with still no significant findings and the behind-back whispers resurged – *'Told you. Kalpenski was right all along about stem cells. She doesn't have the first idea what she's doing'* – the move felt more suicidal than bold. It was OK for Chisholm to push for bright and bold moves, it wasn't his neck on the line. If she failed, he'd merely wheel in the next mug brave enough to risk all to do his bidding.

Maybe that was all Chisholm wanted: the Gifford at any cost, no matter if he lost two or three protégés on the way. She was expendable.

She found herself in a cold panic again, sweating out each day on the lab floor; she could almost feel everyone's eyes on her, questioning, doubting. It was only a matter of time before the whispers, combined with the lack of progress, reached upstairs and they got rid of her.

Then, four months into the project, her nerves by then completely shot from each day coming to work fearing that it would be her last, they finally turned the corner. There had been recent research forays into 'marking' cells to produce antibody reactions and her team discovered that the responses with early stem cells were even more dramatic.

But other research establishments were fast exploring the same area, and it was Senadhira who first suggested using the CELL-ULA to put them ahead of the field. They could take stem cells and computer-age them to provide a far more comprehensive profile of their antibody responses at varying stages. Within only two months they'd already leapt ahead of the competition. The whispers stopped as quickly as they'd started. Suddenly, she was the golden girl and her team basked in her glory, while the rest of the lab floor either wished to touch the hem of her gown to share it or were silently resentful.

But once the success bandwagon had started, it merely gained momentum. Within the year, the Spheros had gained recognition as a world leader in stem-cell research and the phones started ringing for interviews. First, the local Philadelphia press and research journals, then, two days after the publication of their main paper on stem cells and the announcement by the Spheros board that it would be a key plank in their bid for a Gifford Award, a science journalist from the *Washington Post* phoned.

Nothing to stop her.

But she was reminded how close to the edge of the precipice she'd come. And if she'd fallen, Chisholm would have simply let go and brushed his hands. She probably wouldn't even have received an e-mail – which still came through periodically with comments about key events, such as the Gifford announcement – saying sorry or goodbye.

Now that her position was more secure, the time was ripe for her to push back, put Chisholm on the same tightrope she'd been on these past months. Make him aware that if she fell, he'd probably go too. Maybe then if he cared a bit more, or at least he knew he had as much to lose, she wouldn't feel so adrift.

Fourteen months without a bombing.

There'd been four bombings in the three months directly after the Lancaster attack – Sacramento, Salt Lake City, Madison and Raleigh – but they had only caused property damage, no injuries, and likewise no useful clues; then nothing.

For the first five or six months, Todd Wenner hardly gave it a thought. Like most field agents his case load was mountainous, so anything that went quiet or died and gave him more time to free up the remainder of his continually overflowing in-tray was usually welcomed.

He felt sure that any day there'd be another bombing and the game would be on again, next time hopefully with more tangible leads to work on. His exploration of genetic and religious links had thrown up far too many names and possibilities; he desperately needed something else to try and narrow them down.

But as the months rolled by and over a year had passed since the last bombing, the pattern looked increasingly out of step with anything Wenner had previously known and the questions started turning in his mind: Why a chain of bombings only weeks or months apart, then nothing? Had the bombers died, moved on? Or perhaps the bombings had a specific purpose which had since been satisfied or was no longer there?

'What do you think, Batz? What do you think has happened with them?' Having got as far as he could with bouncing it around in his own mind, one bright May morning while checking back through his old file notes for something he might have missed, he decided to get some outside input. Batz, Barry Tzerril, his assistant for the past year. For the first six months Wenner had ignored him, just one more fresh-faced Ivy Leaguer – except that Tzerril was a mix of Armenian, African-American and Latino – straight out of Quantico dumped on him. But still there was the generation gulf to cross, and it wasn't until Wenner discovered that, like him, Tzerril was an 'easy listening' aficionado, particularly Bacharach and the soft bossa-nova/jazz rhythms of Joachim and Gilberto, that he wasn't at all a fan of the heavy rock, grunge and rap that earmarked his generation – that Wenner decided that Batz might after all have half a brain and an opinion worth listening to.

'The animal gene bombings . . . right?' Batz looked up from his computer. It had been almost two months since their last mention, so it took him a few seconds to get his thoughts on track. 'Died, I would say is the most likely.'

'Do you really think so?' Wenner ran one hand over his smooth, shiny crown. 'I don't know. If it was just one man acting on his own, then maybe. But everything's been too well-planned and clean for that. It has to be a team of two or three working together. So that would only make sense if it was the main ringleader who died – otherwise the rest would just carry on.'

'Maybe their situation has changed. You know, ban the bomb and save the planet and save the animals all seems wild and exciting when you're at college. But when you take on a family and a mortgage, suddenly your values change.'

'Is that what happened with you?' Wenner looked at Batz keenly. He knew that Batz had recently got married, only a few months before joining the Atlanta field office.

'No, I'm not there yet.' Batz shrugged. 'I've still got a few wild ambitions and ideals left. You've probably got the main experience there.'

'True.' Wenner smiled drolly. 'When you get to the stage of spending as much time in mall car-parks as on stake-outs, sweating on how big a hole your wife's going to put in your charge card – you'll know you've finally made it, kid. There's no turning back and no more crazy ideals left. Or none that seem worth a shit any more.'

Batz mirrored the smile, though with a faint tease. 'Yeah, but are those mall car-park vigils as exciting as stake-outs?'

As Wenner fixed him with a cool stare, for a moment Batz was unsure whether he'd taken the familiarity and camaraderie a step too far. Maybe he had to wait another six months or a year before he could go that extra yard. But Wenner's smile quickly returned.

'Can be, can be. When she's heading back to the car with so many shopping bags that you can hardly see her beyond them – you get that same gut-wrenching sensation you get when a stake-out suddenly goes wrong.' Wenner shook his head, the smile turning to a tight grimace. 'No. This isn't a case of some college kids or young crazies who've suddenly grown up. Too well-planned and clean for that as well. I reckon these are professionals with a set aim.' Wenner leant back in his chair and eased out his breath. 'And maybe it's just that for the past fourteen months that aim has been answered.'

★

It was another five months before Dani finally raised the courage to re-contact the private investigator she'd used before, Ken Meikle, and instructed him to dig deeper into Julius Chisholm's background.

The main reason for the delay was that since the breakthrough with stem cells, she'd been on a strong roll, her confidence so high that at times she felt almost untouchable. Indestructible.

Nothing to stop her.

The nagging doubts and uncertainty that had made her feel so vulnerable and at Chisholm's mercy when she'd first taken over from Kalpenski seemed a distant dream. When she was on the lab floor – though the occasions she condescended to come down from her office to mix with the mere mortals were far fewer these days – she felt almost as if she were floating. The feeling of superiority – the reverent looks, the eager nods of agreement where before there was doubt or condescension – made her giddy.

She also felt as if it was a position that had long awaited her. Her rightful destiny. Meant to be. She'd finally arrived.

But as much as their progress with stem cells had been remarkable, she was reminded that it still probably wasn't enough to win the main Gifford Award. The two strongest tipped contenders were Dr Douglas Bateman of UCLA for his research into clusterin and cancer-cell survivability, and Professor Aaron Jacobsen at MIT for his work on angiogenesis. And if she couldn't win a Gifford for the Spheros, was she any use to Chisholm? Surely that had been the whole purpose in him getting her where she was.

She started to feel uncertain, vulnerable again, feel that at any second he might pull the rug from under her. And when her lawyer, Silas Merrison, phoned to tell her that they'd finally run out of rope with delays and adjournments with her mother and the court case was in just over two months' time, she hit her lowest ebb and phoned Ken Meikle to put him on Chisholm's back once again.

This time though there was very little file work, except for filling in a few gaps on his last report. Most of it was watching and following a few days and nights a week, and a profile was gradually built up of the various people that Chisholm met with and were dully snapped through Meikle's telephoto lens.

Most of them were nothing out of place, the usual round of present and past business associates, friends, golfing partners and neighbours. The new love in Chisholm's life, a pretty, eight-years younger redhead, was apparently an assistant financial administrator at St Charles's Hospital in Baltimore. So, pretty much the same work as him, but a couple of rungs down. Perhaps that's how he liked his women, Dani thought ruefully: just under him in more ways than one.

But one of Chisholm's past business associates had a decidedly shady background involving three counts of share-dealing fraud, though only one conviction had stuck. And Chisholm met with a man suddenly late one night whom Meikle had yet to identify. Nothing particularly alarming so far that she could hold over Chisholm's head.

Then out of the blue, two days before the court case with her mother, Meikle suddenly phoned her office in a panic.

'I think he saw me last night . . .'

'Look . . . I thought I told you *never* to phone me here.' She looked around nervously. She was in her large private office, not an open lab floor like before, but still she was worried that the phones might be monitored. It would be the ultimate irony if Chisholm heard the conversation.

'I . . . I'm sorry. It's just that I was planning to continue surveillance again tonight, and I wanted to get your feedback first.'

'OK, well. Don't go out again tonight, it's not a good idea. And maybe not for a few nights more. Phone me at home tonight and we'll decide the next move then.'

She got the rest of the details ten minutes after walking in the door. Chisholm had turned round to reverse out of a tight parking space and Meikle felt that Chisholm's gaze had lingered in his direction for a couple of seconds. Meikle wasn't sure if he'd been seen or not. She decided not to take the risk and told Meikle to lay off surveillance until he heard from her again. It was the last thing she wanted to think about now, at least until she had the court case behind her.

But however much she tried to push her darker concerns away, they tormented her increasingly over the next thirty-six hours and her legs were like jelly as she went up the courtroom steps. She must have been mad putting Meikle on Chisholm's back. She'd seen the way he'd so meticulously planned everything to date, what made her think for a minute she'd ever outsmart him, get the jump on him? He no doubt knew all about this court battle with her mother and had meanwhile been biding his time. If it went the wrong way, that's when he'd get someone in to replace her. Save the Spheros any possible embarrassment. Especially now that she'd been stupid enough to get someone to tail him and he'd found out.

Silas Merrison, misreading her concern, assured, 'Don't worry. We're in good shape. It's going to be OK.'

Her nerves only abated slightly, then took a strong grip again when she had to go in the witness box. She didn't put on a good performance. Thankfully, though, her mother, perhaps because of her age and frailty, did equally poorly. But her brother's testimony on their mother's behalf was strong – damn him, always confident even in the face of the most crushing adversity – and swung the balance once more against her. She felt certain she was going to lose.

In the lunch recess on the last day of the trial, her hand was shaking so badly that she could hardly bring her coffee cup to her lips. She must have been crazy to think that she could get away with robbing her mother like this. She was going to lose the case, then her job. She was going to lose everything.

At the time it had only partly been the money, the main thing had been hitting out at her brother – just another of the many man-battles in her life, her way of convincing herself that she was as good if not better than them. Her only grievance against her mother was that she'd nearly always favoured her brother over her. This way she hit back at both of them. Also, it had been so easy robbing her ex-husband of his property that it was hard to resist doing the same again. And now came the payback, the punishment for her sins.

Merrison reached out and gently clasped her hand, the first and only physical contact in all of their almost two-year association.

'I can see that you're worried. But I have to say again: Don't. You might feel that things appear overall to have run in their favour, but don't forget the onus is on them to prove their case beyond reasonable doubt. I don't believe they've quite managed to achieve that. For our part, all we had to do all along was create sufficient doubt – and in that regard I think we *have* succeeded. Also, don't forget there's the thorny trust law issues we raised, which the judge would have to answer in order to rule against you.' Merrison patted her hand once more before pulling his hand back. 'Quite honestly, I think that's one minefield he'd be keen to avoid.'

But she could tell from Merrison's eyes that he was only half convinced by his own arguments. She felt far from assured.

20

André knew that he was dead when he saw that one of the last in the line of tombstones had his name on it.

After the voices on the road, the only other voices he remembered echoed around him in a corridor. A bright light was shining straight into his eyes, then suddenly it shifted and the same panel lights flashed strobes at regular intervals as he was wheeled rapidly down the corridor, the voices suddenly more urgent, barking instructions at each other.

Then the light obliterated everything else and the voices faded, and as he felt himself sinking into the light's brightness, felt its warmth washing all around his body, he wondered whether this was one of those near-death experiences. Except that he wasn't able to look back to see his body, he just kept sailing deeper into the light, and emerging the other side of it he could see that it was a white mist hanging over the tombstones spread below him.

They seemed never-ending, stretching into the far reaches of the city, and when the last of the mist finally cleared and he saw his own tombstone next to Eban's, he knew then that it wasn't near-death, it was death. He wasn't coming back.

He felt salt tears sting his eyes and run cool down his cheeks, but his sorrow wasn't for himself, it was for Eban and the thousands and millions more that now he wouldn't be able to save.

The lines of tombstones had plagued his dreams ever since he was a young child, their spread becoming wider each time; it seemed fittingly ironic that now they should be the last thing he'd see.

He remembered the first time he'd seen them and they'd become etched in his mind. He was only eight years old and it was one of the family's first visits to Paris from their then home town of Amboise. He was excited. But then as the miles rolled by he became tired and eventually fell asleep. He woke up to see the sides of a cantilevered bridge flashing by. *The Seine!* He bolted upright.

Though as he looked out and saw tombstones spread on each side, he was confused. It seemed odd, out of place – a bridge stretching over a graveyard – and for a moment he thought he was still asleep and dreaming or his eyes were playing tricks on him.

He asked his father where was the Seine, had they crossed it already? And his father, Philip, explained that they were heading to the north of the city first, to Sacré Coeur. Then later they'd cut back across the Seine and see the Eiffel Tower.

But the image had imprinted itself strongly. His first view of Paris: a bridge over tombstones spreading into the distance.

And with each traumatic event of his life since – his father's death, then his uncle's – the spread of tombstones would confront him again in the dead of night, always more than the last time, and he'd see their names added to the last row.

When he had been deciding what career path to take, the dreams – combined with an inexplicable draw towards medicine and the fact that he'd lost two of those closest and dearest to him far before their time – he'd seen as a signal that that was what he was meant to do. Try and save them. Cut back the lines of tombstones stretching into the distance.

But he'd been wrong. In the end he hadn't been able to save Eban, or do anything for the countless millions of Ebans who were going to die from AIDS over the coming years. He hadn't even been able to save himself from an early death.

Dani was sure that the heavy exhalation, almost whoop of relief that she let out when Silas Merrison called her to tell her that the judgment had gone in her favour, could be heard beyond her office walls.

A deferred judgment, she'd had to wait ten days for it to arrive in writing at Merrison's office and know its outcome. She'd been particularly tense meanwhile, such a tightly strung bag of nerves that she'd stayed away from the lab floor as much as possible. And at home she'd paced like a caged lion, turning over each and every possibility in her mind, and had been impossible with Allison the weekend she'd stayed over, shouting at her for the smallest thing.

Now it felt as if a heavy, smothering weight had been lifted from her shoulders.

'I said that we'd done enough.' Merrison's tone aimed for reassurance, but his smugness in triumph shone through. 'Also, I'm convinced the thorny trust law issue we threw at him clinched it. He didn't mention it at all in his judgment, completely side-stepped the issue. It took us two weeks to research that alone. A first-level district judge, he'd have had to do the same, and we discovered through one of his clerks that he headed off for an eight-day golf junket in Florida only five days after the case. He dictated the judgment just before he left. You can breathe easy again. You're home and dry.'

'Thanks. You did a marvellous job.' The first time since they'd met that she'd praised him.

Nothing to stop her.

She was floating on air again. Their stem-cell research continued apace and another four news reports appeared about her team before the year was out, one with an interview from her. Though it wasn't until the *Newsweek* article appeared describing her as a '21st-century Madame Curie' that it struck her that she'd finally arrived. She received a congratulatory e-mail the next day through Cyberling Rivalry.

I told you. I told you all along that you were the right one. The image helps: Young, vivacious, smart, female. You're ideal for media exposure, a welcome breath of fresh air amongst a sea of crusty academics. But you're also good at what you do. Very good.

For a moment – *young, vivacious* – she wondered whether Chisholm was flirting with her. But then she remembered long-legged, redheaded Anne Irving from St Charles. She used the opportunity though to draw out Chisholm on the main area that still worried her.

Thanks. I'm concerned though that despite the media hoopla, we still might not have done enough to win over the Gifford committee. Bateman and Jacobsen still appear to be in the front running there.

The answer came back the next day.

Don't worry. You just continue with what you're doing. I'll take care of them.

I'll take care of them. She read the same phrase a few times over. It had a slightly ominous, threatening ring to it, or was she just trying to fathom what on earth he meant? Whatever, it unsettled her, reminded her that she'd probably done the wrong thing putting Meikle on to him. Had he seen Meikle that night?

She didn't put Meikle on the case again after the trial. She lacked the stomach for it and, besides, they'd probably already gained all that they were likely to get. Especially if Chisholm *had* eyeballed Meikle that night. The only question mark remaining concerned the stranger that Chisholm had met with late one night. Meikle said that he'd get in touch again when he knew his identity.

She patted the cover of the *Newsweek* on her desk and leant back in her leather swivel chair. So, now it was official: the general view, but most importantly Chisholm's, was that she'd finally made it. He was going to 'take care' of the rest.

A year and a half since she'd taken over from Kalpenski. Viewed like that, it seemed no time at all. But with everything that had happened in-between – the first anxious months, the court case, the turnaround with stem cells and the various newspaper reports marking progress – it seemed a lifetime.

But right up there on the glee scale alongside her triumphs had been when Russ Hebbard left. He'd invested so much in putting her down and trying to undermine her that her rise to glory had made him look an absolute fool. By the stage of the third newspaper profile, he complained to colleagues that he felt decidedly nauseous and handed in his notice.

He was replaced by a virologist who originally hailed from Baltimore, but had spent the last three years working at one of France's leading research institutes, the ISG. His name was David Copell and she immediately liked him, a welcome relief from stuffed-shirt, stuffed-waistband, stuffy-opinionated Hebbard. His arrival particularly stuck in her mind because only days afterwards she recalled hearing some tragic news about his previous section head in Paris, André Lemoine.

21

Death was a strange journey.

The light was suddenly there again at the end of a tunnel and he was travelling towards it. And as he burst through from the darkness, the light was so powerful that he could feel the raw heat of its brightness wash right through him, touch every nerve end and cell. It felt good, welcoming, as if he was floating in a warm bath of light.

But there was a voice nagging inside his head, trying to pull him away from it.

'You can't leave us, André. Please don't leave us.'

It was Charlotte's voice, pitiful and broken. But it wasn't until he heard Joël's voice, 'Please, *Papa . . . please,*' that he felt something tug inside him.

The line of tombstones was spread once more before him, and as he came to Eban's he knew that he couldn't leave Joël. Charlotte would never be able to cope and Joël would find it insufferable trying to face life without him.

He pushed away from the light and started struggling his way back. But the journey back along the dark tunnel was far more difficult than it had been sailing through. André wasn't sure whether he could make it.

Ken Meikle's call came through within half an hour of Dani arriving home from work for the weekend.

'Sorry it took so long – but I had to jump a few hoops to track down that mystery face Chisholm met with the other night: Grover Kiernan, thirty-six. Works at a metal components factory out at Allentown. But the most interesting thing is that he's got a couple of convictions.'

Meikle left a pregnant pause and Dani dutifully filled it. 'What for?' She leant across with the handset so that she could look out the window towards the front drive. Her ex was due any minute to drop off Allison for the weekend. She was anxious to have the call wrapped by then.

'Grand theft auto when he was nineteen. But the biggy was a conviction six years ago for having pipe-bomb material at his house. He was purported to belong to some right-wing militia group, the Virginia Eagle-eyes, but they were never able to link him to any of their bombings – so he went down just for carrying the material. Got two years and served eighteen months.'

'That *is* interesting.' *Auto-theft? Pipe-bombs?* Far removed from Chisholm's usual high-flying business, golf and Martini crowd. But she was just as far from fathoming how it might tie in.

'The only thing is, I don't have his current address. It seems he moves around a lot, and the address listed with his employer is an old one. But I did manage to speak to one of his old neighbours, and he reckons his housemate –'

'*Sorry . . .*' Through the window, Dani saw her ex's four-wheel drive pull into the driveway. 'I've got to go now. Can I phone you later to get filled in on the rest?'

'Well, that's about it. This neighbour's housemate will hopefully know more – apparently he's actually spoken to Kiernan a few times. I'm seeing him Sunday night, so I can phone you straight after and let you know how it goes.'

As soon as the car door opened, Allison perched her school bag on her shoulder and hustled her way towards the house. Father stayed by the car and looked on expectantly for the front door to open. The closest he ever came to the house; ten paces, pistols at dawn.

'Fine. Great. I'll hear from you then.' Dani sprinted from the phone as the door bell rang and gave Allison a breathless hug as she walked in. 'Mmmm. So good to see you, hon.'

Always the two faces. To Allison, she was nothing but sweetness and light and Dani didn't want that ever to change. Which was why she'd always asked Silas Merrison to call on week-nights with any news on her mother's case, so if she had to let rip cursing for the old crow to die, Allison wouldn't see her other side.

'So good.' She gave Allison's back one last reassuring pat as she broke free from the hug. From Meikle's latest titbit about Chisholm, it looked like she wasn't the only one with a dark side.

André was in hospital for almost three months and when he was due to come out he was informed that he'd need a permanent carer for yet another three to four months. He contacted Bernice, only partly out of pity and their shared loss with Eban; by far the strongest factors were her overall competence and the fact that she was a familiar, friendly face.

He'd suffered a ruptured spleen, a surface skull fracture, three broken ribs, two fractures in one leg, one in the other, and a fractured right forearm and wrist; only his left arm escaped unscathed. As the doctors and nurses were keen to remind him during his first period of consciousness, he was lucky to be alive.

'Am I?' he'd responded caustically one day when he felt particularly low. It was difficult for him to feel good about his situation. Being conscious and the long hours in the hospital bed gave him far too long to dwell on losing Eban and the mess of his life. Every career hope and ambition he'd held sacred had been shattered along with his bones, and there was little doubt in André's mind which was the more painful. His bones would heal, the other André felt rankling deeper with each passing day.

Bernice was just the right person to shake him out of it with a quick rebuke or an easy smile, or, when his despondency was at its lowest and difficult to shift, reminding him that he'd done his absolute best, that it was in fact going that extra distance with Eban that had cost him his career. 'Given the same situation, would you do the same again?' He'd meekly nod or give a subdued 'Yes,' and she'd tell him to stop blaming himself. 'Stop feeling sorry for yourself.'

But at other times, inadvertently, her conversation would touch on Eban, something he'd said or done that had struck her as poignant or had made her smile, and in those moments the cloud of his death would hang over both of them.

She was also good at handling the calls. The first two months out of hospital there weren't too many: the usual well-wishers and condolences, among them Marielle, Marc and David Copell, who had called twice since his new posting in Philadelphia. But the most unexpected call was from Pierre Boisnard, whom he hadn't heard from for almost ten years, though he'd left messages of consolation when Boisnard got ousted from the Cochin hospital research unit for taking his radical treatment methods a step too far. They'd been at medical school together at the Sorbonne, but Boisnard had increasingly become attracted to the less conventional fringes of medicine, particularly those involving natural or genetic solutions.

What was it? Return condolence, reciprocal support, or for Boisnard to say that he knew how André felt: they were now both in the same boat, two radicals ousted by the conventionalists for their beliefs? But from the persistence of Boisnard's calls, two while he was in the hospital and three since, the messages getting longer and more involved each time, it appeared as if Boisnard had something specific in mind about them possibly working together.

It hardly mattered. André never returned Boisnard's calls to find out more, or indeed anyone else's calls. When Bernice answered, he'd wave an arm at her and shake his head and she'd say that he'd call later – but he never did.

The only other human contact he had apart from Bernice were from Charlotte's weekly visits with Joël and Veruschka, a continuation of their regular hospital visits. That had been the only positive thing to come out of the whole mess; the fact that, surprisingly, Charlotte was coping with the dilemma. Someone other than her being the focus of crisis was obviously perplexing, unfamiliar ground for her at first, but perhaps that was just what was needed, centre stage shifted a step away. She either had no time to dwell on her own dramas or felt that for the children's sake they couldn't both be in crisis at the same time.

With the aid of crutches André gained some mobility, and Bernice's care visits reduced to five then three days a week. When she wasn't there, he'd just let the calls mount up on his answerphone – the messages increasingly gaining an edge of concern and punctuated by heavy pauses in the hope that he'd pick up halfway through.

'André. David again. Bernice said that you're a lot better now . . . is that right?' Heavy pause. 'If you're there, pick up. I've got something that will put a smile on your face.' Longer pause, then finally a sigh. 'OK, maybe catch you later or you can call me back when you get this.'

'André. Pierre Boisnard. I'm sorry to call so – but I think this could be a real opportunity for you. Attitudes have changed a lot in the last few years to more natural-based therapies and particularly to genetics, and I think your past work with monkeys could fit in perfectly.' Pause, audible swallow. 'I know how you feel about cancer research because of your family's history with your father and your uncle. But maybe this could be a way of repaying their memory and putting the ghosts to rest once and for all. It would be a shame too for all your past work to go to waste and, as I say, it would tie in so well with what I'm doing here. Please . . . call me sometime, André.'

Boisnard was getting desperate. André wasn't sure whether to be flattered or insulted. The only offer on the table was from fringe medicine. No doubt word had already got round and the mainstream were steering clear of him.

Still André didn't answer, curling up deeper on the sofa with each call, and Bernice continued to take his messages, her excuses becoming more inventive each time. And when finally she lost her temper and snapped at him that he couldn't hide away from the world outside for ever, he lied that he'd returned some of the calls. But when the same people called back again and Bernice answered, she knew that he hadn't.

Then when finally all of his casts were removed and Bernice's care visits reduced to just one day a week, it was just him and the answerphone. Bernice's annoyance was evident as she slammed the door on him at the end of that stint. 'You've got half the world to call back – so I'll leave you to it.'

He tried to summon up the courage to answer the phone, but with each call he found his isolation from the world outside settling in deeper, until finally he started cradling his head with his hands over his ears so that he didn't have to hear the messages.

With his heavy regimen of medication, there were times in the hospital and his first days at home that his dreams were so vivid and his waking moments so murky and confused, he could hardly tell one from the other. That the lines of tombstones and the mist hanging over the city were the reality and he was in fact dead, and the bright hospital lights searing his eyes and the echoing voices were the dream.

But now with the increasingly insistent voices sailing over his answerphone, there remained no doubt: he was alive. The only decision remaining was whether to start living again.

Wenner waved urgently towards Batz halfway through the telephone call. Batz went over to Wenner's desk.

'We got another,' Wenner mumbled with one hand over the mouthpiece. 'Dayton, Ohio.' He brought his attention quickly back to what was being said, nodding at intervals as he made brief notes. 'Yeah . . . Yeah. So they were disturbed, but the bomb still went off? Right. Right. How long between the two do you reckon? Six, eight minutes. OK.' Wenner looked up briefly again at Batz as he wrote it down. 'That's cutting it fine.'

'I know. But that's the timing the guard claimed when we interviewed him.' Dayton PD's Lieutenant Collier mirrored Wenner's doubt. 'Maybe because he started just then to do his rounds, they had to hold back a while before making a break for it. In the end they felt they just couldn't wait any longer, so ran the gauntlet. And that's when he saw them – through a lobby window just as he was making his way back across. He knew that he couldn't catch them, they were already halfway back towards the outer fence. So he set the dog loose.'

That theory made sense, Wenner reflected, because the time-gap estimates on almost half of them were the same: twelve to twenty minutes. On the rest, the explosives had been tied into a computer time-clock the night before. It looked like there were two types of job: rush and pre-planned. Or perhaps it had more to do with whether they could successfully time-clock link to a computer without it being discovered. But every other MO detail tied in: a pound of C4, lab that specialized in genetics and experimented with animals, two-man team – though before they'd only been guessing at that – and all executed within the same time range, 10 p.m. to 4 a.m., with the aim of heavy property damage without loss of life. The one fatality so far looked unintentional, and this one too had come dangerously close.

'How far away was the guard when the bomb went off?'

'Just making his way back across the lobby to the elevators. But if he'd started up, he'd have had it. The blast took out everything on the fifth floor, including the elevator cables. Just lucky that he spent some time checking around the fence where the dog caught the second guy.'

'Please tell me we got some blood – even if we've got to scrape it from the dog's teeth.'

Collier chuckled. 'No, but we've got a patch of fibres from the guy's trousers and there's a stain on it that could be blood. We won't know until later when we run it through PCR.'

'How long?'

'Six, seven hours, latest by tomorrow, we should know. Also there were a couple of stains on the chain link fence where they went over that could be blood droplets. But you know what it's like once it's dried – it could just as easily be treacle from someone's Danish or engine oil. We won't know that either until it's back from analysis.'

Unconsciously, Wenner's fingers were tapping a rapid tattoo on his notepad. Fourteen months with nothing and suddenly there was movement again. Three more bombings in the past month – Chicago, Albany and St Paul – but with the guard disturbing the bombers, this looked like the first where they might get some useful clues. He stopped tapping and glanced at his watch as he made his decision.

'We're heading out to you.' Hopefully by the time they arrived, Collier would know more. 'I'll phone you again from the airport as soon as I know what time we're landing.'

*

'Everything going all right?'

'Yes, yes,' André agreed hastily. 'Everything's going fine.'

Pierre Boisnard asked the same question infrequently now, at most once a week. But during André's first few months at ORI-gene, he'd asked it practically every day, as if hardly believing that André had changed his mind and joined him.

Boisnard took one last survey of the notes spread across André's workbench, nodded perfunctorily with a smile, then continued on through the lab floor.

André watched Boisnard's departing back for a moment before bringing his attention back to his work. Boisnard had put on a fair few pounds since their medical student days together. Almost as broad and rotund as he was tall, he had heavy-lidded, dark-circled eyes which gave him a hangdog look when he was sad or serious. But his smile lifted his whole countenance, and Boisnard smiled often. The dark, hangdog moments were few and predominantly Boisnard was known for his joviality. The Mr Pickwick of medical research. André had always liked Boisnard.

The only worrying thing about Boisnard was his reputation for plumbing the fringes of medical research, consistently going against the mainstream. In that respect his reputation and his appearance were at odds; he looked like the most regular, smiling, two baguettes and pastis man you could think of. Anything for an easy life, the last one you'd expect to rock the boat.

But André knew the dangerous, risk-taking side of Boisnard that lurked close beneath the surface. And what worried him most now was that there'd be two of them pulling in the same direction, without the calming voice of David Copell or his kind to hold them in check should they get close to overstepping the mark.

Possibly, Boisnard's investors – two leading drug companies, one French, one Swiss, and a Paris INSERM – would provide that calming hand. Possibly too, the harsh lessons learnt from his and Boisnard's past débâcles would provide a much needed sobering influence: neither of them could afford to screw up again.

That had been practically his first statement upon meeting up with Boisnard to go through the final arrangements of their working together. When he'd first returned Boisnard's many calls he'd said 'No', he wanted a break from research for a while. He'd either do nothing or take a tame job teaching at a medical faculty; possibly even back at the Sorbonne, where they'd both gained their diplomas. And André kept saying no each time Boisnard periodically phoned him over the next seventeen months with some fresh titbit in the hope of enticing him.

Then the sudden turnaround and his first stipulation laid down that they should be each other's calming influence. 'When one of us starts skirting too close to the edge, the other should rein him in. With two radicals like us, there'll be almost an expectancy for us to be extreme and overstep the mark. They'll be watching out for it.'

Boisnard nodded in sombre agreement. 'And as you rightly point out – neither of us can afford that. Not a second time.'

André's only other stipulation was that Marc and Marielle could join him. Marielle had been biding her time at some nondescript INSERM since leaving the ISG, and while Marc had worked for a while at the Curie Institute, he'd been unemployed for three months at the time that André contacted him about Boisnard's offer. Both were keen to work with him again, and Boisnard readily agreed. André got the impression that Boisnard, still slightly shell-shocked by the turnaround, would have agreed to practically anything within reason.

ORI-gene was a far cry from the ISG. Just two floors of a six-storey building in the Porte d'Orléans district above an assortment of ground-floor shops, with the animal and mice houses in a set of lock-up garages in a rear courtyard previously used by a car body shop. Boisnard had replaced each set of garage doors with frosted glass panels for extra light for the animals, the only change to their overall ramshackle appearance.

But their work was no less exciting than at the ISG. There was a distinct buzz in the air and Boisnard's trademark smile was in place most days. And André said fine, fine, each time Boisnard enquired, because he didn't want to admit that he was just treading water. He'd concentrated most of his work between genetic profiling and further primate research, but none of it was heading anywhere fast. Eight months now that he'd been with Boisnard and still he was no further ahead. And while André didn't want to admit that and possibly dampen the general lab mood, by far the hardest part was facing that himself because of what it meant personally.

Because what André hadn't told Boisnard, or indeed anyone – Marielle, Marc, and particularly his own family – was the reason for his sudden change of heart about going back into research. And thankfully Boisnard hadn't asked – André would have hated to kick off their revived relationship with a lie.

Though what worried André most of all now was that having laid down the law with Boisnard about each of them tempering the other's extremes, his own secret agenda would provide that final weight to tip the scales. Because André knew, if it came to a choice between the two, the decision he'd have to make.

Dani became anxious with Allison around when she remembered that Meikle said he'd probably phone again on Sunday night with news. If it was anything juicy and the conversation started to get involved, she'd have to make sure Allison was out of earshot.

Normally she got Allison to do her school homework Sunday morning so that they had the rest of the day free together. But when it came to this Sunday, Dani decided they'd head out for the day and they didn't get back in until after six. As soon as they walked in the door, she packed Allison off to her bedroom to get her school work done. Then almost two hours later when she'd finished, Dani said that as a treat she could play video games on the TV in her room – something Dani normally dissuaded so that they could spend quality time together.

Allison spent most of Sunday night in her room. But Meikle didn't call.

At first, Dani wasn't overly concerned. Maybe he simply got back too late to call. But when Monday and Tuesday passed and there was still no call, the first seeds of worry began to set in. Wednesday lunchtime she headed out of the lab and called his office from a booth two blocks away. It went into an answerphone. She left a message.

'I thought you said you'd call me Sunday night with news. Can you phone me at home tonight – even if you don't have any news yet. Either way, call. Thanks.'

That night at home, her hands periodically tapping impatiently on her thighs or chair arms and still no call from Meikle, her mounting worries came close to panic before taking a step back again. He must have gone out of town for the week. Otherwise for sure he'd have called back.

That resolution kept her on an even keel over the next day at work, her mind drifted only briefly to it again before she cut herself short. If by the following Monday Meikle still hadn't called, then start worrying again. Until then, push it from your mind.

And that's where it stayed for much of Friday, until mid-afternoon when she went for a quick coffee and cake in the canteen. At first, she found herself staring blankly, unseeing, at the back of the newspaper someone was reading two tables ahead. Yet at some point the name Meikle must have impinged on her subconscious, because suddenly she found herself staring intently. But before she'd strung together half a paragraph in the article concerned, the person reading the newspaper turned the page.

The blood pounded white-hot through her head. She'd managed only to pick out something about a car and a Delaware River black spot – but maybe she was misreading it. Or maybe it was about someone else and the name Meikle had superimposed simply because it was on her mind.

She found herself silently screaming for the reader to turn back again or put the paper down and leave. But he seemed to stay on the same page for an interminably long time, then started to make small circles with a pen near the top of the page and notes on a side pad.

She managed to catch the date though, the 19th, Tuesday's paper. The papers were kept for a week along with some magazines on a side table before being thrown out. The young man reading it, a virology lab assistant, appeared to be looking through apartments to rent in Tuesday's special property section. That's why the keen interest in a three-day-old paper.

She ordered another coffee. Otherwise it might start to look too obvious, her watching like a vulture over an empty coffee cup for him to finish the newspaper. Her hand shook on the cup as she raised it and sipped. She tried as much as possible not to stare at the newspaper, for the most part looked down or to one side, as if wrapped up in her own thoughts.

He scanned the newspaper for another three minutes before finally putting it down. She breathed a silent sigh of relief. But then he perused the notes he'd made for another full minute before eventually getting up.

By then her nerves were at screaming pitch, though again not to be too obvious she waited until he was clear of the canteen before going across and picking up the paper.

Her hands visibly trembled as she hastily flipped back a page, turned the paper over and started picking out relevant portions:

Ken Meikle, 46, of Washborough Drive . . . Pettys Island section of River Avenue, police estimated between 1. a.m. and 1.40 a.m. Monday morning . . . Car found in the river shallows with only its roof visible . . . lost control and hit a tree, though it appears drowning was the cause of death . . . From initial police reports, alcohol and reckless driving are also thought to have been factors . . .

She literally jumped out of her skin when a hand was suddenly laid on her shoulder.

'Everything OK?'

'Yes, yes. Fine.' She swallowed hard, regaining composure. Professor Bradson, one of the Spheros board members. They'd started to take more notice of her – or, more accurately, knew that she even existed – now that she was rising up the ranks. She flipped quickly over to the property page. 'Just looking for a place for a young nephew,' she said, the first lie to come to mind.

She saw Bradson look briefly at the circles on the page. 'Amazing that you've got the time for anything else, what with your work with stem cells. Sterling stuff.'

'Thanks.' She felt her cheeks burning with the panic of the

moment and hoped that Bradson read it as a blush due to his compliment.

'Keep up the good work.' One last reassuring shoulder pat and smile and he headed off.

Her legs were unsteady as she made her way out. The voices in the corridor and the general hubbub as she crossed the main lab floor were nothing more than a dull buzz in her head. She'd have hardly registered whether somebody was calling her name or screaming fire, *fire*! Across one more corridor, punching the elevator button with a shaking hand – thankfully nobody was inside as she made her way up – only seven steps the other side, and finally she was inside the sanctuary of her own office.

With a long, laboured exhalation she shut the door behind her and made her way quickly to the swivel chair before her legs gave way completely.

Perhaps she was making more of it than she should be. Perhaps it was just a coincidence that it had happened the same night Meikle was meant to be meeting up with Kiernan's old neighbour, and it was purely, as the police appeared to believe, an accident.

But then she remembered one of her first meetings with Meikle at a downtown bar when she'd asked if he wanted a beer and he'd said no thanks, he was teetotal. 'Just a coffee, that'll be fine.'

Though maybe he was one of those teetotallers who stayed that way because if they touched a drop, they'd down a whole bottle. Her hands clenched in tight balls as her conflicting thoughts fought for control.

Who was she kidding? Even if he was the type to fall off the wagon, why do it just then? The timing was totally wrong.

Maybe she should tip off the police and let them work it out. An anonymous call urging them to dig deeper that wouldn't link back to her. Then she remembered the message she'd left on Meikle's answerphone, and no doubt he had other notes in his office with her name and number. Once they started digging, she'd get caught in the middle of it.

She slumped her head down between her arms on her desktop.

Was this the price of her ambition? Her payback for all those she'd trampled on and back-stabbed to get where she was?

But was Chisholm just rapping her knuckles for even daring to delve into his background, or had he turned it into yet one more test? He already knew what she was from what she'd done to Hebbard and Kalpenski, not to mention her mother – but he needed one more Dante test to know for sure that her soul was his: 'Turn a blind eye to this, to murder, and I know then that you're mine for keeps. No turning back.' Her head stayed slumped in the same position as the tears started gently rolling.

22

The light through the window was searingly bright. André squinted away from it towards other objects in the room as he opened his eyes: one more bed the other side of a bedside table with lamp and an upright wooden chair were all he could see in the small, spartan room: no dressing table, wardrobe or other furniture.

But through a half-open door was a mountain of clutter: book-shelves piled to the brim with books and files, more files and papers strewn on lab benches between test-tube racks, pipettes and agarose trays.

The shriek of a couple of excitable monkeys burst out, followed by the answering crawk of a macaw. They were from close by, clearly discernible as from within the house, distinct from the steady background hum of cicadas, bird-call and occasional monkey shrieks of the surrounding jungle.

André sat up and rubbed his eyes. At some point in the night, at the height of his delirium, he was back in the tree with the monkeys shrieking all around and the snake's head confronting him. And as he fell into the misty air of a Paris dawn with the tombstones below him, he was convinced that he *had* died, and everything in-between – the hospital lights, the answerphone messages, joining Boisnard – had been little more than a dream. He should have guessed from Boisnard's ramshackle garages housing the animals, the monkeys screeching each time a train rumbled past. Or, earlier, when he'd seen the blood tests that had finally made up his mind to join Boisnard. Only in a mad dream would they take place. Real life couldn't be so crazy or cruel. But then, almost as part of the dream, he was sipping a glass of Coke as he looked out across the taxiways at Belém airport, a few distant lightning flashes showing in the fading light of an Amazon dusk, and suddenly he was confused: he could never recall having visited Belém airport before he died.

Dr Fernand's smiling face appeared at the door, no doubt in response to him stirring and making the bedsprings creak.

'How are you feeling now?'

'I'm not sure.' André tried to swallow against an impossibly dry throat. 'Alive at least.'

'Those stomach bugs can knock you out totally for a while.' Dr Fernand came in close and felt André's forehead for fever. Dr Fernand's dark hair had greyed in distinct sweeps each side, but his features were still quite youthful. André put his age at no more than late thirties. 'But thankfully it's usually only for a short while. What did you have to eat on your way here?'

André thought for a moment. 'A two-course meal with chicken in wine on the main flight. Then just a ham sandwich on the connecting flight to Belém.'

'That should have been OK.' Dr Fernand shrugged. 'They're usually pre-packed in Salvador. And to drink?'

'A Coke at Belém airport.'

'With ice?'

André thought again for a second. 'Yes, yes. There was ice in it.'

'That would be it.' Dr Fernand nodded knowingly. 'They haven't got round yet to making the ice from bottled water. Usually it's just from the tap. Take my advice – always take your soft drinks straight from the bottle. At least while you're here in the Amazon.'

A woman looked in through the door: attractive, early thirties, but looking slightly severe with her dark hair pulled back in a tight bun, no doubt because of the heat. 'So, you're with us again.' She smiled broadly. He'd heard her voice from the next room just before he'd passed out. Dr Fernand's assistant or partner.

Dr Fernand brought his attention back to André. 'You'll probably still feel weak for most of this morning. But after lunch, hopefully, you'll start to feel better. Do you want to look at the macacartos and the samples then?'

As drained and light-headed as André felt, with the reminder of why he'd flown halfway across the world to look at the samples, he suddenly felt driven again. His curiosity wouldn't let him wait that long.

'No, no. I'm OK. Just a quick coffee to wake up, and I'll look at them straightaway.'

Even though André had already seen various lab results e-mailed from Dr Fernand in Manáus, there was something fresh and exciting about viewing them first hand: the fifty or more Petri-dish tests with malignant cells, the mice tumours significantly reduced or completely cleared within only days, the agarose wash-throughs to quantify its strength and effectiveness.

Of the two main areas of André's research – genetic profiling and primate resistance to cancer – the latter had increasingly gained predominance. It was widely known that monkeys didn't get cancer. If given a mature cancer in a lab experiment to see how they responded, the cancer developed as with humans and they were unable to resist it. But in the same way that monkeys carried SIV without it becoming AIDS, there was something in their immune systems that prevented cells from becoming cancerous in the first place.

The main theories propounded were dietary and lifestyle: monkeys had a completely fresh, natural, enzyme-rich diet, whereas humans daily bombarded their systems with a variety of chemicals and additives. But still André burnt the midnight oil for the first few months with Boisnard looking for a cellular or genetic explanation, before finally giving up the ghost. Countless years had been spent looking at P53-linked solutions – the human gene that malfunctioned to cause the onset of cancer – to little avail. It wasn't a path that was likely to be resolved quickly, and with the blood tests that he now took weekly came the constant reminder that time wasn't on his side.

It was then that André spread the net to encompass immune capabilities in other animals: squalamine, shark cartilage, that was supposed to have anti-cancer properties, and magainin, a powerful anti-bacterial found in the skins of frogs and crocodiles. But while Petri-dish tests were encouraging, the results with primates and humans were disappointing.

He spread the net again, contacting researchers worldwide who worked with animals to let him know about any unusual immunities discovered. He received a couple of false starts and a couple more whose initial promise quickly evaporated before Dr Fernand came through about the macacarto. André began to worry that this too, like squalamine, magainin and the others, would fizzle out once it went beyond the Petri-dish and mice-test stages.

'What results, if any, with primates and humans?' he asked Dr Fernand.

'We don't have a humanized version yet, that will take time. Maybe that's one area where you can help us.' Dr Fernand shrugged. 'We simply don't have the test base here in Manáus for human trials – we'd have to make arrangements with hospitals in Salvador or even Rio or São Paulo.' His assistant, Mariah, nodded her accord. Dr Fernand moved closer to the window that looked out on a wraparound veranda lined with cages: marmosets, simian and spider monkeys, and a few at the end with macacartos. 'But as you can see, with monkeys we have a good supply of trial candidates, and the results there have been positive.'

'How positive?'

Mariah stepped forward. 'Well, we've only tested so far with medium developed skin-grafed tumours. But of eleven simian monkeys treated in three dose stages, tumour regression in eight was a hundred per cent. With the other three, tumour regression with the same dosage ranged between eighty-two and eighty-seven per cent, and up to five doses were needed to completely clear them.'

'So in the end, a hundred per cent across the board.' André exhaled with a soft whistle. He'd never before known such strong results with primates, even just with skin tumours. But André told himself not to get too excited. Too early. The high response rate with monkeys might be because the treatment was primate originated. With the crossover to humans and tested on more complex internal and blood cancers, the results might not be the same.

Back in Paris, André worked around the clock to perfect a humanized version from the macacarto samples. The normal time scale for such an exercise was anything from six months to a year. André was aiming to finish within four months. After the most recent blood tests, he was aware that the clock ticking against him had been wound up a few notches. But there were no outward signs of the illness. Yet. Nobody, particularly within the family, was any the wiser.

A month after returning from Brazil, he'd felt weighed down by the burden of work ahead to get the macacarto samples into shape, worried that he might not make it in time. He needed to hedge his bets. The solution might still be found genetically, and for that he'd need to know as much as possible about the family's genetic history. That's why he'd also kept a foot in the camp of genetic profiling; he knew that it would provide the ideal cover.

The first time he'd asked Hervé about taking a blood sample, he'd simply used the excuse of wanting to build up a genetic family profile for his overall data. But Hervé had side-stepped the request, saying that it would be difficult for him given the church's views on genetics. 'Man meddling where he shouldn't and all of that. I'm sorry, André, but I don't think I can help on this one.'

André pushed it from his thoughts. But only weeks later, when he hit a bad patch and his macacarto sampling was going slower than hoped, it was back preoccupying him again. He desperately needed some other family blood samples to narrow the genetic options. Five months more until Eric's release, *if* he got parole. He'd have to give Hervé another push. But he'd probably need bigger guns to shift his position, have to be far more persuasive.

He rang Hervé, saying that his reasons for wanting the blood sample were more personal and close to home than he'd made out initially. 'You know that our father's and Uncle Bernard's death has always weighed heavily with me, and no doubt you and Eric too. It was in fact why I initially shied away from cancer research. Well, we're coming up to age now, Hervé. Next year you'll be the same age our father was when he died, fifty-four, and Uncle Bernard didn't live that much longer: fifty-six. And me and Eric aren't far behind you. If there's a propensity towards cancer being passed down through the generations in our family, then it doesn't give us a whole lot of years left. But detected early, there's a lot that can be done these days with many types of cancer. That's why you should let me take a sample of your blood, Hervé.'

Hervé let out a slow, tired breath. 'You know how I feel after our last conversation; or, more to the point, how the church feels. I don't think I could get involved in meddling with genetics and, as a priest, keep a clear conscience. Whatever might be at stake.'

'Even if it might mean the difference between life and death?'

'Yes, I . . . I suppose so.'

André picked up the hesitance in Hervé's voice. He snorted disdainfully. 'What, God's will and all that? I thought you were the last to be po-faced about religion, especially when it had real impact on people's lives. I remember a few years ago that mother of two in Nemours who died of cancer in her early thirties, and when one of your parishioners commented, 'God's will', you said you'd turned on him angrily and told him that your brother was a medical researcher. That you'd hope God was lending a helping hand to me and my kind, rather than leading young mothers to their graves. Or did you just invent all of that to make me feel good? Because now when I actually want a helping hand, you're turning your back.'

'Perhaps I have more concern for the welfare of others than I do for myself.' Hervé's tone was flat, cool. 'And you know that I feel very differently about conventional medicine than about genetics. Genetics is still a very thorny issue for the church.'

'I know.' André cradled his head in one hand, surveying the lab for inspiration: Marc and Marielle heads-down over workbenches, Boisnard chuckling at the far end with his PA, Cathérine, the background rumble of the RER train punctuated by the occasional monkey shriek. It still felt at times like a mad dream.

For a second he was tempted to tell Hervé the truth. But he couldn't, just couldn't. It would destroy the family, in particular Charlotte. She'd only just entered therapy after her attempted suicide when he'd had his accident. And while at first she'd rallied well and it had in a strange way been character-strengthening, with the length of his illness and his hiding away from the world outside, the first egg-shell cracks in her psyche had begun to show again. Something like this would destroy her.

But he sensed that if he didn't pull something out of the hat quickly, Hervé wasn't going to budge, and he probably never would get another chance later to broach the same subject. The door would be for ever closed on getting a sample from Hervé.

'It's Joël,' he blurted out. 'He has anaemia.' Not true, but at least it was a step closer to the truth and hopefully personal and poignant enough to get Hervé to shift his stance.

'Ohhh!' Hervé exhaled as if he'd received a stomach blow. 'Why didn't you say something earlier?'

'I . . . I didn't want to cause alarm, upset the family. And now that you know – please keep it under your hat, Hervé. Particularly from Charlotte. You know how she is.'

'I know. I know. But how would my blood sample help Joël?'

'It . . . it would help me narrow down the best treatment options, knowing the full family history.' That was the problem with lying. As things became more involved, the lies too became more convoluted. André was careful not to mention genetics, otherwise Hervé would revert to his prior stance. The door would close again.

'I . . . I don't know.' Hervé didn't sound wholly convinced. 'Obviously with it involving Joël's health, I'd like to help if I can. Can I phone you tomorrow and let you know?'

'Yes . . . yes, of course.' André was slightly taken aback. With mentioning Joël, he'd expected nothing less than an immediate about-turn and unreserved offer of help, not more delay and hedging, even if it was only for a day. And it made him wonder for the first time if something else apart from purely religious grounds concerned Hervé about giving blood. 'Call me then.'

'I think we should cool it for a while.'

'You know that that goes against what we originally agreed, and it's important that the MIT lab hit is done quickly.' Chisholm glanced around anxiously from the phone booth on Race Street. Early evening, but the few passers-by were paying him little attention. He was more anxious about himself or his car getting picked out as targets to rob by the area's many floating vagrants and down-and-outs; it wasn't a part of town where he was likely to bump into anyone he knew.

'I know that. But it's too close after the Meikle hit and the problems in Ohio. There's too much heat right now.'

'But the whole thing with Meikle went smoothly, right?'

'Right.'

'From the papers, that's been seen as nothing more than an accident, so won't connect. So it's only the problem with Laine-Metz in Ohio that we need to worry about. You say you think he left some blood there. How much blood?'

'A few spots around the fence. But enough for a lift.'

'Is his blood on data bases anywhere?'

'I reckon so. He spent a four stretch in Penn State a few years back. They take your blood as soon as you walk in – they say for AIDS and other tests. But as sure as the last President got his cock sucked, it goes into some grand database or other.'

Chisholm chuckled briefly. That was the only light side of doing business with Kiernan; at times he had a nice turn of phrase. Kiernan's other facets, in particular his South Virginia drawl and sly, disturbing smile on the couple of occasions they'd met, grated with Chisholm. 'What did he go in for?'

'Liquor-store hold up. Clean hand-over, nobody shot.'

'No bomb-making or bombing links?'

'No. Nothing on that score.'

'Hmm. I doubt that anything would match up just from that.' Chisholm had a sudden image of a giant central computer trying to randomly match millions of CAGT genetic imprints, but he doubted they'd yet reached that level of sophistication. Scientists were still years away from finishing even the main human genome project. No doubt they'd have to key in 'bomber' to be able to narrow things down to a workable list. 'So I don't believe we've got quite the worry on that front that you think. And, as I say, it's important that the MIT lab hit is made quickly.' Chisholm didn't feel inclined to share with Kiernan why it was so important, that with each passing day Aaron Jacobsen gained stronger ground towards a Gifford Award. Nor explain that the Ohio bomb was just a decoy, as were most of the bombings, to obscure the link to the Giffords. The less Kiernan knew, the better.

'There's a . . . aahh, another problem,' Kiernan stumbled. 'After the incident with the dog at the fence, Lee has lost his nerve, at least for a while. I don't think I could get him to move on anything again quickly.'

'Can you get someone else?'

'Yes, but it would take time.'

Chisholm asked how long and Kiernan answered three or four weeks, minimum.

Chisholm fell silent for a second, mulling over the problem. 'OK, let's set that as our maximum target – one month. You find someone else to make the hit on MIT or make sure Lee has found his nerve again within that time – or I find another tag team to replace both of you. And have a nice day, yer hear.' Chisholm hung up abruptly.

Hervé made the call within minutes of putting down the phone from André. 'He's asked me to provide him with a blood sample.'

'What did you say?'

'At first he said that it was for some general genetic research or other, and I said no on religious grounds. But then he said that it was to try and help Joël. That the boy has some kind of anaemia. And it's put me in a difficult position.'

'You can't give him a sample, Hervé. Because as soon as he has that, he'll know. He'll know the truth.'

'I realize.' Hervé sighed heavily. 'But it's just that now he's brought Joël into the picture, it's more difficult to side-step the issue.'

'Do you believe him about Joël? Do you think that the boy really is ill?'

Hervé paused for thought for only a second. 'No. No, I don't. I think it has something still to do with some genetic experiment. But he knows that if he says that, I'll say no to giving a blood sample – so he's brought up Joël to try and shift my position.'

'Then what are you worried about? You can say no with a clear conscience.'

Hervé paused again as he pulled together his final threads of thought. 'Because I think something else serious is troubling him. He wouldn't go to these lengths to lie, particularly by throwing young Joël in my face over just any old genetic experiment. I think it has to be something more personal. Something closer to home.'

'Like what? What could be wrong?'

Hervé explained how André, before finally mentioning Joël, had taken the conversation through an elaborate side-track involving their father's and uncle's early deaths from cancer. 'His general thinking seemed to be that if there was a predilection towards cancer in our family, myself, him and Eric could soon be candidates, because we're now close to the ages of our father and Uncle Bernard when they died. So we should have blood tests as a preventative measure. But I think it goes far deeper than that – and not just because I'm convinced André wouldn't push so hard for my blood sample for that reason – but also because, you know, people have this habit of skirting close to the truth so that they don't have to feel they're lying outright. And I think this was the closest André dared come to the truth.' Hervé took a heavy breath as he came to the crunch of what he'd been struggling to explain. 'I think André has cancer. And I think that, for whatever reason, he doesn't want to come right out and tell us.'

'No. . . . no. Surely not.'

Hearing the sharp, frail intake of breath from the other end, for similar reasons that André felt that nothing should be mentioned to Charlotte about Joël, Hervé wondered now whether he should have openly voiced his thoughts. But he didn't think it would help for him to be yet another trading half-truths and lies. His voice lowered a tone. 'Of course, I might be wrong – I hope I am. But it's the most obvious explanation for how he's acting. And if that is the case, I'm not sure I could forgive myself for refusing to give a blood sample.'

Soft, subdued timbre from the other end. 'I know how you feel,

Hervé. But if you're wrong, could you forgive yourself any less for letting him know the truth after all these years? You know how much it would destroy him.'

'I know . . . I know.' Hervé sighed heavily as he wrestled with the dilemma.

'Also, giving him your blood sample won't help him in the way that he hopes. It would only partially help.'

'The problem is, I can't even tell him that without giving the game away. But even that partial help would be better than sitting by and doing absolutely nothing.'

For a few seconds there was nothing but the faint hiss of the telephone line between them before she spoke again.

'Perhaps you should wait for André to say straight out what the problem is. Deal with it in the same way you do so much else daily at the church: absolve only those who tell the truth, confess. That way you'll know for sure whether you're reading it right, rather than possibly destroying André based on just a strong hunch. Beyond that, I don't really know what to say, Hervé. What you do in the end is really up to you. Between you and your own conscience.'

'As always. Some things never change.' Another heavy sigh. 'But you can see now, *Maman*, why I felt I had to share this with you.'

'Yes, of course.' Lillian Lemoine wondered whether she detected sarcasm a second ago in her eldest son's tone, but there was little point in pursuing it. He'd probably earned the right, and she'd said all she could to both sway and comfort him. 'Really, what you decide in the end I leave to you, Hervé. But phone me either way when you've spoken to André again. When you know more.'

Her legs felt unsteady as she shuffled away from the phone. But it was more a twinge of guilt rather than worry that suddenly made her feel frailer than normal. Hearing that her son might have cancer, and still her strongest concern was that he wouldn't learn the truth that she'd shielded him from throughout his life. And once again she'd left her eldest son, the priest, to play devil's advocate.

23

André put a finger through the cage towards the macacarto, in the same way as he used to with Anouk. It edged forward and gripped the finger hesitantly, only the second time he could remember it doing so – but perhaps that was because it was frightened by the thunderstorm rumbling in the background, needed some contact and reassurance.

André had gone out soon after the thunderstorm started – one of the few he recalled since returning from Brazil – and the monkeys started to become agitated and were shrieking. He was working late as usual, it was approaching ten o'clock when the storm struck. Marc and Marielle had stayed on with him for a while, but had finally left almost two hours ago.

'What is it? . . . *What is it?*' He playfully waggled his finger in the monkey's light grip, looking into its dark eyes, darting between André and the shapes and shadows behind him highlighted by the thunder flashes. He'd have thought they'd have been used to thunderstorms by now. They were a nightly occurrence in the Amazon, within an hour of dusk falling.

André recalled his last night with Dr Fernand, studying the macacartos in their cages on his veranda as the storm raged and water cascaded off his tin roof in almost a solid sheet. On that occasion they'd shrunk back in their cages away from his protruding finger, though he remembered then thinking how odd-looking they were.

No more than sixty centimetres tall, less than an arm's length, the upper part of its body was similar to a common spider monkey, except that its hair was even darker, jet black with no other colourings or relief markings, and was slicked down like an oily pelt. But its lower half was distinctly different, with far thicker, squat thighs, designed for longer-distance leaping and swimming, and its slick, pelt-like skin gradually became smoother and more reptilian. The skin of its calves resembled more that of a lizard than a monkey, with only sparse hair growth, and its feet were slightly webbed.

The reason for this, Dr Fernand had explained, was that the Beruri basin flooded for almost six months of the year. During that period, the macacarto spent as much time in the swamp waters as in the trees above. It was, in fact, known locally as the 'swamp monkey'.

André wondered if the macacarto really could be the key. There had been increased focus in recent years on reptiles having superior immune systems to humans: crocodiles, lizards and frogs suffering gaping wounds and even loss of limbs in fetid, bacteria-ridden swamp water that would infect and kill humans in only days – yet they survived and prospered.

And the 'missing link' theory that we'd originally crawled out of primeval swamps had been the stuff of evolutionary theorists since Darwin. Could the macacarto really be that link? The source of the cure for the scourge of modern man be found through eons-old immunity? Certainly the lab tests were impressive, like nothing he'd previously witnessed.

They'd tested on more complex pancreas, stomach and blood cancers with mice and the results were equally strong as Dr Fernand's initial skin-tumour tests. He'd reached an agreement with Dr Fernand that he would extend the scope of the tests and perfect a humanized version and run human trials, then – if those final tests were positive – they would make a joint announcement and claim at that stage. They also needed a name for the substance, and decided on macaitin, an amalgam of magainin and macacarto.

'Could you really be the answer? *Could you?*' André asked. The macacarto's eyes stared back blankly, its pupils so black that for a moment André felt as if he could see right through them to the dark, primeval swamps of its origins.

Outside, the thunderstorm had started to weaken and recede. Hervé had called earlier, as promised, but had asked for a couple more days to think things over; he had the monsignor visiting from the Fontainebleau parish, and said he didn't have time to focus on anything else. And again, André had the sense that something deeper was troubling Hervé about giving a blood sample. The storm clouds there were still building.

Don't worry. I'll take care of him.

After Meikle's death, Dani's panic that that was how Chisholm took care of things grew stronger each day. A plastic bag over the head and a quart of scotch poured down your gullet, then your car crashed into a tree and rolled into the river so that it looked like an accident.

Was that how she'd end up if she took a step out of place? Was it something along those lines he had planned for Jacobsen? No, too clumsy. But something else leapt from the recesses of her mind in that moment, a recent article she remembered reading about a genetics lab bombing somewhere in Ohio, supposedly by animal rights activists. Could that be another Gifford Awards contender on Chisholm's list alongside Jacobsen?

She was at home when the thought struck. As much as she found the lab claustrophobic since reading about Meikle, could hardly bear to be around other people and felt at times as if the walls and general hubbub of noise were pressing in so hard that at any second her head would burst – the hectic cycle of activity at least kept her from dwelling on the problem for too long. A long, slow exhalation as soon as she got home and unwound over a coffee or herbal tea or, more often of late, something stronger – then within minutes the demons would be back plaguing her again.

The newspaper had probably already been thrown out. She stuffed the old newspapers in polythene bags by the back kitchen door ready for recycling collection. The last had been only six days ago.

She dived amongst the bags and started frantically sifting through. By the time she found the article, in the third bag, she was squatting on the kitchen floor, breathless, surrounded by loose and half-torn newspaper pages in disarray. She let out a little whoop of triumph as she read it: no connection to the Giffords that she could see, and she couldn't remember the lab's name, Laine-Metz, from anything else she'd read regarding the award's contenders.

But to make sure she checked the Net on her home computer, keying in 'Gifford', 'Laine-Metz', 'genetics' and 'bombing'. Nothing came up connecting Laine-Metz with the Gifford Awards, but when she noticed the Giffords mentioned in one of the other animal-rights linked bombings, she decided to spend a while longer checking through. She found one other lab bombed also apparently contending for a Gifford, but then four more with no connection. She sat back in her chair and massaged her aching temples. Two out of seven? Not exactly a strong statistic. The two were probably nothing more than a coincidence. Bomb a dozen genetics labs and it was odds-on that two or three of them would also be contenders for the Giffords.

But the clincher for Dani was the Laine-Metz bombing. Only a week after Chisholm's last e-mail, when their concerns about Jacobsen were at a peak, would he suddenly order the bombing of some obscure lab in Ohio? It made no sense. No, there couldn't be a connection between Chisholm and the bombings.

And as the next few weeks passed with still nothing aimed at Jacobsen, she became even more convinced of that – which also then made her start reconsidering her thoughts about Meikle. Maybe that had just been an accident after all. Another coincidence she'd built up in her mind and made far too much of. Maybe that wasn't how Chisholm operated.

'The problem I have with this, André, is the terrible feeling that there's something you haven't told me. Something you're holding back.'

When Hervé had finally phoned, he'd opened with all guns blazing, caught André by surprise.

'No, no. Not at all. I told you everything.'

'I mean, this problem with Joël. Is it serious? Is it life-threatening?'

'No, no. Of course not.' André quickly back-tracked. 'But it could cause him some problems later, if not treated.'

'So it's something preferable and desirable in the long run, rather than life or death immediately.' Hervé took a measured breath. 'And I'd have thought that yours and Charlotte's blood samples would have had far more relevance to any problem with Joël.'

'Yes, yes . . . of course. I've already taken those and have the data from them.' André could feel himself getting pushed tighter into a corner.

'And even with my limited knowledge, I know that links between families invariably have a genetic connection. Blood groups are usually stand-alone. I mean, look at Eric's blood – right out there on a limb.'

'No, I told you: it's to do with Joël's blood. But as you so rightly say, your knowledge is limited. It would take me far too long to explain.'

Hervé rode the insult as if André hadn't spoken; as if he was reading almost from a prepared script.

'And so the conclusion I came to, what was making me feel so uncomfortable about the whole thing – was that it still had something to do with genetics, but you didn't want to admit that because you already knew how I felt about it.'

André felt Hervé's noose tighten around his neck. No option left but to beat a hasty retreat. 'That's fine, *fine*. If you don't want to give a sample, I understand. I'll find a way of working round it.'

Hervé let out a tired exhalation. 'There's no need to be like that, André. I mean, if you told me the truth, if you told me what the problem really is – I'd feel differently.'

'The truth . . . *the truth*?' André mirrored Hervé's tired sigh. 'For God's sake, I already told you the truth. It's Joël and this anaemia.' But André was sure that the tremor told in his voice.

'All that talk about our father and Uncle Bernard.' Again Hervé was in roll-over mode. 'And the more I thought about it after we spoke last time, the more I was sure. There's something troubling you about your own health, isn't there, André? Some form of cancer like our father or Bernard – but you don't want to come straight out and say anything. Not least because of Charlotte, but probably our mother as well. She's not getting any younger.'

'What me? *Cancer*?' André let out a weak, incredulous guffaw.

But again he wondered whether the tremor in his voice gave the game away. As much as he'd tried not to, had he unconsciously held up an obvious route map?

'Are you telling me that you don't have cancer?'

'No.' Flat, more confident tone this time. 'No, I don't.'

Hervé left a long, uncomfortable silence, as if waiting for André to fill it; a tactic perhaps he used in the confessional.

'I don't know,' Hervé said at length on the back of another heavy sigh. He still had problems coming to terms with André's account.

'Don't worry about it,' André commented, almost flippantly. All André could think of was getting off the line. Hervé had come far too close to the truth for comfort; a second longer and André might be tempted to blurt it out, unburden it all. 'As I said, if you don't feel comfortable about giving a blood sample, I understand. I'll find another way around it. It's no big deal.'

But it was a big deal. For almost an hour after signing off from Hervé, he again found himself frantically scanning the mass of CAGT lines on his computer screen, the genetic codes of his family, looking for something he might have missed before. It was no use. He desperately needed another family genetic pattern to narrow down the options. Five months until Eric's release, even with parole. He couldn't wait that long.

He wondered if he might be able to get a sample from La Santé prison, or maybe track down the sample they'd found at the crime scene and used to prosecute Eric. What was that detective's name: Dounnet. . . . Donnet? Either way, he'd have to think of a good story.

CCGGGTTTTTAA ... TTTAAGGC ... GGGTTTCCC ... CCCAAAAG ... TTTTGGGCCAA ... GGGGAAAATTCC ... CCCAAAAAAG ... AAACCGGTT ... GCCCTTAAA ...

Todd Wenner leant back in his chair and rubbed his eyes. After almost three hours on screen looking at mug shots and accompanying DNA codes, it was all becoming a blur. Over 17,000 in total, split into sub-groups with anything from 50 to 140 names: animal-rights activists and bombers, religious activists and bombers, abortion clinic activists and bombers, general bombers. Every possible candidate for the genetic lab bombings, in turn divided regionally: Mid-West, Pacific Northwest, North-eastern seaboard.

Two hundred and thirty-two sub-groups to search through, Wenner had split the list between Batz and two others: fifty-eight each. Eleven more to go for Wenner. Batz had started on his an hour early and had finished over forty minutes ago, though still seemed to be checking something on screen. The other two, as Wenner looked up, still appeared to be working on theirs.

The program showed three or four lines of string code if there was a close match, indicating it could be a relative, albeit distant. Wenner had had two such close matches, Batz and one of the helpers three each, the other only one. Nine distant cousins, not exactly the result Wenner had initially hoped for. More often than not, close matches simply meant that they originated from the same approximate gene pool: Inbreed, Wyoming, 110 years ago.

Batz's voice broke his thoughts. He looked up to see Batz with one hand raised by his computer. He went across.

'Something interesting here.' Batz brought his attention back to his computer screen and pointed as Wenner leant over his shoulder. 'You remember that a couple of the bombed labs came up as Gifford Award contenders? Well, I checked with the current bombing – nothing there. But when I dug deeper on the other bombings, I noticed another two mentioned in connection with the Giffords. One of them a recent announcement, so perhaps that's why it hadn't leapt out as a factor before.'

'How many of the total, as a percentage?'

'Four out of eleven. 36.4 percent.'

'Mmm. I don't know.' Wenner mulled it over. 'Genetics, right at the cutting edge, and a big prize like that. Might not be that unusual a percentage. Could find that's more or less the proportion of genetics labs that'd be bidding for the Gifford Awards.'

'Seems high to me. And before the Laine-Metz bombing it was riding at forty per cent.' Batz looked up at Wenner with a slightly arched eyebrow. 'If the next one's also a Gifford contender, it's right back up there.'

'Yeah, true.' Wenner sighed and nodded his concession. He couldn't help but feel deflated. After the initial elation of the breakthrough with the blood sample, now they were only a handful of searches away from striking out. Back to square one, back to plodding and fishing in the dark. This was probably just more of the same, but he forced a brighter tone as he patted Batz's shoulder. 'Only one way to find out, I suppose. Check the percentages.'

'How will I do that?'

'Well, I'm sure there'll be some association representing research establishments involved in genetics. And no doubt the Gifford Awards committee will have a list of those who've filed or are intending to file. Compare the two and you're there.' Wenner gave Batz one last shoulder-pat and smiled as he headed back to his desk. 'Good hunting.'

'One of the mice has died.'

André was greeted with the news from Marc as soon as he walked into the lab. He followed Marc towards his section of workbench and immediately vented his surprise. 'But that's one of the seven with which we initially had the strongest results.'

'I know. It's baffling. But we won't know more until I've done a biopsy and run some tests. I discovered it only fifteen minutes ago when I first came in.'

André hovered for a moment more, but there was little he could do to help. For the first couple of hours it was a one-man job, until they reached the stage of studying cell samples. 'Let me know how it goes.'

André headed for his office and shut the door briskly behind him, exhaling heavily as he sat at his desk. He closed his eyes and cradled his forehead in one hand.

Oh God. Was this to be the way of things every time? Hope dangled enticingly within his grasp, then cruelly yanked away at the last moment.

That's how it was for cancer researchers everywhere – why after four decades and countless billions spent, they were still far from winning the battle – why should it be any different for him?

Except that for him the battle was personal, as it had been with Eban. Maybe that's where he made his fundamental, fatal error: he shouldn't get involved with personal battles. They coloured his judgement and made the downside far too harsh and painful to accept. Though in this case, unlike Eban, he hadn't chosen the battle – it had chosen him. He'd had little other option.

André reached for the phone and dialled the number he'd written on his pad for La Santé prison. He'd called Inspector Donnet's office the day before and spoken to a Xavier Bayerge, one of his assistants. Bayerge said that he'd pass on the message, but the main file was with the examining magistrate's office.

'Any decision on release of information would probably rest more with them than with Inspector Donnet, but I'll get one or the other of them to call you.'

No return call as yet, but already the option was looking weak. Weeks of bureaucratic paperwork between the police and the examining magistrate before he could get approval – *if* he was ever able to get it.

Option two: It took a moment for him to get routed through to the clinic at La Santé and finally get passed to a doctor who appeared to know what he was talking about.

'Eric Lemoine. Admitted about three years ago,' Dr Rouilly repeated as he applied some thought to it. 'Before my time, I'm afraid. But he's your brother, you say. And what was this test with genetics that you wanted to run?'

André's mouth was suddenly dry. If he got this wrong, his last option could be gone. 'It's to do with my son. He has a rare form of anaemia, and the best treatment option appears to be through genetic therapy.' André kept the story the same, in case there was some liaison between Eric and Hervé. 'But we need to know which side of the family this strain has predominantly come from. I have some clues of course from my own and my wife's blood samples – but I need my brother's also to be totally sure.'

'I see.'

André wasn't sure whether Dr Rouilly really did see and understand, or whether he'd lost him halfway through. But either way, while he had him swaying he should push a bit more.

'It really could be of vital help. Also, time is very much of the essence.' André's tone lowered, becoming grave. 'That's why I'm calling you now, rather than simply waiting on my brother's release.'

'Well, I . . . I don't really see any problem from my side.' Rouilly hastily cleared his throat as he gathered his thoughts. 'But there may be some other reason, legal or otherwise, why it can't be released of which I'm not aware. So I'd have to check on that: the final word would come from the prison governor.'

'Right.' Some hope. A lifeline, however slim.

But minutes later, staring at the genetic family tree behind Marielle's section of workbench, even if Dr Rouilly came through with the sample, he wondered whether he'd be able to put together the final pieces of the genetic puzzle in the way he hoped. He'd still have by far the larger part of the mountain to climb.

He could feel the sweat still cool on his skin from the nervous anxiety of his conversation with Dr Rouilly. And what if that too ended up as another dead-end?

Marielle's wall chart was a genealogical tree showing all of the women of the Perrigard family – sisters, aunts, mothers, daughters, grand-daughters – going all the way back to 1926, and the respective age each of them had developed breast cancer: 36, 41, 39, 48, 34. The chart had been prepared because of the high predominance of breast cancer within the family, to try and genetically track and identify when the next generation of Perrigard women might be likely to succumb. But it was a chart of hope more than simply a genealogical testament to the early doom befalling generations of Perrigard women.

Boisnard had notched up strong progress with the development of plant peptides to treat breast cancer, which Marielle had shown interest in and was now assisting with: one of her aunts was in her third year of remission from breast cancer. If the cancer was detected early, the success rates were high, ninety-two per cent and climbing. With the aid of the chart, it looked likely that they'd be able to save the next generation of Perrigard women from early deaths.

It could just have easily been the Lemoine family tree, André reflected ruefully: father dead at fifty-four, uncle at fifty-six, and now . . . André shook his head. The chart of little hope. The other side of the coin.

Although ironically his father, the master mathematician and statistician, would certainly have been fascinated by the statistics of it all. So much of André's own life had been modelled on his father: quiet and intense, imaginative and determined in problem solving, and the only one of the family to go into academia. Surely that couldn't all have just been trying to appease his father's memory, make good after his death. Regardless, now he was following in his father's footsteps in yet another way, and that could only be down to genes.

André remembered his introduction to genetics at the Sorbonne, and the prime example used of Huntington's disease. If a person had the genetic string CAG repeated more than thirty-nine times in a row, they would develop Huntington's disease between the ages of forty-seven and fifty-one; if forty CAG strings in a row, deduct four years; if forty-one, another four . . . to the point where someone with fifty CAG strings in a row would develop the disease in their early twenties.

It wasn't a possible or a 'might be', it was a statistical certainty that his father, again, would have appreciated. If they'd been able then to identify the genetic string which led to the Lemoine family's propensity towards cancer at a certain age, his father would at least have been able to appreciate why it struck him when it did. While not making it any easier, his father had always held the view that the first stage of solving any problem was understanding it – so he'd at least have viewed it as the first bright light of hope. Yet even now, after half a century of cancer research, that 'hope' was still slightly out of reach, which is why he desperately needed Eric's blood sample or a breakthrough with the macacartos, or both. And his father would have turned in his grave if he knew what his flawed genes had now wrought on the current generation of Lemoines. If he knew that . . .

'I'm sure it will turn out OK.' Marielle's voice broke his chain of thought. 'The tests with all the others were so positive.'

'Yes, uh . . . let's hope so.' It took André a second to realize she was talking about the dead mouse. 'Marc's running preliminary tests now, so hopefully later we'll know more.'

'I'm sure it's just a one-off.' She reached out and lightly touched his arm, her eyes searching his for a moment. 'So don't worry so. Its death might even be totally unconnected with the macacarto tests.'

'Yes, I . . . I suppose there's that possibility too.' Suddenly he felt good again, more positive, and he wondered how she had that knack with him. As before, he felt instantly wrapped up in the warmth and perfume of her, the tingle of her touch, and perhaps it was that as much as her words. Yet for a second he felt tempted to just sink into those soft brown eyes and her arms and sob his heart out, unburden it all. Tell her everything he'd been unable to share with Charlotte or anyone else. But as he paused to reflect on what that said about him, whether it was just mid-life crisis or because of the mess of his life with Charlotte and now all his other nightmare problems, he felt suddenly vulnerable and uncomfortable. 'I . . . I'm sorry. I'd better get on and see how Marc is doing with those mouse tests.'

24

'Are you OK?'

'Yes, I . . . I suppose I will be.' Dani hesitantly lowered her coffee cup from her lips with an unsteady hand. It was Senadhira who'd enquired. Apart from her e-mail relationship with Chisholm, Senadhira was the only one she felt remotely close to at the Spheros. Perhaps because he'd backed her up over the incident with Kalpenski, perhaps because he often smiled and was jovial with few edges. Though more recently she'd begun to feel that in part it was a front, that like so many others at the Spheros, Senadhira had strong ambitions too – just that they were wrapped in a more friendly, amenable package. He wasn't so overtly grasping. He could see that she was fast rising up the rungs, and so it made sense to stay friendly and keep one hand on her coat-tail. And right now, more than ever, she desperately needed a friend. But she couldn't possibly tell Senadhira what was really troubling her, she couldn't tell anyone. In that way she was truly alone. And yet he could see that she was terribly troubled by something – her hands shaking, her eyes darting nervously and her face flushed – she wouldn't get away with saying she was OK or passing it off as anything trivial.

'I just found out about a close friend's husband dying. Heart attack. He was only forty-six.' The same age Ken Meikle had been. She'd got in the habit of scanning the papers every day to see if anything else had developed on the Meikle case, if it might have suddenly changed from 'accident' status to something more ominous. And while frantically flipping through only a step away from the news-stand on her way to work that morning, she'd seen the story about a bombing at Boston's MIT on page eleven.

Don't worry, I'll take care of Jacobsen.

'I'm sorry to hear that,' Senadhira said, casting his eyes down slightly.

'That's OK. I'm more concerned about how my friend will cope. They've got three young kids.' She'd stood in the same position for almost a full minute while the city spun around her. Her cheeks burnt red hot, though it felt as if an icicle had been plunged through her stomach. Her legs turned to jelly; she was unsure she'd even make it back the few yards to her car.

'I hope it turns out for her.' Senadhira forced an uneasy smile and lightly touched Dani's shoulder. 'I should have those final MGU stromal cell results later today for first thing tomorrow. I'm just running them through the CELL-ULA now.'

'Great. Look forward to it.' Dani took another hesitant sip of coffee. In return for the support and the easy smiles, she'd given Senadhira lead responsibility for a number of the more exciting projects.

As Senadhira headed off, she suddenly became more conscious of the noise and clatter of the rest room around her. She was aware of a few others looking over at her curiously, but Senadhira had been the only one who felt brave or close enough to approach her. She'd cut herself so far off from the rest of them – the 'ice-queen in her lofty perch' with one foot already in the boardroom – was how she'd heard they viewed her.

Perhaps she should have headed straight to her office after reading about the bombing, but as soon as she got in she was usually bombarded by the telephone and messages from her PA. And suddenly her throat had felt impossibly dry and she needed a strong coffee to cut through the woolliness in her head. So she'd braved the rest room.

The daunting question now was whether she could brave the bed she'd made for herself with Chisholm and what the following months held.

In the end, Dani did what she'd done so many times before: she rationalized, told herself that perhaps everything – Jacobsen and the MIT bombing and Meikle's 'accident' – wasn't as bad as she'd worked up in her mind.

She'd done the same when she'd stolen her mother's home. She knew from the outset that what she was doing was wrong, terribly wrong, but then bit by bit came the layers of rationalization: her mother was old and she was better off in any case in a care-home where people could look after her, rather than rattling around in a large house. Besides, the money from the house would have only gone to her and her brother, and her brother would probably have blown it on some wild business scheme or other – which is what had led to the problem with their mother's house in the first place. Worse still, her mother might have left more of it, or indeed *all* of it, to him. Her mother had always favoured her brother, it had been a constant thorn in her side that she'd had to take second place, regardless of her endeavours or achievements. Her brother always seemed to be able to crown her, at least in her mother's eyes.

Then, when her mother had been left with little choice other than to launch a court case against her, that added more fuel to the flames. *How dare she!* Dani cried outrage to other family members caught in the middle about what a terrible thing it was for a mother to take her own daughter to court. And whenever it suited her, she feigned illness – an impending nervous breakdown from the pressure of it all and beta-blockers to ward off supposed heart problems – to gain additional sympathy and divert attention from her aged mother's very real ailments as a result of the terrible ordeal.

By the time she'd worked the whole scenario through enough times in her mind, her mother was a mean and twisted old crab who'd never appreciated her and tried at every turn to put her down, and now came the final hammer-blow of the court case to prove that very point. Her mother deserved everything she got. By that stage, not an ounce of sympathy remained for her mother, nor guilt for her own actions. She'd completely convinced herself that *she* was the injured party. She'd totally reversed the tables.

Though perhaps it had been easier second time around, because she'd done exactly the same with her husband's family's property she'd snatched in their divorce. They were rich, they could take the loss. Besides, look at all the nights he'd left her alone to cope with

Allison while he was off having long Martini business dinners with this one and that. By the time she'd finished mentally re-working her version of their marriage, her husband was a two-horned monster of untold proportions; to support her case, she even went so far as to claim that on a few occasions he'd beaten and raped her, rather than being just the somewhat neglectful – more eye on the money to support his family than the quality time spent with them – husband that had epitomized so many of his generation.

It had been much the same too with Hebbard and Kalpenski. It served Hebbard right for being so grabbing and ambitious. And while she felt sorrier for Kalpenski because she'd since heard that he'd been unable to get another placement anywhere – she told herself that he didn't have too many years left in research anyway. It hadn't been too hard on him. She might even have done him a favour, saved him from high blood pressure and a heart attack by forcing him into early retirement.

She had to admit, the rationalizing became easier every time. Give her a while with any scenario and she'd be able to paint the grey clouds white and herself as a saint rather than sinner.

By the time she'd got to Chisholm, it almost seemed like second nature. She spent a few days agonizing over whether to confront or draw Chisholm out through their e-mail contact, before deciding against it. He'd either completely deny it or, at best, would be defensive. Either way, it would do little to further their relationship, could even seriously harm her future. If he saw her as problematical, he could do what she'd feared at the outset: make sure she was ousted and put his next bright protégé in place. She'd been through too much, invested too large a chunk of her life to throw it all away now. Especially when she was so close, on the brink of what she'd aimed for all along.

Glory. Looked up to and respected by everyone, the top of the medical research tree. Not least because it was the final finger to her mother and brother: she'd at last trumped his successes.

Having made the decision, the pieces fell into place easily: nobody had been injured or killed in the MIT bombing. In fact, the aim in all the bombings appeared to be only to cause property damage, create disruption; the sole fatality had been a worker called back in and so could be put down purely to the error of whoever was working for Chisholm, *if* indeed he was behind the bombings. As for Meikle, perhaps it was, as the police seemed to think, merely an accident. The timing of it could have been purely coincidental.

Then, as if rewarding her for her decision, a few days later the PR department contacted her about an interview with *Time* magazine – which, picking up on the earlier *Newsweek* Madame Curie comparison, heralded her as one of the brightest new stars in medical research and a strong contender for the prestigious Gifford Awards.

The next day there was an e-mail from Cyberling Rivalry:

> Congratulations! Looks like you might have crept just a nose ahead of Jacobsen. You might also want to look at this month's *Pacific Science Journal*.

She found the article Chisholm was no doubt referring to later that same day. Two leading West Coast researchers, one from Palo Alto and the other from Phoenix – and probably in some way connected to or in the pocket of Chisholm – stating that they felt Jacobsen's work with angiogenesis had been overrated. 'Mainly because it represents a somewhat defeatist stance. We can't get to the grass roots of a cure for cancer, so let's just shut off the rooms with the fire. Starve them of oxygen; or, in this case, blood supply.'

Dani couldn't help smiling to herself. Giving her grace and glory with one hand, cruelly yanking it away from Jacobsen with the other. Chisholm was a master player. She'd never known anyone quite like him. Though still she was confused as to whether that was something she should fear or admire. And maybe also it was a subtle object lesson that while he recognized the Machiavellian promise in her, she'd need to raise her game slightly to play in his league. Be prepared to be more ruthless.

★

The *Time* article was seen widely among the medical research community, and was referred to when André and David Copell next spoke on the phone.

'I see that someone at your place is doing well,' André remarked.

'Yeah. Genetics, oncology and molecular biology seem to grab all the limelight these days. Not quite so exciting here in virology, I'm afraid.'

'Why is that?'

'Well, I think it goes back to something we both commented on when the Giffords were first announced. AIDS funding and research was already fighting for equal billing with cancer, and the arrival of the Giffords shifted the spotlight even further away.' David paused as if to choose his words. 'It's not so bad for us in America or Europe, there's been some strong recent progress with combination drug therapies. But as you know, in Africa those sort of options are simply out of reach cost-wise. So it's no wonder they feel forgotten, neglected. And while in research we see little headway towards producing lower-cost drugs that could reach the masses, we're bound to feel frustrated.'

'Yes, I know.' André felt a genuine pang as David said it. His own pet soap box for much of the time they'd worked together, but had he also been guilty of the same after Eban's death? Turning his back at the same time on the bigger picture of what Eban's death stood for: AIDS in Africa and the millions of children who would die this year and next without treatment. But in his case there'd been a very real reason for the switch. One which, when they'd touched on the subject on one of his half a dozen phone conversations with David since joining Boisnard, he'd lied about as he had to everyone else, saying that it was partly Boisnard cajoling and pushing, partly his fascination with genetic trends in cancer and finally getting to grips with what had happened with his father and uncle. And for a moment, he wondered whether to tell David the truth. David was over there and if he swore him to secrecy, it was unlikely ever to get back to his family here. Also, he felt a very real need to ease some of the burden, share the problem with someone, especially after the recent setback with the macacarto samples. The pressure of keeping it to himself, carrying the weight of it all on his own, was becoming unbearable, stifling. At times it felt as if his head were boiling. But as David spoke again, the moment went.

'But hey, not to take anything away from her. She's done some great work, and she's got a good team with her. And some of the fancy equipment they've got up there – especially the CELL-ULA – we get to use too. If you ever need some progressive analysis done in a hurry – cellular or molecular flow cytometry, critical viral load points, likely plateau stages, whatever – it's a real boon.'

'Sounds great.' André was hardly listening. If he didn't say something now to David, he probably never would. 'David, there was something else about why I . . .' But at that moment, Marielle called out from across the room. She was waving and pointing to the phone in her hand.

'It's a Dr Rouilly. Something about him having got permission to release your brother's blood samples.'

'How many have you got it down to now?' Wenner asked as Batz put down the phone and looked up hopefully.

'Twenty-one, twenty-two. But when pushed a bit more, a few admitted that there were really only nine seriously in the running. "But don't quote me".' Batz held up a finger on each hand and twitched them. When he'd phoned the Gifford Awards committee, they'd informed him that they had 114 entries for nominations listed, but couldn't comment on who might or might not be regarded as leading contenders, otherwise it could be construed as undue favouritism. They suggested that some of the medical and science journalists might be willing to be more candid, and gave him some names and telephone numbers. Batz had spent the last two hours on the phone to them.

'At least it's a more workable list, even if we have to cover the whole twenty-two.'

'Yeah. But that's not the half of it.' Batz scanned hastily back through his scrawled notes. 'If we take it just as those nine front runners – four out of five of the Gifford Awards contenders so far bombed, including the recent hit on MIT, are amongst those nine. The other one is out there among a hundred or so also-rans.'

'See what you mean.' Wenner nodded thoughtfully. 'Put like that, it's hard to ignore statistics.' It was looking increasingly like targeted hits: one of the nine trying to knock out the competition, or one of the twenty-two trying to increase their chances by weakening the lead players. 'One thing we've got to keep in mind, though, is that the main Gifford contenders will have been in the news much more than any of the others. That alone might have made them prime targets. We must be careful not to be too one-track and possibly shut out the bigger picture.'

'I know.' Perversely, the note of caution told Batz that Wenner was far keener than he wanted to admit. Perhaps it came from two decades of seeing exciting breakthroughs evaporate to nothing.

'But, hey.' Wenner lifted with a bright smile from his momentary contemplation. 'Well worth a visit to rattle their cages. You got a list of names?'

It couldn't be . . . *It couldn't possibly be.*

André leant back from the microscope and rubbed his eyes, then scanned down again through the DNA chart and side-margin notes he'd made. But there remained no doubt. He'd checked it now twenty times over, and it wasn't suddenly, magically going to change through him looking at it one more time.

It was getting worse by the minute. André could feel everything piling in on top of him until he felt suffocated, the pressure unbearable. Boisnard had put his head through his office door the other day and announced that if the macaitin samples developed as dazzlingly as the early tests indicated, they should enter for a Gifford prize. He'd already spoken to his backers about it, and they were excited by the idea. 'Could be just the boost we need right now.'

André didn't even have the heart to tell Boisnard that one of the mice from the last tests had died. He'd delayed telling him in the hope that the death was unconnected with the macaitin tests, or at least was something minor they could rectify in future tests. And then, suddenly confronted with Boisnard's jovial, hale and hearty manner, it seemed mean and perverse to take the wind out of his sails.

Just before lunch, Marc had given André his initial findings on the dead mouse: the macaitin serum had apparently continued attacking and killing cells, not just those that were cancerous, until finally the pancreas and kidneys malfunctioned. No rhyme or reason as to why, or indeed why it hadn't happened to any of the other mice. Marc's tests continued and meanwhile André made sure to avoid Boisnard for the rest of the day.

André shook his head. Boisnard was busily trumpeting macaitin as a triumph with his backers, while in reality it happily munched its way through the body like a cellular rotavator until the main host was dead. They'd never get within a million miles of human clinical trials. Nothing much changed, André thought ruefully. He'd done the same with the mangabey research at the ISG, holding back the full picture on the early tests in the hope that they'd be able to make good with more positive tests later.

Was that forever to be the pattern of his life? Real success and breakthroughs dangled tantalizingly close, yet always finally just out of reach. And meanwhile he was on one research treadmill after another, a ton of family crises on his back, most of which had no place in his work – yet time after time he'd muddy the line between the two. He wouldn't learn his lesson. If he hadn't been able to save Eban, what made him think this time would be any different?

And now this. Eric's blood sample from La Santé prison. But it was one burden, one secret too many. He couldn't possibly keep it to himself along with everything else. He had to share it. Though he waited until late when everyone had left the ORI-gene labs, biding his time with re-checking the DNA printout, before he finally made the call.

Hervé answered on the second ring. Whether due to André's hesitance or his being too technical, it took Hervé a moment to get clear what he was trying to explain.

'*What?* You can't be serious.' Hervé was almost breathless, his voice quavering. 'Eric – another father? It's ridiculous.' Hervé aimed for an uncertain laugh, but didn't quite get there. 'And how can you be so sure? What blood sample is it you say you have?'

'From La Santé prison.' André eased out a deflated sigh. 'I'm afraid there's no doubt, Hervé. I thought the same as you initially, and phoned back saying that they must have had a mix-up and sent me another prisoner's blood sample. They checked again – *twice*. There's no possible mistake. Eric's is the only vel-type sample in La Santé right now. And equally there's no possibility – having now checked the DNA a dozen times over – that Eric could have had the same father as us.'

'Oh my, it . . . it hardly bears thinking about.' Hervé fell silent for a moment. Then: 'You can't tell him about this, you know. It would destroy him.'

'But . . . I mean, holding something like this back from him.' André was instantly uncomfortable with Hervé's suggestion. He'd shared it not only to unburden himself, but also in the hope of some sage advice. Now that advice was to bury it back where it came from. *Back with all his other secrets*. He'd always thought priests were the first to urge confession, unburdening the soul. 'Something so fundamental. It's wrong.'

'I know . . . I know.'

André could hear rustling against the phone at the other end. Hervé no doubt ruffling his hair as what to do tore at his conscience.

'At least not while he's still in La Santé,' Hervé said at length. 'Hearing news like this while he's still in prison would kill him. He wouldn't be able to take it.'

André could see the rationale in that, but still felt torn. 'I take your point. But he's got to find out at some stage. And what's he going to think then, knowing we've purposely held it from him all the while? He'd feel terribly betrayed.'

'You think he'd appreciate it any better, us dumping something like this on him while he's still in prison?' Hervé retorted. 'You saw how he was the last time we visited. He's at his most vulnerable.'

Apart from the months he'd been hidden away from the world, André had visited Eric in prison along with Hervé every four to six weeks. And on the last couple of visits, Eric hadn't been his normal buoyant, confident, fly-in-the-face-of-all-adversities, self. He looked anxious, his eyes darting nervously as they spoke, and he lost portions of their conversation because his thoughts were elsewhere. The thirty-two months in prison had taken their toll. His focus was obsessively on parole three months ahead, and he was starting to worry what would happen if he didn't get it and had to spend another year inside.

Reluctantly, André had to agree: Eric wouldn't be able to take the news. 'I . . . I suppose you're right.' Maybe another reason he felt uncomfortable about it was because he'd have preferred not to harbour another secret. He was already on overload. And there was still his other problem to tackle. 'Though now, of course, with Eric's blood sample being how it is – I'm back to square one with Joël's anaemia. I really need your blood sample, Hervé, now more than ever.'

Hervé sighed heavily. 'You know how I feel about that from what we discussed last time.'

'I know. But now with Eric's blood sample proving useless, I'm desperate. If there were any other way, Hervé, believe me I wouldn't ask you.'

'I want to help, you should know that.' More ruffling at the other end. More hair and conscience tugging. 'But it's not just how I view it, it's how the church might.'

'The church, the *church*,' André mimicked indignantly. 'This is a young boy's health we're talking about. And not just any young boy: my son, your *nephew*.'

'Really. You shouldn't push me into a corner like this, André.' Hervé was slightly breathless, like a boxer against the ropes. 'You know that I'd help if I could . . . it's not me.'

André sighed tiredly. 'In the past, I've seen you step aside from the strict confines of church rules for far less. So that's what I'm finding hard to accept right now, Hervé. It goes so much against the grain of the brother I *thought* I knew.' André slammed the phone down.

He felt exhausted from the brief confrontation, his head slumping on his arms folded on his desktop. Beyond his office, the lab floor was silent. The last people, Marc and two lab assistants, had left twenty minutes ago. The only sound was the muted background rumble of the RER train, though the monkeys' shrieking in response was less these days. They'd become accustomed to its noise.

He decided to stay for a few hours to see if he could uncover anything beyond Marc's initial results with the dead mouse. He'd phone Veruschka and ask her to grab a takeaway for herself and Joël. But if in the end they had no breakthrough with macaitin, what then? Perhaps the only option would be to tell Hervé the truth about why he wanted the blood sample. Surely then Hervé's stance would change.

'He's close to finding out.'

'How? What happened?'

Lillian Lemoine fell silent as at the other end of the phone Hervé ran through the chain of events that led to André getting Eric's blood sample and then their conversation of only moments before. He'd called his mother straight after putting the phone down.

On the back of a laboured exhalation, Lillian repeated many of her stock, stalwart comments from their previous conversation on the subject. You can't tell him. He wouldn't be able to take the news. It would destroy him.

'But we can't just leave André thinking that Eric has a different father,' Hervé protested. 'In any case, once Eric is out of prison, the cat will be out of the bag.'

'How long do we have on that front?'

'Three months, if he gets parole.'

Lillian fell silent again, and at the other end Hervé couldn't help imagining her thinking the unthinkable: wishing that her son might spend longer in prison so as to delay that now inevitable dark day. He knew she felt aggrieved at the path Eric had taken, but surely she wouldn't take it that far? While he and André had been to La Santé regularly, his mother hadn't visited once, claiming that she was too old and frail for such a journey. This latest downfall she viewed as one upset too many.

'In the same way that you agreed with André what such news

would do to Eric,' she said. 'Just imagine what it would do to André. He's only recently got over Eban's death and his accident, and the long breakdown following. Then there was Charlotte's attempted suicide, and she's still a heavy drain on him. And, unlike Eric, André was far closer to his father, still in fact identifies with him and models himself on him to this day. He wouldn't be able to take it. Hervé. It would completely destroy him, tear down everything he thinks he is.'

Hervé swallowed hard. Their father's death had affected each of them in different ways. Already an altar-boy, Hervé had from then on found the strongest, kindest father figures within the church, whereas Eric had simply become even more rebellious, some child-hood shoplifting giving the first hint of what was to follow, although Eric admitted that he could easily have later stepped back, that his career choice was mainly because it was far more lucrative than the alternative menial jobs open to him. But André had been the only one to follow in Philip Lemoine's footsteps by going into academia.

'I know. I hear you loud and clear there, and I agree. But he's putting on pressure like you wouldn't believe over Joël and this anaemia, *Maman*. I don't know how much more I can take. It's starting to look really bad that I'm not offering any help.'

'But it only *looks* bad,' Lillian said after a second. 'You know that your blood sample wouldn't actually do any good.'

'Of course. I realize that. It's just –'

'. . . Except that it would bring André to his knees, destroy him. That's all it would achieve. And all because of how you might end up *looking* to others.' Hervé was silent for a moment at the other end, and Lillian chuckled lightly to break the tension. 'You know, you're just like André in that respect. Always worried about how things might look in the eyes of others. As if what they thought somehow affected what you are or aren't. If Claude Gallinard taught me one valuable lesson, it was that you can never run your life according to what others might think. You can only follow your own conscience. And you, Hervé, as a priest should know that better than most.'

Hervé wasn't sure what had made him flinch the most: the barb, or the mention of Gallinard. A name from the dark past that he hadn't heard mentioned for years, prompted no doubt because he was at the root of this dilemma now.

'You're right, of course, *Maman*. As always.' His tone aimed between agreeable and patronizing; she could take her pick. 'But the problem now is that things have reached such a stage that if I don't agree to give a blood sample, André and I could fall out in a big way. We might cease to be close in the way we are now. Is that what you would want to happen?'

'No, no. Of course not. But given the alternative, that might be a risk that has to be taken.' Lillian eased another laboured breath, as if trying to free herself of the weight of the years' ghosts suddenly returned to haunt her. When she spoke again, her voice was more subdued, frail; she'd been unable to shift the burden. 'I never said it would be easy, Hervé. But sometimes in life you have to do things that look bad to others in order to achieve good. Claude Gallinard taught me that also.'

One night working late in the lab turned into two; then three; then four . . . and in the end André found himself working late practically every night in an all-out attempt to solve the macaitin anomaly: why it continued killing cells in one mouse but not the others.

Except for the nights they stayed with Charlotte, Veruschka was left in an endless cycle of getting takeaways or having to cook for herself and Joël, which he felt guilty about. But on the one night in the following ten that he'd stayed at home with them, he felt equally guilty and uncomfortable.

It felt wrong sitting with them chatting idly and watching mean- ingless TV while in the lab possibly lay the vital key that might halt the cloud of fate that he knew was fast descending. *The minutes ticking away as the clock ticked for a game-show contestant*. He found it hard to look them squarely in the eye knowing what was coming, particularly Joël. So young, so innocent . . . *so unsuspecting*. Tears welled in his eyes and he turned away from them, the lump so heavy in his throat as he swallowed it felt as if his chest was going to burst.

The less time he spent in their company, the better. One day they'd realize something was wrong and start asking awkward questions. In the same way that Eric wouldn't be able to face hearing that he had a different blood father, he couldn't face them. And so, partly, the late nights at the lab also became a sanctuary, a place to hide away from the truth.

Yet, ironically – as the inevitability settled on his shoulders with each passing day and still no breakthrough in sight – it was also the worst place for that. Because each cell slide, agarose test and flow-chart hammered home that ultimate truth: there was no possible cure and he was foolish to think that he could find one just because of what it meant personally to him and his family.

25

'So, what are the options?'

André looked eagerly around the assembled table: Marc and Marielle, Boisnard and his PA, Cathérine, to take notes.

He'd finally made a breakthrough with macaitin late the night before, so had requested a meeting first thing. The afternoon was the earliest that Boisnard could make it owing to prior engagements, so the five had filed into the room – the canteen area which also doubled as a boardroom when needed – straight after lunch, and André had used the morning with Marc and Marielle to further refine his findings. André's eyes burnt with the intensity of that suddenly revived hope, despite being tired and red-ringed from the succession of late nights leading up to it.

'With any human trials, we're going to have to vet each patient carefully,' Marc offered. 'The levels of cell degradation and therefore vulnerability are going to vary far more there than in the mice tested. We're going to have to measure doses according to each case history.'

Marielle nodded. 'And we're going to find the levels of cell degradation far higher among long-term cancer sufferers who've received prior treatment – such as chemotherapy and radiotherapy – and with the elderly. All of those will be particularly vulnerable.'

Two of the most predominant cancer groups, André thought ruefully. The night before, he'd discovered that the macaitin's abnormally high cell-kill rate with the dead mouse was due to a large number of its cells having been degraded; more so than in the other six mice. André then checked back through file notes and discovered that that particular mouse had been part of another recent test with carcinogens – thus the more marked cell degradation and why the macaitin hadn't had the same effect on the other six. But the finding had serious implications for humans, because the level of cell damage there too was often high: years of abuse with tobacco, bad diet, pollution and food additives – very often cancer was just the final throwing in of the cell-damage towel. The signal that the body had finally had enough. Then, in addition, most of the main cancer treatments caused still further heavy cell damage, killing or degrading a number of good cells along with the bad.

Marielle was right. Give macaitin to most of today's cancer sufferers, and they were more likely to end up like the dead mouse rather than the other six.

But get the balance right, get it so that the proportion of extra cells killed wouldn't harm the patient, and André sensed that they could be on the verge of one of the most important cancer breakthroughs of the decade.

Boisnard proposed proteolytic enzymes and high protein supplements. Reduce cell damage from previous cancer drugs and raise the body's own immunity before treatment.

Marc said that their current dilemma probably wasn't that different from that confronted in the early days of chemotherapy. There too, a large number of extra cells were killed. 'Particularly those rapidly dividing in the stomach and gut and in hair follicles.'

Concurrence was nodded from around the table. That's why the main side effects with chemotherapy were stomach upsets, diarrhoea and hair loss.

'Much the same too with thalidomide,' Marielle threw in. The scourge of pregnant women in the sixties, what then had caused horrific birth deformities by cutting off the blood supply to rapidly growing cells in the foetus had recently been discovered as similar to the angiogenic process – cutting off the blood supply to cancer cells. So, by default, thalidomide had made a comeback. The only group it couldn't be administered to were women of child-bearing age.

But where macaitin differed from chemotherapy or thalidomide, or indeed any other cancer treatment André had previously known, was that all of these generally killed cells by being only partially discriminate, targeting cells that simply had certain characteristics:

new, crudely developed, rapidly growing and dividing cells. But at the same time these characteristics also defined other, non-cancerous cells, and so these were also affected. In any case, that partially discriminate targeting rarely eradicated more than eighty per cent of cancer cells – more often than not the hit rate ranged between thirty-five and sixty per cent, and sometimes there was no effect at all.

But with the macaitin tests so far, it had been one hundred per cent effective, killing *every* cancer cell. And therein also lay its problem, its Achilles' heel. It was *too* effective, continuing its rampage beyond taking out every cancer cell to also encompass damaged and degraded cells. André had only run preliminary tests with two of the other mice so far, and there had been additional cells affected there as well – just not enough to kill them. André would bet anything that it was the same with the other four mice.

Yet if they could somehow control that rampage, get the balance right . . .

'I think the first thing we have to establish,' André said, 'is what ratio of additional cell targeting is acceptable. Fifteen, twenty, thirty per cent?' André shrugged. 'Because, obviously, some degree of taking out additional degraded or damaged cells could be viewed as a plus rather than a minus. It's just once a certain line is overstepped.'

'Also, the rate at which macaitin attacks cells,' Marc commented, looking at André and then around the table.

André nodded. This was something they'd discussed that morning while collating their notes. 'OK. The rate at which macaitin kills cancer cells is quite rapid, which initially is a definite advantage. But as it continues its forage into other cells, it becomes a problem. The body simply can't keep replacing those cells at the same rate. At least not in the case of the mouse that died.'

Getting the balance right. They continued throwing the pros and cons around the table for the next few hours, and at one point André began to wane, the succession of late nights catching up with him. But by that stage the full weight of what was within their grasp – *the cancer breakthrough of the decade* – had hit Boisnard, and

286

he was the one sitting forward keenly, eyes alive, his arm motions suddenly animated.

And looking at Boisnard, André wondered whimsically if it had been the same when Madame Curie had isolated radium in her garden laboratory, or for Mendel laying the foundations of genetics in a monastery. Certainly, it was an equally unlikely setting. Boisnard had put a potted palm in the corner to add some ambience, but it was badly in need of watering, its fronds light-brown at the edges. Dust motes rose slowly up by the window as they became disturbed from the sill by the vibrations of the RER train rumbling past.

'If we can get those ratios right,' Boisnard said, waving one hand for emphasis, 'do you think then we might have a strong enough package for a shot at the Gifford Award?' Obviously Boisnard had talked further with ORI-gene's backers, and had a far keener eye on the Giffords than André had appreciated from their earlier conversation.

'Yes. I . . . I suppose we would.' It probably made perfect sense, André reflected: the cancer breakthrough of the decade – you'd naturally want to enter it for something like the Giffords. It was only because of what the breakthrough meant to him personally that that consideration was further from his mind.

But as they started mapping out the stages involved – having quantified cell-kill ratios, refinement of the macaitin serum and finally choosing the ideal vector for its application in humans – André's concerns began to rise again. He could see eight to ten months of tests stretching out ahead, maybe even a year, and he doubted he could afford anything like that sort of time. 'We're going to have to somehow short-circuit that process,' he said, tapping his pencil rapidly on his pad.

'Why? What's the hurry?' Marielle opened out her hands on the desktop.

'Well, I . . . I.' As her eyes met his, again he had the feeling that she of all people sensed that something deeper was troubling him. He dived for cover under Boisnard's mention of the Giffords. '. . . It's just that if we hope to make a play for the Gifford Awards, we'll have to get in shape before then. Otherwise we'll end up waiting another four years.'

'Of course,' Boisnard swiftly supported. 'With something like this, you'd want to go for a main award rather than just one of the annual associate awards. And those are only every four years.'

The main focus was quickly back on the enormity of what was within their grasp: the cancer breakthrough of the decade, and now the possibility of a Gifford Award. But from the way Marielle's eyes lingered on him, André could tell that she was the only one not convinced that that was foremost on his mind.

'The only way to cut that time,' Marc said, 'would be to use one of those flow cytometry machines that actually projects likely cell reactions based on a few models that we provide. But as far as I know, there's only five or six of those machines worldwide. And they're booked solid – at least three or four months lead time to get on one. So in the end I'm not sure how much we'd gain there, time-wise.'

André was a second slow tuning in to what Marc was saying. Then he recalled his last conversation with David Copell. '. . . *But we get to use some of their fancy equipment.*' He held up his pencil. 'Except that I happen to know where one of those is located: the Spheros Institute in Philadelphia. An old colleague works there – so hopefully we'll be able to jump the queue.'

Dani paid little attention at first when David Copell, whom she'd only spoken to a handful of times before, approached her and asked if an old work colleague from Paris could send over some samples to run A.S.A.P. through the CELL-ULA machine.

'Yes, no problem,' she said. 'Tell him ten to fourteen days. We should be clear by then.' That should allow enough for the priority work already scheduled, she thought. She waved a rushed goodbye and continued along the corridor.

David Copell caught her on the general lab floor the next day and confirmed that his friend was sending the samples, and forty-eight hours later they arrived by courier. The ice-packed samples were tagged and put in one of the store-room refrigerators, and the accompanying file was placed on the end of her desk. Still she paid it little attention.

By that time she had something else on her mind.

Craig Berwick, head of security, had sent her an e-mail informing her that a certain Todd Wenner of the FBI would be visiting to advice about the recent rash of lab bombings. They'd recently uncovered a worrying trend that could make the Spheros Institute a possible target. Berwick requested her presence at the meeting in two days' time, or whoever she wished to nominate to represent the lab floors. Berwick had also apparently advised the Spheros administration about the meeting, should they wish to have someone present.

She was in a blind panic for much of the next day, spinning the possibilities around in her mind. If it was just a general warning, surely they'd have just phoned or written, wouldn't go to the trouble of a personal visit. After all, how many labs were there that could be potential targets? Hundreds. They couldn't possibly visit them all. No, they knew something. They'd picked up or traced something through one of the bombings and the trail had led back to Chisholm and the Spheros. So now they wanted a personal, face-to-face confrontation – all under the guise of an innocuous general meeting – to test if their information was right.

She was so troubled by it that she didn't think she'd be able to attend the meeting; her intense nervousness would surely give the game away. But then sending someone else and not knowing first hand what was going on would be just as excruciating. She wondered whether Chisholm was going through the same battle of conscience.

Probably not. Mr Ice Cool, he'd no doubt bluff it out with ease, shrug it off as if it were nothing at all. Certainly he wouldn't want to trust such a meeting to anyone else.

Maybe she should just follow his lead. Shrug and smile and hide behind his coat-tails as he parried whatever the FBI threw at him. Watch the master at work. Another reminder that she'd have to be bolder, tougher, to play in his league.

Bolder, tougher.

She e-mailed Berwick back next morning to say that she would be at the meeting, then through much of the rest of the day, when nobody was watching, found herself repeating those two words like a mantra to herself in preparation. It hardly helped, so late afternoon she popped a couple of diazepam.

She was still feeling mellow and in a slight daze from them when she picked up the report at the end of her desk. With her preoccupation with the FBI meeting and taking care of a pressing workload over the last few days, it was the first chance she'd got to read it.

At first the words washed over her, held little import, partly because of the diazepam, partly because her thoughts were still elsewhere. Then they hit her like a fireball and she found herself frantically reading and re-reading whatever hadn't fully sunk in the first time.

It was almost twenty minutes before she finally looked up. There had been four calls during that time, but she'd just let them go into voice mail.

She let out a slow deflated sigh and shook her head. *Jesus.* If this one panned out how its report read, she and Chisholm would have wasted their time with all their grand plans for the Giffords. Hebbard, Kalpenski, Jacobsen and the other bombings . . . and now this visit from the FBI. All of it would have been for nothing. Out of the blue this obscure researcher from Paris with his even more obscure monkey from the Brazilian rain forests was going to romp home, sweep the rest of them off of the board. *If* these final tests went how he hoped. She waved the report contemptuously, as if about to fling it across the room, before throwing it down again on her desk. And now he wanted *her* to help him achieve that. She smiled thinly at the irony.

The first thing she'd have to do was tell Chisholm. This changed everything. Her hands hovered over her computer keyboard for a moment before the right words fell into place.

We've got a fresh problem just come up. But this time it's from a French research lab, so I'm not sure how easy it will be to take care of. It might also be difficult to sort out purely by e-mail, because it involves a detailed report that I think you should see. So we should either meet and talk or you tell me where to send the report. It has to be dealt with *urgently*.

She leant back and closed her eyes after hitting the send key. *Oh God*, of all the times for this to come up. Though at least she felt slightly more settled: she'd shared the burden.

But over the next hour before she finally headed home, she began to have second thoughts about sending the e-mail. She desperately needed a quick response, but would Chisholm read it that night, or indeed within the next few nights? Then again, maybe it wasn't the best thing for him to read just before the FBI meeting. It could throw him off his stroke. Put a dent in his confidence that would make all the difference between it going smoothly and a disaster. And if the FBI did have the Spheros in their sights over the bombings, what if they'd already started monitoring staff e-mails? She checked quickly back over its wording. She hadn't given much away, except her mention of the lab's French location making it not so easy to 'take care of' could be construed as hinting at US-based bombings – not least to Chisholm. She'd let on that she knew.

Her hands shook on the steering wheel as she drove home, despite the diazepam. The same bubbling cauldron of doubt, possible options and ramifications plagued her for much of the night.

She picked sparsely at her dinner, and soon afterwards, her stomach still writhing with butterfly contortions, she took two more diazepam. But by that stage she was a complete wreck of muddled thoughts and frayed nerve ends and their effect lasted for little more than an hour. She slept fitfully, woke up at 4 a.m. to pop two more – then in the morning, after two mouthfuls of Danish pastry that she feared she might bring straight back up, she reached for the diazepam bottle again before staying her hand. No, she'd take them just before the meeting. She'd need them more then.

She drove into work with her hands once again shaking uncontrollably on the steering wheel, numbly fended early morning calls while her stomach did somersaults, and then, after swallowing the last two diazepam, took slow, even breaths as she made her way along the corridor to where Berwick had convened the meeting, silently repeating the mantra with each breath, each step.

Be bolder, tougher.

Dani found herself strangely perturbed by Wenner's baldness. To her, he appeared as if off a garish poster for the latest freaky axe-murder film rather than the more noble examples of *Kojak* or *The King and I*. It did little to help her already fever-pitch nerves, quelled only slightly by the diazepam.

Chisholm was indeed there, and she was dying to know if he'd read her e-mail. Just a small nod or raise of an eyebrow would probably have been sufficient, but she was careful to avoid much eye-contact, keenly aware that any guarded or anxious looks between them could easily give the game away.

Wenner's colleague, Barry Tzerril, younger, swarthy, four inches shorter, with a crop of wild dark hair and equally wild, darting eyes, stayed silent through most of the meeting, as did Berwick apart from initial introductions and a brief mundane question-and-answer interlude about general security arrangements with Wenner. But Tzerril had the unsettling habit of shifting his eyes rapidly from one party to another, zeroing in particularly when key questions were asked, as if keenly weighing reactions.

For the next half-hour, Dani's nerves wavered wildly. She relaxed a bit when Wenner in his introduction said that it was just a general visit they were making to a number of research labs, then tensed again when he mentioned the Gifford Awards. 'We're in fact seeing all the main contenders, because we're concerned they may be potential targets.'

The worst moment was when Wenner, looking directly at Chisholm, asked, 'Do you happen to know why one of the Gifford contenders might try and knock out its competitors?'

'No, not really.' Chisholm looked lost, perplexed for a moment, then smiled disarmingly. 'Though that would certainly put us out of the running as suspects. We're probably the prime contender, so perhaps should be more concerned about one of the others trying to knock us out.'

'Yes, sir. That's why we're here.' Wenner fixed Chisholm with a cool stare. 'To warn all the main Gifford contenders that they could be targets. We're not specifically looking for suspects here.'

Wenner held the stare a second longer before diving into the statistics of why they thought Gifford Awards contenders could be at risk.

Over those moments, Dani felt the intense nervousness of the past forty-eight hours rise to a pitch. She felt hot, flushed, her breath suddenly constricted, and was sure that if nobody else, Wenner's colleague, Tzerril, had noticed. She could feel his eyes boring into her for a moment. But still she resisted the temptation to look towards Chisholm. Obviously he'd made sure to put some non-contenders into the target mix, but not enough. Statistically, Gifford contenders had still shone through as by far the strongest targets. The first chink she'd seen in all of his planning to date. She felt strangely assured: he wasn't perfect after all.

But he was still good, oh so good, a consummate performer in a league above anyone she'd known before. He parried and shouldered Wenner's questions with ease, for the most part came across as gracious and thankful for the visit and the warning, with the balance of concern just right that the Spheros might be among the next targets. At one point, he even gestured towards Dani, perhaps to answer why she'd been so quiet and looked anxious, perturbed.

'You'll have to excuse our Dr Stolk. She's been working practically around the clock for the last month to conclude some research, and now with your visit she's going to have to be the one to organize the copying of all data on the lab floors and its transfer outside. One hell of an undertaking, but we simply can't risk losing even a part of it.'

As Wenner and Tzerril looked towards her, she smiled thinly through her veil of anxiety and fatigue.

Oh, so good. Within no time, Chisholm had turned the tables, was in control again, playing Wenner and his colleague masterfully, as he had done with her from day one.

Towards the end of the meeting, she risked a searching glance towards Chisholm to judge whether or not he'd read her e-mail; but she couldn't discern anything either way. The same poker face he'd held throughout with Wenner, it gave nothing away.

For the time being, it looked like they'd got over the hurdle of the FBI. But with the fresh problem now from this Paris lab, by far their biggest hurdle was yet to be crossed.

26

André decided to take a taxi to Sacré Coeur. He still cycled back and forth to work, but that was only two kilometres. Sacré Coeur was on the other side of the city, and his right leg still played up whenever he attempted long journeys. But most of all the long trawl across the city would give him far too long to dwell on the nightmare events of the past few days that had led to this meeting now with Hervé. And he'd pass too many city landmarks on the way that would bring back memories.

Not least the Rue Caulaincourt bridge with its row of tombstones beneath. Even without his leg problem, he didn't think he'd be able to cross there on his bike, not now. He simply didn't have the strength or resolve.

The first upset had come with the call from Joël's school yesterday afternoon. Then the update from David Copell in Philadelphia. *'There's been a problem, I'm afraid.'*

But it would take a while for Hervé to get there from Nemours, so they'd arranged to meet in an hour and a half, and biding his time meanwhile around the lab – avoiding Boisnard, shying away from eye contact with Marielle in case she saw the truth that lay there, tapping his fingers impatiently on his desk and handling calls numbly, mechanically, the dead time allowing him far too long to churn over yet again the crushing problems plaguing him – was just as bad.

His nerves were at breaking point by the time the taxi came.

With the call from Joël's school saying that he was ill, he knew then that he couldn't keep the truth to himself any more. Events had overtaken him.

As the taxi approached the Caulaincourt bridge, he closed his eyes, couldn't face seeing the tombstones. Though as he heard the wheels rumble across the bridge's rough-ridged surface, for a moment he wondered if he opened his eyes whether he might break the spell. He'd see that the tombstones didn't spread as far as he pictured in his dreams. Then again, if he hadn't opened his eyes in the first place halfway through his father driving across, he would never have had the recurring dreams . . . and with the moment's indecision, by the time he opened his eyes they were already past, he could only catch a glimpse of tombstones above the bridge's railings, couldn't gauge how far they stretched.

Is that how it would be now with Joël? Leaping between macaitin and a genetic solution, and back again, and by the time he'd finally decided, it would be too late. The moment would have gone.

Except that right now it looked as if he was going to be too late with *both* options. All he could do was push both as hard as he could, and hope, and pray.

Pray. André looked up at the daunting edifice of Sacré Coeur. He'd arranged to meet Hervé at the top of its wide approach steps.

Having already arranged for Bernice to be there to help when he got Joël home from school, he'd put in another call to David in Philadelphia. Over three weeks since he'd sent over the samples, surely they'd have the test results by now? When he'd called David four days earlier, he was told that the delay was probably because of other things already in the system that had to be processed first. 'But I'll find out more and call you back.' Still no call back after four days, and Joël falling ill at school was a sudden, harsh reminder that they simply didn't have the time to wait. And when he'd made that second call, David had told him that there was a 'problem', but he didn't yet know exactly what. Or indeed whether it was a short- or long-term problem. 'Though the department head, Danielle Stolk, has promised faithfully a full explanation by the end of this week. I'll call you straight away then, André.'

André was slightly out of breath as he reached the top of the steps. No sign of Hervé yet. The view over the city was open and invigorating, but André felt nothing but hemmed in, restricted. All of his options seemed to be rapidly closing down. He still had to hope that, once told the truth, Hervé would finally agree to give a blood sample. And what was this truth that Hervé said he in turn had to share?

When Hervé arrived a few minutes later with a wave from halfway up the steps and an apology about the traffic being heavy coming off the Périphérique, André had his mind as much on that as Hervé's reaction to what he had to tell him, and so he rushed at points, garbled his words, didn't quite lend the gravity he'd have liked. He'd held the terrible secret to himself for so long now that perhaps he'd become partly numbed to it.

Joël has leukaemia.

Even saying it now on a hushed, tragic breath in front of Sacré Coeur to his ordained brother somehow belied the weight it had laid on his shoulders these past months. The words just seemed to get lost on the wind and drift across the city.

Hervé stopped walking and looked down as he fell silent. Stony silence in which the activity of tourists milling around became brutally intrusive. They'd decided to stay ambling in front of the cathedral rather than go inside. The pin-drop silence inside and the echo from its hallowed walls wouldn't have allowed them to talk freely and easily. Though maybe hearing those words echoed back from its High Altar would have lent them the gravity they deserved.

After a moment came the questions: How long? What type? How's he being treated? What's the prognosis, surely there's reasonable hope? Does anyone else know? Does Joël himself know?

And André tried as best he could not to sound like he was reading from a patient report: Almost a year. ALL – Acute Lymphoblastic Leukaemia. Protease inhibitors initially, then more recently chemo, which is why he's been tired at school. Poor prognosis, because there's been virtually no initial response or remission, with both haemoglobin and platelets falling rapidly below the critical 100 mark, and now aplastic anaemia had developed. Hope was at best slim and time was against them. Without a breakthrough soon, there'd be absolutely no hope. No, nobody else knew. And no, even Joël himself didn't know: the same as Hervé, he'd been told that he had a treatable condition, so that his tiredness didn't perplex him. Joël had also been sworn not to say anything to Charlotte or Veruschka. It would worry them unnecessarily.

Hervé shook his head. 'You mean for all this time you've –' He stopped short. He could hardly admonish André, given the lifetime that his mother and he had held back *their* secret. The comment would come across as hypocritical. And as he thought about it, even though over the years he'd rehearsed this moment in his mind many times, particularly over these past weeks, and had built himself up as best he could on the drive from Nemours – now the moment was upon him, he wasn't sure he could do it. André's son dying, and now he had to tell him that . . .

'How could God be so cruel as to strike twice, Hervé?' André waved one arm in despair. 'First with Eban, now with Joël.'

Hervé felt a light sweat break out on his forehead. It was getting more difficult by the second. 'He's only struck once, André. You chose Eban yourself, took on the task of trying to save him. Fate or God, or whatever you wish to call it, has only picked you out once – now, with Joël.'

André smiled awkwardly. 'You know how they say that God doesn't give anyone a burden that's too much to carry? Well, in this case they're wrong. I feel as if I've already used up everything I have, all my reserves, trying to save Eban. And now I've got nothing left to give. Nothing left to try and save Joël.' André shook his head wearily. 'I just couldn't face going through the same again. And it's almost as if I know already that everything I try will be useless. I've already been that route with Eban. No point in fooling myself a second time.'

Hervé swallowed hard. *Oh God.* How could he possibly dump this on André at such a moment? Another mountain of earth on top of a man who was already half-buried? How would he even start? He surveyed the city ahead in search of answers, wondering after a moment if that was symbolic: when the moment had finally come, he had his back to the church.

'Let's walk,' he said.

They headed back down the steps towards the Willette Square gardens. Halfway down, André started speaking again.

'You can see now why it was so important I gained your blood sample.'

'Yes I . . . I can.' Hervé closed his eyes for a second, praying for strength.

'And now that you know everything, can you help?'

Hervé could feel André's eyes on him hopefully, pleadingly. He turned and gripped André by the shoulders.

'I want to. I've wanted to all along.' He looked down, couldn't meet André's pitiful stare for any longer than a couple of seconds. 'But it wouldn't help. We have different fathers, André.' He looked up to meet André's eyes directly at that moment, letting the words out with a weighty exhalation as a coach went by.

André searched his face questioningly for a second, one eyebrow arched quizzically as if he hadn't heard right. Then, as it became clear that he had and the comment sank home, André let out an abrupt, disbelieving snort.

'What, *you*? It's you . . . not Eric?'

Hervé lightly shook André by the shoulders and said simply, 'No,' letting his eyes do the rest, willing home the message.

André's eyes continued searching his, but this time what they found was pushed away, seemed impossible for him to accept, the snort of disbelief this time turning to a half cry as he shook his head.

'No, no . . . *no!*'

André's eyes darted imploringly towards passers-by, as if they might tell him something different, then finally he looked up towards Sacré Coeur for divine intervention, help or mercy.

Hervé didn't join him in looking back towards the church. This was something he had to do alone.

After the first question of 'Who, *who*?' and Hervé's answer, 'Claude Gallinard', André stayed silent for much of their slow walk through Willette Square as Hervé related the full story, going back to a long-forgotten place and time: Monteroule, Provence, 1943.

An Italian regiment had occupied the village and, with the Vichy regime of the time, had practically free rein. Its commander, Captain

Vitielli, took a shine to their mother and, when he learnt that their father was a statistician who had done some previous work with aeronautics, hatched a plan that he be sent to the Taifun/Nord factory in Bourges to help out.

Of course, everyone suspected it was to get him off the scene so that he could have a free hand with their mother, but what could they do? In the end, Gallinard was the one to intervene. The area's most prominent businessman and already in everyone's eyes in thick with Vichy and the occupying forces, he felt he was the only one who could help. More wine, food produce, gave over even more of his château on the west of the village to accommodate Italian soldiers – he traded all manner of favours over the following months to keep their father in the village at their mother's side.

Gallinard felt that she'd find it hard to survive on her own, particularly with Captain Vitielli pressing his advances on her. Worse still, Gallinard feared he might be violent if she resisted.

'Our mother never forgot Gallinard's kindness and compassion, saw him in a completely different light from that day on.'

Then, in the fifties, when their father went north to Reims to take up a work commitment with Aérospatiale, travelling back to see their mother only once every other month, she felt deserted. She felt that all that Gallinard had done had been wasted and their father had put his career first and the family second. That was when she and Gallinard became close and finally had an affair.

André had little memory of the village, the family had left when he was only seven. Most of what he knew about the village and events there had been through family stories related over the years since.

'I thought that was because they couldn't sell the house and you'd just got settled into school there,' he said.

'Yes, it was. But he could have waited. She still felt that he'd put career first, family second.'

André nodded thoughtfully. He wondered whether he'd been guilty of the same. Except that for the past few years his family and career had been muddled, and now the hammer blow that Philip Lemoine wasn't his father. No inherited genes or traits. No nothing.

At the end of Willette park they walked across to a bar with its pavement terrace facing the park and Sacré Coeur. Hervé ordered a sparkling water, André a Calvados. He felt he needed something stronger.

André shook his head. 'But Gallinard . . . *Gallinard*?' He smiled crookedly, incredulously. 'If it had been Eric, it might have made more sense. The thieving, the cavalier attitude . . . we could have said to ourselves: oh yes, well, he's got different genes to us. That's where he gets it from: Gallinard, the sly-handed manipulator and con-man. The bad blood wins through.'

'You're being unfair to him. There was a lot more to Gallinard than people saw on the surface.'

'What?' André raised an eyebrow. 'You mean the stories about him doing deals with Vichy and the occupying forces just to suit his own pocket during the war weren't true? That he didn't smuggle and bootleg and pay them to turn a blind eye? That he wasn't like Monteroule's Citizen Kane, as the villagers described him. Tell me which part I've got wrong?'

'I know. I know.' Hervé nodded in acquiescence. 'That's the image everyone saw on the surface. Our mother too, before the incident with Gallinard trading favours to keep our father in the village. That's when she saw the other side of Gallinard, and discovered that that wasn't the first time he'd done such favours for the local villagers.' Hervé took a sip of his water. 'Gallinard was a marvellous pragmatist. He knew that Vichy and the occupying forces were there to stay – at least for a while. And he'd seen also what had happened in nearby villages where they'd put up resistance against them. There was more looting by the soldiers, more village houses occupied and their occupants evicted. More hardship overall. They suffered. So he made it comfortable and welcoming for them in Monteroule. He plied them with wine and good food, even supplied them with bootleg cigarettes and nylons to send home for their women when he could get them. So, yes, he did all manner of deals with them, sold his soul to the devil. But it also put him in a strong position to trade favours when need be – such as the problem with our mother. And the village also got the benefit of much of the spare produce and contraband, when Gallinard could get the occupying forces to turn a blind eye. Unlike so many surrounding villages, Monteroule prospered during the war. Gallinard made sure of that. And that was the side our mother saw increasingly after Gallinard helped her.' Hervé took another sip of water and grimaced. 'More like Monteroule's Oscar Schindler than its Citizen Kane.'

André took a heavy slug of Calvados and shook his head. 'So how come I'm being told all of this marvellous information now? To make me feel better about him being my father?'

'No. There was simply no reason to tell you before. Besides, it might have made you suspicious that we were angling at something. But it makes the information no less true.'

'Who else knows about him being my father apart from you and mother? Does Eric know?'

'No, he doesn't. It's just the two of us . . . and now you.'

André knocked back the last of his Calvados. 'So, he was a marvellous fellow after all.'

'Well.' Hervé shrugged. 'He at least had a far larger heart and stronger morals than most people saw on the surface. You could have had far worse blood.'

André reached across the table and gripped Hervé's arm. 'But don't you understand – I *had* the blood I wanted. I felt I was so much like our father . . .' André's eyes flickered uncomfortably to one side for a second. 'Who I *thought* was my father. And I modelled so much of my life on him, as if trying to please him after his death. Look Father, look what I've done! You'd have been so proud! And all the time I was screaming at the sky to the wrong man.'

André suddenly became aware that he had raised his voice and was gripping Hervé's arm too tightly. Some of the people at nearby tables were looking over at them. He let go of the arm and sat back.

Hervé had expected no less. In only minutes, he'd turned André's world upside down. Hearing that his father wasn't who he thought was bad enough, but coming on the back of the crushing burden he was already carrying over Joël must have made it unbearable.

Hervé could see the pain etched deep in André's face, but most of all the total incomprehension. Coming to terms with it would be a struggle; perhaps he never would.

Hervé reached across and gently clasped the back of André's right hand. 'To all intents and purposes, he *was* your real father, André. He loved you, cared for you, brought you up no differently from me or Eric – as his own. You weren't wrong to model yourself on him. The rest with Gallinard, well, that was just biology. Genes.'

'*Genes*,' André repeated, smiling crookedly. 'The very things you've been telling me all along aren't so important.' André patted Hervé's hand as if to say, thanks, but empty consolation, before moving his hand away. 'And now you've proved the point.'

They were silent for a second, then André asked, 'Did Philip know?'

Though said as if an afterthought, Hervé could tell from André's tone that it was vitally important to him.

'No, he didn't. He came back on one of his home visits a few weeks later, and our mother covered up by claiming that you were premature. So he never knew, or even guessed.'

André slowly nodded. One more piece of the puzzle that might help him battle his way finally towards acceptance.

'And when did you get to know?' André asked.

'Not until five years after father's death, two years after I was ordained. Our mother felt she couldn't bear to shoulder the secret alone any longer. She had to share it with someone.' Hervé shrugged uncomfortably. 'I'm not even sure whether she told me as a son or as a priest.'

Another slow nod, then André stared into the mid-distance between Hervé and Sacré Coeur. Neutral ground, because that's where he felt right now, his thoughts too numb to fully put his feelings into words or to even know where he belonged, let alone where he should head.

'You should speak to Gallinard,' Hervé said.

'Why? Why should I do that?' André said vacantly. 'I hardly even know the man, have only spoken to him once in my life.'

'He knows that you're his son, André, and knows how you've

fared over the years. And he's proud.' Hervé stared the message home, but after a second André's gaze shifted uncomfortably. 'And also because if you wanted my blood sample, then certainly you'd want one from Claude Gallinard.'

'I'm not so sure now that was a good idea. Probably just clutching at straws.' André shrugged. 'Probably my best chance still lies with the macaitin serum, however difficult things might look on that front right now.'

Hervé watched André stare again into the mid-distance, as if he'd suddenly lost all interest in life, but particularly in the family who'd so disappointed him.

Hervé gripped his hand again across the table. 'You'll want the sample, André, because there's something you don't know about Gallinard. Something that goes way back, three years before our family even arrived in Monteroule.' André looked back slowly, dispassionately. But at least Hervé had his attention. 'Gallinard had a daughter. And she died then, at the age of only four. Of leukaemia.'

27

On the taxi journey back from Montmartre, André kept his eyes open as they crossed the Caulaincourt bridge and the tombstones. It was as if it suddenly held no fear for him any more, no secrets.

His father wasn't dead and buried after all, wasn't among the tombstone rows. He was still alive and as well as could be expected at ninety-four. According to Hervé, Gallinard had suffered a stroke a few years back, but it was only mild, he was still reasonably mobile and active – and still lived in Monteroule.

Even his uncle was somebody else, *if* Gallinard had a brother; one more to be deducted, André thought, as he coolly surveyed the tombstone rows.

The first thing Hervé had urged him to do was confront Charlotte and tell her the truth about Joël. 'Head straight over there in a taxi now.'

But André had argued that she wasn't ready yet. While coping with the aftermath of André's accident and his breakdown soon after her own, she'd avoided any relationships, as if she couldn't handle both at the same time. Or perhaps it was too soon after her last disastrous relationship and she didn't want to get hurt again.

Then, when he'd recovered, she'd had a brief dalliance with a late-thirties fashion distributor, but at the first mention of 'business' arrangements and her concern that a money motive might lurk beneath, she'd steered clear, fast. She was learning at last.

More recently, Henri Porcelet at the bookshop below had made approaches to her and they'd had a few dates together. 'He's too old,' she'd commented at first, before André reminded her that he was only three years older than her. He'd been tempted to add that it was just that he was a lot older than the last few men she'd gone for, but that might have come across as rubbing salt in the wounds of her past disasters.

He had to agree with Hervé, she'd been far more stable since seeing Porcelet, but still he felt the timing was wrong. 'It's too soon. It would seem as if just when she's got her shop-front back in order and tidy for the first time in years, we come along and throw another brick through it.'

Though he agreed with Hervé that he had to tell her something to answer Joël's recent tiredness, because she'd soon guess that something was wrong, so he decided finally to go halfway – as he had done with Hervé the past month or so to try and get his blood sample – and say that it was anaemia.

But he didn't think that he could confront Charlotte to tell her, feared that she might see in his eyes that it was something far more worrying and tragic – and so he had to wait for the lab offices to clear to make the call.

'Is he going to be OK?' she asked uncertainly, as if desperately afraid of the answer.

'Yes . . . yes. He's going to be fine.' Yet even with half the city between them, he feared that she'd pick up on his hesitancy and know intuitively that something deeper was wrong. 'It's complex, but very treatable. In a few months, we should see a big improvement. He's going to be very tired in the meantime, might miss a few days from school.'

If nothing else, he'd covered for what would be the main outward symptoms over the next few months. Maybe she'd be ready for the truth then.

'He's in good hands, at least,' Charlotte said reassuringly. 'He's so lucky to have you there for him, André.'

So lucky. André shook off a shudder as he hung up, felt sick to his stomach at the deceit. Joël fast fading, and meanwhile all of his main options seemed to be getting further out of reach.

He tapped thoughtfully at the receiver for a second. He didn't want to call Gallinard, not yet. Still his main option lay with the macaitin serum. Two more days to know what was happening on that front from David. If in the end everything went well there, perhaps he wouldn't even bother to call Gallinard.

*

Two days later he was in the same position by his phone with his office door closed, waiting for the last people to leave the lab before he put through a call to David. If it was going to be bad news from Philadelphia, he didn't want anyone to hear, particularly Boisnard or anyone who might feed the information back to him.

From the first mention of a possible Gifford Award in connection with the macaitin serum, Boisnard's enthusiasm had grown by the day, and the last two days had been unbearable.

'I think our backers are right. Something of this size could give our shares just the boost we need. Some new equipment, certainly. Maybe get those monkey houses sorted out once and for all. Aren't you meant to have heard from them by now?'

Boisnard was suddenly like an eager child looking forward to Christmas, impatiently counting down the days.

'Yes, but they've had some delays clearing the CELL-ULA of work before they can get ours on. Shouldn't be long now.'

André cradled his head in his hands as Boisnard nodded with a satisfied smile and left his office. It was getting worse by the minute. Not only did Joël's life depend on what news came from Philadelphia, but now ORI-gene's future as well.

Though that night he couldn't get hold of David, it just went into voice mail, and although he did speak to him both of the next two nights, David had no firm news, still hadn't managed to tie her down. 'If I didn't know better, I'd think she was giving me the runaround. Probably just busy. Normal crazy workload.'

And when three more days passed with still nothing conclusive from Philadelphia and the pressure from Boisnard by then was insufferable – his beaming face confronting André on the lab floor or peeping through his office door at every opportunity, 'Any news yet?' – in the end he openly lied and said that the macaitin samples were finally being run through the CELL-ULA at that very moment. 'So, barring any complications, shouldn't be long now.'

Lies and half-truths to Boisnard now as well as Charlotte, and questioning glances from Marc and from Marielle – though some-how more searching, as if she, more than anyone else, intuitively knew that something deeper was troubling him.

He'd hoped that his catharsis with Hervé would have helped. But he was still lying to everyone else, so the burden was still there. And now, in sharing the truth with Hervé, he'd been thrown an even larger one to shoulder – and he wasn't sure if or when he'd be ready to share that with anyone else. *His whole life a lie, the very core of who he thought he was, not just the past frantic months of his cover-ups.*

Joël's condition was also rapidly getting worse. It had taken four days for André and Bernice to get Joël well enough to go back to school, then late yesterday afternoon his teacher had phoned again to say that he had a fever and had been nauseous. His soft, innocent eyes were heavy and questioning as he asked why it took so many pills and injections just for simple anaemia? And would it really make him feel that tired so much of the time? Joël too was beginning to doubt.

Though in the 'accelerated phase' now for the past four months, apart from the recent downturn, the drop in Joël's main indicators – haemoglobin and platelets – had started to level off; the 'plateau phase', as it was termed. And that was often how it felt: driving fast across a high plateau, never sure when the cliff-drop ahead, the 'blast phase', was going to come.

So when André did finally get hold of David, over a month after first sending over the macaitin samples, and was struck with the bombshell of exactly what lay behind the hold-up and 'problem', it simply felt as if he'd hit the cliff-drop early. Certainly the sensation of falling was no less sickening, and the end result was the same: once they hit the drop, there was no hope left for Joël.

Yet along with the terrible shock, André felt strangely relieved. Because now that he'd hit this brick wall, he'd have to tell everyone. He couldn't possibly keep it secret any longer. The burden would finally be shed.

'I'm sorry, André. So sorry. I had no idea. If I had, I would never have . . .'

But in the middle of David's awkward apologies, André stopped him short. 'Wait a minute!' The hairs on his skin bristled. He thought he'd heard something outside his office and caught a shadow of movement through his glass partition that was quickly gone as he looked up. Yet he'd made sure the lab floor was empty before making his call. Every nerve end was suddenly attuned to the sounds around. But all he could hear was the faint clatter of a passing RER train and the hum of city traffic beyond. 'David. Can we talk again later? I think someone else might be here when they shouldn't be.' André hung up and headed out of his office to check.

Dani could hardly bear the wait for Chisholm's reply. The tension in the lead-up to the FBI meeting had been excruciating, and the respite from the relief that they didn't appear to be directly under suspicion and weren't about to be handcuffed had lasted only a few hours before her nerves kicked in again, with a vengeance.

But she avoided taking any diazepam, went cold turkey with her hands trembling lightly but uncontrollably through the rest of the day. After all, the first thing she'd need was a clear head to enact whatever plan of action he thought best – *when* he deigned finally to respond.

She'd hoped to get an answer sometime that afternoon, or at the latest when Chisholm went for his normal seven o'clock call-in at Cyberling Rivalry. She waited on to see. But when by 9.30 p.m. there was still no answer, and the security guard, George, had passed her office twice with a tight smile, everyone else having left almost two hours before, and she'd in turn acknowledged him with a brief glance up from the files she'd flicked through blankly for hours without reading – she finally gave up the ghost and left.

She slept fitfully that night, images of Wenner's bald head and Chisholm's smug, taunting smile, playing through her thoughts. *'You'll have to excuse our Dr Stolk.'* Perhaps he'd decided finally to ditch her. Decided that she was too nervous, anxious, too much of a liability. She couldn't cope at his level.

She managed only half a cup of coffee that morning before she felt like retching, her nervous system already on overload, her stomach in butterfly contortions. But at least there was an e-mail message from Chisholm when she got into her office. He must have gone to Cyberling Rivalry late last night. She opened it with trembling, uncertain hands. It read simply:

> Get this report optically scanned and send it to me as an e-mail file attachment. I'll decide when I've seen it what action should be taken and whether or not we should meet.

She could have got the scanning done in the IT department, but she wanted to keep the whole thing as tight under her hat as possible, so went to an outside bureau. For the same reason, and the fact that the FBI might be monitoring, she sent her e-mail with the file from a Netcafé on Spruce Street. She explained in her cover note that given the sensitivity of the file and the recent 'visit', she no longer felt comfortable sending or receiving e-mails in the lab.

Then followed another excruciating three-day wait before Chisholm finally answered, with her checking the Netcafé each lunchtime and straight after work.

By that time she was completely neurotic, couldn't concentrate on any of the other work piling up on her desk for more than a few minutes before her thoughts drifted back to the macaitin samples and Chisholm. A feeling of despondency that there was no point working on anything else, because unless they got over that high brick wall – everything they'd so far worked towards would be futile. So she turned her attention exclusively to the macaitin samples, partly as an escape valve, and used the three-day wait to run them through the CELL-ULA herself. After all, if the results didn't come out as this André Lemoine in Paris hoped, they were all panicking for nothing.

But the results were startling, only served to further fuel her concerns. She ran through two of the samples sent from Paris, then three random internal oncology samples. Secrecy was paramount, so she processed everything herself, using lab assistants only for basic fetch and carry, not any hands-on assessment.

Chisholm's reply was, as usual, curt and to the point:

Sorry about the delay, but apart from assessing the best way to handle this, I've used the time to start putting things into motion. I can now speak with more confidence that those envisaged plans will work. And yes, let's meet. It's time. Also, the game plan this time would take far too long to explain simply through e-mail tennis. Hannigan's on Filbert Street, 7.30 p.m. tomorrow night.

With the build-up of the past months, but particularly the last few panicky days, and the fact that this was the first time she was meeting Chisholm under these circumstances, everything was suddenly in the open – she was like a schoolgirl on her first date. Nervous, apprehensive, hands twitching on the hem of a wrap she'd put on.

And Hannigan's, if anything, supported that illusion. A popular downtown yuppies' and singles bar, its back booths were tailor-made for first dates and romantic liaisons, though obviously Chisholm wanted the privacy for other reasons.

Brief, terse smile in greeting, 'How are you? Had you already guessed it was me?' Then, without waiting for an answer, he made the question almost rhetorical by looking towards the waitress to order their drinks – a white wine for her and a whisky and soda for him – before launching into his plans to deal with this new dilemma of the macaitin samples from Paris.

A genetics lab in Sacramento. A researcher in Recife, Brazil, he'd had previous dealings with who'd play ball. The New Sciences Council.

Dani had to admit, he *had* been busy, and seemed to have it all worked out. She started to make notes: names, contact numbers, order of play that Chisholm envisaged – but as he continued, she was struck by the sheer scale and audacity of the scheme.

She shook her head. 'I'm not sure I could handle this. It's too complex. Too many things could go wrong.'

'It's no different to what you did with Hebbard.' Chisholm took a quick sip of his drink and smiled ingratiatingly. 'And you pulled that off in grand style.'

'That was simply claiming an internal file as my own,' she protested. 'This would be falsely claiming an entire breakthrough discovery, a vitally important one at that. And soon to become a very public breakthrough, given their intended bid for a Gifford Award.'

Chisholm sat back and held out one hand. 'Just look at it as a larger version of Hebbard's internal file – because that's all it is in the end, some internal research that's showed sufficient promise to be shared with a broader audience – and you'll be fine. You can pull it off. I have confidence.' Chisholm took another quick slug of his drink. 'Each stage has been carefully worked out. Follow them and there should be no problems, no repercussions. Or at least none that we can't handle. Just take it one step at a time, you'll be fine.'

Those same words echoed through her head, *you'll be fine . . . you'll be fine*, as over the next few weeks she meticulously followed each stage of Chisholm's plan. The back-dated file from GNC in Sacramento took only three days to arrive and made her relax a bit, thinking that everything was going to go smoothly after all. But then the file and fresh macaitin samples from Chisholm's tame researcher in Brazil took almost two weeks to arrive, and put her in a flurry again. She was already getting pressure from David Copell as to when she'd have the test results on the Paris samples, and she probably needed at least another ten days to process her own samples and get her final report in shape for the NSC.

So when Copell asked again two days later, she admitted that there was a problem, but she'd report fully in a few days. The following week became a hop-scotch of avoiding Copell or putting him off with more excuses, and meanwhile grabbing every spare daytime minute and late-night hour she could in the CELL-ULA room in a frantic bid to get her own house in order, every possible angle covered, before finally showing her full hand to Copell.

On the last night, she worked until almost midnight checking and re-checking every last detail in her report and those from GNC and Brazil, slept well that night for the first time in weeks, and, an hour after sending off a duplicate package to the NSC, phoned Copell to drop the bombshell.

'I'm sorry. I think you can probably now appreciate, given the sensitivity, why I couldn't say too much earlier. Certainly, though, it would be wrong for us to process these samples given the obvious conflict of interests that could arise.'

She let out a deep breath as she put down the phone, as if all the problems and panics of the past weeks were suddenly ebbing away from her. She felt strangely serene, in control again, as Chisholm had suggested she might be: *you'll be fine . . . you'll be fine.*

But it made her thoughts suddenly turn towards some of Chisholm's other words towards the end of their meeting. When he'd seen that she still harboured some doubt and nervousness about the task ahead, he'd reached out and gently clasped the back of her hand.

'You're a lot better at this than you probably even realize: claiming someone else's property as your own. It's one of the reasons I chose you in the first place.'

It struck her then that he was probably referring to the débâcle with her mother; it was the only incident she could think of that preceded their clandestine association. And it suddenly made her feel naked, vulnerable again; a reminder that he knew everything about her and she practically nothing about him. All the questions that had raged through her mind over the past weeks about Meikle and the lab bombings had remained unanswered, shrouded in mist.

'I was wondering,' she said, fighting hard to swallow back her anxiety. 'You know, what that FBI officer, Wenner, said the other day about the high incidence of Gifford contender bombings. And just a few weeks before the MIT bombing, after I'd expressed concerns about Jacobsen, you told me not to . . .'

The gentle clasp of her hand suddenly became a tight grip on her wrist.

'I want to make one thing clear about our association. I'll let you know only what I want you to know about me. And don't *ever* trouble to ask or dig any deeper.' Chisholm's eyes burned straight through her, then softened after a second. 'It's for your own protection as much as anything else. If it all goes wrong, you don't know anything. You might have hunches or suspicions, as may the

FBI or others – but you don't know anything directly. You're not implicated.'

As Chisholm's cool blue eyes searched hers, she had no doubt in that moment that he was behind the bombings and Meikle's 'accident'. And she couldn't help feeling that his precautions were to protect him more than her. All of his e-mails were completely anonymous. She had absolutely nothing to prove that all along he'd been guiding her. If it all went wrong, she would probably be the one left holding the baby.

It was Marielle outside of André's office. He saw her as soon as he opened his door, in the shadows just beyond the view through his office glass partition.

'Oh, it's . . . it's you.'

'Yes, I . . . I forgot something and came back for it.' She glanced down and skewed her mouth slightly, as if feeling uncomfortable with the lie. She looked at him more directly. 'Well, it was more than that, actually. I could see that you've been troubled for a while, but particularly over the past few days, and it began to bother me. I came back to talk to you about it – thought you might feel awkward opening up while everyone was around. And when I came up, you were already on the phone.'

'Oh.' It was his turn to glance down uncomfortably. 'How long were you there?'

'Long enough.' She held the same steady gaze, unflinching.

It hit André in that moment that she already half-knew; and what parts she didn't know she'd already guessed. And it somehow felt right that she should be the first to know everything. She'd been the most intuitive, suspecting all along that something was troubling him, and had stronger shoulders to take the burden than the likes of Charlotte.

They went to the rest room and he poured the last of the day's coffee as he started to relate the whole sad saga: Joël's illness and why he'd suddenly changed his mind and joined Boisnard in the first place; the blood tests with Eric and Hervé and the revelation that he had a different father from them; keeping Joël's illness secret from Charlotte all along, and now yet another secret to share with her; finally, the brick wall he'd hit over macaitin with David in Philadelphia.

As he described Joël's fast-worsening condition and saw her melt, her eyes moistening – 'Oh, God, André, I'm sorry. So sorry' – it struck him that there were other reasons why he'd chosen her to confide in: she was warm, compassionate, and he had deeper feelings for her than he dared admit.

'At the outset, I felt sure I'd save Joël in time, or his leukaemia wouldn't be so aggressive. But with each passing month, hope has slipped away.' André gestured helplessly back towards his office. 'And now this, the final grain of hope gone.'

His eyes welled and he felt a single tear cool against one cheek. She leant in close and hugged him, kissing the tear softly away. He never intended to break down, or even to become maudlin – but as he felt himself gently trembling against the warmth of her body, he started softly sobbing. And once he'd started, the floodgates opened, a catharsis of all the pent-up anger, sorrow and frustration of the past long months.

She hugged him closer and kissed a few more tears away as they flowed. And at one point they froze and looked at each other, sudden recognition of an invisible electricity sparking between them beyond the catharsis and compassion. He thought: I'm too old, too worn down by events, too exhausted and defeated to be of any earthly use to you. But she just continued to kiss the tears from his face, as if to say, 'I don't care,' lingering on a few close to the corner of his mouth before finally closing her eyes in abandon as she kissed him fully on the lips.

It was a moment, though – feeling like a breathless lifetime as he sank into the warmth of her kiss – before he too abandoned himself completely, gave in to the last of his raw emotions. And as she pulled him down to the surface of the rest-room table and they started gently to make love, with the intermittent rhythm of passing RER trains and occasional monkey shrieks in the background, he wondered whether it was fired by his long-suppressed feelings for Marielle, or whether it was just another catharsis. Proving to himself that he was still alive and vital and functioning when in every other area of his life he felt impotent and useless.

28

'So, what do you think?'

They were at Denver airport as Batz asked the question, having just left the last of the twenty-two main Gifford Award contenders.

'That guy in Houston was a definite oddball. Like Jim Carey on speed.' Wenner had to raise his voice to be heard above the hustle, bustle and the flight announcements. 'And that woman in Philadelphia and that ferret with the squint in Oakland seemed a little anxious too.'

'Not forgetting that old guy in Seattle,' Batz offered. 'Kept mopping his brow all the time.'

'That's because the air-conditioning was broken.'

'That's what *he* claimed.' Batz smiled. They sat in silence for a moment, brooding over the question more seriously.

'I don't think we should expect too much clarity straight away,' Wenner said. 'That'll take more time to filter through, *if* it's going to. But at least we've rattled their cages.' Wenner looked up as he heard their flight called. They stood up and headed towards the flight gate. 'I think we're going to learn a lot more from what happens next: whether the bombings stop, or, if they do continue, who's the next target.'

'I'm sorry,' André said as he lay back next to her, still catching at his breath.

'Don't be,' she said. 'I wanted it to happen.'

He looked across at her, a faint sheen of sweat glistening orange on her body with the streetlight filtering in through the window. He traced one finger lazily through a droplet below one breast.

'I mean for burdening you so with everything. Not for what just happened between us, of course not. Except perhaps the feeling that maybe it wouldn't have happened if I hadn't poured my heart out to you like that.'

She looked back directly at him. She reached out and traced one finger slowly down one cheek, as if she were still searching for tears.

'I didn't make love to you because I felt sorry for you, André. I did it because I wanted to.' She shrugged and looked slightly away. 'I have done for a while, though only recently did I fully realize it.'

One thing they had in common, André thought, except that he was still pushing away that realization even as they sank down to the table.

He kept his hand below her breast, gently stroking, and could still feel the electricity there, a faint trembling beneath his touch: her body bore out her words. But much of what had happened still felt unreal, as if as soon as he touched her she'd evaporate and he'd wake up to find that it was all a dream. He shook his head.

'I'm too old.' He watched her brow furrow, as if puzzled by the comment. 'And I feel too tired, too worn down by everything to –'

She put one finger by his lips at that moment, smiling faintly and shaking her head. 'You're not *too* anything, André. Except perhaps too good. Look at the men I've been with so far: the woman-beater, the mind-controller, the mother-obsessive finding fault with everything because the replacements never quite live up to her. And all you're worried about is your age?' Her eyes flickered down for a second. 'In fact, their age has probably been much of the problem. They just haven't experienced enough of life to feel good and confident about themselves, so they try and bluff it out, compensate in other ways – but never quite make it. You're twice the man they are, André: warm, sincere, caring, compassionate. And you *are* secure and confident within yourself.'

André nodded lamely. Except that at that moment, with everything in his life fast falling apart and now this final blow from Philadelphia, he didn't feel secure and confident about anything. And he wasn't sure if it was that ideal an accolade: the best of a bad bunch. But Marielle's words, misplaced or not, certainly made him feel good – how long had it been since any woman had complimented him like that? Certainly not Charlotte, constantly obsessed with her own problems. And maybe at his age that was as good as it got. Small mercies. But the reminder of Charlotte also made him think about the future.

'What do you want from this now, Marielle? Where would you like it to go?'

'Well, I . . . I'd like it to continue. Would you?'

'Well . . . yes.' He glanced down uncertainly for a second before looking back at her. 'But there's Charlotte to consider. I'm not sure how she'd take it.'

Marielle shrugged. 'How long has it been since she's been going off with this one and that? And I thought she'd recently settled into a more stable relationship, found someone who might be suited.'

'I know.' André nodded hastily. Henri Porcelet. 'Looks that way. But you know how she is – so frail and often troubled. Unpredictable. And right now, on top of having to break the terrible news to her about Joël, I'm not sure how she'd take it.' The irony alone would strike the wrong note, he thought: telling Charlotte all along that she should avoid partners so much younger, then him doing exactly the opposite.

Marielle nodded, her expression mirroring his concern for a moment before breaking into a faint smile. She reached out and gently stroked his cheek.

'You know, if you have a fault, André, that's it. If you're *too* anything, it's being too caring about others, too concerned how their lives may be affected.' She traced her fingertips down, then brought one of his hands up to touch her cheek. 'And maybe it's time, André, to think what you want for yourself. What *you* want from life.'

André felt himself start to tremble, not just from the intimacy of her touch, but because of the chord she'd struck. As soon as she said it, he realized how right she was. He spent so much of his life caring for others: Eban, the legions in Africa under the scourge of AIDS, Charlotte's ups and downs, now Joël – that there was never any space left for what he wanted for himself. He'd become so selfless and altruistic, that what was left of him, his own wants and desires, was little more than a shell. But it had been that way for so long that he just didn't know how to change.

Perhaps what had happened now with Marielle was the first step towards that change. He wasn't sure that the old André would have made that bold a move. And maybe it wasn't just about mid-life crisis and a catharsis of all the problems on his shoulders at that moment – but because he'd suddenly found out that he wasn't who he thought he was. He was no longer bound by the rules of the old André. The careful, caring academic, very much like the man he'd thought was his father, would never have been so bold and daring. It had taken the buccaneering, opportunistic, grab-what-you-can-while-you-can spirit of Gallinard. Perhaps no longer having such a strait-laced father figure to live up to would make that bridge easier to cross. He could think of himself more, *live* a bit. Except that right now with the Joël nightmare, once again there was simply no space left for himself. And still he was nervous about Charlotte.

'At least until she's over the initial impact with Joël or there's some brighter hope there, I don't think Charlotte should know anything about us,' he said. 'I don't think she could take both at the same time.'

'Yes, I can see that,' she said. A faint smile creased her seriousness after a second. 'Except that it's yet another secret for you to shoulder.'

He nodded, tightly sharing her smile. The mention of Joël suddenly brought back the problems in Philadelphia, and Marielle asked a few questions to get everything clear in her mind.

'. . . So David says that they can't process or indeed have anything to do with the macaitin samples because they were already working on some in conjunction with another lab?'

'Yes. For the past five months, they claim. And they can't have anything to do with handling them because it could cause a possible conflict of interests.'

'Do you believe them?'

André paused for only a second. 'No. I think they've seen the potential and are trying to claim it as their own. But that could be hard to prove, and meanwhile doesn't help me in getting tests run quickly.' André shrugged. 'And there's always the possibility that I'm wrong. That by coincidence two people hit on a breakthrough with macaitin at the same time.'

'And they're claiming precedence in the discovery?'

'Yes.'

With each answer, André felt the hopelessness weigh heavier on his shoulders. He felt punch drunk after the events of the past months. 'And now with this final blow, I just don't know how to get up from it. Or even if I could work out how – if I have any fight or energy left.'

'There's still hope, André.' She shook him by the shoulders, her eyes burning into his. 'There's always hope.'

And as she talked fervently about the remaining options – sending the samples to other institutes, arguing the Spheros's claim, getting the NSC to arbitrate – her eyes fiery, hand gestures animated – he was reminded why he'd told her rather than Charlotte. Charlotte would have simply sunk into despondency along with him and accepted that it was all hopeless. There was nothing left but to let Joël die. Maybe Marielle's exuberance came partly because it was all new to her. He'd been battling it for almost a year now, although it felt like a lifetime. She had no idea how tired he felt.

Her enthusiasm, though, was infectious, for a moment had him swayed, except for the timing. That put the last two options – arguing the toss with the Spheros and NSC arbitration, both of which could eat up six to nine months – out of the question.

'And with only another five of these machines worldwide and the normal delays to use them, trying the others would delay things probably two to three months. I'm not sure we can afford even that time.'

'Five slim hopefuls is better than nothing, André.' She shook him gently by the shoulders again, her soft brown eyes pushing home the message. 'And you never know, if you plead the case strongly one of them might relent and put you on the machine straight away. Or there might be a gap where someone else lined up can't be processed then for whatever reason.'

Hope. She exuded it from every pore, and he wondered whether that was what had been missing half his life: someone to fire him up with passion, hope and enthusiasm, rather than drag him down with problems and neurosis. Then quickly reproached himself that that was unfair. Charlotte too had been full of verve and passion in their early days together – which brought him full circle again to mid-life crisis: whether he was trying to grab a chunk of the past that could never be re-lived in quite the same way again. Exactly what he'd been telling Charlotte to avoid these past few years.

Marielle's breasts had gently jiggled as she'd shook his shoulders, giving her nakedness an almost comic eroticism – but all he could see in that moment was her beauty: the sheen of sweat still on her skin, her full lips where she'd teasingly slid his finger, her warm eyes imploring him not to give up hope – and he felt totally swamped by her. Filled to the brim with a heady elixir of hope and desire that he couldn't recall feeling before. And whether he felt he desperately needed her to be able to make it through the next few months, or because she made him feel good after the drought of passion and his loneliness of these past few years, or something deeper – all he knew in that moment was that now that he'd found her, whatever problems it might bring on top of everything else, he didn't want to let her go.

'. . . And Dr Kalmann from Celtech phoned again. Asked if you could give him a call back. Also Professor Sommerton wondered if that review on stem cells he'd asked for a few days back was ready yet? Left the reminder that he leaves for the Boston conference in only three days, and he'd like it in hand at least twenty-four hours beforehand to review it . . .'

Dani half faded out her PA Joyce's voice at the other end of the phone as she updated the morning's calls. It had been much the same the morning before, and the morning before that . . . calls returned sporadically or late, or never, as meanwhile the paperwork and files mounted on her desk. Sommerton was one of four research heads on the Spheros board, who, because his oratory skills were superior to his three fumbling, bookish counterparts, was regularly called upon to represent the Spheros at conferences. Senadhira,

John Page and Andy Luttman were also pressing her over internal projects in urgent need of her input. The only one internally not calling urgently on her time was Chisholm, because he knew what she had on her plate at that moment. Only one thing dominated her thoughts.

'Has there been anything from the NSC yet?'

'No. Nothing's crossed my desk.'

'OK. Thanks.' Dani sighed heavily as she hung up.

Despite everything she'd already put in place, all now hinged on what happened next with the NSC. The NSC, New Sciences Council, had been set up four years ago to deal with the increasing number of precedent and patent disputes due to the explosion in genetic research. As soon as a research institute had reasonably complete papers, they were urged to file with the NSC before going public or sharing the information with other institutes to help avoid possible later compromise with precedence and patents.

She'd already been held up a week with the delay in getting everything from Brazil and putting her paperwork in sufficient order to file with the NSC; now, on top, another ten days had passed without hearing anything from them.

And this was by far the most crucial juncture in the whole operation. She and Chisholm knew that the moment Lemoine in Paris realized he wasn't going to get anything from them, that they weren't going to play ball – he'd immediately try his hand with the other five CELL-ULA machines worldwide. They'd do exactly the same in his position. But they couldn't block his progress with any of the other CELL-ULA establishments until they received an official acceptance of their filing from the NSC.

Ten days. Why the delay? Normally they stamped these things and turned them around within a few days, a week at most. As panic began to bite, she'd phoned four days ago to press about progress, and was told that there'd been delays overall because of the volume of new filings over the past few months. 'Call again in two days if you haven't heard anything by then.'

When she'd phoned, she was told that there was still nothing firm to report. 'I'm afraid I can't even see it logged on the computer

– which means that it's still at the review stage. Try again in three more days.' Her worries settled deeper with each call. Could the delay be because Lemoine had already filed and therefore there was a conflict? If so, they were sunk before they started. With Chisholm she had discussed the possibility and quickly discounted it. Lemoine didn't look in good enough shape to file – in fact, that had been the main rationale behind him contacting them for vital extra data. Without it, they doubted he'd be ready. But with the delay, she'd begun to wonder.

Dani looked at the files piled on her desk. Another day before she said she'd phone again, *if* nothing arrived by the next morning. Perhaps she should use the time to clear some of her mounting backlog of work. It wasn't like her to let things slip, get so behind; people were no doubt beginning to talk.

The problem, though, as she'd found over the last week when she'd tried, was that she couldn't concentrate on it for any length of time before her thoughts drifted back again to the main problem at hand. It overshadowed all else, and each extra day with no news was dragging her further down.

She should never have agreed with Chisholm to go ahead. She'd had doubts at the outset that she could pull it off, but the first few stages had gone smoothly, lulled her into a false sense of security. As she sat surrounded by mounting files and unanswered messages that she couldn't lend even the first bit of clear mind-space – she could just imagine this André Lemoine in Paris urgently making calls to the other institutions with CELL-ULAs to get their co-operation.

Perhaps he already had, and one of them was by now halfway through processing the samples and about to send back their report. *Game over.*

Chisholm had e-mailed her last night, asking what news from the NSC. He was probably expecting an answer back directly. Should she answer and say how seriously worried she'd become by the delay, or wait until tomorrow when hopefully there might be . . .

Her phone started ringing, crashing into her thoughts. She

stared at it as if it were an alien, picking it up finally on its third ring.

'Dr Stolk. John Page here. Sorry to chase you so on those cardio myocytes. But I can't start on the second stage until I have your file notes and comments back on the first stage agarose results.'

'Yes, I . . . I'm sorry.' She frantically scanned her desktop for the file. It was exactly where it had originally landed three days ago, but was now buried under five more files. 'I started on it yesterday, but then got interrupted by something else,' she lied. 'I'll get it back to you by tomorrow.'

Page audibly sighed, almost a groan. 'The problem I've got is a real heavy thirty-six hours completing flow cytometry from midday tomorrow onwards – so unless I start some time this afternoon, I'm just not going to have time to –'

'*John!*' she cut in sharply. 'You're one of the best people I have on the lab floor at picking up infinitesimal cell movements through a microscope. So you should have no problem watching my lips move – even a floor away at the end of a phone line. *Tomorrow,* John!' She slammed the phone down.

Her hand was trembling uncontrollably as she took it from the handset, the blood pounding red-hot through her head, rushing to her cheeks.

Of all the battles she'd been through to get where she was, this was the most vital. Everything hinged on what happened next. Make or break. Do or die.

How long before Lemoine in Paris got co-operation elsewhere and it was then too late to block his progress? Hopefully all the CELL-ULAs would be booked solid for months, which was normally the case. But if he pleaded his case hard, it wasn't unreasonable to assume that he could get *one* of them to put him on earlier, perhaps even within a week. Then say another five or six days to process everything. She was already approaching that sort of time, and still she had yet to hear from the NSC.

She cradled her head in her hands, massaging her pounding temples. It was going to be close. One hell of a horse race.

*

'So. Mid-October is the earliest,' André confirmed, lifting his eyes from the phone to the lab activity beyond his office glass screen. Marielle was the only one fully in view – Marc was at the end of the lab and Boisnard in his office at last check – and appeared to be busy studying through her microscope and making notes. But André picked up her regular, surreptitious glances to each side checking on everyone's movements, particularly Boisnard's.

'Yes, October 11th to 15th.' The flicking of paper from the other end, diary pages or a calendar being checked. 'Or the week after. That's the earliest.'

The Sanger Institute in Cambridge, England. The third of André's calls so far. The first, because of the time difference, had been to Japan. Then the Curie Institute in Paris – the only machine practically on their doorstep. Two to go.

October 11th? Nine weeks, André calculated. Better than the two so far – three and four months respectively – but still a serious delay that they could ill afford.

'The problem I'm facing is that there's a group of young children aged eight to eleven proposed for a clinical trial, and this treatment could be ideal for them.' André pleaded his case the same as with the earlier two. Saying that it was his own son might have come across as too dramatic, and one boy had suddenly become a group because that was more standard with clinical trials. '. . . And given their condition, I'm not sure we can afford that sort of delay. I simply don't think we have the time.'

'I see. Well . . . we do have some flexibility, but only for very extreme, urgent cases. Whether this falls into that category, I'd have to confer with one of the directors. I can't make that decision on my own. But if you could meanwhile fax or e-mail me the main details?'

'Yes, yes . . . of course.' The first glimmer of hope. 'I'll get them straight off.' André raised his eyes hopefully towards Marielle as she glanced back just after he'd hung up. She flashed him a quick smile.

She'd stayed in view while he made the calls mainly to act as look-out for Boisnard and signal if he was approaching. They'd agreed not to tell him about the problems in Philadelphia until they got someone else lined up to help. Faced with a complete brick wall and the Giffords suddenly out of reach would be too bitter a pill for him to swallow. If they got agreement elsewhere, they could gloss it over. 'They couldn't help in the end – possible conflict of interests. But we've got someone else to help and their report should be back with us by the end of next week.'

At least that's what they hoped. Quite a few hurdles yet to go, André reminded himself. Only one slim hopeful so far. Two more to go: one in Mexico, and a second USA-based lab, this time in northern California.

The first seemed promising. Dr Moragues in Mexico City started to ask questions about the four young boys he had lined up for clinical trial.

'Ages ranging from eight to eleven, you say. And what type of cancers?'

'Leukaemia,' André said.

'What, all of them?'

'Yes.'

'And all the same type of leukaemia?'

'No. Three of them have ALL – two of those in the accelerated phase. The other one, AML, first stage.' André was making it up as he went along, but as he feared losing track of what he could bring to mind quickly or repeat accurately with successive questioning, he reached for a few files at the end of his desk and flicked rapidly through until he found some useful papers. 'Chemo with Ara-C was only partially successful in that case, and it was much the same in the other three. And one of those also now has aplastic anaemia and B-cell complications. That's the most worrying factor about all of these cases. At this stage they're so advanced that . . .' André faltered as Boisnard walked in. He'd been so absorbed in leafing through the files that he hadn't noticed Marielle gesturing in the background. '. . . that . . . that I'm not sure we have the time to wait. Sorry, one minute.' André put his hand over the mouthpiece and said to Boisnard, 'I'll come into your office in just a minute.'

'It's OK. It's just something very quick.' Boisnard shrugged. 'I'll wait.'

André went back hesitantly to his phone conversation. 'Yes, yes . . . OK . . . yes.' He kept his end as bland as possible, but still felt his stomach in knots. The deception, the constant shell-game of lies, was wearing him down to a frazzle; and while sharing the burden with Marielle had helped, he was on his own at that moment. She was in the background, looking on anxiously past Boisnard's shoulder, redundant. André felt his stomach pull even tighter as Dr Moragues asked what sort of lead time before possible relapse with any of the boys, 'And what was the name again you've given this substance you want tested?'

'Relapse could hit at any time, of course, but I wouldn't like to push my luck beyond six or seven weeks. And, er . . . I'm not sure of the exact spelling . . .' André glanced down, doodling on a pad, then stopped as he realized it made the shaking of his hand more noticeable. He could almost feel Boisnard's eyes boring into the top of his head. 'I haven't got it in front of me right now. But I'll put it in the e-mail request I send through.'

'Just very quickly,' Boisnard said the second the handset hit the cradle. 'The Bern conference is in only six weeks, so I wondered what sort of shape we're in.'

André tried to detach his thoughts and focus as Boisnard ran through a quick check-list of the progress of projects in hand – peptides, genetic profiling, cytokine responses, enzyme support therapy – and in a brief lull in their exchange, Boisnard looked towards the phone as if to say, now I've shared my thoughts with you, it's your turn. André was a beat slow catching on.

'Oh, just a lab in England. Chasing up on some genetics data.' It was all that sprung quickly to André's mind as to why he'd been conversing in English, the only shared language between him and Dr Moragues. He couldn't think of a good cover excuse why he'd be phoning Mexico.

'Right.' Boisnard nodded thoughtfully. 'I thought it might have been the States. Their report should be arriving any day now.'

'Yes . . . yes.' André felt his cheeks flush and he shielded any shadow in his eyes by glancing down momentarily. He forced a tight smile as he looked up. 'Should be.'

'I was wondering if we might be in shape with that too for the Bern conference.' Boisnard shifted his weight and waved one arm in emphasis. 'Short notice, I know, but now with the report we should have more than enough for an early splash. The first hint of how big this is going to be. Big enough, hopefully, to wipe everything else off the board at the Giffords next year.' Boisnard swept his arm out theatrically and beamed. 'Get the press and market pundits warmed up.'

André looked at Boisnard soberly. More talks with his backers, no doubt. He was talking more like them every day. The truth was going to crush him, destroy him, like throwing a brick through a child's favourite candy store window. André felt the weight of his deception pressing unbearably on his shoulders. For a moment he wondered whether to tell Boisnard everything here and now, stop torturing him with false hope. But then Boisnard's beaming smile had almost a life force of its own, was infectious, hard to defy, and so he found himself simply smiling along, agreeing, 'Yes . . . let's hope so.'

André shuddered with the release of pent-up tension as Boisnard left his office. He shook his head and silently mouthed '*Mon Dieu!*' as he caught Marielle's eye.

They waited until Boisnard had left for the day before making the last call to the States, another no-go, then headed to a nearby brasserie where over strong coffee and cognac he related the full account with Boisnard while she intermittently soothed his brow and kissed one cheek.

Hope. In that moment it felt as if she was the only crutch to help him through the coming days and weeks. They sank back probably one too many cognacs, and she reminded him of the two hopefuls notched up that day.

'There's still hope, André. Cling to that.' She kissed him repeatedly as she pressed home the message, like a mantra. 'Cling to that.

Don't give up.' And on the last couple of kisses on the cheek, she slid into a more passionate kiss on the mouth – an old man a couple of tables back smiling at André over Marielle's shoulder.

But that hope felt further out of reach when they returned to the lab and he checked his e-mails to discover that the earliest Dr Moragues could help was five weeks. And further still when he phoned Veruschka to say that he'd be working late – hoping to grab a couple of hours at Marielle's apartment, the only place they could be together and keep their relationship secret – and heard that Joël hadn't been well. With a quick parting kiss to Marielle, he raced home in a taxi.

Joël had a fever of 101.7, was nauseous and had diarrhoea – the most common side-effects of his chemotherapy. Another day or two off from school only three days after the last, and no doubt more questions from Charlotte. But looking into Joël's haunting, questioning eyes as he mopped his brow in the dead of that night, the thing that hit him hardest was just how long he could keep from telling the boy. A part of Joël already half knew, André could see it in his eyes. *Oh God, help me. Help me!* André turned away before Joël saw the fear and uncertainty in his own eyes.

But the next morning there was an e-mail from the Sanger Institute in Cambridge. They could put the samples on the CELL-ULA in nine days. André phoned straight away. They could process them and have their report back to him within another six or seven days.

Hope again.

It was another five days before Dani finally heard from the NSC, by which time her nerves were past breaking point. She'd reached the stage of all but giving up hope. Telling herself that it didn't really matter was the only way she could relieve the stifling tension to tackle her mounting backlog of work. But that in itself felt partly self-defeating: what was the point in catching up when the game would soon be over, everything she'd worked towards swept away? All else became pointless.

After two days of battling through the files on her desk and fending and returning calls, she was back to square one, head in hands, shaking uncontrollably, viewing the situation ahead as hopeless. *Twelve days?* Lemoine would surely by now have secured help elsewhere.

She'd finally answered Chisholm's e-mail after three days with still nothing from the NSC. His response, which returned within hours – she e-mailed from the Netcafé at lunchtime and his reply was there when she returned on her way home that night – was understanding and supportive, but she could sense even his panic between the lines. Unusual for Chisholm.

I suppose we should have waited a bit longer before letting Lemoine know that we couldn't help – but then we'd probably pushed things as far as we could putting off Copell with excuses. One more excuse and they'd have probably suspected something was wrong anyway and started fishing around elsewhere. No point in reproaching ourselves. We did the best we could under the circumstances. We just have to hope that the NSC answer within the next few days and that meanwhile Lemoine doesn't strike gold with another CELL-ULA lab.

She got in an hour earlier to work the next morning and prepared her letter to go off to all five other labs, so that if the NSC letter arrived in that morning's post, she could messenger everything straight off to them – but when it didn't arrive she felt strangely powerless, redundant, sitting there with all the letters prepared and ready to go and having to wait yet another day, or two, or . . .

By mid-morning with the letters in a neat pile at the end of her desk along with all her other untouched or half-finished work, the sight of them began to grate on her nerves. She went back on her computer and tapped in an extra line to the effect that the Spheros's full report on macaitin had already been filed with the NSC and their answer was due any day, which she'd send on to them. She reprinted all five letters, enclosed a copy of the Spheros report and covering letter to the NSC, and sent them off by messenger.

She felt far better afterwards, felt some of the weight ease from her shoulders and was able to focus again on tackling the other work on her desk. It was simply a holding letter and might only gain them a day or two. But at this stage of play, a day or two could be vital. She only prayed that she wasn't already too late.

The first hint André had of any problem was Dr Moragues phoning that afternoon, 10.18 a.m. in Mexico.

'I've received a letter that I think you should know about. From the Spheros Institute in Philadelphia.'

'What does it say?' Although André had already half-guessed. He felt a tingle along his spine while the rest of him became numb as Moragues related its highlights.

'. . . And so given this background, they would consider any help given to ORI-gene with macaitin tests as a serious infringement of their own patent and precedent rights over same.'

Dr Moragues was obviously reading that key portion of the letter verbatim, and had trouble wrapping his tongue around some of the English, particularly inferrr . . . ingement. He took a breath at that point. 'It's quite a long, involved letter. Would you like me to fax you a copy?'

'Yes . . . yes.' André was a second slow detaching from his numbness and clearing his thoughts. 'That would be good of you.' His first thought was what would happen if and when the Sanger Institute in Cambridge got the same letter. 'Look, I know this is a difficult situation . . .' André gave a quick potted history of his side of events: that macaitin was something ORI-gene had been working on for months and samples had been sent to the Spheros some five weeks ago. Sleight of hand by the Spheros was suspected, though it might be difficult to prove. '. . . But overall, we're confident that any claims of precedence would in the end fall in our favour. And, given that, would the offer of a five-week turnaround still hold? Would you still be able to work on them?'

'I . . . I thought you had someone else to work on them sooner?'

'Yes, we do. But with a letter like this in circulation . . .' André let it hang in the air, unsaid, that that situation might now change. From the moment's silence following, it was clear that Dr Moragues felt wrong-footed, awkward, and André wondered whether he was checking back-up options should the worst happen with the Sanger Institute – or as a dry-run of how they might react.

'Well, it's . . . it's not the sort of thing I could decide on my own. Something like this, I'd have to get the input also of one of the other directors. I . . . I'll let you know how things stand on that front later. When I send you a copy of the Spheros letter.'

André got the impression that Moragues couldn't wait to get off the line. It didn't look promising.

He found himself clock-watching for much of the rest of the afternoon, checking his computer regularly for e-mails, tapping his fingers nervously on his desk and anxious each time he answered his phone in case it was the Sanger Institute to tell him that they'd received the same letter.

There were nine calls over a two-hour period before it fell quiet again, no calls at all for forty minutes; then, just before he was preparing to leave, his phone rang again. He stared at it apprehensively, his breath suddenly falling short. They'd waited till the end of the day to break the bad news to him, didn't want to embark on what could be an awkward exchange while the lab was in full flurry. He left it until the fourth ring before he finally picked it up.

'André. Oh, you're still there. I wasn't sure if you'd have left for home yet.' It was Charlotte. The easing of his breath must have been audible at her end, because she asked, 'Are you OK?'

'Yes . . . fine. Just another lab that's been chasing me on something not yet ready, and I was worried it might be them.'

'Oh, right.' She launched into the main reason for her call: Henri had asked her to go on holiday with him, a ten-day break to Tunisia. Should she go?

'Yes, you should,' he said, perhaps a little too quickly.

'It's not just what it represents on the surface, the chance of a nice holiday,' she said. Yes, she could do with the break, but her main worry was giving Henri the wrong signals. If she agreed to it, he'd then take it that things were serious between them, when she wasn't quite sure yet. And if she broke things off afterwards or the relationship didn't progress anywhere, Henri might feel used. Again she raised the concern that he was too old.

'No, of course not. He's only a couple of years older than me, and I don't consider myself old.' Again, probably too quickly. He didn't want to come across as too eager to get rid of her, even though the instant she mentioned it he knew it would solve so many of his problems: her more attached to Henri so as to lessen the impact over Marielle, a breathing space while she was away to at least allow some of the dust to settle over the dilemma with Joël; and with her generally more settled with Henri, she'd have someone else's shoulder to cry on if and when she fell off the wall again.

'Yes . . . you've got a point.' She was silent, thoughtful for a second, and he could tell that shifting the ideal image in her mind of her last few toyboys and thirty-somethings to Henri Porcelet was taking a bit of mental gymnastics.

His incoming e-mail symbol flashed on his screen. He clicked it open. It was from Dr Moragues. He quickly scanned through, homing in on the key portion:

'. . . If it was just up to me, I think something could have been done. But we have close ties with two large US-based drug companies, and so our directors are obviously nervous about possible lawsuits.'

André felt his stomach sink, and he missed most of what Charlotte said next. 'Sorry . . . what was that?'

'I said, the other thing that concerned me about going away was that Joël has been ill recently. Are you sure you'd be able to cope on your own?'

'Yes, yes . . . no problem. I've got Bernice too to help out when need be.' For a second he wondered whether Charlotte had heard or suspected something and was testing him. Had there been an edge to her voice? 'Anyway, he'll be back at school in a couple of days.' At least that was what André was hoping for if Joël's temperature and haemoglobin count stabilized; if not, he'd still be laid up when Charlotte got back from holiday. Then he wouldn't be able to delay telling her any longer.

'I suppose you're right,' she said finally, a reluctant concession. 'I should go.'

He looked pensively at the phone for a second after hanging up. Three days before she left. Ten days away. At least one less thing to worry about for that time. He glanced up as he noticed Marielle looking at him through the office partition. She fired him a quick smile. Old life, new life. *Hope.*

He went back to Marielle's for a couple of hours that night and they made love, but he couldn't help feeling as if it were the last, desperate action of a condemned man. He found what was hanging over him at that moment difficult to shake free, and reminded her that if the Sanger Institute went the same way as Moragues, all was lost. And again she shook him out of it, told him not to give up hope.

The tombstone spread came for him again that night in his dreams, and his main emotion at first was surprise: he thought that now he knew that his real father was still alive, wasn't among the tombstones, the nightmare wouldn't plague him any more. But the dream this time was somehow different: as he tried to see the names on the last row of tombstones, a bright light came from behind, blinding him, and he wondered whether that symbolized the hope that Marielle urged. But as the light fell into focus, he could see that it was the headlamp of an RER train hurtling towards him – the screeching of the macacartos getting louder and more frantic as it approached – and each side were dark tunnel walls. No escape. And as the rumble and rattle of the train bore down on him, he could suddenly hear Joël's cries above the cacophony from the monkeys: '*Papa . . . Papa!*'

He awoke with a jolt before the train hit him – but he could still hear Joël calling out. He jumped out of bed and ran towards his room.

29

Todd Wenner stood by the fourth floor window, looking out over Atlanta's Century Parkway. The first rush-hour traffic had started edging its way home and dark storm clouds hung overhead, threatening rain. Half of the cars already had their lights on.

'I don't like the silence,' Wenner said.

Batz looked up thoughtfully from his computer. 'At least it's told us one thing. That we probably hit a nerve with our recent visits to Gifford contenders.'

'True.' Wenner nodded, still surveying the street scene ahead, not troubling to look back. 'But that still leaves nineteen possibles. And don't forget, last time we had a lull between bombings, it lasted fourteen months. If we get the same this time, it could easily end up a dead file. For ever buried.'

Though as Wenner looked blankly ahead into the gathering storm clouds, it wasn't the worry of a long silence that he felt hanging over him, but the unsettling feeling that something at that moment was brewing and would soon break. The quiet before the storm.

The storm cloud hanging over the ORI-gene labs was also intense. It began to mass within hours of them hearing from the Sanger Institute in Cambridge that with the recent letter from the Spheros and the, 'obvious change this makes to circumstances', they could unfortunately no longer process the macaitin samples, then ebbed and flowed on Boisnard's rapidly shifting emotions: shock, bewilderment, disappointment, and, finally, abject concern and worry.

At first, after a panicky corner consultation with Marielle, they'd decided not to tell Boisnard until they'd at least tried to get more hopeful news elsewhere, but halfway through a desperate scramble

336

to drum up something with the remaining CELL-ULA options, Boisnard burst into André's office waving a piece of paper. 'What on earth is this?'

André recognized it immediately as the Spheros letter. It had been faxed to Boisnard by a colleague at the Curie Institute. André should have realized that at their level the research community was small and Boisnard was bound to find out – but it was the worst possible way for it to happen, smacked of them purposely going behind his back to cover up.

'You should have told me all this earlier,' Boisnard said at the end of their almost hour-long meeting. His expression was hangdog, defeated, his shoulders slumped like a boxer who'd taken too many stomach punches, each struggling explanation from André a blow to sag him deeper.

'It became more awkward with each passing day,' André said. 'Each time I saw you, all you talked about was how you or your backers saw macaitin as a likely Gifford Award winner. It became more and more difficult to take the wind out of your sails – until, hopefully, there was light at the end of the tunnel. That's what we were trying for now.' André gestured towards the phone. 'Better news from one of the other labs.'

'We?'

'Yes.' André sighed. It wasn't at all how he'd wanted to tell Boisnard, but that had been the pattern recently. Every secret, imparted or received, seemed to catch him unawares. 'Marielle knows too. She's the only other one here that does. Nobody else knows.'

Boisnard kept an eyebrow raised a second longer, but didn't pursue it. The eyebrow sank again, along with his general countenance, back into despondency. After a moment: 'Does Charlotte know?'

'No. Like you, I was hoping for more positive news before I let her know.' André's shoulders slumped in sympathy with Boisnard's as he let out another sigh. 'Otherwise I don't think she'd be able to take it.'

Boisnard nodded thoughtfully, his eyes cast down. He was slow in looking up again. 'And when did you first know about Joël's condition?'

'Just before I joined you here. That's what finally gave me the kick over the edge.'

'Oh, that was the reason for the sudden about-turn. And here was me thinking that it was because I'd finally convinced you that what I was doing here was worthy and noble.' Boisnard smiled ingenuously, the first levity to touch his face since he'd walked in.

'It was. And maybe everything I'd done before at the ISG was too. But when that final jolt came, there was simply no other choice. I couldn't stay hidden away from the world licking my wounds any longer.'

Boisnard's heavy-lidded eyes sank down again for a moment before slowly lifting to contemplate André levelly. 'I suppose all that's left is for you to continue trying with the other labs, as you were before.'

'There are still a couple of possibilities,' André said. 'I should know where we stand by close of play tonight – at the latest tomorrow.'

Boisnard nodded sombrely as he started making his way out. 'I should know a bit more from my end by then, including hopefully what to do should the worst happen.'

Boisnard looked ponderous, hesitant, as if he in turn held a secret that he was uncertain about sharing with André as he paused for a second by the doorway. Then, finally deciding against whatever he was about to say, with a perfunctory nod he closed the door.

André had his answers by 5.40 p.m. that night, but Boisnard had left the office almost two hours before and hadn't been seen since. André waited on for him, and when Boisnard rolled in back through the doors forty minutes later, André could smell the cognac on his breath.

Boisnard had had a drinking problem when he'd fallen from grace with the Cochin hospital eleven years ago, but recently André had never seen him indulge in anything but light social drinking, and *never* in office hours. But at least there was a wry smile back at the corner of Boisnard's mouth, his sombre mood had mellowed.

André explained to a weary-eyed Boisnard that they'd struck out, no go anywhere, and Boisnard simply shrugged, as if to say, 'We expected no less.'

They agreed that the best back-up options were to initially go in strong to try and get Spheros to relinquish their precedence claims – unlikely given their NSC filing and letters to the other labs, but worth a try – or get their agreement to share the discovery, as in the case of the Gallo–Pasteur dispute. They were the only two ways they could see of avoiding a lengthy dispute and therefore get early release of the macaitin data to be able to help Joël, and others.

At the mention of the boy's name, again André noticed Boisnard look nervous, anxious.

André got hold of David later that night, just after lunchtime in Philadelphia. He'd agreed with Boisnard initially not to mention Joël; while nothing might be stronger to gain sympathy, it also raised possibly awkward personal-involvement/ethical issues. But when David started to complain that it could be awkward for him to be caught in the middle of the whole affair – 'If I'm the messenger of all this bad news, they might decide just to shoot the messenger. And I'm not considered young bones in this business any more. It could take me a while to find another position' – André decided to play the card.

It took four days for David to return with an answer, and meanwhile Boisnard's mood became darker and more volatile. More than a few times, André heard him shouting openly across the lab floor to his PA Catherine or one of the lab assistants. It was as if he knew the news would be bad before it came.

When André finally brought him into his office to tell him that it was no on both fronts, Boisnard simply stared blankly at the floor and slowly shook his head, like a condemned man hearing that his last reprieve had gone, even though he'd expected no different all along.

'There's only one way they'd release the CELL-ULA data

straight away, they say. A sort of reversal of our first offer to them: if we sign to relinquish any and all precedent claims to macaitin.' André shrugged. 'I know it's far from ideal – but at least I can feel assured that there's *one* route whereby I'll be able to save Joël's life.'

Boisnard didn't answer, simply closed his eyes and shuddered. As he slowly opened them again to look steadily across the table, André noticed that his hands were trembling uncontrollably, and was aware for the first time of the intensity of whatever had been tormenting Boisnard these past days.

'I think we need to talk, André.' Boisnard tried to maintain eye contact, but as André saw the anguish and awkwardness there, they shifted down again, then towards the open lab beyond his glass partition. 'I . . . I don't want to do this here. Let's go for a drink.'

I've been approached by David Copell. He's had a response from Lemoine in Paris with a couple of offers. We need to talk, urgently.

Chisholm's e-mail reply was there when she went by her regular Netcafé on the way to work the next morning.

OK. Let's meet tonight at 7 p.m. Same place as before, back booth.

Hannigan's was busier and noisier than last time: there was an amateur fifties and sixties night in full swing, with a succession of singers trying their luck on karaoke as Peggy Lee, Frank Sinatra, Chuck Berry or Patsy Cline. It was an annoyance, but at the same time masked their conversation. Nobody could possibly listen in.

Dani started explaining the two offers relayed through Copell as soon as their drinks were ordered. 'The first is an obvious non-starter, but I think the other offer is well worth looking at. We'd still get a shot at the Giffords, even though we'd have to share the glory. Plus we'd avoid any forthcoming lawsuit – which could affect our chances if it gets messy. Also, we could . . .'

Chisholm held one hand up, stopping her at that point. A wry smile creased his mouth. 'We don't need to. I don't think they'd even trouble to go to court, not now we've got this.' Chisholm produced a small tape recorder from his pocket and tapped it reassuringly as he placed it on the table. 'Or if they did, their case would look in such doubt from the outset that it certainly wouldn't cut any ice with the Gifford committee.'

He pressed play, and a tinny voice sailed free, competing weakly with a Frank Sinatra contender just stepped up to the mike. Dani had to lean close to the recorder to hear. It was David Copell.

'Oh God, André. That's terrible . . . *terrible*. And after all you went through with Eban. How long have you known?'

'Almost a year. That was why I joined ORI-gene in the first place.'

'And you kept it from Boisnard all of this time?'

'Yes. Up until today, when the whole thing blew up.'

'And it's now accelerated-phase ALL with Joël?'

'Yes. Has been for the last four months now.'

A heavy pause, the sound of Copell swallowing hard. Then: '*Jessssus*. André . . . this is a nightmare. A fucking nightmare. I can understand your rationale, believe me I can. I'd have done exactly the same. But after the whole mess with Eban and the ISG – if this ever got out, you'd be sunk before you even started. The same old cry of personal involvement and ethics would come up again.'

'I know . . . I know. That's why you can't say anything to them about it. I'm only telling you because you're a close friend.'

'Thanks.' Copell's tone was light-heartedly sarcastic, attempting to lighten the burden suddenly thrown on his shoulders.

Chisholm stopped the tape at that point as the waitress returned with their drinks. When he pressed play again, the rest of the tape was Copell confirming that he'd help – but he'd have to be cautious because of his position. 'Let's talk again in a couple of days.'

Dani took a sip of her wine and asked: 'When did you think of taping Copell's conversations?'

'As soon as the whole thing blew with Lemoine. Having used Copell as a go-between – if Lemoine was going to confide in anyone, it would be him.'

Dani nodded and smiled, 'Good thinking,' but inside she was squirming. She couldn't help wondering if Chisholm had monitored her calls too, feeling her face flush as she panned back for any awkward or incriminating calls. 'It's hot in here, and noisy.'

Chisholm simply smiled tightly.

She glanced back at the tape. 'Do you think Lemoine is telling the truth – about his son?'

'Yes, I do. I think it's too dramatic and personal for him to use just to get Copell's help through sympathy. And it could as easily have backfired. Copell brings up the ethical and personal-involvement angles – but he could have cried it stronger and refused to help.'

That too made her uneasy, gave her a cold feeling in the pit of her stomach. Certainly the stakes had raised: a few weeks ago they were robbing a man of one of the main research breakthroughs of his career – which at the time she'd complained to Chisholm she wasn't sure if she could handle. Now they were possibly taking away his last chance of saving his son's life. But after everything else so far – Hebbard, Kalpenski and what she'd done to her mother – surely she should simply take this in her stride? Having made the decision to sacrifice all for her ambitions, see this as just one more rung on the ladder?

'What we need to do now is find out more about what happened at the ISG with this Eban,' Chisholm said. 'Get a final trapdoor prepared should we need it with the NSC – or maybe even leak it to the press.'

'Yes.' She nodded pensively. 'That should hopefully cut off any of his last possible escape routes.' Certainly, Chisholm seemed to be unfazed by it. Just another day. Another life ruined. If she hoped to follow fully in his footsteps, she'd have to be more like him, be prepared to go that extra step if need be; and, in turn, he'd seen that initial spark of ruthless ambition in her, which was why he'd singled her out. But as she looked across and saw him eager, almost gloating, at this final cornering of Lemoine, she was reminded of Meikle, the bombings and the recent FBI visit, and suddenly the space between them felt like a cold dark river that she wasn't sure she could take that final step across. They were closer than they'd ever been, sitting a foot across from each other in a private booth like two lovers, but at that moment the gulf between them felt as if it had never been wider.

A fresh singer had taken the microphone with a rendition of Ben E. King's 'Stand By Me', and Dani felt the solid, insistent bass beat pounding that dark river of uncertainty through her veins, her pulse suddenly heavy at her temples. She sipped nervously at her wine.

'Whichever way Lemoine's going to jump with this, we should know over the next week or two. The phone lines will be red hot between Lemoine and Copell.' Chisholm raised his glass towards her and smiled thinly. 'So we should meet up like this every other day to keep on top of everything. Things are going to be hotting up from hereon in.'

'Yes . . . OK.' She sipped again at her drink. *Hotting up*. She could feel the heat and activity of the room pressing in on her, every nerve end in her body suddenly alive with a volatile mix of adrenalin and dread.

Chisholm picked up on her anxiety. 'And if you're worrying about this new situation with Lemoine and his son – *don't!* As Copell rightly says, he shouldn't even be trying to juggle that situation with his work. And we can't be bothering ourselves just thinking about one boy. If we get this right with macaitin, we'll be saving millions. Hardly anyone else at the Giffords will get a look in.' He reached across the table and clasped her hand. 'Just think of all the kudos and glory. We could go down in history, have our names right up there alongside Pasteur and Mendel.'

She looked down at her hand in his, and was sure he could feel it trembling. To anyone looking on, it was probably the final confirmation that they were just another couple out for the evening. Except that there was still that dark gulf between them, and what they were planning was more momentous than any onlooker could possibly imagine. Two people suddenly isolated from the noisy throng around by the sheer scope of their vision; and, by extension, the world beyond.

'Yes . . . you're right,' she said breathlessly, closing her eyes for a second. *Glory. In History.* Everything she'd aimed for all along, and more. She shouldn't trouble herself with what she'd had to do to get there. The end more than justified the means. And suddenly the dark river between them became warm, welcoming, as she took the final step across it. 'I shouldn't worry.'

'I was all but washed-up, finished, when I first made contact with you,' Boisnard said, eyes downcast, his direct eye-contact with André since he'd started talking, fleeting, minimal. He took another quick slug of Calvados and, as he put it back down, waved his cigarette hand away from it dramatically. 'Or at least the writing was already on the wall. That's why I pursued you so hard.'

They'd gone to a café a couple of streets away so that they wouldn't be disturbed by Marc or Marielle or one of the other ORI-gene lab assistants. It was a large café with old marble tables and wooden benches. A lot of new bars had adopted the same style for period effect, but this was one of the originals, and its chequered cream and terracotta tile floor bore the wear and grime and the countless stubbed Gauloises of its age. It was quiet, only a couple of other tables were occupied, the lull between the lunchtime and evening crowds.

Boisnard did most of the talking; this was his unburdening, his catharsis.

He explained how his two main backers, both sizeable drug companies – one French, one Swiss – held a sixty-five per cent shareholding in ORI-gene. André simply nodded. He knew that they were majority shareholders, but no exact figures had been quoted before.

'The INSERM holds only five per cent, and I the remaining thirty.' Boisnard prodded his chest with a couple of fingers. 'But the thing is, to support that share, I've had to mortgage practically everything I own. As appointed managing director it gave me the control I wanted, but it also made me ultimately responsible if anything went wrong. I was surprised at first that with their level of shareholding they didn't put their own man in as well – but they said that they didn't have enough expertise in the field of natural-sourced medicine or genetics to get directly involved. They preferred a more "hands-off" approach. They'd leave me to it. They trusted me, they said.' Boisnard took another quick slug of Calvados. 'At first, everything went well. I enjoyed the latitude and freedom given me, and the only checks and controls were that their appointed accountant do the quarterly figures – at which time I would also prepare a progress report to accompany them.

'But as time went by, I came to realize that the main reason they'd taken a "hands-off" stance was because the whole business of natural-sourced medicines was so new and controversial: they wanted the flexibility of being able to jump either way. If it started to shape up and look sexy and therefore boost their shares, they'd stay aboard and perhaps even increase their investment. If it wasn't heading anywhere fast or looked risky, they'd jump ship, dump it. And that's what they looked ready to do when I first contacted you.' Boisnard shrugged. 'Squalamine and Lyprinol had flopped miserably, and although there was some progress with peptides, at that stage it looked like a couple of other labs had stolen the march on us. Too little, too late, they said. So I held them off by saying that you were going to join me.'

'How on earth did you manage to stave them off for so long?' André asked. 'What . . . it must have been fifteen or so months before I finally relented and joined you.'

'Don't ask.' Boisnard shook his head wearily. 'Still recuperating. Finishing off some private papers before he joins us . . . Just another month now to wait. Believe me, I was running out of excuses by the time you finally joined, and their patience was wearing thin. But it also built up their expectations. The golden boy had finally arrived! Lemoine, the mover and shaker. Far better than tired old Boisnard – well past his sell-by date.' Boisnard smiled awkwardly.

André reached across and lightly gripped Boisnard's arm to lift him out of his mood. 'I'm sure that's not how they thought of you.'

'Maybe not early on. But by then it certainly was. If you hadn't joined me, I'd have been sunk.' Boisnard looked to one side for a moment as two men a few tables away got up and left. 'Though that long build-up also brought its own problems. Expectations were high from the moment you arrived, and when for a while at first nothing dramatic happened, there were a few touch-and-go moments then too with my backers. That's why I latched on to macaitin so quickly. It was the pot of gold I'd long promised them, finally arrived. They recommended the Gifford Awards almost immediately, and the bandwagon rolled rapidly forward from there.' He drew anxiously on his cigarette. 'I should have waited for at least some of the dust to settle.'

'You weren't to know what was going to happen.'

'No?' Boisnard looked at André aslant. 'I should have known that alone from the pattern of my life so far. Known that it was far too good for anything to go so smoothly, without problems.'

Boisnard's eyes shifted down hesitantly, and it dawned on André where he was heading. 'Your backers. They're not going to budge on macaitin, are they?'

'No. No, they're not.' He met André's steady gaze only fleetingly. 'The only hope would have been sharing the find, but even that I wasn't sure they'd go for. Relinquishing any claim in order to get the key data released early, there'd be absolutely no chance of.'

They were silent for a second, the only sound that of the waiter clearing the glasses from a few tables away.

André felt his stomach sink as the realization fully settled. 'But . . . but what about Joël? And surely they wouldn't want to face a lengthy legal battle?'

'With Joël, they'd no doubt say it was just one boy, and they have to look at the bigger picture of the millions that could be saved. And that besides, from an ethical standpoint, you shouldn't even be mixing your personal life with your work. I'm not even sure it's wise to mention it to them. As for the legal battle – while they're fighting it and there's still the chance of them winning, their shares will ride high. If they throw in the towel early, they'll drop straight away.' Boisnard watched André's eyes dart for a second, as if searching for other options. He slowly shook his head. 'I'm sorry, André. You know what it's like at this level of research. So much of it is about money. If it was just up to me, you know I'd help. But it's not – and they'd pull the rug from under me for sure. I'd be ruined. If I was younger even, I . . . I might be able to face that. Be . . . be confident of being able to pull my way back up again.'

As Boisnard started struggling with his words, André noticed his eyes welling up. Despite the sting of what Boisnard was saying, André's immediate reaction was to offer solace, comfort. He reached across again to gently grip Boisnard's arm. 'It's OK . . . it's OK. I understand.'

Yet André's touch and words, perversely, made it all the harder for Boisnard. Getting André on board to save his own neck, and now telling him that he couldn't help save his son for much the same reason. Boisnard felt the guilt and shame of it pressing down hard, the nape of his neck aching with tension and weariness.

'But I'm too old now, André. It . . . it would be one fall too many. I'd never be able to bounce back.'

André was able to hold Boisnard's gaze for only a moment before Boisnard's eyes shifted again to look absently at the waiter wiping off the next table. Perhaps because Boisnard couldn't bear to look at André a second longer with the hurt and desperation he saw there – or maybe as a stark reminder that if he fell from grace at his age, he'd be fit for little better.

But André too found himself staring numbly towards the waiter, a somewhat lost and solitary figure wiping away the day's dregs, along with any last hopes he'd clung to of being able to save Joël.

'I found out something about what happened with Lemoine at the ISG,' Dani said.

'Me too.' Chisholm sipped at his coffee and held one hand out to her. 'It's OK. You first.'

She was sitting alongside him, leaning in close so that she couldn't be overheard, her tone eager, excited. But suddenly she felt slightly intimidated, hesitant, as if what she had to offer might not measure up.

She'd made sure to bump into him in the corridor earlier, and, checking that nobody was within earshot, muttered under her breath, 'I've found something out. We need to talk early.'

'OK. Tonight, then. Same time and place as we'd originally arranged to meet tomorrow night.'

To anyone looking on, they'd be sure that something was going on between them. And again now they were huddled together like two secret lovers. But at least it was quieter than last time, a Starbucks café on Arch Street.

'I got the information from Savaitin-Keller in Paris. We did some work with them last year.' She leant a few inches closer as the espresso steamer threatened to drown out her words. 'Apparently Lemoine adopted a young African boy who was dying of AIDS, and he was chasing down a breakthrough treatment in the hope of saving the boy. Word has it that when the boy's condition took a dive quicker than anticipated, Lemoine jumped the gun on treatment.' She arched one eyebrow dramatically. 'The boy died as a result.'

'Any proof?'

'No, just rumours. Scuttlebutt.' Dani tapped her coffee-cup rim. 'The ISG hushed it up pretty quick. Lemoine left within days of the boy dying. "Compassionate grounds", was the official ISG line.'

Chisholm sat back. 'Well . . . you've done better than me. My guy only found out about the boy dying and Lemoine leaving in a rush – but hasn't yet pieced together the reasons why. Except that when he digs a bit deeper, maybe he'll get a bit more of the background details and proof we don't yet have.' Chisholm took a sip of coffee and smiled. 'Private investigators. You can't beat them when you want to dig down to get the whole picture. Like a terrier with a rabbit.'

Dani flinched and looked away from his searing eyes and smugness, any elation she'd felt from his praise quickly dying in the pit of her stomach. Like nobody else, he had the ability to make her uneasy at the click of a finger, play with her emotions as if turning a tap on and off. And his enigmatic smile, like so much else about him, could be read either way. His own emotions were always a closed book.

'David Copell left the ISG at exactly the same time,' she said.

'He was probably involved with it too, or at the very least knows the details of what happened.'

'Yes . . . probably so. Probably so.' Chisholm pondered briefly as he took another sip of coffee. 'But we can't push him on the issue. Right now we need him to talk openly and freely with Lemoine. And he's not going to do that if he thinks he's under the spotlight.' Chisholm was lost with another thought for a second, then raised his cup towards Dani. 'But good work. Looks like we might have shut down what few options Lemoine had left before he's even started. Though let's see what my man comes up with and what goodies pass between Lemoine and Copell over the next few days before we drive the final nail into his coffin.'

'I know we haven't had any contact over the years,' Gallinard said. 'But Lillian phones me every now and then to keep me up to date with your progress. And I have to say – I'm very proud of you.'

'Thank you . . .' André paused for a second. He had trouble wrapping his tongue around 'father' or '*papa*', but then Gallinard hadn't yet referred to him as 'son', either. 'That's very kind of you.'

It was late, the only sounds from the apartment that of Veruschka watching television in the next room. But André's ears were tuned to the other direction, to Joël's room. He'd been feverish and nauseous again and Bernice had stayed late to settle him down; it sounded as if he was asleep at last. He'd lied to Charlotte that Joël was all right, he'd be going to school the next day, because she was threatening to cancel her trip to Tunisia with Porcelet. The last thing he wanted was her staying and panicking, phoning him every other hour. But the hard truth was that Joël's condition hadn't improved at all, in fact, if anything, it had worsened, and him returning to school still looked a while away. The day after Charlotte left, Hervé phoned to say that he'd spoken to both Lillian and Gallinard – they'd arranged that Hervé would clear the ground first before André finally made contact with Gallinard. But with the problems with the Spheros and Boisnard, this was the first opportunity he'd had to call.

They spent a few more minutes with pleasantries, then got to the subject of Juliette, Gallinard's daughter who'd died at the age of four.

'I'm so sorry that the ghost of Juliette has revisited you in this way,' Gallinard said, his breathing suddenly laboured, heavy. 'She was treated at L'Archet hospital in Nice, the only cancer centre at the time. They wouldn't have any papers or samples still – it's too long ago. But I have some of the old hospital papers here, and I can send my own blood sample, if that will help.'

'Yes, it would. *Anything* would help at this stage.' André found it hard to keep the desperation and despondency out of his voice. Maybe that was why he was finally phoning Gallinard; now that hope was fast dying on every other front. Clutching at straws.

'I know there's probably little point in telling you to "be strong", because no doubt everyone else is telling you that right now. But you know, Juliette's death changed me, made me stronger in so many ways that I couldn't have imagined before. Not through trying to save her: in those days there was no hope for leukaemia victims, it was an absolute death sentence. After her death, I tried for a while to make sense of it, but could only see it as dark, bad. What possible good could ever be seen in a four-year-old child being taken from this earth? But then with the war and the Italian soldiers occupying Monteroule, I started to see it. I started to see Juliette's face in the children of Monteroule, pleading help me, save me!

'Up until then, I'd only been consumed with making money, building my little empire in Monteroule. But with the advent of the war, I realized I was in a position to actually do some good. In other towns and villages in Provence, we'd heard how hard the occupation had been at times: looting, stealing, property and businesses taken over, families split apart. By buying favour with the occupying soldiers, I was able to soften the impact on Monteroule. Your mother and father were just starting to think about having children when Captain Vitielli was keen to have Philip sent away. God knows what would have happened from thereon in. And there were many others. A Jewish family ran a small grocery and provisions store, and there was talk of having them sent away and their business taken over. But I swore blind that they were Catholic, even conspired with the local priest to have false Holy Communion papers prepared for them.

'From then on, every child laughing or playing in the streets of Monteroule, I'd see Juliette's face in them. And my step felt freer and lighter than it ever had before. It felt suddenly as if her death hadn't been for nothing.'

'Hervé told me what you did,' André said. 'I had no idea before that. And I think it's marvellous . . .' Still André had trouble saying 'father', even though at that moment he'd have been proud to call Gallinard father.

'But with you and your son, Joël, now, it's different, André. As I said, in those days with leukaemia, there was absolutely no hope. But now the success rates are a lot higher, and nobody is probably in a better position than you to take advantage of that.'

Success rates. Hope. Yet another singing from the same song-sheet as Marielle – but after the calamitous chain of events with the Spheros and Boisnard, the chances of saving Joël had never felt further away. He hadn't planned to say anything, but perhaps because Gallinard had in turn poured out his heart, he found himself sharing with Gallinard the tumultuous past week: an unscrupulous research institute stealing his discovery one side, a partner and his backers unwilling to budge on the other, and he and Joël caught in the middle with little other hope in sight.

Again Gallinard's breathing came across heavily, laboured, his words forced as if they were taking all of his strength.

'I had to learn how to be good, André. But from what I hear, you're a good man already. And maybe that's part of your problem: you're too good, too trusting. Maybe you have to take a leaf out of my old book: learn how to be tricky, devious. Not be afraid to break the rules. Because when I think back to it, I had to draw on a lot of those old wily ways in order to save Monteroule. And you might have to do the same now in order to save Joël.'

30

'Please, David . . . you've got to help me. I'm begging you.'

'You know it's difficult, me getting caught in the middle like this. I could lose my job.'

'You know I wouldn't ask if there were any other choice. And Joël is slipping fast. The way he is now, I can hardly see him lasting more than a month or two.'

'Oh, *Jesus* . . . André. You shouldn't do this to me. Put me in this position.'

Copell's tone became distraught, his breathing fractured, as he struggled with the conflicting emotions. There was a heavy pause before Lemoine spoke again.

'How long have we known each other, David? Over twenty years. Half a lifetime. And so you know I wouldn't claim precedence on macaitin without being a hundred per cent sure of my ground. And I think in your heart you know it too. You know they've pulled a fast one. I mean, look at that five-week delay without them saying anything – then the first thing they do is file with the NSC. And had you heard any mention of macaitin before at your end?'

'No . . . that's true. But then I'm in a different section to Stolk and her team. There's a lot of projects they work on that I don't get to hear about.'

Heavy sigh from Lemoine. 'Look, all I'm asking is that you dig about a bit and ask a few questions. And if, after doing that, you're satisfied that their claims over macaitin are just and true – it stops right there. I wouldn't expect you to help. But if you're not satisfied . . . I know you of old, David. You wouldn't rest easy with the knowledge that they'd done something like this. Even without the terrible extra pressure that Joël's illness has put on the whole affair.'

'OK . . . *OK*.' Copell's return sigh carried exasperation as much as defeat. 'Let me see what I can find out over the next few days. But no promises.'

Chisholm pressed stop and leant back in his chair. This time he'd be the one calling for an early meeting.

Marielle kissed his brow and lightly stroked one cheek as André put down his beer glass from a heavy slug.

'Don't worry . . . don't worry. He'll come through.'

'I'm not so sure.' André looked down despondently, and, after a second, took another strong gulp. By the second day with no response from David, he'd already started worrying. Now, day four and still nothing, he'd sunk back into abject gloom. All of Marielle's and Gallinard's urging not to give up hope had been for nothing. Without Copell's help, there was no hope, no chance left of them being able to fight back.

They'd gone to Jacques Borchaud's Bar Soupçon so as not to bump into anyone from ORI-gene – but unconsciously perhaps also as a reminder of happier times: himself, Marc, Marielle all together at the ISG, Eban still alive and Joël in perfect health. The bar was busy and becoming progressively noisier with its usual after-work crowd.

Charlotte was arriving back from Tunisia in only two days, and Joël was still off school. If he could get him back by tomorrow, at least then maybe he could fluff his way round the fact that he'd been off for so long, then . . . André stopped himself abruptly. What was the point? He'd have to tell her soon about Joël, as well as about his relationship with Marielle. The crushing inevitability of that made the game he was playing – choosing when and to whom he told the truth or lies just to buy time on confrontation – somehow pathetic. Or maybe he did it for some feeling of control; the last, pitiable vestige of control he had over anything. His life lay in tatters around him, and it was time to admit that – *to everyone*. Maybe then he'd also accept it, stop fooling himself and . . .

But as he looked across at Marielle, it felt wrong giving up. Gallinard too was telling him to be strong, fight back. Perhaps the two of them were there for him at this moment for a reason. Most of all, as the noise of the bar swam around him and he shuddered with the reminder – he couldn't give up because of Joël. He could almost hear his small voice like a shrill bell cutting through the cacophony of voices around: *'I feel sick again and can't stop shaking, Papa . . . What's wrong with me? What's wrong with me?'*

Marielle saw the pain etched in his face and the tears well quickly in his eyes, and she reached out and gripped a hand tightly, repeating, 'Don't worry . . . David will come through. I'm sure of it.'

But he had trouble focusing on her through his tears, the bar seeming to sway lazily around her, and among the echoing blur of surrounding voices, it became his mother's voice: *'I'm sorry, André . . . so sorry. I wanted to tell you earlier, but never found the courage. It would have broken your heart to know.'*

Maybe that's where he got it from, withholding the truth from everyone until the last moment. She'd hidden that secret from him for over forty years.

His mother had phoned him the day after he'd spoken to Gallinard; obviously they'd spoken together meanwhile. Then the next day he had Hervé on the phone telling him that Eric's parole had been successful. 'He's being released in ten days.' Some good news, at least.

André felt as if all the strands of his life were racing towards a crucial crossroads, yet he'd long ago lost the route map to any part of it. Worn down by fitful sleep from caring for Joël and the nightmare roller-coaster of the past weeks, André felt he couldn't make sense of anything any more. And now he'd probably had one drink too many to try and drown it all out. Even if he could find any clear direction as to how to fight on, he felt he no longer had the strength left.

He clutched Marielle's hand. 'Help me . . . *help me!*'

They went back to his place, again on the pretext of her helping out with Joël, but André was exhausted and fell asleep early while Marielle cradled and soothed him as if he were a child.

The rows of tombstones rose up quickly in his dreams, like dark ghosts that couldn't wait to mug him – though thankfully this time the mist obscuring them became steadily thicker, almost impenetrable, saved him from fully seeing them. Yet that quickly brought another fear: he couldn't see where he was going, and he could feel the mist thick and cloying in his nostrils and throat, choking him, as a harsh ringing suddenly broke him out of it. He heard Marielle's voice faintly in the background just before she called out to him.

'It's David!'

He jumped out of bed quickly and grabbed the phone. He was still clearing his head as David spoke, and for a moment the words felt unreal, still part of the dream and he hadn't yet awoken. Then he started repeating like a mantra, 'Thank you . . . Thank you, David . . . *Thank you*,' nodding eagerly with each one. 'You don't know what this means to me.' Then, as he hung up and the exhaustion and pent-up emotions of the past weeks finally became too much, he burst into tears and once again Marielle cradled him like a child.

André prayed that David had saved him from his nightmare in more ways than one.

The lab floor was quiet, and David Copell had a keen eye on a couple of lab assistants at the far end of the room, the only other people still there at nearly 7 p.m. – when Dani Stolk's voice came from the side, startling him.

'Were you planning to stay late tonight, David?'

'Yes . . . looks that way.' He glanced back at the file open on his desk. 'Something I'm a bit behind with, I was hoping to finish off.'

'Well . . . if it could wait until tomorrow night. There are problems with one of the elevators, and George downstairs has got them coming later to fix it. Both elevators will be out for a while, so he asked me if all the floors could be clear before they came – and I said I'd make sure everyone was gone by seven-thirty.' She shrugged. 'Sorry. But should be OK tomorrow. Also there's something I'd like virology to take a look at for me, if you've got the time, then?'

'Yes, yes ... sure,' he said, quickly snapping out of his disappointment.

For a moment, he'd worried that she'd cottoned on to his wanting to snoop around and was trying to prevent him staying late. But the offer seemed open for the following night, which became practically a re-run: the same file open before him, the same eagle-eye watching for everyone else to finally leave – except that this time there was a group of three labbies lingering on, and for a while he wondered whether he would ever be on his own.

Then, when they finally left, it was eerily silent. He could hear his own breathing, the tick of a clock on the wall, the hum of the mainframe and spectrometer at the far end of the room.

He honed his hearing beyond that for any sounds from the floor above. Dani Stolk had left an hour before with a quick look-in and nod in his direction. 'Hope you're OK with that stuff I left you. Let me know tomorrow if you have any problems with it.' Fifteen minutes later a labbie and a secretary left, then John Page shortly after. Nothing after that. Certainly, it sounded quiet up there, as if there was nobody remaining. Only one way to know for sure.

He headed out and up the marble staircase, his steps echoing ominously in the silence. He'd never stayed this late before, when nobody else was there. The weight of the silence felt alien, unsettling. As did the wide, empty space as he swung open the door to oncology and saw nobody there. But it was what he wanted. He went over to Senadhira's desk and opened the file Stolk had left him. Its words swam blandly in front of him, practically a blur. He hadn't read a single word of it earlier and certainly couldn't concentrate now.

He felt hot, his throat constricted. He looked anxiously towards the wall clock, its ticking now merging with the solid pounding of his pulse. He'd make as if he was looking through Stolk's notes for five minutes and hope meanwhile his nerves calmed down, then head up towards her office. If anything could possibly be found that would help André, it would be there.

*

356

'You managed to delay him, then?'

'Yes, till tomorrow night. Some story about the elevators needing maintenance.'

Another rushed after-work coffee-house meeting, this time at the XandO Café on 36th Street.

'OK, fine.' Chisholm nodded thoughtfully. 'A couple of days' delay would have been better – but if that's the best that could be done.'

'He seemed very anxious, said he had a file he was keen to work on. I thought pushing for an extra day would have been awkward.'

'Don't worry. It's tight, but I'm sure I can get everything set up by tomorrow.'

After a heavy pause, she asked, 'Just what is it you have planned for Copell?'

'I think this is one of those "Better you don't know" situations. That way, you don't later have to feel nervous or implicated, because, in the end, you didn't know what was going to happen. But put it this way – it gets rid of a number of our problems in one go: Lemoine and Copell, and the FBI snooping around.'

'Oh, right.' She was even more baffled and unsure, and although she felt the first pangs of warning, misgivings, she didn't pursue it. Chisholm's countenance, looking determinedly ahead, seemed to warn her off: that door is closed.

Chisholm took a sip of coffee and quickly moved on. 'Thinking about the FBI. The file back-ups we discussed shortly after their visit – have the copy files all been moved now?'

'Yes . . . everything was wrapped up over a week ago.'

'Good. Good.' Another couple of rapid, anxious sips of coffee, then Chisholm ended their meeting by mentioning that he'd decided to run with a press leak on Lemoine's past problems with the ISG now rather than later. 'Losing Copell's help is going to hit Lemoine hard, but I want to catch him with this while he's still winded, kill any possible chances of him fighting back.'

'OK.' Rain spots on the café window merged with those on her front window at home as she gazed out absently and replayed the previous night's conversation in her mind. In retrospect, she was able to home in on its small signals and nuances now more than then; at the time she'd been slightly numb and unfocused, straight after rushing from work and putting Copell off till tonight.

She looked at the trees at the end of her garden swaying in the breeze. She was alone that night, Allison was with her father. Copell would be alone in the Spheros building at that moment, too. What *did* Chisholm have planned for him?

'I'm sure I can get everything set up by tomorrow . . . Gets rid of a number of our problems in one go . . . Have the copy files all been moved?' As she trawled back through the conversation, she could feel the answer almost there, tantalizingly within reach. But then as her thoughts turned to Meikle and the FBI visit about the bombings, a part of her pushed it abruptly away again. Perhaps she was simply following Chisholm's dictate that it was best she didn't know – or was her own self-protectiveness kicking in because she didn't *want* to know, didn't want to face it?

Chisholm had given the story to Ben Flavell, one of the best East Coast stringers he knew to get a good medical story spread quickly and effectively.

Primary targets were the main US and French medical journals, then Philadelphia and Paris general press. Outside of that, whatever national and international journals would be interested in picking it up.

For Flavell, Chisholm's criteria list was all but redundant; that was more or less already how he saw the lie of the main interest areas, and he planned his calls accordingly.

Within an hour, he'd made his national medical journal and Philadelphia press calls, then he phoned Paris. With each call, he made sure to pass on Chisholm's stipulation that the story be held back for two days, and this in turn was dutifully passed on by the news agency Flavell regularly used in Paris.

But one evening newspaper, *Le Soir* – perhaps because that delay would give their main daily competitors several hours lead on them, or because they interpreted that with the time difference, by the time most of their readers saw the story it would be early morning in Philadelphia in any case – decided to jump the gun and run the story the day before.

The first of them to see the *Le Soir* story was Marc Goffinet, who had stopped for a coffee at a nearby café on his way home after another late night at ORI-gene, where André and Marielle were still finishing up.

His cup froze midway towards his mouth as the article caught his eye, two columns at the bottom of page five, stayed in that position for almost a minute as he rapidly scanned through, then was put down with a jolt. He slammed down some coins equally noisily and bolted from the café.

André heard the urgent voices seconds before Marc and Marielle came into view through his glass screen and then burst into his office. Marielle was waving *Le Soir* in one hand.

'We've got a problem, André. A big problem.' She had the paper already folded at page five, and prodded a finger at the offending article as she laid it on his desk facing him.

One step behind her and breathless, Marc simply nodded. And something else in Goffinet's face at that instant – as if he was hurt and confused as much as worried – that André didn't comprehend until he started reading the article. Goffinet knew the full history with Eban and the ISG, but little of this new dilemma now with Joël being so ill. Yet another on André's long list for truth-telling that he hadn't yet got around to.

'Oh Jesus!' André jumped up from his chair, clutching one hand at his hair. *'Jesus!'*

'I know.' Marielle nodded forlornly. 'Now with that story out, it makes trying to fight back almost impossible. They've won before we've even started. And once Boisnard's backers see it, no doubt he'll have even more problems with them. They'll probably pull the plug straight away.'

André caught the quick look from Goffinet to him and Marielle. Something else he hadn't known about.

'Not just that,' André said. He looked anxiously at his watch. 'Charlotte arrives in half an hour. If she sees this . . . it will tear her apart.'

'But you were going to tell her soon anyway.'

'I know . . . I know.' He bit lightly at the back of his knuckles, then gestured theatrically with the same hand. 'But not like this . . . with half the world knowing before her.'

Marielle nodded and looked down like a chastened schoolgirl. Perhaps she'd meant that because he was dreading telling Charlotte – someone doing the job for him partly let him off of the hook.

'I need to get out to the airport before she has a chance of seeing this.' André lifted the paper and slapped it with the back of one hand.

'I'll . . . I'll run you out there,' Marielle offered. 'I'm parked just down the road. It could take you a while to find a cab this time of night.'

'Thanks.' André grabbed his jacket and glanced again at his watch as they headed out. Orly airport from the city centre was normally thirty-five minutes' drive. 'If her flight's on time, she'll already be through customs by the time we get there.'

'Well – let's just hope that it's delayed.' Marielle gave a taut, challenging smile. 'Or that I can beat the traffic.'

The drive to Orly through the night-time traffic was hair-raising, yet strangely exhilarating. Marielle wove and threaded her small car, a blue Renault 5, through seemingly impossible spaces, accelerated maniacally on clear stretches, and, when the path ahead again looked blocked, would at the last moment find another gap and cut across and through once more.

Her dark hair flipped wildly from side to side as she swerved, spun and fish-tailed through the traffic, traded words and gestures with the occasional irate car- or truck-driver – yet at no time did she appear anything less than in complete control. And André was reminded not only just how good she was for him, but of the strong contrast to Charlotte – whom they were now racing towards so that he could save her from breakdown number three. Or was it four? He'd lost count. And perhaps that too was part of the attraction: Marielle's strength and confidence. The world's healer, if some of his more illustrious past press were to be believed – but now he felt so worn down and battered, it seemed he hardly had the strength to take care of one person more, let alone . . .

And what were the press saying now:

'Compassionate grounds' was the original claim, but it appears that the main reason for 'Darwin Man' André Lemoine's sudden departure from the ISG three years ago was his chancing his arm with a radical cure for his adopted son, Eban, who died only days before him leaving . . . Now it looks as if much the same situation is rearing its head again in Lemoine's battle with Philadelphia's Spheros Institute over macaitin, a revolutionary new cancer treatment. Lemoine is claiming precedence in discovery of macaitin, but what he has not openly declared is that his biological son, Joël, is dying from leukaemia . . . History is repeating itself, the Spheros Institute claim: 'Yet again, as with his past débâcle with the ISG, it appears that Dr Lemoine has not heeded the ethical divide between work and family. And this, we are convinced, is largely behind the current unfortunate situation with Dr Lemoine's false claim over macaitin,' Spheros Institute Director, Julius Chisholm, said yesterday.

The article seared through André's mind as Marielle picked up speed through the city outskirts.

Marielle was right. There was little or no hope remaining . . . unless David could find something that would point to the Spheros making a false claim. He'd be there that night, clandestinely searching through computer files. Apparently he'd been delayed from doing so the previous night.

Marielle parked in South Terminal short-term stay, and they quickly became out of breath as they ran along the long concourse towards international arrivals. André's head was spinning as they finally stopped and looked up at the arrivals board. He had trouble focusing, and it was Marielle who spotted it first.

'Air Tunis. Delayed.' Marielle let out a relieved breath and gave André's arm a reassuring squeeze. 'We got here in time.'

But in the end the delay was almost two hours, and André

became anxious again during the long wait. Over a chain of coffees to kill the time, Marielle's placating words and occasional hugs did little to calm him before they finally went across to join the taxi drivers holding up placards. Maybe he too should hold up a placard: Charlotte Lemoine to see her husband before reading *Le Soir*. He needs to tell her that her son is dying, because half of Paris already knows.

'There! *There!*'

Marielle's shout came almost at the same time he spotted Charlotte and Porcelet. She smiled as she saw him, but it quickly took a quizzical turn. He returned it tightly, anxiously.

'André, nice to see you!' she exclaimed as she approached. 'But you needn't have come out to meet me, you know. I'm a big girl now.'

'There's something I have to tell you,' André said, guiding her lightly by the arm away from blocking the exiting throng.

'Couldn't it have waited?' She put down her suitcase and flipped back her hair. 'Oh God. It was so hot on the flight back. And the stewardesses so slow. It took me a lifetime to get a drink.'

'No, no. It couldn't wait.' His tone lowered. 'We need to talk.'

Porcelet picked up on the signal and nodded towards them. 'I . . . I'll just grab a couple of things. I won't be a minute.'

But Charlotte was oblivious, still caught up in the rush and excitement of the trip. 'Tunisia was marvellous, but, oh, the women. Still stuck in the dark ages, no dress sense. And the driving! You took your life in your hands every time you . . .'

'Charlotte, *please!*' His grip on her arm tightened and he led her a couple of yards further away from the exiting crowd. 'This is serious! It's about Joël.'

Her eyes narrowed. 'What about Joël? What's happened to him?'

But now the moment was upon him, looking into her pleading, desperate eyes, he didn't think he could say it. *Our son is dying!* Not here amongst the crowds and turmoil, his head spinning with the echo of the flight announcements and the thrum of activity, his legs feeling suddenly weak, about to give way, his pulse pounding. He swallowed hard. 'He . . . it's . . .'

Over on the far side of the terminal, Porcelet had picked up a newspaper and a packet of mints, and, with a quick glance across to see that they were still engrossed in conversation, went to the nearest bench seat and opened the paper.

'*What is it?*' Now it was Charlotte's turn to grip André's arm as he fumbled for the words. 'What's happened to Joël?'

'Let's . . . let's go over there.' He nodded towards the nearest seats. He needed to get away from the main throng. Trembling and his legs like jelly, he feared he might collapse at any second.

'What is it?' she pressed. 'Is he ill again? Has he been in an accident?'

'No, no . . . not that. Well, he's been ill, but it's more than that . . . *he* . . .' He looked desperately around the milling crowds and at Marielle for inspiration for how best to say it, and suddenly the thought struck: *David!* The newspaper story had without doubt been fed from the Spheros – but how had they known about Eban and the ISG, and now Joël's illness? The only way was through them listening in to his telephone conversation with David. And if they'd listened in to that – they'd have also have heard when David offered to stay late and snoop around. That's why there'd been a day's delay! They were setting him up. It was a trap!

'Oh God! . . . *Jesus* . . . *no!*' He fumbled for his mobile and address book and quickly flipped through for David's number. He started dialling.

'For God's sake, André, what is it with Joël?' Her grip was now so tight on his arm that her nails dug in painfully. 'Don't leave me hanging like this!'

'Please . . . *please!* Only one second.' André held a hand up defensively, half turning from her. 'Someone trying to help Joël . . . I suddenly realized he's in danger.' It started ringing.

Charlotte's face was contorted in confusion and panic. A nice holiday to get her calm and settled, her equilibrium back, and André had reduced her to a quivering wreck in only seconds. Maybe they were simply no good for each other.

It kept ringing: two, three times . . .

As André looked aimlessly around the terminal, he met Porcelet's

363

eyes looking keenly up from his newspaper across at him. And as Porcelet folded the newspaper closed, André caught a glimpse of its banner – *Le Soir* – and in that instant, with Porcelet's gaze staying steadily on him, he knew that Porcelet had worked out the reason for the panic to meet Charlotte at the airport.

Porcelet looked down at the floor for a moment, as if uncertain, undecided – then stood up and started his way across.

Four rings . . . *five*. 'Come on, David! *Come on!*' André started to sweat with the heat, noise and panic of the moment. Porcelet was a good forty yards away at the far side of the terminal, but picking up pace towards them. He'd have to ring off and explain before Porcelet got to them with the newspaper!

Of all the times he'd mentally prepared for this moment, it had always been in a quiet restaurant or the privacy of his place or hers, clasping her hands tight as he looked soulfully into her eyes; not surrounded by crowds and noise and with his mind half on something else. Yet that had been the pattern of so much of his life: continually putting off anything he didn't want to face, until in the end events overtook him – he had no choice on how or where they happened.

Porcelet was only thirty yards away, sifting his way rapidly through the crowd. If David answered now, he wouldn't even be able to start explaining to Charlotte before Porcelet reached them. One more ring, then he'd give up.

The clock ticking on the far wall seemed louder with each moment David waited. He tapped a couple of fingers on the desktop as a distraction, but that too seemed ominously loud; and, as it fell in time with his pulse, he stopped abruptly. Only the ticking clock was left.

And beyond that, as his hearing became sharply attuned, sounds reached him that he'd never been aware of before: the faint thrum of traffic heading along Chestnut Street, a siren drifting from the far reaches of the city; but, overlaying that, threatening to smother all else, the sounds from his own body: his breath falling, shallow and erratic, his heart pounding, almost a drum-beat as it pumped the pulse at his temples. He gently rubbed them to ease his tension. *Relax.* Take a deep breath . . . for a second all he was left with again was the ticking clock and the background city thrum before his heavy exhalation drowned it out, like a tidal wave.

Over five minutes had passed. It was time. He looked from Senadhira's computer towards the stairs leading to Stolk's office as if they were a gallows or green-mile walk. He was dreading it.

With another heavy exhalation he went across and started his way up, his legs leaden and his hand shaking as it gripped the stair rail.

'Please, David . . . you've got to help me. I'm begging you.'

Despite the emotional plea and his long friendship with André, he would probably have balked at helping if he hadn't also gained some inside information to add ballast to André's claim. The first couple of days that hadn't been forthcoming, everyone he spoke to was full of nothing but praise for the venerable Dr Danielle Stolk: *'She's turned that department around . . . I doubt her predecessor, Kalpenski, could have put them in the running for a Gifford Award.' 'She's young – so maybe there's a few that'll speak bad about her out of professional jealousy. Not me.'* His concerns dug deeper. He wanted to believe André, but what if – as had happened with Eban – Joël's illness had pushed André's professional judgement a step too far. Then he spoke to Kirsten Bremner.

Stolk's office was before him, some faint light filtering in from the corridor. He swung open the door, his hand pausing for a second by the light switch before flicking it on. He could work just with the glow from the computer screen, but if George came up it would look as if he was snooping if he worked in the half dark. He sat at her desk and booted up her computer.

'Yeah. It wouldn't surprise me if she pulled a stunt like that. She did pretty much the same with me over a P53 paper I prepared a few years back. She claimed its main findings as hers rather than mine. But you really want to speak to Russ Hebbard. He got shafted big time over something similar. Claims that was the main reason she got promoted instead of him. He left about the time you joined – he's with IME now.'

As the program symbols and files showed on screen, he stayed perfectly still and held his breath, listening to the same background thrum of traffic, another clock ticking from the adjoining office. There were no other sounds. No footsteps on the stairs or corridor, no elevator rising with George to check the floors again. He keyed in the linked access he'd read over Senadhira's shoulder the day before, then started double-clicking symbols and checking files.

'Oooh! Our dear Dani Stolk. Better known by those she's crossed as "Dagger Stalk" from the way she sneaks up and plunges home the knife without them hardly noticing. Oh, she caught me good. Real good. That's why I left in the end. She took the main position I was after – so there wasn't much point in hanging around. But what she did to me was nothing to what she did to Murray Kalpenski. He's all but washed up from what I hear, still hasn't found a placing anywhere else. He's the guy you really want to speak to.'

He'd got hold of Hebbard the day after speaking to Kirsten Bremner, but Kalpenski was more elusive. After getting no reply to his three messages left over the next thirty-six hours, he phoned André back. He had more than enough already to believe André's claim, and couldn't afford to lose more time.

'. . . Joël is slipping fast. The way he is now, I can't see him lasting more than a month or two.'

David went immediately for the private, non-networked files, sifting swiftly through for anything that looked like it might have a macaitin or Gifford connection. Two groups of files tagged *maitl1–4* and *Gifd1–6* looked the most likely, but when he opened them up they were just general, non-related correspondence. He kept hunting through, trying a succession of more obscurely named files, but nothing there either.

Where? For God's sake, where? His head ached, felt close to bursting with tension.

He tried half a dozen more possibles with no joy, then in desperation went into file history and deletions. After only seconds of scrolling through, a group of files – *maict1–14* – made him sit forward sharply. Then, half a page down, another set: *Giffa1–19*. The entire first batch and six of the Giffa files had been transferred and then deleted two days ago, the rest yesterday afternoon. He attempted recovering one of the Giffa files, but its contents had been emptied before deletion. He tried four more 'Giffa's and six 'maict's with the same result.

Whoever had transferred and deleted the files had covered their tracks, almost as if they knew somebody might come looking. *Two days ago?* Only the day after he'd spoken to André to say he'd help. Surely not? Surely they hadn't known he'd come snooping? But then there was that one-day delay from Stolk. What was that for? And she'd also conveniently given him a file to handle: the ideal cover if he wanted to snoop on her computer.

David's breathing fell fast and shallow, his heart pounding so hard that it took him a moment to pick out the ringing beyond it. He'd heard an internal phone ringing on another floor shortly after everyone left, but this was different; fainter, barely discernible, but familiar: his own mobile ringing! He'd left it downstairs on his desktop.

It seemed to go on ringing for ever. Who could it be? He'd told Pamela he'd be working late – but maybe she'd remembered something she wanted him to pick up on his way home. Finally, it stopped ringing.

Knowing that they might have suspected he'd snoop made it all the worse, as if there were invisible eyes watching him from every corner. He looked around. There was a CCTV camera in Stolk's office, but, with only so many monitors downstairs, George would probably have the view fixed on the corridor outside.

He was suddenly keen to shut down and get out before George came up to check. He quickly scanned through for any other likely files, found two, and was halfway through writing down the two main file groups, when – as if on cue and George had silently read his thoughts – he heard the swish of the elevator starting to rise. Or was he imagining it? Again he held his breath and homed in on sounds beyond his own heartbeat pounding – but there was no doubt: the steady swish and hum of the elevator rising sounded ominously loud in the cavernous silence of the building. He quickly noted the terminal the files had been transferred to, No. 38, and came out of file history.

But just as he clicked to exit Windows, the computer screen went black and all the lights went out. His heart froze. All the lights on the floor were off too – it was pitch dark. He shuffled over to the window and looked out: lights were still on in buildings close by, but he couldn't see any light coming from the floors below. It wasn't a general power outage – only the Spheros building was affected.

Now the cocoon of silence around him was total: no elevator rising, no ticking clock. *Nothing*. Only the sound of his own breathing and rapid heartbeat.

Surely the emergency generator and lights would come on at any second? But it stayed obstinately dark, only a weak diffused glow filtering in from the city lights outside. David tentatively made his way back to Stolk's desk.

He should wait for the power to come back on, then shut down her computer properly; otherwise she'd know in the morning that it had been in use when the power went. Also, if he tried to make it out now, negotiating the stairs would be a nightmare: pitch black without the benefit on any irradiated city light.

A sudden sound made his nerves jump: faint shuffling and movement on the stairs, not clear at first beyond his own fractured breathing. He attuned his hearing: footsteps on the stairs! Then he picked out the faint, shifting beam of a penlight. George had come out of the elevator and made the rest of the way up by foot.

'George!' he called out; a strained, hoarse whisper.

No answer.

'*George!*' Louder this time, clearly audible on the stairs.

Again no answer, though this time the footsteps froze and the penlight went out. After a few seconds, they continued moving up towards him.

David felt his skin prickle with fear, as if invisible electricity in the air was drawing every nerve end to the surface. His whole body felt alive with it, plugged into each small movement of the person approaching. No, two people! The shuffling merged at points – it couldn't be the footfall of just one person.

'George!' David called out once more in desperation. Then, when again only silence returned: 'Who's there? *Who is it?*'

His voice, cracking with fear, sounded strangely distant, disembodied, and his heartbeat and the rush of blood through his head was now so loud that he had to strain to hear above it. But still there was no answer, only the same shuffling footsteps moving steadily towards him.

Patrol Officer Frank Jukes was slightly out of breath from the adrenalin rush of the car chase as he confronted the two youths: late teens, early twenties, both Hispanic-looking, the driver with his hair slicked back tightly into a small pony-tail, the other with a half-inch cut the size of a skull cap on top, graded down at one-inch intervals like a Javan mountain rice terrace until completely shaved at mid-ear.

It had started off a quiet night. He'd positioned himself in an ideal blind-spot pull-in off Walnut Street, one he'd used several times before with great success – but after forty minutes he still hadn't seen a speeder. Perhaps because it was a weekday and not particularly late. He started to become tired and irritable, lulled into a half-sleep by the steady, almost predictable flow of traffic – when a steel-blue Pontiac Sunbird with a dark-blue, red-edged flame motif along each side flashed past. He was slow in pulling out and putting on his siren, and it took him almost half a mile to catch up and for them to finally slow so that he could pull them over.

They looked a lively pair, so he took no chances. He got them both out of the car and gave them a rapid pat down before asking for licence and registration.

'So, what's the rush?' he asked pony-tail. He angled his torch to reduce the glare from the licence: Hector Duran. Twenty-two years old.

'I was rushing to see my sister. She's ill in hospital.'

'Well, that's original.' Jukes smiled incredulously. 'At least it's not your dying mother?'

Java-cut sniggered. 'No, that was last week.'

'*Callate*, man!' Pony-tail hissed at his friend. 'You trying to make it worse for me.'

Jukes studied them warily, trying to weigh them up. Java-cut looked gone, his eyes distant, unfocused. His friend seemed more alert, but also more nervous, frantic, as if he had something to hide. One of his fingers tapped nervously against the side of his car.

'OK. What have you been taking?' Jukes asked.

'Taking?' Java-cut rolled his eyes and sighed. 'We nooo been taking nothin', man. We're no thieves. Just ask my mother – or his. She out of hospital now.' He guffawed wildly at his own joke, alone. His friend and Jukes remained stony-faced.

Jukes was fast losing his patience. 'You know what I mean.'

'Ooooh, that kind of taking.' Java-cut rolled his eyes again, this time heavenward. He waved one arm theatrically. 'Everything, man. You name it.'

'Don't listen to him,' Pony-tail cut in. 'He don't know what he's saying.'

'What . . . is he drunk? Drugged?' Jukes pressed. 'Which is it?'

'No . . . no. Well, you know . . . I mean, even if he is.' Pony-tail's gestures became more desperate as he struggled to explain, then he prodded his own chest. 'Me . . . I ain't taken nothing. All night, I . . .'

They were disturbed by the sudden screech of tyres from a turning sixty yards away on the opposite side. A grey van with tinted windows pulled out and quickly picked up speed along 23rd Street. Jukes looked at it thoughtfully for a second before bringing his attention back. It was turning out to be a lively night after all, but he couldn't chase every errant car in the city.

'. . . I never took a thing,' Pony-tail finished. 'Clean, man . . . clean.' He held both hands out imploringly.

'Look, I don't know if this is a routine you use every week, or it's just something you've borrowed from Cheech and Chong, but . . .'

'*Who?*' Java-cut squinted.

'Never mind.' Wrong generation. 'The thing is, I'm going to have to take you in and run . . .'

Jukes instinctively ducked and put one hand over his head as the explosion came. It boomed like thunder and lit up the night sky, and he felt his ear-drums press in as if his head was going to burst. He felt a sting to one cheek, and as he straightened up he saw a couple of blood specks on Java-cut's neck and forehead. He'd stayed open-mouthed staring at the building along the street: twenty-plus storeys with a wedding-cake formation for the uppermost floors, the explosion had taken place about six floors from the top.

'Wow!' Java-cut exclaimed. 'Is that just in my head, man, or for real?'

Jukes wished now that he'd pursued the van, rather than waste his time with these two dopers. Unless he tweaked the details, his later report could read embarrassingly. He hadn't noted any part of the registration or even what State it was from.

'I . . . I've got something to do now,' he said, running back to his car.

'No shit,' said pony-tail, a sly smile crossing his face for the first time.

His friend stayed open-mouthed, staring at the residual fire and smoke streaming from the building. Two stark sirens sounded in the distance, moving closer.

31

'When were you finally planning to tell me?'

'Soon. Soon.'

'What? When he was virtually on his death-bed and so ill I couldn't miss the symptoms – then you'd finally tell me what was wrong?'

'No, no. Of course not.' André cradled his head in one hand, as Charlotte had done when he'd first told her the news. Except that she'd stayed in the same position for almost a full minute before anything more was said. The hustle and bustle of the terminal around them hadn't helped. He'd held off Porcelet with an outstretched hand and a muttered, 'I'm dealing with it now,' as Porcelet had come within a few yards of them – but Porcelet's step had already slowed as he saw them start talking, and André's glare at the *Le Soir* in his hand did the rest. Porcelet heeded the warning and backtracked to take a seat eight yards from them. 'I . . . I kept hanging on for brighter, more hopeful news to try and soften the blow. And time just drifted by.'

André reached out and clasped her hand reassuringly, as much for him as for her. 'Also, you had so many of your own problems and pressures that there never seemed a right time to tell you something like this. I . . . I felt that I just couldn't burden you. You'd completely cave in.'

'*Don't* . . . don't blame me for this.' She chewed at her bottom lip and pulled her hand away, her eyes darting rapidly at the floor, as if it might hold some answers.

When she looked up again, she asked a chain of questions to get everything clear in her mind, and André painted things as best he could without being openly misleading.

Her spirits raised a bit at the mention of the possible breakthrough with macaitin, then immediately slipped back when he came to the current battle with the Spheros and the newspaper article. He gestured towards Porcelet and the *Le Soir* folded in his lap.

'*What?*' Charlotte's breath seemed suddenly trapped in her throat. She waved one hand wildly, almost slapping his arm. 'Is that why you're telling me now? Because half of Paris already knows?'

He felt his face flush with the directness of her stare and the hurt he saw there. There was little point in denying it. He gripped her hands tighter. 'You think I wanted to do this here? Telling you that our son is dying surrounded by all of these people . . .' He waved one arm equally wildly. 'While the PA announces that the flight to Istanbul is delayed? Of course not. I had a quiet night planned in a restaurant or at home to tell you. But in the end events overtook me, and this –' he gestured again towards Porcelet and the newspaper – 'would have been no way for you to find out. Through *Le Soir*'s medical correspondent.'

Charlotte nodded knowingly, and in that moment something sparked between them; a soulfulness and understanding in her eyes that hadn't been there for many years.

Her eyes filled, but she held back from completely breaking down. Perhaps the one advantage of where they were – she'd have felt awkward, embarrassed with so many people around.

But he felt her hands trembling as she fought to keep control, with the strength of her emotions shown most as she pulled her hands free and gripped his shoulder, shaking him to emphasize her words.

'Fight them, André. Fight them with whatever it takes.' Her fingernails dug into him as she gave him one last shake, then hugged him. 'Don't let Joël die.' A hoarse, tremulous whisper close to his ear that sent a shiver down his spine.

'David's in Philadelphia trying to get some information right now. Trying to help us.'

It reminded André that he still had to contact David urgently, and, after a parting hug with Charlotte, heading back to the car with Marielle, he tried again – but his call went into an automated carrier message service. Then the same message the four further times he tried later.

Marielle stayed with him for the rest of the night – though mainly as an emotional bolster; he felt too drained for them to make love. Yet, along with his mounting worries over David, what remained with him most during those hours, particularly as he was struggling to get to sleep, were Charlotte's eyes as she'd implored him and shaken home her message.

'*Fight them, André. Fight them with whatever it takes.*' Her pitiful, pleading eyes haunted him as he finally drifted off, and at some point in the night he felt her shaking him again in his dreams. '*Don't let Joël die.*' Her touch so real that he felt his whole body shudder in response.

'André, André . . . *André.*'

He woke up with a jolt as he realized that Marielle was shaking his shoulder. He'd been sweating heavily, and it felt suddenly cold against his skin. He blinked and focused on the telephone in her hand.

'It's Pamela Copell, calling from Philadelphia. It's about David.'

What stuck in Wenner's mind most was looking down through the ragged hole left by the explosion in the elevator shaft.

'That's what caused the critical injury,' said Philadelphia PD's Lieutenant Jack Farrell, staring down through the hole alongside him. 'The elevator got trapped between the sixth and seventh floors when the power was cut, then the explosion severed the cables. The fatality was in the office just behind. They caught the worst of the explosion. Couldn't have been more than fifteen, twenty feet away from it at the time.'

Wenner trawled back in his mind for key clues and anything he might have missed on the flight back from Philadelphia, the first chance he'd had to draw breath in what had ended up being a long night. The call had come through from Philadelphia PD to the Atlanta field office just before 11 p.m., and they'd phoned him at home straight away. He raised Batz the minute he'd put the phone down from them, and an hour and a half later they were on a red-eye flight bound for Philadelphia.

'Do we know who they are?'

'George Hanley, the building's security guard, was the one in the elevator. And a researcher, David Copell, the fatality. He was so near the blast that it's doubtful we'll get a match on dentals, just DNA on the bones we found, pretty heavily carboned from the fire. But there's no doubt it's him. He was identified on a security video by head of security, Craig Berwick, only minutes before the explosion. Copell was in the office just back there.'

'Any chance that he could have made it out in that time gap?'

'Doesn't look like it. No elevators working, and no light to find his way on the stairs. But just to make sure, we phoned his home and spoke to his wife. She hadn't seen him and expected him back hours ago. He didn't make it out.'

Farrell confirmed that he'd have the DNA results in three or four days. Berwick had come along with one of the Spheros directors, Donald Bradson, but Farrell had spoken by phone to another of the directors, Julius Chisholm, in San Francisco on business. He'd finished with them just over an hour ago. Wenner nodded, commenting that he'd met both Berwick and Chisholm along with another doctor only a couple of months back when he'd been doing his rounds warning about possible bombings.

'Seems ominous, that warning, now.' More ominous than he'd thought at the time, he contemplated on the return flight, staring beyond his brooding reflection in the plane window at the mist and clouds drifting past. The second fatality, another critical, and only a couple of months after the last bombing. Both the body count and the frequency were on the up.

Some distant lights appeared through the clouds. Charlotte or Greenville: it was too early to be Atlanta.

'At least it narrows things down,' Batz commented. 'Like ten green bottles.'

'Yeah, ten green bottles,' Wenner echoed drolly, a wry smile creasing his lips. Hopefully it would be that simple. Now that it couldn't be the Spheros either – that left only seven more prime Gifford contenders. And among those, who would see MIT and the Spheros as the most threat? With any luck, it might narrow down to only two or three possibles. But still he had the nagging feeling that he was missing something vital in the pattern.

Perhaps he'd gain more clarity when he'd got some sleep. One thing would certainly change now with the second fatality, he reminded himself. His section head, Mike Leverett, had promised him the help of an extra four or five staffers, and the prospect of half the squad room at full steam at his every command and finger-click was irresistible. He doubted he'd bother going home for a sleep break, he'd head straight in and work through.

The case having simmered slowly for so long, he had the unsettling feeling that the heat had suddenly been turned up high. There was no time to lose.

'I had no idea you were going to do what you did. I'd have never agreed to it.'

Dani had tracked down Chisholm to San Francisco's Palomar hotel, and the anger in her voice was evident. The first time Chisholm had heard her like that.

'This isn't either the time or place to talk about this. Where are you calling from? Home? Give me the number, I'll call you straight back.'

Dani waited almost forty anxious minutes for the return call. Typical Chisholm, she thought. Playing her, making her hang on and sweat. But it sounded as if he'd also used the time to prepare; a cool, measured monotone that abided no interruption.

'It was the only way to deal with everything. We had the FBI on our backs, snooping around, and Copell left out there wouldn't have gone away. If we'd ousted him like Kalpenski, he'd have simply gone to the NSC and reported that he suspected wrongdoing – that Lemoine contacted him way before our filing with them. He'd have caused all manner of problems. This way – as I say, the *only* way I'm afraid that I could see – we got rid of both problems in one. Now the FBI will be convinced that we can't be behind the bombings and will focus on other Gifford contenders.'

Dani felt herself go cold. She'd always suspected, but this was the first time Chisholm had openly admitted being behind the bombings. She felt immediately uncomfortable at the use of 'we'.

'If you'll remember, I didn't know about those either. Once again, like now – you were acting very much on your own.'

'Don't get all sanctimonious with me. Not after what you did to Hebbard and Kalpenski – not to mention your own mother.'

'*What?*' Dani wheezed as if she'd taken a stomach blow. 'You know about that?' Again, it was something she'd suspected before, but this was the first time it was out in the open between them.

'Of course. I've known about it right from the start. It was one of the things that I thought would make you ideal. Maybe I was wrong.'

Dani swallowed hard, struggling to gather her composure. 'But this is different,' she spluttered. 'We're talking about you taking a man's life.'

'Yeah. Someone that I hardly knew, meant nothing to me. Whereas your mother . . . ooooh, different ball game, I would think.'

Dani sensed that Chisholm was purposely teasing and taunting her, but she couldn't resist countering. 'You can't compare what you've done to that. And there's a lot you don't know about what happened with my mother. There's two sides to the story.'

'Oh, I know a lot more than you realize. Your mother suffered a stroke not long after, and her health has declined a lot more since the court case, I understand. You're a doctor – you'd have known full well what something like this would have done to her at her age.'

'I suffered too,' she defended. 'Particularly in the run-up to the court case.'

'Yeah, in the same way that you suffered with the rape attempt from Kalpenski. Good heart-on-the-sleeve job that was to get the family sympathy vote. You should have got an Oscar.'

'That's ridiculous. I was bound to be upset.' She tried to sound bold, despite the tremor in her voice. She'd phoned Chisholm to give him a piece of her mind, but he'd quickly flipped her over and given her far worse back. As ever, the master.

'She loved and trusted you,' Chisholm said. 'You couldn't have hurt her more if you'd run a knife straight through her. And perhaps, given how everything turned out, that would have been less torturous, less cruel.'

Dani felt tears welling, tears she'd long held back. 'You don't understand,' she protested. 'It wasn't just about her, it was about . . .'

'What? Your brother?' Chisholm taunted. 'Aaah. Did she always favour him over you? Not appreciate you as much as you felt you deserved? Is that what you want from me and the rest of the world: appreciation? To make up for what you felt you didn't get from your mother. Is that why the relentless pursuit for glory?'

Dani felt Chisholm's words cut her to the bone, strip her psychologically bare in a way that nobody had done before. But he was certainly right about one thing: he knew far more about her family background than she'd realized.

'I . . . I don't have time for this now.'

'No, no. Of course not. You sound upset, distraught. But before you go – do you know what the investigator I put on to you said?'

Despite herself, despite her skin crawling as Chisholm gloatingly laid bare her emotions, her curiosity stayed her. And Chisholm knew it.

'. . . He said that in his line of work he'd dealt with the lowest of the low: drug dealers, mafia villains, you name it. And he couldn't imagine even them doing to their mothers what you did to yours. In fact, despite their many, many failings – most of them revered their mothers. Put them on a pedestal, would do anything to protect them. Not exactly an ideal epitaph: "Worse than the lowest of the low".'

Dani's stomach sank. Is that what people thought about what she'd done to her mother? So far she'd only been able to guess at the behind-the-back jibes and whispers. 'I . . . I've . . .'

'I know. You've got to go.' Chisholm's voice suddenly dropped, becoming menacing. 'But don't ever again admonish me, tell me what I should or shouldn't be doing. You're simply not in a position to moralize.' The phone was slammed down abruptly.

Dani stared numbly at the dead receiver for a moment, her

breath falling fast and shallow, before finally, with a trembling hand, she placed it back.

She gently closed her eyes and started weeping.

'What did you say your name was?'

'Tim. Tim McKay. I'm a friend of David Copell's. Just before he . . . well, before the bomb incident, he told me he talked with both Kirsten Bremner and Russ Hebbard about Danielle Stolk's more underhand, duplicitous side – and Hebbard mentioned your name. David was interested because an ex-colleague in Paris has accused her of claiming a breakthrough find of his as her own. But unfortunately he never got the chance to speak to you before the bombing.'

'Terrible business that. Terrible,' Kalpenski mused. 'And I'm so sorry for what happened to your friend.' He coughed and took a fresh breath, as if he was also gathering his thoughts. 'She's certainly bad news, that Dr Stolk. And of course what's happened with this fellow in Paris has her trademarks all over it after what happened with Bremner and Hebbard – not to mention myself.'

McKay listened carefully and made occasional notes as Kalpenski related the sorry saga of his run-in with Stolk and him finally having to resign.

'Part of the deal was that it would be clean, they'd keep quiet any claims of sexual harassment. But I suspect they didn't even bother to keep to that part, because one way or another rumours seem to have spread on the grapevine. Certainly, I haven't been able to get a whiff of a placement since. However, at least all of that free time has had one benefit: the chance to dig up a bit of dirt on our dear Dr Stolk.' Another deep breath, which lapsed into a fit of coughing before being cut short. 'Her brother was an absolute mine of information, and what happened between her and her mother made my run-in with her pale in comparison. A real Cane and Abel tale.'

McKay sensed from Kalpenski's build-up that this was a pivotal story, and he stayed silent as it unfolded.

'Their mother, seventy-six at the time, owned a big house in the Manayunk area of Philadelphia that had been left in trust in the brother's name for years. The reasons for this were partly to avoid inheritance tax, but also because his company – he was a property developer – had paid for some improvements to her house a few years before. There was an agreement between them that should anything happen to her, the house should be sold, and, after repayment of the cost of the improvements – which amounted to no more than fifteen per cent of the value of the property – the proceeds should be divided equally between her two children: Simon and his sister, Danielle.

'But Simon's business started to have problems. The mother agreed he could take out a loan equal to the improvements he'd made to the property, but things got steadily worse from there. Teetering on the edge of chapter eleven and fearing bankruptcy, he suggested that his mother's house go into his sister's name under a similar trust arrangement to protect it from the bank and other possible creditors. As part of the agreement, the sister increased her own mortgage to cover the bank loan, and so the trust arrangement became a mirror image of that previously with the brother: if the property was to be sold, she'd deduct the fifteen per cent to cover the loan and the rest would be her mother's; or to be shared equally between Dani and Simon should anything happen to their mother. The only problem was that everything was done in such a rush that they didn't put the trust arrangement in writing. Besides, they trusted her. She was family.'

Kalpenski took a fresh breath, and already McKay could see what was coming. 'Move the clock forward four years, and the mother wants to sell the place, clear the small loan, and move into a smaller place. Also, she says she wouldn't mind creating a bit of cash from the deal to take a few autumn-day holidays. Dani dives in and says that as far as the holidays are concerned, take a break straight away courtesy of her and her boyfriend. For the past few months she'd been going out with a car dealer who had a small condominium in Cancun. Take a month off there, Dani says. When you're back, we'll talk some more about selling the place. The minute her mother's on the plane, Dani sells the place and dumps her personal stuff in rubbish bags on her brother's doorstep. Her mother pleads and begs on her return, so does the brother – but Dani breaks off all contact and refuses even to answer the phone. A court case ensues, but Dani claims that the house was a "gift", that her paying off the business loan was part of the deal, the rest was her inheritance. With little or no paperwork on the mother's side to support the trust arrangement, Dani ends up winning the case.'

'What happened to her mother?' McKay asked.

'She was left with nothing. She had a stroke from the shock of it all shortly after, and, unable to care for herself, ended up in a nursing home.'

'And the brother?'

'Oh, he came out of chapter eleven and is now firmly back on his feet. But he was almost in tears when he told me all about it. Not just because of what had happened to his mother, but also what came out from Dani about him during the trial. He had no idea that her resentment, almost hatred of him, ran so deep. And most of it stemming from Dani's belief that her mother favoured her brother over her – which he had little or no control over. But she used the court case very much as her soap-box, her big chance of payback. She made much of his business collapse, making out that he'd been a serial failure virtually throughout his life. And at the same time she elevated herself, claiming that if she hadn't stepped in, her mother's property would have been totally lost in any case through bank and creditor actions from her brother's business collapse. It was as if to say to her mother: "Look, look at me! I'm the one you should have been favouring, *not him*! He's a failure!" And to the court that she somehow deserved the property through her actions.

'Simon was destroyed. Not least because when he vented his surprise at her attack on him to friends and other family – he discovered that she'd always talked him down to correct this favour-itism imbalance she'd fixed in her mind. It came as a shock that someone he'd always talked up and defended was doing exactly the opposite in return.'

Kalpenski coughed and cleared his throat. 'I know what a broken man looks like, Mr McKay, mostly because of what I've seen staring back from my mirror the last couple of years. I spent almost four hours talking with her brother, Simon, and at the end of it he looked worse than me. Each time he dug deeper about his sister, the picture got blacker. He discovered that she'd done much the same with her past husband over the home they shared. The husband's father had made a private mortgage with his son – but when it came to the divorce, she claimed that the house was a "wedding gift". Perhaps that's where she first got the idea from, Simon admitted. He felt foolish, betrayed, and also terribly responsible. Because it was he who first proposed that the property go in his sister's name; and if he'd had any idea how she felt towards him and his mother – let alone this run-in with her ex-husband and father-in-law – he'd have never suggested it. Certainly, her relationships with her mother and brother go a long way towards explaining her later actions.'

'In what way?'

'Well, for a start her relentless drive and ambition – her need to always prove herself. Prove that she's better than her brother. Also, her resentment, practically hatred of men, because she feels that they start with an unfair advantage through being naturally favoured over women. And so she feels justified in playing dirty to even the balance. You can see it behind what happened with her ex-husband and her brother, then Hebbard, myself . . . now this colleague of David Copell's in Paris. And how many more that we don't even know about?'

McKay had heard that Kalpenski had become consumed with wanting revenge against Stolk, spent much of his time, between sending off résumés, tracking down any past enemies she might have made – but he hadn't appreciated the intensity of that campaign until now. And it looked like he'd found most of those enemies within her own family.

It brought McKay around to the other main aspect he was interested in, and whether Kalpenski might also have a view on it. But he'd have to be careful how he broached the subject. He didn't want to inadvertently give away who he was and the real reason for his interest in the case. Not yet.

*

'André, André . . . *André!*'

André slowly roused from Marielle shaking his shoulder and peered up through bleary eyes.

'You can't stay here like this,' she said. 'We need you back at the lab. And, more than anything else, Joël needs you right now.'

'What's the point?' He shook his head. 'I can't help him any longer. And every time I try, look what . . .' His voice trailed off. He closed his eyes as if to shut out the unwanted images as he shook his head again.

It was the third day that André had stayed at home after hearing about David, and Marielle was beginning to worry about him, fearing that he might be settling in for another long session hidden away from the world, as he'd done after Eban's death.

She'd spoken to him on the phone the evening before and he'd said that he'd be coming in the next day, probably late morning, about 11 a.m. When by 11.50 there was no sign of him, she phoned, but it went into answerphone. She tried again at thirty- to forty-minute intervals with the same result, leaving three messages. Then finally, at just after three o'clock, exasperated, she jumped into her car, and, after a flying stop at a couple of shops, turned up at his door.

Bernice answered, mumbling her apologies as they headed along the hallway. 'Sorry, Marielle. He told me not to answer the phone. Said he didn't want to speak to anyone.'

Marielle looked in on him briefly, then decided to prepare everything in the kitchen before waking him.

'Come on, André. I've made fresh coffee, and some Singapore noodles. One of your favourites.'

André peered up again. He could smell the aroma wafting in from the kitchen. She smiled at him, some small beads of moisture on her forehead and above her top lip from the rush over or the steam in the kitchen. Or perhaps it was raining outside. André had no idea, hardly even knew if it was night or day. She was so good for him. But she was just a dream, a foolish illusion. Like so much else in his life that had been good before being taken cruelly away, he knew that it couldn't last. Past her shoulder, Bernice looked on concernedly from the doorway.

Everyone concerned, worried about him. *André the healer, the saviour.* But then everyone he touched . . . André felt the tears close again, and blinked heavily, trying to push them away.

'He had two young children, Marielle. How can I even begin to come to terms with what's happened to his family, their loss – and all just to make good on the problems with mine.'

Marielle squinted at him sharply. '"Make good"? "Problems"? Joël is *dying*, André. David knew that and fully weighed that up when he offered to help.'

André shrugged. 'More like he felt forced into a corner by Joël's predicament. Felt that he couldn't say no.'

Marielle sensed that she wasn't going to get anywhere fast on that front. She deftly changed the subject. 'Hervé phoned as well, twice now. Said for you not to forget that Eric comes out tomorrow. La Santé, ten a.m.'

'I know. He phoned here yesterday. That's why I just let it go into the answerphone. I couldn't face it.' André shook his head. 'I couldn't face anyone right now.'

'You surely wouldn't do that to him again.' Marielle recalled how strongly André had regretted not showing up at Eric's trial. 'Not when you know how much it hurt him last time.'

'I'm no good to him like this. I'm no good to anyone.' He sat up slightly, gesturing helplessly. 'I'm sure he'd understand. Especially with what's happened to Joël – and now losing David like this.'

'Oh, yes. I'm sure he'd understand,' she echoed caustically. 'He'll understand that whenever there are other problems in your life – he takes second place. This is a big day for him, André. His first day of freedom in three years. You can't let him down.'

She saw him slowly close his eyes and shake his head again as he struggled with the conflicting emotions. But it sparked anger rather than pity in her. She lambasted that he couldn't just hide away from everything he didn't want to confront, and it quickly descended into their first argument, with her throwing at him that he hadn't even told Charlotte about their relationship yet, which he'd promised he'd do – despite understanding why he hadn't, that it would have been too much coming on top of telling Charlotte about Joël.

'Well, maybe I won't have to now,' he said.

'What does *that* mean?'

He reached up and gripped her arm, his eyes filling, close to tears. 'You don't want me like this, Marielle. I'm no good for you. Like I said, I'm no good to *anyone*.'

She searched his eyes for a second, biting her lip as she looked down, hurt that he'd discard their relationship so easily. Just because, like so much else in his life, he felt he couldn't face a confrontation over it.

'No, you're right. I don't want you like this,' she spat back. 'It was the other André I fell in love with: caring, selfless. Not the one acting as if he couldn't give a damn because all he's consumed with is self-pity.'

André's grip on her arm tightened and his other arm went to her shoulder, lightly shaking her. 'You don't understand, Marielle. I'm frightened. I'm frightened because every time I go out there, somebody dies.'

Seeing the hunted look in his eyes, Marielle understood only too well. Most people would have crumbled long ago with everything he'd had to face: Eban, Charlotte's neurosis, Joël's illness, his family's recent revelations. David's death was one burden too many, the straw that broke the camel's back. And because André gave so much of himself to his work and to others, when the crashes finally came, they were spectacular. But the last thing she wanted to do was condone his actions, give any hint of support.

'The thing is – Joël is going to die in any case if you do nothing to help him. Is that what you want? To stay here feeling sorry for yourself and just let him die?'

André flinched sharply as if she'd slapped his face, and for a second she thought she'd gone too far in trying to snap him out of his self-pitying stupor. But then she realized that he was looking just past her shoulder, and she turned as she too registered faint movement behind her.

Joël, drawn from his room by their raised voices, stood a couple of feet behind Bernice in the open doorway.

'Oh God, I'm sorry. So sorry.' Marielle's shoulders slumped and she prayed that Joël hadn't been there long, hadn't heard the worst of what she'd said; but as she met the hurt, bewildered look in his eyes, she knew that he had.

32

'OK, what have we got?'

'For my money, Nimbus Corporation and Bio-TX have to be top of the list. If you take MIT and Spheros out of the picture, they're the two with the strongest shot at winning a Gifford.'

'I don't think we should overlook ZML and Thorne-Paget, falling close behind. The aim could be taking out all four main contenders above them. Nimbus and Bio-TX could be next on the list.'

'If we follow that route, then we might as well also not discount all the other Gifford contenders, with the aim that there's *six* above them to take out, including ZML and Thorne-Paget.'

The squad room was buzzing, with comments winging in from every corner of the room. Wenner sat on the edge of his desk, pointing his finger like an erratic conductor. Stan. Tom. Dougy. Batz took notes to his side and made only a few brief comments; Wenner already had the benefit of his thoughts, it was what the rest of the squad room had found out in the last forty-eight hours that he was eager to know.

'There's a new suspect also come into the frame. ORI-gene in Paris. According to some recent press reports, their Dr Lemoine has had a run-in with the Spheros over a new anti-cancer agent known as macaitin which could have a serious shot at the Giffords.'

Wenner mulled it over for only a second. Batz had put a clipping on the same subject under his nose just the day before.

'Don't think so. Too recent. It could only possibly be linked to the current bombing – not any of those preceding.'

But Wenner began to wonder when two hours later the same name came up in an e-mail sent to him. He'd wrapped the meeting up forty minutes before and was just skimming through Batz's notes for anything important he might have missed when his computer flashed, *You've got mail.*

He read the first few lines, then looked to see who it was from: mckay808@hotmail.com. It wasn't an internal e-mail, or from an e-mail address he recognized. He started reading it through again:

> You should look closer at the Spheros Institute. Because it's my belief that they arranged to have themselves bombed to throw you off the scent. They had a recent conflict with a company called ORI-gene in Paris and a certain Dr Lemoine. David Copell had previously worked with Dr Lemoine and was his main contact at the Spheros. Copell had started to snoop around on Lemoine's behalf, and so with the bombing the Spheros got rid of both of their problems in one: Copell, and any suspicion of them over the other bombings.
>
> But don't pre-warn the Spheros that they're under suspicion, otherwise they'll simply shift any incriminating information from their computers and bury it for good. You need to go in there and raid all of their computers without any forewarning. Trust me. You'll find everything to back up my claims there somewhere.
>
> Good hunting!

Wenner was still on an adrenalin high from the meeting, but this made him feel positively electrified. He felt his face flush as if he'd read a shock admission from a lover.

He stared at it blankly for a moment before re-reading it. Then he picked up the phone to speak to Mike Leverett.

The lab was buzzing, comments winging in from every corner of the room.

'What do you have for haemoglobin and platelets on sample four?'

'Seventy-five and sixty-seven,' Goffinet shouted back.

'And sample two?' he asked Marielle.

'Sixty-three and fifty-four.'

André did a quick calculation. They were all up slightly by three or four per cent, except the platelet count on sample two, which inexplicably had dropped a fraction. He could still feel a little woolliness from the earlier drinks as he applied his thoughts to why that might have happened.

Together with Hervé, they'd picked up Eric at the gates of La Santé and headed to the Soupçon for some champagne to celebrate.

'So,' Hervé said as he offered a toast and gave Eric a quick hug with his other arm. 'You're only going to go on the straight and narrow from now on. That's a promise?'

Eric had half an eye on a willowy brunette across the room. 'Yes. Find me a narrow woman and I'll head straight for her.'

They laughed. It was good to see that Eric hadn't lost his edge and sense of humour, hadn't been completely worn down by the three years in prison. The shadows of those years could only be seen in brief lulls in the conversation when Eric appeared to grab a moment's reflection. Or maybe it was fear and uncertainty of what was to come.

André too felt carried along on the spirit and warmth of the reunion, was glad he'd made the effort to be there – but when Eric asked after Charlotte, Veruschka and Joël, it reminded him of the impossible burden that awaited him. All fine, he'd answered, except Joël had been a bit poorly recently – though hopefully nothing serious. Now that everyone else knew, he felt guilty not telling Eric the truth. But he didn't want to dampen Eric's big moment, his first taste of freedom in years.

In a strange way, it also felt like a fresh start for André. He'd already been on the verge of being swayed by Marielle's bombardment of arguments: he couldn't just give up on Joël; there was still time to work out a macaitin formula independently that could save him; if David was looking on, he wouldn't want André to give up, otherwise it would mean his death had been for nothing: saving Joël and fighting the Spheros over macaitin was the ultimate payback. But what had finally galvanized André into action was that now that Joël knew he was seriously ill, he couldn't possibly just vegetate in the next room. It would seem as if he'd purposely given up; he wouldn't have been able to meet those pitiful eyes head-on: *Am I going to die? Is there nothing that can be done?*

'No, you're not going to die,' he'd assured with a heavy hug just after Joël had overheard Marielle. 'I won't let that happen.'

Then first thing that morning, Marielle had phoned to say that the blood sample had arrived from Claude Gallinard in Monteroule.

'Your father.' She seemed hesitant as she said that, as if sensing he hadn't fully got used to it. 'We'll start working on it straight away, start building up some data. You get here as soon as you can.'

Shortly after Eric asked about Joël, André found himself periodically checking his watch. Finally, three glasses of champagne for the worse, he managed to get away and head for the lab. Things were already in full swing as he walked in. Marielle informed him that Boisnard, buoyed by the fact that they aimed to formulate macaitin treatment data independently, had sent a challenging letter to the NSC and the Spheros to that effect – and there was an energy and enthusiasm about the lab room that hadn't been evident for many months. The fightback had begun.

Marielle handed him a few sheets with their calculations so far, and he spent another hour making his own notes before finally lifting his head.

Joël had been at the accelerated phase of ALL for some while, abnormal lymphocytes multiplying alarmingly and crowding out his healthy red blood cells and platelets. Protease inhibitors and now two stages of chemo had produced only minimal responses before relapse, and with the B-cell and anaemia complications, stem-cell and bone-marrow transplant hadn't even been an option.

André rubbed the bridge of his nose. Three or four months at best at the current rate of haemoglobin and platelet decline. Could they possibly make it in time? The sheer volume of data, tests and cross-checking before they got even close to a final treatment procedure, seemed insurmountable, impossible.

The only thing that offered some fresh hope was the arrival of Claude Gallinard's blood sample to help narrow down the options. In a way that felt strangely prophetic, meant to be: Gallinard's genes at the root of his daughter's illness half a century ago, and now Joël's, reaching down through the ages to aid a cure.

Though there was one final, daunting factor starting to prey on André's mind: something he'd noticed while tucking Joël into bed the night before that could firmly close the door on any slim hope they carved out now, make it impossible to save him. But as test results and comments started flying back and forth between himself, Marielle and Goffinet, André pushed it resolutely to the back of his mind, let himself get swept along on the fresh energy of the lab room and the new hope that Gallinard's samples had brought: *meant to be . . . meant to be . . .*

'If everything worked out as claimed in the e-mail, we'd be home and dry. We'd split the case wide open and go from A to Zee in one. But if it doesn't, if we find nothing, then we're in trouble. Big trouble. Because this isn't just some John Doe or small, backstreet company. This is a giant research establishment, and they'd have their equally giant, heavyweight lawyers on our backs quicker than you could strike a match.'

'Yes, I appreciate.' Wenner gently massaged one temple as his section head, Mike Leverett, laid out how he saw everything. Pretty much as he'd thought, but it had been worth the try.

'And then would come the question of why we'd acted so hastily based on such flimsy information. Because, for all we know, this communication could in fact have come from those behind the bombings, eager to throw us off track.'

'Yes, I see. Or indeed any of the other Gifford contenders – as if the bombing wasn't enough – looking to add to the Spheros's problems and put them further out of the running.' Wenner was keen to show that he'd also been considering the alternative possibilities; he didn't simply leave all deeper reasoning to Leverett. Lemoine was another possibility on that front, but he hadn't yet shared anything about that scenario with Leverett.

'Yes, there's . . . there's that too,' Leverett agreed after a second. He took a fresh breath. 'The thing is, we just don't know who or what is behind that message. And until we do – we simply can't act on it. If some of the gaps were filled in, then maybe everything would become clearer and the risks of making a move on it would also diminish. That's where your activity should be focused right now: trying to find out more about the sender. Motive for sending you the information, anything else they might know, and, most importantly, *who* they are.'

André hadn't dreamt about Eban for some while, and at first the images were warm and welcoming, pleasant: Eban playing football with a group of other children on the Ruhengeri plain as André looked on.

After a moment, Eban broke away from the other boys and, from a few paces away, beckoned back towards one of the other boys playing. Initially, André couldn't make out the other boy who joined him, the heat rising from the baked earth between them shimmered and wavered, blurring his vision. But as André squinted and focused, he could see that it was Joël. The two boys joined hands and started walking steadily towards the far ridge.

The sight at first made him feel good, the two of them together again – but then the underlying message suddenly hit him, and he stepped forward, frantically waving and calling out.

'No, Joël! You can't go with him!'

They kept pacing resolutely towards the far ridge without looking back, appeared not to have heard him – and he started running to catch up with them, shouting out as he went: 'No, Joël, stop! Don't go with him . . . *Stop!*'

He was panting heavily, breathless as he passed the other boys playing, the searing heat burning the back of his throat and robbing his voice as he gave one last scream for Joël to stop before they reached the top of the ridge – but the two boys didn't look back, simply paused for a second as if contemplating what lay ahead beyond the ridge before pacing resolutely on.

André scrambled desperately up the ridge to reach them, his legs aching and lungs gasping from the effort, the two boys gone from view for a moment before becoming clear again through the shimmering heat. And as he saw where they were heading – endless rows of shadowy tombstones stretching out in the valley ahead –

he started crying, one hand reaching out as he made a final, desperate plea.

'Don't go, Joël, *please* . . . I can save you. I can . . .'

'Mister André . . . *Mister André.*'

André broke out of his dream and focused on Bernice. She'd stayed over for the last few nights as Joël's condition had worsened.

'Mister André . . .' She looked agitated, worried, a rash of tiny sweat beads shining on her forehead. 'I think you should come and see.'

He leapt out of bed and followed her into Joël's bedroom.

I appreciate the information you sent, but as things stand now we simply don't have enough to instruct a search. We need to know a lot more. For a start, who you are and your motives for sending this information. You could be anyone – even someone trying to throw us off track of the real culprits. Also, while I accept your point about not forewarning the Spheros because they'll shift anything incriminating – how do you know they haven't shifted it already? We would like nothing more than to act on what you've sent, but we desperately need to fill in some of these gaps. If we raid the Spheros and get it wrong, we'll never get the chance to go in there again later.

Wenner found himself becoming increasingly anxious as he waited on a response to his e-mail. If it was a ruse, somebody trying to throw them off track or add to the Spheros's problems, they probably couldn't give any more information without risking putting their head in a noose. He doubted he'd hear anything more from them. But if they answered, there was a chance that it was real and the sender knew something vital. And if so, as Leverett aptly put it, they could split the case wide open and go from A to Zee in one. Home dry.

The thought of that turned the flame up high on his nerves as the minutes, then hours, ticked by. He'd finally got the back-up on the case he wanted: Batz and another half-dozen staffers burning up the phone lines and their computers almost constantly for the last forty-eight hours. But it had come at the cost of an increased body count, and he was keenly aware that it could still take weeks or even months to crack the case. And as time dragged by with no results, his 'team' would be reduced to five, then four, then . . . until finally it was just him and Batz again.

Yet if this came through, he'd short-circuit all of that grief in one, be able to smugly announce to the squad room that while they were all busy trying to find their asses with both hands, he'd solved the case.

Come on. Come on! He tapped his fingers impatiently on his desktop as he sat down with a fresh coffee. Five hours now and still no answer. It was just a ruse. A phoney. A . . .

He jolted forward, spilling part of his coffee in his lap as his screen flashed that he had mail. But it was just an internal memo.

'What's up?' Batz enquired, noticing him anxiously checking his computer every other minute.

'Someone sending me supposed information about the case. But it looks like just a hoax.'

Wenner was convinced of that when another hour passed with still nothing, his nerves by then completely worn down from waiting. Though just as he was about to call it a day and head home, a message finally came through:

I'm a friend of David Copell's with a strong interest in this case, particularly in light of his death. More than that I can't say without possibly putting myself at risk. The Spheros shifted all vital data two days before the bombing – so it hasn't set them back at all work-wise or in their aims for a Gifford Award. But interestingly, some of this was simply shifted to a computer on a higher floor, clear of the bombing area. Which then starts to look not only as if they knew when the bombing would take place, but also *where*: exactly which part of the building. And the only way they could have known that was if they'd organized the bombing themselves.

Wenner sat back and eased out a slow breath. The possibility that it was real, though no more than that. It told him a little more, but still nothing concrete. And certainly not enough to shift Leverett's position and get him to sanction a raid. He'd have to go back to his sender and push some more. He was halfway through his third re-read and starting to word his reply in his mind, when Batz, waving the phone receiver from a few desks away, broke his concentration.

'Jack Farrell from Philadelphia. He's got the DNA results in from the Spheros bombing.'

Joël remained asleep, even though he was wheezing quite heavily. His breathing seemed more laboured each day.

'Here . . . and here too.' Bernice pointed. 'It seems far worse than the other day. More swollen.'

André gently felt under Joël's left armpit and the side of his neck: the lymph nodes were severely swollen. They'd been swollen at times before, but never to this extent. It was what André had noticed when tucking Joël into bed the night before – but in the hope that in a day or two they'd go down again, he'd suppressed the most worrying explanation: that Joël's condition might soon slide from the accelerated to the blast phase, or had already done so.

Over the last two months of Joël's accelerated phase, his haemo-globin and platelet counts had fallen from the mid-seventies to late forties; but in the blast phase, with malignant lymphocytes exploding wildly and now little effective chemo to halt their pro-gress, that same drop could occur in only ten to twenty days. The cliff-edge looming ahead that André had always hoped and prayed would come later rather than sooner, or never.

But now he had to face that Joël might have already hit the blast phase, or that it was imminent. He could no longer push the portent away.

'Have you taken a blood test today?'

'Yes.' Bernice pointed towards the vial on the dressing table. 'Just a couple of hours before he went to sleep.'

André looked accusingly at the vial. Perhaps that's why he often withheld the full truth from others; because at the same time, part of him also didn't have to face it.

They wouldn't know for sure until he'd analysed the fresh sample in the morning; but if Joël had already entered the blast phase, all of his efforts along with his bold assurances to Charlotte and Joël would have been for nothing. Empty promises. The last door would have closed on him being able to save Joël.

33

Wenner freeze-framed the video, studied it for a couple of moments – then rewound it a fraction and played it back to the same point before pausing again. He leant in closer to the screen the second time, trying to pick up on the finer details.

What is it that you've seen or heard at that moment, David Copell? Someone coming up the stairs? The elevator starting its way up? Or just one of your regular look-over-your-shoulder checks because you're where you shouldn't be?

Farrell's words seared through his mind: 'That means that on the bone samples we tested, not only do they *not* match David Copell's DNA – they're also between twelve and fifteen years old.'

Farrell had blurted it out impatiently when Wenner interrupted his recital of DNA sequences from forensics to lend weight to his statement.

Twelve to fifteen years old? Obviously bone or skeleton samples of some type. Wenner had immediately asked Farrell to examine any bone fragments found in the adjoining offices. 'Maybe he moved slightly away from Dr Stolk's office before the explosion, or the blast scattered his remains wider.'

Could Copell have possibly made it out before the explosion? He'd replayed the security video of the last few minutes before the power was cut more than a dozen times looking for clues to what David Copell might do next.

He was where he shouldn't have been, and the building was empty – so the smallest thing would have spooked him. But as Farrell rightly pointed out, there would have been no light on the stairs, so getting out would have been difficult. Difficult, but not impossible. Though Pamela Copell had said that she hadn't seen her husband.

Shortly after Farrell dropped his bombshell, Wenner had phoned

Pamela Copell and asked if there was any other place her husband might have disappeared to for a couple of days other than home.

'No . . . nowhere that I can think of. *Why?*'

'Nothing. Just exploring every possible option.'

He didn't want to reveal the latest findings and raise her hopes that her husband might still be alive – only to dash them a couple of days later when Farrell came back with the forensic results from the adjoining offices.

He also stayed his hand on sharing the news with the Spheros. The e-mail claim from David Copell's 'friend' that the Spheros was behind the bombings, and would quickly shift anything incriminating if they feared things were closing in on them, lingered at the back of his mind. He decided for now to play his cards close to his chest.

Though as he looked again at the frozen, flickering image of David Copell glancing past his shoulder just minutes before the explosion – it suddenly occurred to him: how did Copell's 'friend' know that the Spheros had shifted anything vital just two days before the explosion?

The most likely place for anything sensitive would have been on Stolk's computer, or with Chisholm or another board director – not on the general floor with any of the minions.

And the most likely time for Copell to discover that vital files had been shifted were those moments just before the explosion when he was searching on Stolk's computer. Yet if he hadn't made it out, how could he have possibly passed that information on to his 'friend'?

Wenner picked up the phone and buzzed Maurice Wasserberg on the next floor.

'Maury. Todd Wenner. How long would it take you to trace an e-mail IP address for me?'

'Give me an hour or two, I should have it.'

André swilled the Pernod around in the bottom of its glass. He stared thoughtfully into the milky liquid – misty, clouded thoughts – then with one last swill, knocked it quickly back. His second of the day, and it was barely 11 a.m. He'd hoped they might settle his nerves, but as he put the glass back down, his hand was still shaking.

Joël's test results from an hour ago resounded in his head like a bad dream: haemoglobin, 39; platelets, 34. It looked like Joël had entered the blast phase two or three days ago, and if the decline continued at the same rate, he'd have only about a week left. Shortly after the results, he'd announced over his shoulder to Marielle that he needed some time alone, feeling all eyes on him as he left, worried that he might be headed for another long spell shut away at home. He'd gone a few streets away before stopping at a bar. He hadn't wanted anywhere that Marielle or Marc would find easily if they rushed out after him.

As he looked up from contemplating his empty glass and ordered another, he noticed an unkempt middle-aged man, one of only three other people in the bar, peering at him through bleary eyes. Silent recognition of someone else who appeared to have as many problems as him, or welcome to the pre-midday heavy-drinking club? André knocked back only half of his next Pernod before paying and leaving. He stepped out into the cold Paris air, the Pernod burning strongly in his chest, and flagged down a taxi.

'Montmartre, please.'

André sat silently as the city rolled past his taxi window. He could never remember exactly where the bridge was until he was actually approaching it, and so his request to stop came abruptly.

'You don't want to go all the way to Montmartre?'

'No. Stop here. *Here!*'

He paid the bemused driver and took a deep breath as he looked out from Caulaincourt bridge across the rows of tombstones. A faint mist hung in the air, but unlike his dreams it wasn't dense enough to obscure anything. He could easily see the full expanse of the graveyard.

Much smaller now than he remembered from his dreams or as a child, it held no fear for him any longer – though perhaps that was because he'd misread its messages all along. At first, he'd thought it was because his father and uncle had been claimed so young by cancer; then it became a siren call to try and save the legions dying from AIDS; then, when he'd discovered that Joël was ill, finally cancer.

But in the end, when he'd found out that Gallinard was his father and learned about his half-sister, he'd convinced himself that that's what it had symbolized all the time: Gallinard's flawed genes reaching down through the decades to now save his dying grandson. Something destined, meant to be.

And now that that last, desperate hope had also slipped through his grasp, it felt as if the graveyard had been taunting, playing with him all along. It hadn't symbolized anything – it had just been a combination of his own paranoia and trying to make some sense, some order of everything.

Yet, if his years in medicine had taught him nothing else, he should have known that nature was random, cruel: it struck down young and old alike, often without rhyme or reason.

His hands gripped tight to the bridge railing, the graveyard becoming blurred as his eyes swam with tears.

'If you have to take anyone, take me!' he called out challengingly. *'Take me!'*

At that moment, death would have been a welcome release; he didn't think he could bear the days ahead, watching helplessly as Joël died. And he was certainly no longer any use or help to him, or *anyone* for that matter. In the end, he hadn't been able to save any of them.

'Take me instead. *Take me!'* His voice rose to a near scream – loud enough to make two people further along briefly turn round – his hands gripping the bridge railing tighter with each shout as his tears flowed freely.

But his plea was lost as quickly as his breath vapours on the misty air, the graveyard answering with silence, defiance.

'You've won,' André said, his voice lowering to barely a whisper. 'You've won.'

Wasserberg came back to Wenner with an IP address for mckay808 @hotmail.com just before lunch.

'Jack Burridge, 435 Albemarle Drive, Greenville Golf Estate, Laurinburg, South Carolina.'

'Thanks.' Burridge? *Burridge?* It rang a bell from somewhere, and after twenty minutes of checking through files, he found it: Burridge had been Pamela Copell's maiden name.

Wenner didn't want to lose any time, so he phoned through to the Charlotte field office and asked them for a team of three or more to be dispatched pronto. Eight minutes later they were rolling.

A fifty-minute drive, they arrived at the Greenville Golf Estate entrance at 2.24 p.m., where they milked whatever information they could out of the gate-guard, Warren Danbury. He was helpful with letting them know where the house was on the estate – but said he knew little about the family or their movements. Danbury waited until their car had gone from sight, then immediately phoned the house.

'Jack? Warren here. You said for me to call if anyone official-looking came asking about you. Well, they did. Just a minute ago.'

'Good going. Thanks. That's another case of prime Kentucky on its way to you.' Then, as he put down the phone: 'They're here. You'd better move.'

'Sooner than we thought, but still.' Tim McKay grabbed his bag from the corner, hoisted it over one shoulder, and gave a quick captain's salute as he headed out the back door.

He crossed a busy highway and two more roads before spotting a phone kiosk a few hundreds yards along that looked safe enough to make the call from. He was still heavily out of breath from running as he spoke.

'Pamela. It's me. I think it's time I called André in Paris. Came in from the cold.'

'I've got another couple of jobs for you.'

'What? Like the last one – somebody taken out?'

Chisholm inwardly flinched, but remained deadpan. Kiernan's lopsided smile, as if he'd actually taken pleasure in killing Copell, unnerved him. To Chisholm, it was just numbers on a balance sheet, ambition; means to an end. Maybe it was the scientist in him, but he couldn't bear excessive or warped emotions, those that defied logic. That was why he always avoided personal contact with Kiernan, if he could. Though this was one conversation he didn't want to risk over the phone.

'No. It's back to just collateral damage again. But probably no less awkward, because they're abroad this time. France. One in Paris and one in Lyon.' Now it was Chisholm's turn to smile wryly as he watched Kiernan get to grips with the prospect.

They paced deeper into the patch of wasteland in Woodbury, their breath condensing on the cool air. To one side, a giant billboard announced that 19,700 sq. ft. of prime warehouse space was planned for the site.

Kiernan asked a succession of questions about the position, size, height and security arrangements of the buildings, and Chisholm answered in similar bullet-point fashion.

'As you can see, access to both is fairly easy, and security minimal. I purposely chose them as such, so you could pull them off alone.'

Kiernan nodded thoughtfully, then after a second his lopsided smile resurfaced. 'Not content with blowing up half of America – now you want to start blowing up the rest of the world.'

'Something like that.' Deadpan again. 'The Lyon hit should be made first, then three days later – Paris.' There had been an animal rights group fairly active for the past few years in France, though the last lab bombing had been almost a year ago. Two bombings in quick succession would look like they'd re-ignited their campaign, and Chisholm had noted in the French press that Lemoine was often referred to as 'The Darwin Man'. He was a prime target for animal rights activists. Though, as usual, Chisholm didn't share the background details with Kiernan. He wouldn't know which of the two bombings was the decoy.

'When do I leave?' Kiernan asked.

'First thing tomorrow.' Chisholm took an envelope out of his coat pocket and handed it across. 'There's your ticket and your phrase-book.'

Kiernan's face betrayed the hint of a smile, but with no reaction

402

from Chisholm, it quickly died. One small consolation of his meetings with Kiernan, thought Chisholm. Kiernan was so easy to make a fool out of, because half of the job had already been done.

'I . . . I don't understand. Why couldn't you have told me? Why did you have to make out to everyone that you were dead like that?' After the initial shock and elation of learning that David Copell was still alive, André started to get angry. 'You have no idea what I went through. I hid away at home for days, all but gave up on everything. Including trying to help Joël when he most needed me.'

'I was afraid, André. Desperately afraid. I thought: if they'd go to those lengths to get rid of me, destroying half their building – knowing I was still alive, they'd simply try again. A handy road accident, an injection to make it look like a heart attack; any number of ways without anything tracing back to them.'

'But why couldn't you have gone to the police . . . asked for their protection?'

'Think about it, André. This all started because you didn't even have enough proof to back up your claim with the NSC, let alone the police. And we're still in that position: no proof. If I told the police that the Spheros blew up their own building to try to kill me, at the least they'd be highly sceptical; at the worst, they'd think I was mad. All I've been able to find out so far is where possibly incriminating information has been shifted. So I wanted to test the waters as a shadowy figure from the outside, see how open the police were to the suggestion that the Spheros bombed themselves, with the aim of getting them to raid the Spheros. If they'd agreed to a raid, hopefully we'd have got the proof we wanted, so would they – and I could have come out into the open. Whoever was behind this at the Spheros would have been roped and tied and I'd have got the protection I wanted.'

'And how did the police react?'

'It's with the FBI now, because apparently there have been other bombings. I sent them some e-mails – but the bottom line was that they needed more to be able to instigate a raid.'

'Other bombings?' André felt slightly winded by the bombard-ment of fresh information, and his voice came over as strained, almost disbelieving. '*What* – possibly linked to the Spheros?'

'Yes, looks like it.' David exhaled wearily. 'That was the other advantage of staying a shadowy figure for a while. I was able to dig around in the background without problems or risk. If anyone I contacted fed back to the Spheros, inadvertently or otherwise, I was little more than a ghost.'

André fell silent for a moment. 'I mean, Pamela too,' he said, easing into an awkward half-sigh, half-laugh. 'She was the one who phoned and told me that you were dead. And she sounded so convincing. Crying and in a terrible state, almost beyond consolation.'

'I know. And I'm sorry for what I might have put you through these past few days – particularly with all else you've got on your plate now with Joël. But Pamela was the first person the police would have checked with, so it was vital that she was convincing.' David mirrored André's sigh, as if also sharing the gravity of what he was feeling at that moment. 'And I hope that you can understand now my reasons for doing it. Because the largest part of that was to hopefully put us in a stronger position to help Joël.'

'I . . . I'm sorry.' André took a quick step back as he reminded himself: it had been due to him pressing David to help Joël that David's life had been put at risk in the first place. 'It couldn't have been easy . . . coming so close to death like that. And knowing that you're still in danger.'

'No, it . . . it wasn't.' His skin tingled with the reminder, the images still too close, too vivid: the darkness and silence closing in even more after the footsteps had receded. And something about the urgency with which they'd moved away that made him, after a moment, decide to brave the impenetrable blackness of the stairway. He had to make his way mostly by touch, and the blast came when he was only four floors down, its air-rush throwing him suddenly to the ground. He could almost still feel it now, like the warm blast of a hair-dryer against his back and neck. He could hear loose debris and dust falling all about, and felt some small fragments hit him; then after a moment – though it felt like a lifetime – he got up and desperately fumbled the rest of his way down, uncertain how much damage had been done and whether the rest of the building would crumble around him before he made his way out. 'It wasn't easy.'

They were silent for a second, gathering their thoughts, then David started relating what he'd found out while posing as Tim McKay: Stolk's relentless rise to power, much of it through similar tactics of deception and false claims, then finally her getting the support of Julius Chisholm, one of the main directors. 'That's where the smart money lies as the main mentor behind her rapid rise to power. She wouldn't have been able to do it on her own. It's all quiet whispers, though, nothing proven. Chisholm keeps very much at arm's length in the background. But it is *his* computer, the floor above Stolk's, where all of her key files were transferred. That's the main thing I was able to discover just before the power went down and I got out of there.'

'So, that was the aim of getting the FBI to raid? They'd have picked that up in the sweep?'

'Yeah. As long as they did it without warning. Otherwise anything potentially damaging would have just got moved again. But maybe now if I come out fully into the open, they'll shift their position. It's a gamble – but I'm stuck for what else to try.'

'I . . . I don't know if we have the time any longer.' With the shock of hearing from David and their preoccupation with what he'd been able to uncover, André hadn't yet mentioned the recent rapid decline in Joël's condition. He brought David up to date. 'He entered the blast phase just a couple of days ago.'

'*Oh Jesus*, André. I'm sorry . . . so sorry.' He felt suddenly numb and hollow, and only the reaction of his body's extremities – his hand gripping the receiver impossibly tight, as if he was tempted to smash it repeatedly against the kiosk glass – told him he was also angry. While he was battling away in the shadows, at André's end the last strands of hope were slipping from his grasp. All of his efforts had been for nothing. Joël was going to die, while Stolk and Chisholm sailed into the sunset with little to hinder their progress

– and next year would no doubt step up on the rostrum to smilingly collect a Gifford Award. The thought stuck in his throat. 'There must be something that can still be done. If we can get the FBI to raid the Spheros, then push them to –'

'It's over, David. *Over!*' André exhaled tiredly. 'As you say, getting the FBI to raid is at best a hopeful shot. And even if they do – how long before they'd release information to us from an investigation? Two months, three? From the tests we ran the other day, we'd be lucky if Joël lasts another eight or ten days.'

'I . . . I suppose you're right.' Hearing André's tone of total defeat, it struck him that André had probably gone through the same cycle he was going through now – pushing it away, refusing to accept – a few days ago when he'd run his final tests. That was no doubt why André had sounded slightly numb and distant through much of their conversation; at first, David had put that down to André's shock at discovering he was still alive. David sighed. 'Even if we push with a court order for them to release the information, it would take six or seven weeks. Longer, if the Spheros lawyers opposed it – which odds-on they would.' Suddenly, getting the FBI more deeply involved was the last thing they wanted to do. But however much the situation seemed totally hopeless, David still found himself searching for options at the back of his mind. He looked up as a car passed by, its front passenger glancing at him momentarily. He was reminded not to stay too long in view from the road. The FBI could soon start trawling wider from his brother-in-law's house. 'It's not like you to give up like this,' he said in a lighter tone, trying to ease the tense silence that had settled.

'I know. That's what Marielle said.'

'You're usually the one fighting to the end, and I'm the one with the voice of reason.'

But the silence settled quickly back, the two of them, three thousand miles apart, finally accepting that they'd exhausted every possible option. There was nothing left they could do.

'Except there's one thing,' David said breathlessly, the thought rising suddenly. 'One way we might be able to help Joël quickly.'

But as it gelled, he thought: it's too audacious, too risky. André would never go for it. 'I know exactly where the macaitin data has been shifted to: which computer and which office and floor.'

'How will that help us?'

'If we wanted it quickly, we could steal it.' David drew a sharp breath. 'That is, if we can find a good thief.'

34

Grover Kiernan caught an overnight flight from JFK to Paris, arriving just after midday.

After clearing customs, he spent over an hour with his contacts for some C4 in a dingy basement in the Belleville area – al-Faydir, an Algerian splinter group, the only people he could find that actually sold *plastique* to fund their other activities – and by mid-afternoon was on a TGV speeding south towards Lyon. By the time he'd hired a car and driven the twelve miles to its L'Islon industrial estate, it was dusk.

As Chisholm had said, security was almost non-existent. Three-storey warehouse unit with basic alarm and monitoring, a chain-link fence that a five-year-old could climb, and only two roaming guards for the whole estate.

He went to a Routiers café and had a *menu du jour* surrounded by truck-drivers en route to Avignon and Nîmes, and returned at 9.50 p.m. Waiting for the ideal gap when the two guards were at the other end of the estate, he leapt the fence, by-passed the alarms and cut the glass in a downstairs window, went up one floor and placed the C4 in a bag under a desk, and made his way swiftly out again. Set with a one-hour delay, he was on the TGV back to Paris when it went off.

He normally only used the throw-it-in-and-leave tactic when the strike came at short notice or Chisholm was in a rush. But this time it was because Chisholm had specified a three-day delay between the Lyon and Paris hits – and Kiernan didn't want to hang around in France any longer than necessary.

He checked out the second target, ORI-gene, early the next morning. Again, virtually nil security. The only minor obstacle was that he'd have to get above the ground-floor shops to gain entrance

– but he'd noticed a small yard with garage units at the back where he could climb with ease without being seen.

He'd place the C4 in a computer this time, linked to its timer. Set it one night to go off the next so that it satisfied Chisholm's three-day delay; but also, and more vitally, so that he'd be well clear of French soil when it went off.

Wenner's hand paused for a second above the receiver before making the return call to Julius Chisholm. When he'd phoned earlier, he was informed that Dr Chisholm would be tied up for at least another hour. 'Please try later.'

This time he was told that he'd be just a couple of minutes, 'If you don't mind holding?' Normal delay while Chisholm disentangled himself from other calls and work, or was he mentally preparing himself? As before, Wenner held up one hand towards Batz – bringing it down finally as Chisholm came on the line. It was vital that both calls were made at the same time.

'Dr Chisholm. Good of you to spare the time. This shouldn't take long.' Wenner started by talking about the FBI's angle on what had so far been established: two-man team, power cut initially, C4 left with only a few minutes' delay, elevator cables severed . . . 'Though perhaps Lieutenant Farrell will already have gone over some of this with you?'

'Yes . . . well, he's been in touch throughout with Craig Berwick – who in turn has kept myself and Professor Bradson up to date.'

'That's good to know. It's just that when I visited straight after the bombing, you were away. San Francisco, I believe. And after our meeting a couple of months back – I wanted to make sure that you were kept in the information loop.'

'That's very kind of you, Agent Wenner.'

'My pleasure.' Wenner could feel Chisholm's tension coming across in waves. As with their previous meeting, Chisholm was trying to spar with him – but this time the syrupy overtones weren't completely covering the tightness in his voice. 'And also to be the first to let you know the good news: George Hanley, your building guard, is going to make it! He's off the critical list. Lieutenant Farrell called earlier to tell me.'

'Oh, that *is* good news. I'm so pleased.' This time the syrup caught in Chisholm's throat, his voice croaking slightly.

'Yes, isn't it?' Wenner was enjoying this much more than their last conversation. If his phantom e-mailer was to be believed, Chisholm was probably starting to panic whether Hanley might have seen anything before the explosion. 'The second bit of good luck.'

After a pause: 'In what way?'

'Well, if I hadn't come and warned you a month or two back about moving files because you could be a possible target – you really would have been caught out.'

'Yes . . . of course. That was very helpful. But unfortunately we were only halfway through that process when it hit. It still knocked us sideways on a lot of vital research.'

'I'm sorry to hear that.' Wenner resisted reaching for the syrup bottle; he didn't want Chisholm to focus on the topic any more than necessary. 'But I wanted to be first to tell you about George Hanley pulling through. All we need now is a bit of luck with the investigation.' Wenner could see Batz putting down the phone from his call. Wenner was eager to sign off and find out how it went – but then at the last second Chisholm asked him about the DNA results from the bombing.

'Lieutenant Farrell said that he'd let us know – but then we didn't hear anything.'

'Oh, right.' Wenner had instructed Farrell under no circumstances to share the DNA findings with the Spheros; in fact, because everything was at such a delicate juncture, leave *all* contact with the Spheros to their Atlanta office until further notice. Now it was Wenner's turn to feel on the spot, tense. It wasn't the sort of thing he could fluff around and say that they didn't have them yet; in Chisholm's line of work, he'd know they should have something by now. 'From the tests run so far, it looks pretty conclusive that it's David Copell. We'll know a hundred and one per cent in a couple of days. But of course, we have to inform his relatives first – so that's unofficial. Just between you and me.'

'Of course.'

As soon as he was off the line, Wenner confronted Batz. 'What did Stolk say?'

'She said that *all* the files had been moved. It was lucky we warned them.'

Wenner nodded and smiled. Batz had been instructed to similarly bury the question, make it incidental, in his case among a chain of questions about how they were coping after the bombing. A floor and a half had been boarded off – but were they managing to function OK in the other three and a half floors? Or had some of them had to transfer to another building? No, they were managing to cope. Just. 'But it's a bit of a squeeze. And still very disorganized.'

Wenner scratched his chin. 'So at least we know one thing – *everyone's* lying. All we've got to do now is work out why.' His last couple of calls had been to Pamela Copell and her brother, Jack Burridge. Burridge claimed that it was him who'd been sending the e-mails, because of concerns about the Spheros that David had shared with Pamela before the bombing. Wenner had hit them both with the DNA findings of twelve- to fifteen-year-old bone fragments, and as a result it was their belief that David was still alive. 'Have either of you seen or heard anything from him?' They'd both answered flatly, No.

Straight afterwards, Wenner asked Maury Wasserberg to get phone records on both of them for the past month – 'Outgoing and incoming.'

They arrived late afternoon, and Wenner spent almost half an hour going through them before finally lifting his head. An increase in calls between them since the bombing – which you'd expect, even if David Copell had been caught in it and died. But it was a call to Pamela Copell from the same exchange but a different number to Burridge, about the time of the FBI visit, that caught his eye. He checked and ascertained that it was a phone booth about two miles from Burridge's home – then phoned the Charlotte field office to tie down the exact time of their visit. He tapped one finger pensively by the entry as he put down the phone after speaking to them.

If David Copell had rushed out the back door just before the FBI arrived, the timing was perfect, and his wife was probably the first person he'd want to call. Wenner was convinced now more than ever that not only was David Copell still alive, but he was also his mystery e-mailer. The only puzzler remaining was why Copell was still hiding in the shadows and didn't want to come into the open.

'Vince. Long time no speak.'

'Yeah. Fair few years. *Too* many.'

After the pleasantries, Eric Lemoine got to the point of his call: another job; a sixteen-floor climb of a twenty-two storey building in Philadelphia.

'Big prize?'

'No. It doesn't involve art or jewels.' Eric glanced towards André and Marielle as he provided a potted history: the Spheros stealing some research from his brother, his brother's son falling ill, and now them hoping to steal the research back in order to save the boy's life.

'So, we're the good guys for once.' Desouza sighed light-heartedly.

'You could say that. But it doesn't pay big, either, Vince. Ten thousand dollars – that's all we could raise.'

André nodded as Eric looked towards him again. Boisnard had offered to pay sixty per cent of it – but in every other way he wanted to be kept completely out of it. If his backers ever got wind of his involvement, he'd be out on his ear, no questions asked. They'd gone back to André's apartment to make the call. Hervé too was ready with a lot of arm's length advice. When Eric first said that he knew the ideal man for the task, one of the best cat burglars on the East Coast – Hervé was immediately against the idea. 'Eric's just come out of prison. We couldn't possibly put him at risk of going straight back in again – whatever's at stake.' Eric assured him that he'd just set it all up and act as liaison – he wouldn't get directly involved in the robbery. Reluctantly, Hervé had given ground. 'As long as you're sure that's the case.'

André brought his attention back as Eric told Desouza that it was a two-man job. 'For something like this, he'll have to be fairly seasoned. Someone you know you can rely on.'

'You know as well as I that the only two people I'd trust as back-up on anything big are Terry Steiner and yourself. And Terry's doing a five-year stretch in Elmira right now.'

'OK. We'll talk more about which one of them will be best when I get there.'

Desouza realized that Eric couldn't talk freely on the subject at his end. 'Yeah. We'll talk more later.'

For Julius Chisholm, the pressure built steadily through the day. He was used to being in control, staging and tracking every last detail. But he had the feeling that at that moment there were elements he couldn't possibly plan around, because they were unseen, taking place without his knowledge.

The call from Wenner hadn't on its own unnerved him. In fact, apart from informing him about George Hanley pulling through – it seemed to be fairly lame, lacked purpose. The only thing had been a slight teasing undertone, as if Wenner were saying: I know something you don't, so now I'm going to play with you a bit, see if what you say ties in.

And then when he'd spoken later to Dani Stolk to go over final details from her section for his speech that night, she said that she'd got a call too, from Barry Tzerril.

'Why didn't you say something earlier?' That wasn't like her; usually she'd panic and jump with the slightest sneeze from the FBI, would have e-mailed or phoned him straight away.

'Because there really wasn't much to the call. Just conversational, asking how we were coping after the bombing. Oh – and he told me about George Hanley being out of danger.'

'Nothing else?'

'No. Not that I can recall.'

Chisholm started to feel uneasy. Two calls about the same time to tell them little more than Hanley's good progress? It could have been a coincidence, but Chisholm wasn't convinced. Something was going on – though he couldn't immediately put his finger on what. And it was the worst possible time for it to come up. He had a keynote speech to make that night – 'Short- and Long-term Financing in New Medicine,' at Penn State University – and was only halfway through his preparation notes, with a mountain of other work to clear from his desk before the day was out.

He tried to push it from his mind, tell himself he was worrying for nothing, but with each passing hour fresh questions rose. Why hadn't Farrell called for a while? Three days now, when before Farrell had called either Berwick or himself every day, sometimes twice a day. Three days with nothing, then suddenly two calls from Wenner's department within an hour? And Farrell had said that he'd have the DNA results the next day – yet three days later Wenner was saying that the results still weren't totally conclusive. The one moment in their conversation when he'd sensed Wenner was off balance.

But while the questions multiplied, the answers remained tantalizingly out of reach. Between preparing his speech – a mass of scribbled notes that he was still far from happy with – clearing the rest of his work and fending off the afternoon's calls, his head was bursting with it. He massaged his temples, edging into an uneasy chuckle as the irony hit him.

Stolk was usually the one to panic – yet this time she seemed unruffled by the FBI call. And last time, he'd been the one playing Wenner on a string. Maybe that was what so unsettled him: the sense that everything was suddenly upside down, out of kilter.

He stayed an hour late to finally knock his speech into shape, and screeched his Saab sharply out of the Spheros underground car park into the early evening traffic. He glanced over at his passenger seat to ensure he had all the files he'd need: with his speech preparation taking up most of his time, he'd have to finish off his other work at home afterwards – then braked sharply as he looked back up at tail lights in front of him.

He surveyed ahead. It hardly seemed to be moving, appeared jammed solid for two hundred yards or more. All he needed; it was already looking tight for him to make it in time. After a couple of minutes of edging forward only a few yards, he started banging his fist on the wheel in frustration – stopping abruptly as he noticed a woman in a car alongside looking over at him.

Oh Jesus. He was losing it. It had only happened a handful of times in his life before, but he detested the emotion in himself as much as in others: the feeling of being totally cut adrift, powerless. And what made it doubly frustrating was that he could sense that the key was close within grasp; just find that, and everything would start to fall into place again. He'd start to wrest back control. Familiar ground.

Though it wasn't until almost an hour later that he thought he might have finally found it, a lightning-bolt as he adjusted his bow tie in the mirror, with only minutes to leave for the dinner: *Files!*

He'd need to speak to Dani Stolk though to be totally sure. But when he tried her number, it rang without answer. He tried again as he was halfway to the dinner, speeding across Market Street bridge. This time it rang engaged. He was quickly back to banging his fist on the steering wheel. Come on! *Come on!*

The key to it all was David Copell, Wenner decided. If he was the mystery e-mailer, then he knew everything: the whys and wherefores of the Spheros's bombing campaign, their current run-in with ORI-gene in Paris, where they'd transferred the vital files that could prove his claims, and, most importantly, what was going on at that moment that made him want to continue playing dead and keep out of sight.

The only ways he could get to him, apply some pressure to hopefully bring him out into the open, were by e-mailing mckay808 or through Pamela Copell. He decided on the latter. But there was one thing he wanted to put in place before making the call, so that they got what they wanted either way she or her husband decided to jump.

He buzzed Maury Wasserberg and asked him how long to put a tap on the Philadelphia line he'd earlier gained records for.

'Four, five hours is the normal. But I'll go through to the Philly FO and let you know.' Two minutes later Wasserberg was back with the answer: 'They're keen – hoping to get Boy Scout's badges. They say they'll do it in three.'

'OK. Tell them to go ahead – and call me back the second it's in place.'

It took precisely three hours and fourteen minutes. Wenner knew, because he'd started looking impatiently at his watch as it approached three hours, and had anxiously drummed practically every second since on his desktop or the phone receiver.

He gave the receiver one last finger-drumming before picking it up and dialling out. He could tell from Pamela Copell's faint intake of breath as he announced himself that she was instantly nervous, perturbed.

'Sorry to trouble you again like this, Mrs Copell. But there were a few things left hanging from our conversation yesterday. First of all, your husband still being alive is no longer just supposition on our part – it's a fact. An absolute. As I mentioned the other day, all the bone fragments studied were either aged or their DNA didn't match your husband's. So if you haven't seen him – I think you'd better start accepting that he's used the explosion as a cover to set up a new, secret life somewhere. Is that still your claim – that you haven't seen your husband?'

'Yes . . . yes, it is. I haven't seen him.'

Her voice noticeably quavered, but she didn't scream outrage at the suggestion. And the incredulity she'd displayed when he'd first told her that her husband was probably still alive had come across as forced, staged. She knew he was alive and where he was. Wenner decided to push harder.

'You don't know of another woman he might have been seeing, or problems with creditors? Any reason he might want to disappear and start a new life? Why that might suddenly become an attractive option?'

'No. No . . . I don't.' Pamela Copell sighed heavily. 'The last I saw of him was the morning of the bombing when he left here. The next I knew was Lieutenant Farrell calling at my door to tell me that David was probably dead.' A faint croak came into her

416

voice. 'And there was such devastation caused by the bomb that identifying David could be difficult.'

'David's *not* dead, Mrs Copell – so you can save the emotions.' Wenner's tone was cool, flat. He wasn't going to be taken in by it. 'And if you stopped fencing with us, we might actually be able to help you. For one thing – those e-mails we received that your brother claimed he sent: we're sure it was David who sent them.' Wenner was careful not to mention the call trace that had strengthened that suspicion in his mind; it might stop her from what he hoped she'd do as soon as he hung up. 'And in those e-mails he made various claims about the Spheros Institute, trying to get us to instigate a raid in order to substantiate them. We didn't say no – just that we'd need more information to go ahead and raid. And your husband coming forward and telling us everything he knows could give us that extra something we need.'

Wenner took a fresh breath, his voice softening. 'Now, I know your husband might be worried about issues of safety – who wouldn't after just missing being killed by only minutes? But if he came forward, we could offer the protection he'd want. Of that, you've got my assurance.' Wenner left a marked pause, but it was a second before Pamela Copell filled it.

'OK. I . . . I understand.'

'So I want you to think carefully about what I've said, Mrs Copell. Very carefully. And pass it all on to your husband if you hear from him. Or should I say *when* you next hear from him.'

Another mumbled, subdued, 'OK.' It was difficult to tell if Pamela Copell was really taking in what he was saying, or just eager to get off of the line. 'I will.'

The second he hung up, he picked up again. 'Maury. I want any and all calls made to or from that Philadelphia number e-mailed to me as voice messages with the time underneath for identification. Thanks.'

Again he was back to finger-tapping, this time by his computer. The first e-mail message flashed up after only a minute. Too soon: it was the call he'd just made to her.

The next message he waited six minutes for. Wenner's hand was trembling as he clicked it open and played the voice-mail:

'David. I've had Todd Wenner on to me again. He *knows* you're still alive, has completely turned his back on all other possibilities. And he suspects too that it was you who sent him those e-mails – not Jack. He says that he can offer you protection if you go to them with everything, and I want you to think seriously about it, David. Because I'm not sure how much more of this I can take.'

'Just hang on, Pamela. We're sooo close. If all goes well tonight with André and we get what we want from the Spheros – tomorrow I can come out with my hands up and reveal all to Wenner.'

'And if it doesn't?'

Heavy, tired exhalation. 'Not worth thinking about. Let's just set our sights on tomorrow and talk again then. He's unlikely to call you back again today, so stop panicking.'

'Put like that, I suppose it doesn't seem so bad.' She lapsed into a strained chuckle. 'You know, he was even suggesting you might have another woman you were making a new life with.'

'He's only trying to get a rise out of you, draw you out. As I say, just hold tight, try and stay calm – it's only until tomorrow.'

'OK. I'll try . . . I'll try.' Quick blown kiss. 'I love you.'

'Love you too.'

As soon as it finished, Wenner went back to Wasserberg and got an address in Philadelphia's Clifton Heights area that the call had been made to.

'Looks like one of David Copell's cousins.' They'd earlier spent time putting names and addresses to the numbers on Pamela Copell's phone records. 'Do you want me to alert Philly FO to pay him a visit?'

'No.' Wenner noticed Batz looking keenly towards him, picking up on the urgency of his activity of the last few minutes. He beckoned him with one hand as he hitched his jacket from the chair-back. 'This is going to be delicate, need kid gloves. I'd better do it myself.'

*

418

The French boast one of the world's best anti-terrorist intelligence services. This stems primarily from being beleaguered by three decades of Algerian separatist-linked bombings, mostly in and around Paris, and is split into two divisions: DGSE for external intelligence, DST for internal.

They'd been the first to pre-warn American intelligence services about September 11th, having only weeks before foiled an attack on the American embassy in Paris, and French counter-terrorism had gone into even higher gear post 9/11.

As a result, they'd infiltrated every terrorist group of note, among them the Algerian splinter group, al-Faydir. The DST had placed a sleeper agent inside al-Faydir five months before Grover Kiernan's visit, but by the time he dutifully passed the information on to his DST unit chief, a bomb had already gone off at what they suspected was the first target in Lyon. Thankfully, no loss of life.

That left one remaining, unnamed, target in Paris to be hit within a day or two, and very likely in the same line of work: genetic research.

DST thought it particularly worth sharing with their intelligence-gathering counterparts in America and Europe because, unusually, it involved an American visiting French soil to carry out the bombings. Within an hour of them passing the information on, it had been transcribed and security coded by Quantico and fed out, in turn, to their field offices.

35

'I think the best way is, we get up to that bit of flat roof two floors up – then make our way up the back of the building from there.'

'You don't think the left side would be better?' Eric offered. 'At the back we'd still be visible from the road running behind the block.'

'Yeah – but it's further away and not too busy.' Desouza scanned the building again. 'The most difficult part will be where it spreads out into a sphere. But at least we've got only one floor of that before we're able to get in.'

Eric found himself go slightly dizzy as he studied the four floors that made up the sphere, sixteen floors up. He looked down again and rubbed his eyes.

'You OK?'

'Yeah. Just a bit tired still from the flight.'

They went back to the hotel and Eric phoned André to confirm everything. 'We've checked out the building, and everything's set for tonight. Ten p.m.'

'Is it possible to pull it forward a couple of hours?'

'A couple of hours earlier?' Eric was repeating for Desouza's benefit. Desouza simply shrugged. 'I suppose so. Why?'

'Because Joël is slipping far faster than anticipated. So I'm going to have to pull everything forward and administer the treatment as soon as you have it.' Originally, they'd agreed that the treatment data would be stolen one night, administered the next. 'Joël's immune system is rapidly closing down, losing the ability to respond to *anything* – even if macaitin proves successful. So the earlier I do it, the better.'

'I . . . I understand. No problem.' Seeing Joël for the first time after his years in prison had come as a heavy shock: eyes sunken, little more than skin and bone, his breathing laboured and shallow as he forced a smile. '. . . *Uncle Eric!*' It had been the main catalyst behind what he was doing now: not just to hopefully save Joël, but the chance to do something good, worthwhile for the family for once. Make amends. And it made the lying easier now as André asked if Desouza had found someone as his partner.

'Yes. Terry Steiner. One of the best.'

'And you're not going along on the robbery itself – you promise? You know how important that is to both me and Hervé.'

'No. I won't get directly involved. I promise.' Eric felt a faint shudder run through him. André had made a point of eliciting the same promise from his as he left Paris, clasping both of his hands tight and staring soulfully, unsettlingly into his eyes as they'd parted at Orly airport. '*You promise, Eric. I'd never forgive myself if anything happened to you – especially after all you've been through.*' But all he'd pictured at that moment was Joël's sunken, haunted eyes, making him reflect all the more on his own worth. My God, his mother thought he was so worthless that she hadn't even visited him once in all of his years in prison. A chance to make good at last. Perhaps the *only* chance he'd get. '. . . I promise.'

But as he felt himself still gently shaking after he hung up, he realized that it wasn't just the deceit that was troubling him, but the feeling that had suddenly gripped him earlier while staring up at the Spheros building. He'd thought that it was just a momentary blip while he was in prison, a reaction to what was happening at the time or perhaps the flu medication he'd been on – but now he began to worry that it was something deeper.

He quickly shook it off. When he got up on the building, he'd be fine: it was just that he hadn't done it for three years.

'Why didn't you tell me that before? I asked you *specifically* if they talked about anything else.'

'It . . . it just didn't seem important.'

'*What* – that I knew?'

'No . . . *no*. The way that Tzerril asked about our files being moved before the bombing. It came across as . . . as purely incidental. By the way.'

Chisholm's head was boiling. He was sitting in the car park at Penn, watching through a rapidly misting windscreen as people in evening wear drifted past. He had only minutes before he'd have to head in.

'You know, for somebody supposedly intelligent – sometimes you take the prize for dumbness. If it didn't strike you at the time as important, then surely when I asked?'

She became flustered, countering feebly that it wasn't always possible to cover *every* angle. 'I mean, look at that Lemoine in Paris. After all our efforts – it appears he's still trying to fight back.'

'Sorry, but you're wrong on that front too. That problem is being taken care of as we speak. Because, unlike you, I *do* take care with the details. Any last hope he had of fighting back will soon be gone.'

'What does *that* mean?'

'Last chance to avoid the dumb prize: *you* work it out.' He hung up abruptly. Now, of all moments, he didn't have the time to banter with her. OK, he'd worked out that the question of whether or not they'd transferred their main files before the bombing was important to the FBI, but why?

The same thought was buzzing in his head ten minutes later, unanswered, as he milled through the main hall at Penn, being greeted by old friends and well-wishers, patting him on the shoulder and asking how everything was going, and he'd smiled back tightly and said that everything was *fine, fine, never been better* – when at that moment everything was far from fine; in fact, had never been worse. I can't do this any longer, he thought. He felt hot, the buzz and throng of the room pressing in on him. He eased his collar and glanced at his watch. They'd be starting the dinner soon, and he'd be up on the rostrum straight after. His head was bursting, his mouth dry. He couldn't wait till after then; he'd have to sneak some time out beforehand. He headed out into the foyer area, dialling Wenner's number as he went.

Maybe he could use the same tactic: talk generally, lightly, about the investigation, and slip in the key points he was keen to know amongst it all. But the agent answering in Wenner's section informed him that neither Agent Wenner nor Agent Tzerril was there.

'And I'm afraid they're not contactable right now on their mobiles either, because at this moment they're in flight.'

'Do you know to where?'

'Philadelphia. Try them again in an hour, they might have landed by then.'

'Thank you.' Chisholm felt a tingle run up his spine. *Philadelphia!* 'I will.'

It was looking more ominous by the second. Within hours of speaking to himself and Stolk, they'd grabbed a flight heading their way. But surely they weren't coming to see him? If Wenner had troubled to check, he'd have known that he had an unbreakable speaking engagement. Perhaps they were going to see Farrell: an update run-through on the investigation. Maybe by phoning Farrell he'd be able to fill in some of the gaps, find out why the three-day silence. But it looked like it was officers' night out: Farrell wasn't there either, and he ended up speaking to a duty sergeant, Alex Corcoran.

Chisholm introduced himself and explained that he was calling about the recent bomb attack to the Spheros Institute. '. . . The investigation of which your Lieutenant Farrell is in charge of.'

'Yes . . . I know the case.'

'Right. Well, I also spoke the other day to FBI Agent Wenner, and he said he was planning to meet again soon with Lieutenant Farrell to discuss the matter. I was wondering if he might be seeing him tonight.'

'No . . . not that I'm aware of. Lieutenant Farrell has now left for the night, and to my knowledge has nothing diarized for a meeting.'

'I see. OK.' He was starting to feel adrift again. Why was Wenner coming, and who *was* he seeing? 'I was wondering if – '

'Julius . . . *Julius Chisholm!* It must be two years, if it's a day.'

Chisholm turned sharply towards the voice booming across the foyer. Simon Fen-something. Fenmann? Fenton? They'd met at a convention in New Orleans, and he'd spent half the night trying to get away from him. Looked like he'd put on a fair few pounds since. 'Yes, I'll . . . I'll be with you shortly. Just finishing this call.'

'I noticed your name-card – you're just a couple of tables away from me. So I came looking.' He beamed apologetically. 'I think they're starting to serve now.'

'OK . . . *yes*. Just one minute.' Chisholm held one hand out and turned his back on Fen-something. He wasn't sure now that he could face going back in there to see *anyone*. He could hear the hubbub of voices in the grand hall rising, making his head swim, threatening to drown out any clear thought as he turned his attention back to Sergeant Corcoran. 'As I was saying, Lieutenant Farrell also mentioned that he was going to phone me with the DNA results on one of our employees who died in the explosion: David Copell. I was wondering if you might have that now.'

'Yes, we do. I remember Farrell and his team talking it over a few days ago now, because it was so unusual. Not the normal sort of DNA readings we get. The bone fragments that we tested were old.'

'*Old?*' Chisholm felt his stomach twinge.

'Yeah – as in over ten years.' Though Farrell had found Wenner's request to withhold the DNA information from the Spheros odd, he'd duly passed that on to his two main assisting officers, the only other people who'd had any contact with the Spheros. But the message hadn't worked its way through the rest of the division. 'Well, they were either old or didn't match the guy who was missing.'

'Are you trying to tell me that David Copell wasn't killed in the explosion?' Chisholm felt the twinge work deeper, his legs starting to shake and feel unsteady. 'That he *isn't* dead?'

'From the DNA results, sure doesn't look like it.'

Chisholm felt his legs giving way, as if the floor were suddenly opening up beneath him. But at least he finally had the key he'd been desperately seeking these past hours.

'Hold on . . . *hold on!*' André leant over and lightly kissed Joël's cheek as the ambulance sped through the Paris night.

They'd managed, through Bernice, to get the help of one of

Necker Enfants' ambulance drivers. It was important that they monitored Joël's respiration, pulse and temperature every second, even for the two-kilmetre drive from Montparnasse to the ORI-gene lab.

Boulevard du Montparnasse was heavy with traffic, so the driver was taking a series of back-street short-cuts, and André had to brace Joël at moments as the ambulance turned and swayed – taking the opportunity every other time for another reassuring hug or hand clutch. '*Hold on!* Not much longer now.' A breathless whisper that he wasn't sure Joël could even hear any longer.

Joël's face was pallid, ghostly white, the only colour from the emergency light as it strobed between him and Marielle, leaning over to take his readings.

'101.3. Pulse, 46. Respiration still weak at 14.'

Bernice was alongside Marielle, her expression taut, fearful. For her, like him, the ordeal held extra weight. She'd nursed Eban in his final weeks, actually been there when he died, and the worry that this might be a replay was etched deep in her face.

Marc was already in the lab, preparing everything. André glanced at his watch. They'd soon be starting their climb in Philadelphia. If everything went well, within half an hour they'd start receiving the data.

The cliff-drop of Joël's blast phase had accelerated alarmingly two days ago, his platelet and haemoglobin counts dropping 10 points in just twenty-four hours. The next day had been even worse, 12 and 14 points respectively. Joël's system was in free-fall, the only question remaining as to when he'd finally hit ground. Three hours? Four? Certainly, he wasn't going to last the night.

André closed his eyes, a cold hand gripping tight inside his chest. Suddenly the shadows between the streetlights crossing his shoulders felt like the city's tombstones rising up into the night, telling him: *It's too late. We're going to claim this one as well.* André shook off a faint shudder, steeling himself against it. Hold on! *Hold on!*

Maybe now with David Copell still alive – one pulled back from the graveyard that he thought had been lost – he'd be able to save another. But he reminded himself that he faced his toughest challenge yet, with the odds stacked heavier against him and the stakes higher than they'd ever been. Trying to process a cancer cure in only hours that would normally take months, and all of their hopes now resting with two thieves.

36

'*So lonely . . . So lonely . . . So lonely . . . So lonely . . .*'

Dani abruptly hit stop on her CD player and sank back into the couch with an audible exhalation, swirling the ice in her glass for a second before taking another heavy slug of bourbon. Third now, or fourth? Who was counting? Certainly not Sting, he was too busy telling her that she was sooooo fucking lonely.

She'd put on the compilation primarily to listen to 'Fragile', because that's how she felt at that moment: fragile, swept along by circumstances. But then that had been the pattern of her life of late: she'd start with one intention, one aim, and it would soon divert into something else.

She took another quick slug and raised her glass into the air. So lonely. All gone. All deserted. Who, in fact, was there left to care any more? She'd driven them all away in her rise to glory: her husband, her mother, her brother – everyone she'd ever been close to. Sent them packing with knives plunged through notes on their backs proudly proclaiming: *I've won!* And a fair few too with her work: Bremner, Hebbard, Kalpenski . . . now David Copell and this Lemoine in Paris.

And who was she left with: Julius Chisholm.

'*You know, for somebody supposedly intelligent – sometimes you take the prize for dumbness.*'

He didn't care about her. In the same way that he perceived much of the rest of the world, he had little more than contempt for her. She was below him: a pawn, a means to an end. And as soon as that end stopped being served, she'd become dispensable. She'd simply be cast aside and the next golden protégé put in place.

It was lonely at the top. And her staff all hated her, thought she was too aloof; or at the very least they resented her. Even those who were reasonably friendly and supportive, like Senadhira, wouldn't miss a step if she fell from grace. He had far too much of an eye on the corporate ladder to get anywhere near a sinking ship. The smiles and eager nods would soon stop.

Soooo lonely. The only one left was Allison. Though that was probably because Allison had little other choice: she was reliant on her and far too young to make up her own mind. And of late she'd noticed that when she threw her usual aspersions at her ex, Allison would often defend him, stoically claiming that he was a 'good father'. Allison was starting to make up her own mind about the world outside. What would happen when she got fully out there?

'. . . He said that in his line of work he'd dealt with the lowest of the low: drug dealers, mafia villains, you name it. And he couldn't imagine even them doing to their mothers what you did to yours . . . Not exactly an ideal epitaph: "Worse than the lowest of the low".'

The moment the words left Chisholm's mouth, it had hit her like a sledgehammer. That's what everyone thought of her! What lay behind the wary glances and muted whispers that she'd catch every so often. She wasn't looked up to and respected. She was hated! She hadn't succeeded an inch in being able to trump her brother in her mother's eyes, or anyone else's. Empty glory.

And her medical glory would also quickly dissolve to ashes if and when the macaitin/Lemoine scam went sideways – which sounded sooner rather than later from Chisholm's last call. It looked like the FBI were closing in. *Fast.* She knocked back the last of her drink and immediately poured another, smiling crookedly as she took the first swig. The only bit of perverse satisfaction she'd gained. Chisholm was rattled for once. Mr Ice Cool was suddenly red-hot, steaming.

Yet if she was hated now, what would they think when they discovered that in falsely claiming the macaitin formula from Lemoine, she'd let his ten-year-old son die? My God, Allison was only a couple of years older than that! And what was it that Chisholm now had planned for them?

'Last chance to avoid the dumb prize – you *work* it out.'

Another bomb, no doubt. Lemoine would be on a tight schedule as it was to prepare the missing data. A month or two's setback would finish any last hope he had.

And when it all went wrong, she'd no doubt get the blame: it was her name on most of the files and contacts over macaitin, Chisholm's probably wouldn't appear anywhere. He'd walk clean and clear of the whole mess. And, *oh God*, what a mess it would be. Her career would be ruined and she'd spend years in jail. Years in which Allison would be brought up by her father and she'd lose her only friend, while everyone finger-pointed: *'Told you so. Told you she was bad news.'*

She noticed her hand shaking heavily on the tumbler as she took another slug. The tumbler and the floor beyond also seemed slightly blurred, out of focus with her eyes suddenly moistening – though as she reached with her other hand to steady the tumbler, she fumbled, the glass slipping clumsily from her grasp.

And as she sank to her knees to pick up the tumbler and spilt ice, the floodgate of tears opened fully. *Oh God, I'm sorry. Sorry. So sorry.* Though she was no longer sure who she was lamenting: her mother, her brother, David Copell . . . Lemoine; so many now that she had to make amends to. Or to herself for the mess she'd made of everything, or Allison, for the years that now she'd have to spend without her. She cried and wailed until she was almost breathless, gasping, her chest aching with it. Making up for all the years that, bent on little else but her own ambitions, *glory*, she'd harboured a cold heart, hadn't shed a tear. In fact, she'd revelled in that, looked up to people who could remain calm under pressure, *calculating* . . . like Chisholm.

But as she looked up and caught her reflection in the mirror across the room: on her knees, distraught, mascara running, a woman on the edge who'd finally tipped over . . . her anger rose. That was no doubt what Chisholm expected of her! Weak and ineffectual; after all, *everyone* was weaker than him, less capable. Clutching at the tumbler, she hurled it towards the mirror – though missed. She took a deep, fresh breath as she got shakily back to her feet. She was damned if she was going to give him the satisfaction!

Amends! Maybe it wasn't too late to make some of them. Chisholm seemed to be worried that the FBI were asking about them moving files. The most incriminating ones were now on his computer, but carrying her name. If she was going to re-write history, then she'd have to get to them and do a bit of name juggling: diminish her involvement and elevate his.

But there was one call she needed to make first. She wiped at her smudged mascara, grabbed her coat and mobile, and started dialling as she headed out towards her car. It answered as she swung out of her driveway.

'Yes. A number in Paris, France . . . ORI-gene.'

The first eight floors went well, without problem. Eric had taken a deep breath as he looked up at the building, and hadn't felt dizzy this time. He'd taken that as a signal that everything was going to be fine; that what had happened while he'd been in prison had been a momentary blip, wouldn't be repeated.

And he'd followed the basic climber's rules: concentrate only on the next hand- and foothold, don't look down – even though looking down had never troubled him in the past. He'd always found cityscapes from high up quite exhilarating, a breath of freedom.

But at some stage halfway up the ninth storey, everything changed. His mouth felt suddenly dry, his palms sweaty, and it felt as if either he or the building were swaying slightly. He could feel the wind whipping steadily across the building face, threatening to pull him loose on some of the stronger gusts.

He clung on tight, kept himself pressed firm against the concrete and glass as he stealthily followed Desouza's lead. Tenth floor . . . *eleventh.* Only five more floors.

His heart was pounding hard and fast, his palms sweating so profusely that it made each grip perilous, uncertain. And as a sudden, violent gust of wind hit him and almost tugged him loose – he shut his eyes and clung hard to the building. But could still feel his body swaying sickeningly seconds after. Or maybe it was the whole building moving?

'Are you OK?' Desouza asked.

Eric simply nodded, his mouth too dry and tight to speak, hardly daring to open his eyes again.

'Are you sure?' Desouza pressed.

This is André's affliction, not mine, Eric told himself. But he felt himself continue to sway and spin, and saw again the dizzying view from the third-floor rampart into the ground-floor well at La Santé prison.

There'd been a disturbance between prisoners, and in the ensuing fight Eric was almost pushed over the edge – only saving himself at the last second by gripping tight to the rampart rail. But the sensations that flooded him in that instant warned him that his relationship with heights might never be the same again.

'I . . . I've got a problem,' Eric muttered, risking a squint towards Desouza. 'I think I've developed a fear of heights.'

Desouza chuckled uncomfortably. 'You're kidding?'

'No. Not the sort of thing I'd kid about.' He closed his eyes and shuddered. He felt suddenly frozen rigid, his hands gripping so tight to the building that his muscles ached. 'Not at a moment like this.'

'I suppose not. A floor or two up would certainly have been better timing.' Desouza's incredulous smile quickly died. 'But you've done this a hundred times before. What happened?'

'I'm not sure. But my last job – I fell. The only small warning I got was feeling dizzy once when looking over a rampart in prison. But when we started up, I thought I'd be fine.'

They were silent for a second, then Desouza said sharply: 'Look up!'

Eric squinted up uncertainly, and Desouza barked the order again. 'Now I'm not going to ask you to look down – you know how many floors you've already climbed. But it's less than half that to where we're going. Five floors, that's all.'

'I . . . I can't do it.' His shuddering ran deeper, his muscles screaming as he clung tight. He feared that if he eased his grip for even a split-second to try and move, the wind would sweep him off the building and he'd fall.

'So what are you going to do?' Desouza quizzed challengingly. 'It's longer down than up.'

'Don't know.' Eric slowly closed his eyes again. 'Just . . . just leave me here. You do it on your own.'

'I can't do that. You know that it's a two-man job. One to take care of the cameras and play look-out while the other raids the computer.'

'But . . . But I can't move. You can *see* that. It's not a game I'm playing.'

'Not a fucking game for me either. I'm stuck halfway up this building too, and suddenly I got no back-up.' Desouza grimaced awkwardly, glancing up. 'So what do you want me to do? Get up there and phone your brother to say I can't help him any more, his son is going to die – because you got cold feet and got stuck halfway up the building. Oh, and your brother's probably fallen by now – so you lost him too. But hey, have a nice day.'

Eric smiled weakly. 'You've got such a way with words, Vince. Anyway, as far as my brother's concerned – I'm not even meant to be on this climb. Remember?'

'Yeah, well.' Desouza shrugged it off as an annoying detail. 'Just that I don't like bullshit. And this is fucking bullshit supreme! It's only half the distance already gone, and you've done it a hundred times before. You can make it!'

Eric peered up, warily eyeing the remaining five floors. It was going to take every ounce of will just to move an inch, let alone cross the chasm Desouza was suggesting.

Another cool whip of wind suddenly hit them, carrying with it the sound of a siren from the streets below. Eric glanced down, but still everything seemed to be swaying, a lazy blur of distant orange streetlights marking grey street-grids. He quickly shut his eyes again. He was shaking so heavily, he feared that that alone would make him lose his grip.

'Besides, we can't stay up here too long,' Desouza said. 'We're gonna get seen.'

'True. True.' At that moment, the prospect of more years in prison was more worrying than plummeting to his death. But either way, he'd be letting André down. And Joël.

Desouza sensed he was on the edge of a decision. He smiled disingenuously. 'And if you're worried about falling – forget it. If you stay here, your muscles are going to lock up and cramp, and in ten or fifteen minutes you'll fall anyway. So if either way you're going to go – you might as well do it climbing. Better to die trying than not trying. Right?'

'Right. Like I said, Vince . . . such a way with words.'

The first clear thoughts hit Chisholm as he was walking back into the grand hall. The first couple of moments he'd been too numb, shaken, to think anything worthwhile past the fireball confusion in his head.

But his legs still felt weak, unsteady, and the throng of voices and clatter of cutlery of a hundred or so people dining didn't help. The sound seemed magnified tenfold, threatening to smother what little clarity of thought he'd been able to muster.

Copell still alive! *Still alive!*

One possibility he'd never have been able to guess. No doubt why he'd felt so adrift. But most damning was that Wenner had chosen not to mention it; in fact, had openly lied about the DNA results.

A venison carpaccio was put in front of him soon after he sat down, but he ate slowly, unenthusiastically, found it hard to swallow.

'Got your speech all prepared?' Lawrence Turnball, one of the dinner organizers, smiled at him from across the table. 'Going to tell us all how to turn those half-dead projects into gold mines?'

'Yes . . . yes. Something like that.' He smiled back, fumbling instinctively for his notes. He couldn't even remember which pocket he'd put them in, let alone how he'd planned to knit the jumbled mass of scrawl into anything cohesive.

Maybe that was why Wenner was coming to Philadelphia that night: to see Copell! But why straight after he'd quizzed himself and Stolk on what files they might have transferred before the explosion? Why was that so important?

Pamela Copell too had said that she hadn't seen her husband – which meant that she must be in on it as well. Chisholm cleared his throat from a bit of venison that got stuck for a moment – but it rapidly turned into a coughing fit that had him reaching for his water glass.

The main thunderbolt of clarity hit him mid-sip, took his breath away – though he quickly covered it with another cough.

He recalled looking at the security video of David Copell's last few minutes before the power went off. When Pamela Copell said he hadn't come home, they hadn't even troubled questioning whether he made it out in the three minutes between that and the bomb going off. Yet at that moment, Copell had been on Stolk's computer, and so he'd have seen exactly where and when they'd transferred all the vital files. *And if Copell had made it out, he'd have passed that information on to Wenner!*

'Are you OK?' Turnball asked.

'Yes, will be . . . will be.' Chisholm coughed again and took another quick sip. That's why Wenner had been so interested in what they said about transferring files. *He was hoping they'd still be where David Copell said they were.* He felt everything around suddenly pressing in on him: the heat, the noise, the hubbub of voices echoing deafeningly in the high-domed hall, Turnball still looking at him slightly questioningly. He had to find a way of getting out of here, *quickly.* He lapsed into another sudden coughing fit, and as he went to sip this time, he fumbled, dropping his glass.

He meant just to spill the water down his shirt-front, an excuse for a hasty escape to the washroom – then out. But the glass caught on the edge of his plate and smashed, and as he jumped up and brushed himself down from the spilt water, he caught his right hand on a shard of glass, cutting it. He dabbed it and then wrapped it quickly with a serviette.

'I'm sorry. Plea . . . please excuse me for a moment.' Now that Wenner knew the files were probably still there, no doubt he was organizing a raid.

'That looks bad,' Turnball commented. 'Do you want someone to look at it?'

'No . . . no. It's OK. A quick swill in the washroom, it'll be fine.' And probably it was going down that night, knowing that he was tied up at a dinner function. *Another reason for Wenner's rush trip to Philadelphia.*

'Roomful of doctors.' Turnball gestured to the throng around with a pained smile. 'If you're going to cut yourself, no better place to do it.'

'No. I'll be fine. Thanks.' He walked rapidly away to deter anyone from following and possibly fussing, and barely paused half a step by the washrooms. Wrapping the serviette tighter around his bloodstained hand, he made his way through the foyer and out into the night.

The member of Wenner's team to pick up on the French bombing alerts put out by Quantico was a new recruit of ten months, John Hooke.

Hooke tried Wenner's number, but it went into voice mail. He left a message, tapping his fingers anxiously as he hung up. Until Wenner came back to him, he was on his own with what to do next, and he wasn't sure that waiting until Wenner landed in Philadelphia was the right thing to do. Events might have progressed too far by then, be impossible to stop.

He decided to meanwhile work on his own initiative, and within an hour had the names of all American citizens on flights returning from Paris within twenty-four hours each side. He then cross-compared that with their voluminous list of potential bombers: the computer came up with two matches: Jack Geddes and Grover Kiernan.

Geddes had arrived at LAX nine hours ago, but Kiernan's flight had been delayed, wasn't due at JFK for another hour and twenty minutes.

Hooke alerted the Los Angeles field office to pay Geddes a visit, then did the same with a New York team to greet Kiernan as he arrived.

Hopefully, meanwhile he'd get a call back from Wenner.

*

Jack Geddes rapidly slipped out of the frame. The visiting field agents discovered that he was in his early sixties and had been on holiday in France with his wife and his son's family of two young children: an unlikely bombing trip.

Whereas Kiernan was in his mid-thirties, travelling alone, and a search of his luggage uncovered a TGV ticket to Lyon for the day of the bombing there. He quickly became the prime suspect.

Though three field agents had been grilling Kiernan without much joy for almost an hour when Wenner's return call came through.

'What the manual tells us to expect, I suppose,' Wenner said with a sigh after Hooke brought him up to date. 'Standard first-stage denial. But if that bomb is going off tonight – we simply don't have the time to wait for him to open up.'

'I know. Do you think we should work on the assumption that it's ORI-gene and call them anyway to warn them?'

'Yeah, good idea. Phone and warn them that that's what we fear. Make sure the building's clear of personnel or records of value.' Wenner glanced at his watch as the streets of West Philadelphia rolled by his hire-car window. Batz was driving. 'We're gonna be at Copell's door in ten or fifteen minutes. Maybe something he has to say too will give us a handle on the next best move. But call ORI-gene, and let me know the minute Kiernan starts to break. *If* he does.'

Hooke looked up ORI-gene's number and dialled. With the time difference, he doubted there'd be anyone there: the most he'd get was an emergency contact number or night security – in which case he'd have to quickly grab an interpreter.

37

Each foot up the building had to be fought for; with each step and fresh handhold, Eric felt his body's shaking worm deeper, every muscle and nerve-end aching and screaming with the effort and tension.

At moments, Eric thought it would have been preferable to fall just to be free of that pain, and on two more occasions on his way up he was completely frozen rigid, felt he couldn't go on another step – and Desouza had to coax and cajole him again, finally losing all patience and grabbing and pulling by his shoulder.

'I'm not leaving you on this fucking building – you hear! Only a floor and a bit to go. *Come on!*'

But as they came up to the part of the building where the sphere angled out, Desouza's expression dropped sharply. Eric slowly shook his head. They'd miscalculated. Rather than being able to crawl straight in where the explosion had left a gaping hole, the first gap didn't start for a good six feet; for that distance, unless they could get ropes attached, they'd have to crawl almost upside down before being able to get in.

Desouza forced a tight smile as he took the rope and grappling hook out of his knapsack. 'I reckoned on maybe a few feet gap. Just looks like I'll have to swing a bit wider.'

'We'll never make it.' Eric continued shaking his head. 'Getting the right angle on something to grapple on to from this angle will be near impossible. And even if you do – we'll be dangling in mid-air with nothing else to grip to before we even knew if it's going to fully take our weight.'

'Never know till you try.' Desouza started swinging.

For the first fifteen minutes, from a chain of stumbling explanations and head-shaking excuses from David Copell for his actions,

Wenner learnt little of value that he didn't already know or had half-guessed: Copell was the mystery Tim McKay who'd sent him the e-mails, and he hadn't come forward before because he was convinced his life was still in danger.

'Yeah, I understand that.' Wenner nodded pensively. 'But when your wife passed on to you that we'd offer protection, and pressed you once again to come in out of the cold – you said that you couldn't until tomorrow. That is, and I quote – "If all goes well tonight with André and we get what we want from the Spheros."' Wenner narrowed his gaze on Copell. 'What is it that's happening with your old friend André Lemoine and the Spheros tonight that's so important that your life – or should I say death – must be put on hold until tomorrow?'

'Nothing, it . . . it was just an expression. I wanted overnight to think about what she'd said. Think everything over.'

'I see.' Wenner remained thoughtful, forcing a tight smile. He noticed Copell glance again at his watch, for now the third or fourth time since he'd arrived. He'd struck a chord. Something *was* happening that night, probably even as they spoke.

But when he pushed more, Copell simply dug in his toes, and he could see himself fencing with Copell for half the night without getting anywhere – until Hooke's second call came through.

'*What?* There's people in the ORI-gene lab in Paris right now?' Wenner kept his eyes firmly on Copell as he spoke, watching his reaction. 'What are they still doing there?'

'Some procedure involving a young boy. And the other strange thing is that they said they had a call earlier warning them about a possible bomb. From a woman.'

'A woman? Do they know who?'

'No. Anonymous call – she didn't give a name. All they passed on to me was that she spoke no French and had an American accent – and that she sounded very nervous, troubled.'

'Right.' Someone in the know perhaps at the Spheros, but surely Chisholm would keep something that sensitive tight to his chest? 'So if they've already been called and warned – why haven't they left?'

438

'That's the problem.' Hooke sighed heavily. 'This procedure they've got on tonight with the boy. They say they can't possibly leave the lab until the procedure's finished. That if they do, the boy will die.'

'If they leave, the boy will die?' Wenner repeated mainly for Copell's benefit. 'But have you explained to them that their good friends at the Spheros have sent them a bomb-greeting – probably set to go off tonight?' The shadow of worry that had crossed Copell's face at the start of his conversation quickly darkened. Copell looked down and chewed at his lip. 'And if they don't get out of there quickly – they could *all* die.'

'Yes – I've explained that. But they say that while that remains only a possibility, or even a probability, they can't do anything. They just have to continue in the hope that there isn't a bomb. Because with the boy, that is a certainty. If they try and move him at this juncture, he'll die.'

'*Oh Jesus*. That's all we need.' The tension of his approaching confrontation with Copell had steadily mounted on the way to Philadelphia. Then had come the call from Hooke about Grover Kiernan; now an anonymous warning call and the news that there was still activity at the ORI-gene labs. And while at first he'd hoped that all of that might provide the final push to get Copell to open up – with the alarming detour it had suddenly taken, it was one pressure, one emergency too many. For the first time he was uncertain what to do next. Both Copell and Batz were looking at him expectantly as he dabbed at the sweat beads on his forehead with the back of one hand. '*OK*. I think it's time for me to speak directly with Grover Kiernan. Ask him if and where he's planted a bomb. As soon as New York have him on the line, get them to call me.'

Wenner waggled his mobile threateningly towards Copell. 'And meanwhile I suggest you think long and hard about telling me *exactly* what's going down tonight. Because, believe me, if I can find any way of holding you accountable for what happens – I will. Starting with obstruction of justice and working the list from there.'

★

It took nine throws of the grappling hook for Desouza to finally attach to an object that felt solid. He'd felt it catch on to something three throws ago, but as he pulled hard, the rope and hook quickly sailed loose. This time, after three firm tugs, it seemed to be holding. With one last tug to make sure, Desouza held one hand out to Eric.

'OK. You first.'

Eric eyed the rope uncertainly. 'I thought you'd want to go first. Show me how it's done.'

Desouza shook his head. 'First one up gets the best shot – because the other one's here holding the other end of the rope. It's not swinging so wild and loose.' But the main reason was because he feared that if left behind, Eric might freeze again and say he wasn't coming up. Desouza wanted to make sure Eric made this last leg.

With another uneasy look up, Eric reached out and gave the rope his own couple of reassuring yanks.

Desouza patted his shoulder encouragingly. 'It's OK. I'll be right behind you. With you every inch of the way.'

Eric nodded and tried to force a smile, but his throat was too tight, too dry. And he was even more conscious of his body shaking as he gripped the rope and swung fully on to it. He shut his eyes and tried to imagine he was doing something simple, like climbing a gym-rope or up to a tree-house as a child – not dangling in mid-air two hundred feet from the ground. And the sickening swaying he'd experienced earlier this time was for real. He felt his stomach lurch, and thought for a moment he was going to vomit.

He swallowed it back, keeping his eyes clenched tight as he desperately clawed his way up. *Gym-rope. Tree-house. Gym-rope. Tree-house.*

But at some point, he felt something different: a bit of give in the rope? Though maybe he was imagining it, his mounting catatonia producing all kinds of illusory demons. But as it happened again, he opened his eyes wide in shock to see the shadow of something beyond the glass – *a chair on its side?* – shifting rapidly back.

He quickly shut them again before the chair, and his grappling rope caught on it, sailed free into the air – couldn't bear to see the fall and the city below rushing towards him, the sensation on its own was bad enough. And this time it was impossible to stop being sick, coughing and choking as he felt himself falling, *falling* . . . feeling like a lifetime, the city lights swirling and spinning . . . though it was little more than a second before the rope suddenly jolted tight again, almost ripping free from his grip.

He let out a sharp gasp, shock as much as relief, and peered up uncertainly: the chair appeared to have caught on another desk eight feet from the first. Though he was now that much further down, five feet beyond where he'd started.

'OK. Easy, *easy*.' Desouza made a calming motion with one hand. 'The worst is over.'

André glanced anxiously at his watch. They'd expected the first contact from Desouza over twenty minutes ago. *What on earth was happening?*

Marielle had urged him to stay calm: 'Shouldn't be much longer now.'

But now she too was starting to look perturbed, biting at her lip as she looked at Joël. His blood-pressure, pulse and respiration had all weakened markedly since they'd first wheeled him in forty minutes ago. His breathing was so shallow it was barely discernible. The only thing that hadn't changed was his temperature – though at this late stage that wasn't a particularly good sign, signalled that his immune system was no longer fighting back.

When the call had come through from the American woman, they'd thought at first that that would be Desouza. Then just minutes ago the second warning about a possible bomb – this time from an FBI agent! Their nerves had leapt again with expectancy when he'd rung – *surely this time it was Desouza?* – and probably Marielle had came across as both disappointed and oddly complacent when she took the call. '*Oh, yes. A bomb. We've already had a call about that.*'

But the second call had made the threat suddenly more immediate, pressing. With the first it had merely been a possible event, 'happening soon . . . that's all I know', or perhaps could have even been disregarded as a hoax.

One thing was certain: if they didn't hear from Desouza quickly, their last chance to save Joël would have gone, he'd have passed the point of no return to be able to respond to *anything*. Then they might as well all pack up and clear the lab, however indeterminate the threat of a bomb might be.

It had taken them only eight minutes to set up everything: connections to monitors for pulse, respiration, ECG, and the computer links to both receive and process the data from Philadelphia.

But listening to the repetitive, bit-by-bit weakening beeps fast ticking down the minutes that Joël had left, now possibly also counting down a bomb while they all stood powerless, waiting, sweating, watching the telephone – their only remaining lifeline of hope – it felt as if everything was crashing in on them at once. And André wondered if that was to be the unbreakable pattern of his life: just when he overcame one set of obstacles, more would suddenly be put before him. The graveyard was determined to win, claim Joël no matter what he did. Maybe it was some sort of divine intervention for meddling where he shouldn't. Only days ago, when Joël hit the blast phase and it looked as if their last options were rapidly slipping away, he'd confronted Hervé with the same.

'Maybe this is God's way of telling me that I'm not meant to interfere. That mixing animal and human genes and characteristics is wrong, against nature and His will. I should stop fighting, just let Joël go peacefully.'

And Hervé had quoted from the Bible about hiding your light under a bushel. 'If God has given you a particular talent, it's wrong not to use it. If you weren't meant to save Joël and others, André – you simply wouldn't have that ability.'

So now, suddenly, it was God's will. But all that André could see – with hope offered with one hand and then cruelly yanked away with the other – was that God hadn't made his mind up yet.

Eric was still catching at his breath as Desouza slumped down beside him. As soon as Eric was up, he'd wound the grappling rope more securely around a pillar before Desouza followed.

'We made it!' Desouza exclaimed breathlessly, the comment

aimed mostly at Eric; it had taken him seven torturous minutes to Desouza's two to make that final leg. Desouza looked around after a second, forcing a wry smile. 'Now comes the difficult part.'

The floor where the bomb had struck had been cleared of glass and small debris – all that remained were half a dozen carbon-stained desks and chairs – then boarded off from the rest of the building. It took Desouza less than a minute to cut a hole through the boarding for them to clamber through. They slipped on their ski-masks, and while Eric systematically spray-painted each security camera on their way up one floor to Chisholm's office, Desouza cut the electricity for all the lights.

Eric found his way across Chisholm's office with a torch. 'Here it is!' he announced after a second. 'Computer number thirty-eight.' He switched it on and sat down.

Desouza was only half paying attention. 'Doesn't look like he's taking the bait.' He listened out a moment more for sounds from the corridor. 'Can't hear no elevator rising.' Their aim had been to wait until it had started on its way up, then cut the power to that too between floors.

'You'll need to do this bit,' Eric said, as the main screen came up with a code entry box.

Desouza took a little black box from his pocket and plugged it into the CPU. Within two minutes it came up with seven series of combined numbers and letters – the first key strokes made on the computer at the start of each work session. Desouza started through them – glancing anxiously every other second towards the corridor and the elevators – and with the fourth code, he was in.

Eric took over again while Desouza went back to listening out. Checking between File Manager and the information André had scrawled on a bit of paper, within a minute he found the first file. He took out his mobile and started dialling.

Desouza held out one hand. 'Don't you think that's a call *I* should be making. So that your brother doesn't know you lied about making the climb?'

'No, doesn't matter. Not much he can say now.' Eric shrugged. 'Fait accompli. Besides, if that security guard does start making his way up, you're going to have to be there to cut the power off fast.'

'*This is Anna Stolk. I'm afraid I'm not here to take your call right now. But please leave a . . .*'

Dani hung up, wiping at her eyes with the back of her hand. Her tears had been streaming so hard as she'd dialled her mother's number that the road ahead had been little more than a watery blur. And now, when she'd finally built up the courage to make the call, try and make some amends, her mother wasn't there. She bet that she'd have been there for her brother. She was always there for him. '*Oh, Simon, so good to . . .*'

She swung out as a cyclist suddenly loomed in front of her. Pulling back in, she felt the car slew slightly. Or perhaps it was her? *Everything* around her – not just her life at that moment – felt strangely adrift.

She looked sharply to the side as her mobile started ringing, finally picking it up on the third ring. *Chisholm!*

'. . . When those macaitin files were transferred from your computer to mine – did you bury all traces on your Norton Delete and file register?' His voice was hesitant and stumbling, almost frantic, far removed from his usual Mr Cool and Calculated.

It took her a second to focus her thoughts. 'No . . . why?'

As Chisholm breathlessly explained his concerns – Copell still being alive and the FBI probably planning to raid his computer to get the vital files – she felt a chill run down her spine like a cold razor. Her foot eased on the accelerator pedal.

'*Still alive?* Are you sure?'

'Absolutely. From the DNA tests, the bone fragments they found were twelve to fifteen years old.'

The skeleton she'd put in the corner of her office! A reminder of med-school days. The chill settled like an icy stone in her stomach.

'I'm heading there right now to bury everything possibly incriminating,' Chisholm said. 'Where are you now?'

'Nowhere.' That's exactly what it felt like suddenly: *heading nowhere.* But no point in saying she was at home; Chisholm could probably hear background traffic sounds. 'Well, heading to a Seven-Eleven. We ran out of milk.'

'Hopefully I'll get there before it's too late. Wenner apparently left Atlanta for here mid-afternoon. I'll . . . I'll phone you tomorrow and let you know.'

'OK.' *Adrift. Heading nowhere.* She stayed on the same road for almost a mile, staring blankly ahead through the steady sweep of her wipers, before the conversation she'd just had fully sank home.

It looked like Wenner was closing in far faster than she'd anticipated, and now their only hope lay with Chisholm getting to the files in time. Certainly, she couldn't also now head there. But Chisholm sounded far from certain, a tentativeness that was both alien and endearing; for the first time he sounded vulnerable. Maybe he knew he was already too late. Or maybe, knowing he had only hours left, he had the same type of file manipulation as her in mind: clean any possible links to his involvement and put her even more in the frame!

Whatever, it looked bad for her. She was going to go down, with or without Chisholm. David Copell too, now that he was still alive, had probably been eagerly spilling to Wenner about how she'd been a prime mover in the macaitin scam as well as making sure he stayed late on the night of the bombing. And now with her call to France, no doubt they'd match that on voice analysis and know it was her! Proof positive that she knew about the planned bomb attack there too.

She banged her fist on the steering wheel. *Shit,* how could she have been so stupid! The drink might have given her the bravado to fight back, but it had also obscured all the possible repercussions. And now she couldn't seem to filter a clear thought through it to know what to do next.

Even if she did now speak to her mother to make some amends, it would appear that she'd only done it because she knew she was about to fall from grace. And what a falling from grace it would be! Her eyes started to fill as she thought again of the finger-pointing and condemnation, '*Worse than the lowest of the low,*' and the years in prison away from Allison. She wiped at her tears to clear her watery, skewed view of the road ahead. *Oh God, I'm sorry, Mom. Help me. Help me!*

Maybe that had been part of the problem all along. Heading on the same road when the main purpose had long ago been lost. What had she been after by even attempting to make amends? To make people suddenly like her, say that she was a good person after all she'd done? Or was the power and the glory, following in Chisholm's path, still more important? That if she did that, they'd respect and like her anyway? Only now was she realizing that those two aims were different and she couldn't have both. And, faced with having to make the choice, she wasn't sure what she wanted from anything any more.

Her mobile rang again. She looked at it accusingly. Who this time? Chisholm again, her mother phoning back? No. It was a number she didn't recognize – and right now she didn't feel like talking to anyone.

She let it continue ringing, and as she looked back up she was late seeing the red light. Whether because of the distraction of the phone, her tear-blurred vision, or the drink dulling her reactions, she wasn't sure.

The red light imprinted itself on her mind almost at the same time as the car flashing across the junction only yards ahead of her. She braked hard – but with the wet road her wheels locked and she slid at an angle for eight yards before finally coming to rest. *Lights and screaming*. That's all that she was suddenly aware of as the headlights, screeching brakes and blaring klaxon of the truck fast bearing down on her swamped her senses.

And at the last second, her foot paused on the accelerator to get out of its way: whether because she realized it was already too late, or because she saw it as a welcome release, an oblivion from everything she saw ahead, she wasn't sure. She wasn't sure of anything any more.

'Tell me, Kiernan . . . *tell me*. Or, by God, if anyone's killed tonight, I'll make sure the key's thrown away for so long that you'll forget what women and Big Macs look like, let alone taste like.'

When Wenner had first mentioned that there were people in the ORI-gene lab that night, Kiernan commented, 'Simply ask them to shift – then you've got no worries,' and Wenner had explained about the young boy that would die if they moved him. So what they needed to know, *right now*, was where the bomb was and what time it was set for. But still it had been heavy going from there, as if Kiernan thought it might be an invented story just to get him to open up – and it wasn't until Wenner openly lied and said that they'd picked up *two* DNAs from past bombings, 'And I'll bet anything one of those is going to match yours,' that he sensed Kiernan was on the edge of breaking.

Wenner could almost hear Kiernan's mind totting up everything stacked against him: positive ID on him buying C4 in France, train ticket to Lyon, match on that same C4 on both the Lyon bomb and the one set for that night in Paris, now a likely DNA from a past bombing. Kiernan knew that he was all but roped and tied.

'OK . . . OK. But if I give you what I know and the people behind it, I want a deal just on property damage – no talk of manslaughter or indictment under any terrorist acts.'

It wasn't a difficult deal for Wenner to make: on the one accidental fatality so far, with no DNA or other possible links, they had nothing to get near securing a conviction against Kiernan for that bombing. But Kiernan sounded put off stride when Wenner accepted so lightly his grand announcement of Julius Chisholm being behind it. 'Yeah, we already worked that one out. What we need to know now is where and what time that Paris bomb is set for?'

'I . . . I remember the time: Half-past three in Paris. Well, tomorrow morning. Late, because when I reccied the area early evening it was pretty busy. I didn't want any bystanders to get hurt.'

'Really considerate of you.' Wenner found Kiernan's sudden soft-soap act sickening. He was already practising his trial testimony. 'Now where, Kiernan? *Where?*'

'Inside one of the computers. But . . . but I don't remember exactly which one.'

'You're kidding me?'

'It was one hell of a rush . . . there were sounds outside. I thought someone might be coming into the building. It was a computer in the open general office – not one of the private offices. That . . . that's all I remember.'

'What about even an approximation: second, third or fourth computer from where you came in?'

'Sorry . . . can't be sure. I just picked one at random with my penlight and went to work as quick as I could. Then out again.'

Wenner sighed heavily. The most he was probably going to get from Kiernan. He got put back to the field agent in charge and said that he'd want to speak to Kiernan again later after he'd made some notes. 'Meanwhile, hold your questioning. Just let him cool his heels.'

Wenner noticed that Copell had looked anxious through much of his conversation with Kiernan, chewing at his bottom lip and checking his watch at intervals.

'We'll talk in just a minute,' Wenner said. He kept his eyes resolutely on David Copell as he dialled ORI-gene's number, even after Copell – obviously perturbed by the pattern of events – cast his eyes down and cradled his head in one hand.

'Yes, I know I promised. And I know that Hervé would go mad and never forgive you if he ever found out . . . and I'm sorry. But with us being let down at the last moment like that – there wasn't much else I could do. It was either I made the climb with Desouza, or there was no climb.'

From his position by the doorway, Desouza waved impatiently with one hand: a 'get done with the apologies, let's get on with it' gesture.

'Yes . . . yes. It went well. No problems at all.'

Desouza shrugged incredulously and smiled.

'We . . . we were held up because there were a couple of people in a car close by the building. We had to wait for them to go. Now . . . do you want that data or not? We can't hang around here long. I've got the screen open in front of me right now.'

'Of course,' André said, the sudden edge in Eric's voice sparking an uneasy bond between them: Eric thousands of miles away in a strange building in the dead of night, somewhere he shouldn't be, and both of them united in that instant in trying to save Joël's life. 'Send it through.'

'There's a lot of files with the maict prefix. More even than you put on the list.'

'That's OK. Just send it all, as Marc instructed. We'll sift through the files at this end to find what we're after.'

Marc signalled from his desk to André's side. 'Everything's ready to go here.' One computer to receive the data, another two to process and analyse it.

'Right. I'm making the connection . . . *now*.'

And as seconds later André heard the shrill beep by Marc's computer, the link, the bond between them was complete: the metronome-beat tension from Joël's monitors suddenly reflected in Eric's shallow breathing as he waited expectantly at the other end.

'Is everything coming through OK?' Eric asked after a moment.

André watched as the first text and columns of figures appeared on Marc's screen. 'Looks like it . . . looks like it.' And suddenly, after the long, anxious wait, the lab was a flurry of activity as Marc started calling out numbers and Marielle sat at the computer alongside him to hurriedly feed them in and start analysing them. 'Got to go now. All hands on deck time.'

In contrast, Eric and Desouza's end was strangely passive at that moment, waiting and silently watching the light flickering on Chisholm's computer as it fed through the data that could save Joël's life.

'I don't like it,' Desouza said, half an ear still on the corridor. 'It's too quiet. The guard sees us spray the security cams, and just sits there. Doesn't come up to investigate.'

'Maybe he was taking a leak, or somewhere else at the time.'

'Yeah. And he comes back to find the security cams for two floors blacked out and half the power gone – and he's not a teensy bit curious? No. Something's wrong.'

38

The lights of Philadelphia's Schuylkill Expressway flashed by Wenner's side window as Batz drove.

Everything had gelled for Wenner halfway through his call to ORI-gene: people in the lab that night, a procedure that couldn't be interrupted, Copell looking anxiously at his watch. He wheeled on Copell as soon as he put the phone down.

'Somebody's sending through the data from the Spheros tonight, aren't they?'

And although Copell didn't answer, the look in his eyes and him anxiously rubbing his forehead with one hand said enough.

'Why didn't you just continue with trying to get us to raid the Spheros files, as you'd pushed for in your e-mails as Tim McKay? If you'd come out into the open – we'd have probably been able to do that.'

Probably. That was half the problem, Copell explained. There was no guarantee. And even if they had raided, the vital files would have been tied up for weeks or months with lawyers. 'And right now, Lemoine's son simply doesn't have that sort of time. He's only got days left.'

Wenner closed his eyes for a second in acknowledgement. 'Why tonight in particular? Not yesterday or tomorrow night?'

'Chisholm's indisposed. An important dinner function where he's one of the main speakers.'

'*Yeah?* Let's see if we can make sure he's *indisposed* for a while longer.' Wenner smiled wryly: the thought of arresting Chisholm in front of all his contemporaries particularly tickled him. But when he got through to Penn Hall to find out Chisholm's table so that he could instruct the local Philadelphia PD officers, he was told that Chisholm was no longer there.

'Left in quite a hurry. Missed his speech and most of the dinner, in fact.'

Within two minutes they were on the Schuylkill Expressway, heading for the Spheros building. Wenner sat in the back with Copell as Batz drove.

'Looks like I'm not the only one the last shoe has just dropped for,' Wenner commented.

Copell was back to cradling his head in one hand as the city lights flashed by. 'They're in the middle of the procedure right now. I only needed another hour or two – then I could have told you everything.'

'Yeah, well. Turning a blind eye to a felony in progress for an hour or two?' Wenner shrugged. 'Under the circumstances, I could probably have accommodated. But I doubt that Chisholm's going to cut anything like the same slack. So right now let's just worry about getting there before him. And hope that in Paris they can find the computer with the bomb – or finish what they're doing in time.'

As soon as Chisholm had left the dinner, he'd phoned the Spheros reception foyer desk and spoke to the relief security guard for the past ten days, Bill Mathieson.

'Has anyone turned up at the reception desk tonight?'

'No.'

'Well, if they do . . . however official they claim their business might be, whether they're FBI or local Philadelphia PD – you're not to let them pass reception, is that clear?'

'Yes, sir . . . that's clear.'

'I'm on my way to you right now – so if they do show, tell them you're under strict instructions not to let anyone pass until I arrive. When I get there, I'll have the Spheros lawyers deal with whatever warrants they might show. And meanwhile, whatever happens, don't leave your post at the reception desk. You must be there to confront and stop whoever might approach. Is that also clear?'

'Yes . . . yes. That's also clear.'

Then he called Dani Stolk, with the main purpose to sound out if Wenner might have got to her already – but she seemed to show genuine surprise at all the right moments. The only thing was that she sounded slightly distant, subdued, though that might have been through shock at the sudden turnaround of events, or because he'd shouted at her on his last call. He made sure this time to keep an even keel, appear anxious because of what had happened, obviously, but not let rip full-bore with the abject panic he felt at that moment. It was play cards close to your chest time again.

But as soon as he put the phone down, staring emptily, icily ahead as the road spun below his wheels, the pressure-cooker panic was back like a tight knot in his chest. He sped through an amber light ahead, turned sharply on to Walnut Street bridge, then put his foot hard down again. He could almost imagine the smiling, back-patting, appreciative faces from the dinner he'd just left, suddenly becoming sneering, disdainful, finger-pointing.

No! No! *No!* He banged his fist on the horn at a car ahead uncertain about which lane to take, swung out, and accelerated past. He was brighter and sharper than the lot of them put together, let alone the likes of Wenner and his monosyllabic spic sidekick. He was damned if he was going to let them get the better of him.

He hit the end of bridge ramp so hard that his suspension shuddered, swung with a screeching slide into 24th Street that started to go into a spin before he straightened and sped up again – and by the time he reached the Spheros building his whole body was shaking uncontrollably from the breakneck drive and what might await him there.

Security guard Mathieson had watched in numb horror as a ski-masked figure successively sprayed three of the security cameras between the sixteenth and seventeenth floor – then seconds later two more cameras had suddenly gone dark. Probably the power had been cut, Mathieson surmised: both had gone at the same time, and Mathieson hadn't noticed anyone approaching them.

He'd have gone up there, except for Chisholm's stern warning about leaving the front desk. Possibly it was a set-piece distraction to get him away from his post so that others meanwhile could gain entry. He decided to sit tight. Chisholm said that he'd be there soon: let him determine what should be done when he arrived.

Mathieson got to his feet the second that Chisholm, breathless, eyes darting anxiously around, burst through the main doors and approached him.

'Nobody turned up yet?'

'No . . . not down here. But something's happened up on the sixteenth floor.' As Mathieson hesitantly explained, the darting uncertainty in Chisholm's eyes became more intense, finally settling with a fiery focus on Mathieson.

'How long ago was this?'

'Four, five minutes ago. Not long after you called.'

'And why on earth didn't you go up to deal with it?' Chisholm waved one arm wildly in exasperation.

Mathieson thought for a moment that Chisholm was going to hit him, and noticed for the first time Chisholm's bloodstained hand. A couple of blood droplets spattered his uniform jacket with the motion.

'Be . . . because you told me to stay here. Not to move under *any* circumstances.'

Oh Jesus. The lack of initiative of the everyday worker. Chisholm rubbed his aching temples. The fireball smouldering in his brain since leaving the dinner exploded in a blinding white light, stinging the back of his eyes, and he swayed unsteadily for a moment, as if he were about to faint.

Wenner obviously had kept one step ahead of him. Knowing that he'd probably block a conventional raid and tie it up with the Spheros lawyers for weeks, he'd arranged this little unofficial visit.

Chisholm focused again on Mathieson. He reached out and touched Mathieson's shoulder. 'You got a gun? Know how to use it?'

'Yes . . . yes, sir.' Though Mathieson sounded far from certain.

'Then follow me.' Chisholm headed swiftly across the foyer and punched one of the elevator buttons, then suddenly paused, remembering that on a few occasions Kiernan had cut the power to the elevators, trapping the security guards inside. 'Let's take the stairs. If the power has gone for two floors, it might go for the elevators too.'

They started their way up at a run, their urgent footsteps echoing ominously on the marble staircase.

Eighteen minutes until the bomb went off.

André knew that they wouldn't even be halfway through the procedure by then. They'd only just started getting to grips with the first few sets of macaitin data when Wenner's second call came through.

'We can't shift *all* the computers on the open floor,' Marc argued. 'This one we've got to keep linked, and Marielle's already deep into processing on hers. We simply don't have the time to start all over again.'

'But we've got to do something,' André protested. 'It's not a might-be any more – it's a certainty. In eighteen minutes it's going to go off!'

Marc glanced towards the private offices to one side. 'I suppose we could do one thing. Use the computer in your office as the second one for processing, where we know there's nothing planted. That at least reduces the risk.'

André quickly surveyed the room, counting: eleven computers on the open floor. More than a one in five chance if they removed nine of them. Better than the odds for Joël, he reminded himself sourly.

'OK . . . OK. But let's break the back of this data, see where we stand first with Joël. Has the data on Joël's sample come through yet?'

'Looks like just through on this second batch,' Marielle called out, her eyes glued to the screen. 'Sample MC-3.'

'What does it say?'

'Just processing it now . . . *Yes!* Here it is, 6.41 to 6.43 millilitres per litre.'

André went into his office, leaving the door wide open, and started furiously tapping out on his computer. He looked at the results after a moment, banging the flat of his hand against his forehead as if it might force home some clarity. The sample had been sent through when Joël's haemoglobin had been 54 and his platelets 48; now it was a world apart from that, and there were simply too many possible variables to work out in between.

'Has the sample I sent through with low haemoglobin and platelet counts come through yet?' He shouted towards Marielle. 'MC-7, I think it was.'

Marielle shrugged and looked towards Marc. Marc answered.

'No . . . Not through yet.'

André leapt up and came to look over Marc's shoulder. 'We desperately need that. Joël's haemoglobin and platelet counts have shifted too far in the meantime to work the calculations through with any accuracy.' André looked anxiously at his watch. 'Especially in the time we have.'

They all silently watched the data feeding through on Marc's computer for a moment.

'Pulse 38, respiration 13,' Bernice called out, as if as a stark reminder. There simply wasn't the time to stand immobile staring at a computer screen.

André checked his watch again, *fifteen minutes*, as he made the decision. 'Let's shift the computers now! Until that data's through, we can't do anything – so we might as well use the time!'

They agreed that it would take far too long to go up and down the stairs with each computer – so they'd simply dump them out of the window at the far end where they'd fall into a side courtyard by the rubbish bins, away from the front street and the monkey houses at the back.

André and Marc unplugged and shifted them while Bernice tended to Joël and Marielle kept watch on the data feeding through. They knew nothing about *plastique* and whether or not it might explode on impact, but as a precaution they stepped back from the windows and hunched down with each computer dropped. The shrieking of the monkeys seemed to increase with each one that crashed to the courtyard below, and the rattling of the trains was also stronger through the open windows, adding to the mayhem of the moment.

Eric's faint voice came over the phone by Marielle's desk. They'd left the line open so that they could tell Eric when they had what they wanted. Marielle picked it up.

'Everything OK your end?' Eric asked with an edge of concern.

'Yes. It's just the monkey houses next door. I think all the activity here has got them a bit excitable.' Marielle smiled tightly. Eric knew nothing of the added problems their end. André hadn't wanted to worry him, with everything else Eric had on his plate at that moment.

'And is everything still coming through all right?'

'Yes, fine. We're just waiting on one or two bits more, then that should be it.'

'OK. I'll speak to you again in a minute.'

André was heavily out of breath after shifting only his second computer, and with everything else happening around him at that moment – the shrieking monkeys, the rattle of the train, his breathlessness reminding him of his cycle-ride after Eban's death, Marielle smiling tightly at him as she traded another half-truth on his behalf, the beep of Joël's machines struggling to keep a bizarre rhythm to it all as Bernice stood watch, her face fearful that she might lose this one too – it felt as if half of his life was funnelling into that single instant. Though André wasn't sure whether that signalled that this time he'd finally win through, or whether . . .

'It's coming through!' Marielle screamed. 'MC-7.'

André ran across, hastily signalling to Marc. 'Can you take care of the rest on your own?' Three computers left to throw out.

André's whole body was trembling from the exertion and his legs felt weak, and he steadied himself with one hand on the edge of Marielle's desk as he looked over her shoulder. Or maybe it was also from the blind panic and sleepless nights of the past days and weeks. The text on screen swam in and out of focus for a second before finally becoming clear, and André let out a small gasp, almost disbelief, that it was coming through in time. The first part was preamble and patient history, information they'd originally supplied to the Spheros, but next up would be the vital macaitin data.

If any of them had listened to the telephone laid on Marielle's desk for the last couple of minutes, they'd have heard the excitable voices at the other end. But the shrieking of the monkeys and the crashing of computers had drowned it out.

The first sounds to reach them were two gunshots. Then a second later the computer screen went blank.

Desouza first picked up the rapidly approaching footsteps when they were two to three floors below.

He signalled frantically to Eric to keep quiet. Eric was at that moment on the phone to Paris, and Desouza started to panic that that would pinpoint their position. Without that, those approaching – two or three people by the sound of it – might start searching the floor below where they'd come in. They'd gain a couple more vital minutes.

'OK. I'll speak to you again in a minute.' Eric put the phone down hastily.

They both stayed silent, breath held, as they listened to the approaching footsteps. They heard a bit of shuffling on the floor below, as if one of them had broken off to do a peremptory search – then they continued up towards them.

'Is it still feeding through?' Desouza asked; an icily urgent whisper as he looked hastily around.

'Yes . . . *yes!*'

Few places to hide effectively, Desouza noted, especially for Eric. Although he was behind the glass screen annexing Chisholm's office, the door was wide open and he was highlighted in the glow from Chisholm's computer screen.

They didn't even bother to try. Desouza simply took a few steps back and raised one hand in mute greeting as Chisholm and the guard burst through the door.

'They're armed!' Chisholm screamed, catching heavily at this breath. 'Shoot them!'

The guard raised his gun, already pulled from its holster, a few inches higher.

Desouza raised both arms defensively. '*No* . . . no we're not!'

'We're not,' Eric echoed, following suit.

Chisholm smiled thinly as he picked up Eric's French accent. 'I should have known! Lemoine's behind this little soirée!' He should have guessed that this was a step too far for Wenner's blood. Apart from anything else, the scream of falsely gained evidence would probably have knocked any prosecution down at the first hurdle.

Chisholm only then noticed that his computer screen was on. They were sending the information through to Lemoine as they spoke!

'Give me that!' he snapped at Mathieson.

Mathieson put up only brief resistance, as if unsure what Chisholm intended to do, before letting the gun free from his grasp.

Chisholm's first shot went high, shattering his office glass partition and an entire section of the glass wall behind. A few papers wafted loose from his desk with the cool wind suddenly drifting in as Eric and Desouza instinctively ducked. But the second shot was on target, hit the computer screen square-on. It flashed and sparked as half of its screen and side-casing flew off.

'There! That's put paid to your little game!' Chisholm smiled cynically, though part of his mind was still doing somersaults as to whether he'd got there in time. What if the main data had already been sent through? And after French Accent's initial glare, Chisholm noticed his eyes drift to something else just below his desk – then quickly back up again.

The information was still feeding through!

Chisholm hustled quickly into his office, keeping Eric at bay with the gun, and went around to see the tell-tale orange light flickering on the CPU below his desk. He pointed the gun at it.

'*No!* No, you don't!'

The jolt from French Accent suddenly lunging across caught him by surprise, throwing his shot off as they tumbled backwards.

There was a yard between them at that point, and Chisholm eased off his next shot directly at French Accent, hitting him in the shoulder. Chisholm gloated as he saw him flung back, and levelled and aimed again at the CPU.

Eric was blind to all else at that moment: his shattered shoulder, the fact that Chisholm's next shot would no doubt finish him, Chisholm smiling crazily as the breeze through the shattered window behind lifted at his hair, and the sickening, swaying drop only feet away that he'd spent the last forty minutes clawing desperately, inch-by-inch, to escape from. In that instant all he focused on was the information feeding through that could save Joël's life; a sense that his own life was worthless in comparison, spent.

With a rousing grunt, Eric threw himself again at Chisholm – the shot sounding deafeningly over his shoulder – unsure whether or not it had struck the CPU as they flew irresistibly back towards the void of the sheer drop behind.

André banged his fist on Marielle's desk as the screen went blank, imagining the spread of tombstones suddenly rising up from it as he realized he was too late. The pattern of his life wasn't going to change: as ever, he'd been brought to the very edge, hope dangled enticingly in front of him, then . . .

'André . . . *André!*' Marielle shook his shoulder brusquely. 'It's coming through again.'

André opened his clenched eyes – the first time that he'd closed his eyes to the world outside in the hope that meantime it would change and it had actually worked – to see the data continuing to spread out on screen.

Marielle pulled the phone back to her ear, shouting again urgently, '*Eric!*' Still no response; she'd already called his name out twice with no answer.

Then suddenly, as three more gunshots sounded in quick succession, she shouted his name repeatedly again – the last a frantic scream that had everyone in the room looking expectantly at her for a long, frozen moment. But still nothing. The screen suddenly went blank again in time with the last gunshot.

'Is it enough?' she asked André anxiously.

'I . . . I don't know. Probably.' At least the main body of the data had started to feed through: 11.54 to 11.57 ml. But half of his mind was still on what might have happened to Eric. Focus . . . *focus!*

Marielle clutched at his right arm. 'Just do your best. That's all anyone could expect of you, André.'

He closed his eyes for a second and nodded solemnly, then rushed across to his computer. He could probably work the calculations from there, but under this sort of time straitjacket it was excruciating. His fingers started to ache as he tapped relentlessly at his keyboard, sweat drops blurring his vision at intervals as they ran into his eyes – but feeling as if he could hardly even spare the time to wipe them away. Within minutes, he'd filled almost two pages with calculus, and his head was spinning with it.

At the end of the room, Marc boldly announced that he was throwing out the last computer. He huddled down, but there was no explosion.

'Only 36 and 12 now!' Bernice shouted, the tremor clear in her voice; and coming almost as an echo, Marielle called out a series of figures from her own calculations. André fed them in, did some rapid cross-calculations, then anxiously checked his watch again: *six minutes until the bomb!*

André mopped at his brow with the back of one hand as he continued tapping furiously – *no time* left to dwell on what else was going on around him at that moment, his jaw working tightly, the muscles at the back his neck knotted and screaming with tension, his head feeling as if it was about to burst.

Five minutes . . . four. 35 and 11. 12.55 to 12.57 . . .

André leapt up as he hit the final result. He did the last calculation for Joël's blood volume standing, leaning over the keyboard, then shouted out the result to Marielle.

'The median is 47.64!'

They already had a flask with the macaitin formula by Joël's gurney, and Marielle rushed over and started measuring into a syringe. André did the last of the measuring as he came over, then, with a brief look heavenward as Bernice raised the vein in Joël's left arm, steadily pressed it home.

And watched and waited expectantly.

Three minutes twenty . . . three minutes ten . . .

'34 and 10,' Bernice announced.

Joël's pulse and respiration were still falling.

And as they came under the three-minute mark, Marc shouted: 'We'd better move it now! I don't think we can afford to wait any longer.'

They'd agreed that just before the bomb went off, they'd shift to the end of the room furthest away from where they'd dropped the computers, and move the three remaining computers to below the window. Marc and André shifted the computers while Bernice and Marielle moved Joël and his surrounding monitors.

Two minutes forty . . . thirty . . .

'*33 and 10 . . . 32.*'

But halfway along, with a computer in his arms, Marc announced breathlessly, 'We can get rid of these too, now! We don't need them any more!' And he hoisted and threw the computer out of the window.

André followed suit, still no explosions, the crashing bringing a renewed flurry of screeching from the monkey houses.

'*32 and 9 . . . 31. 30!*'

Bernice had to scream to be heard above the bedlam, and as André and Marc ran back and started shifting a couple of desks into position as a final barricade to their huddled group, André saw the sudden shudder in Joël's body and heard the dull, monotone buzz from the ECG machine before Bernice's screams.

'Flatline . . . *Flatline!*'

Marielle barged past the half-upturned desks and grabbed the defibrillator. André took the pads and leant over Joël's body.

'*OK!* Stand clear!'

But as he hit with the charge, Joël's body suddenly struck him as abhorrent, obscene: eyes sunken, skin ghostly and pale, mouth drawn tight in a rictus, his body so frail and skeletal that as the charge jolted through him it looked as if it might shatter what was left of it – a lifetime apart from the smiling, loving Joël he knew – and André began to question what he was doing. For the past ten months pumping Joël with one drug after another, and now one last, desperate attempt with a drug that had never been tried before, a supposedly eons-old link yanked from some dark jungle depths –

while he risked the lives of his own brother and all those around him.

One minute thirty . . . twenty . . .

Still an ECG flatline, as if the monotone beep were urging: *Let him go . . . let him go!*

Maybe he'd been right: he wasn't meant to meddle. And maybe Hervé had simply been humouring him, telling him what he wanted to hear when he told him otherwise: that God wouldn't have given him the ability if he hadn't wanted him to . . .

'André! . . . *André!*' Marielle's sharp voice snapped him to, reminding him to try again. As ever, her soft eyes imploring him not to give up.

Yet suddenly he wasn't sure what he wanted any more. And as he hit again with a charge, like so much else in his life, he felt as if he was doing it mostly to please everyone else. His own thoughts and emotions had ceased to have relevance . . . he was just a passenger.

Fifty seconds . . . forty . . .

Still flatline.

But at that moment André noticed something that sent a chill through him: the main junction box at the far end where the bomb was going to go off. If he didn't restart Joël's heart before the electricity went down, all hope was lost in any case. God would have made the decision for him, taken the last chance of saving Joël from his grasp.

'Help me . . . *Help me!*'

The dizzying, swaying view of Philadelphia streets far below was suddenly there again, and for a moment Eric wasn't sure if he'd actually fallen and his mind was replaying the last thing he'd seen as he lay on the ground, dying, or whether he'd somehow, miraculously, clung on. He just couldn't work out how. He hadn't reached out for anything.

Then he noticed his legs and part of one thigh caught around a small section of glass wall left in place, and felt himself slip another inch as Chisholm, grunting and wheezing, eyes wide with fear, clutched at one arm.

'Just let the fucker go!' Desouza screamed, moving towards them.

'I can't! He's got hold of me as much as I've got him.'

Desouza clutched desperately at Eric's trouser leg and waist, but with Chisholm's weight the other end it took every ounce of his strength to hold Eric where he was, let alone pull him back in.

Below them, a car swung into the car park and three men got out, looking up, and the sound of sirens drifted from a block away. Seconds later, two squad cars also swung in – the sudden activity going in and out of Eric's vision as Chisholm swung below him in the wind whipping around the building.

Chisholm suddenly gasped, eyes widening, as he slipped down a few more inches.

Desouza had yanked hard, putting all his strength into it, and managed to pull Eric back an inch – but at the same time the movement had dislodged Chisholm slightly.

'Lose him! *Lose him!*' Desouza screamed. 'Otherwise I won't be able to hold you any longer.'

Mathieson, who'd followed a few steps behind Desouza and looked on bemusedly for a moment, leant over to help at that point – but was only able to get a partial grip with Desouza in the way.

Eric felt Chisholm sliding inexorably down his arm as he lost all strength to hold on – but it seemed somehow wrong to just let him fall to his death, and Eric suddenly clutched tight to Chisholm's hand.

'Hold on! *Hold on!*' he shouted. But Chisholm's hand was slippery with something – despite his best efforts, Chisholm continued to slide from his grasp – and at the last second Eric closed his eyes in resignation. '*Sorry.*'

Though as Chisholm fell away, in his cynical mind – how he viewed everyone and everything, and probably what he'd have done with the situation reversed – he was sure that French Accent had smiled wryly as he'd said it.

*

The blast was an unstoppable maelstrom, smashing every window and half the masonry at the far end and hurling the fragments in a whirlwind across the room.

André and Marielle huddled over Joël's body to protect him, and André felt the sting as the fragments hit his body and heard Bernice grunt as she was hit by a larger chunk of masonry. André felt that one cheek and his neck were damp, probably cuts from flying glass, but he couldn't see how badly anyone else was hurt: it was dark, the air filled with dust.

André thought he'd heard Joël's ECG heart-rhythm start up again just before the blast, but he couldn't be sure: the deafening explosion quickly drowned out all else, and now with no instrument readings, all he could do was feel for Joël's pulse.

The shrieking from the monkeys outside was now deafening, and everyone in the huddle around Joël was coughing intermittently. André had to concentrate and stifle his own coughing to pick up anything from Joël's pulse: it was there, but weak!

André ran across the room, feet crunching on the broken glass.

'What are you doing?' Marielle asked.

'Adrenalin . . . *adrenalin!*' André shouted back. He knew that Joël's pulse wouldn't hold unless he did something quickly.

Though there was another worrying factor discovered with this particular sample, probably because the haemoglobin and platelet counts were so low . . .

They'd treated Joël with high-dose enzymes for the past five days to make his cells more receptive to the macaitin, but with his haemoglobin and platelets at this level, they needed an extra kick-start. He was sure that's what the last test report from Philadelphia was about to say before the link was cut.

André fumbled frantically among the flasks and vials in the cabinet – but it was impossible to find anything under these circumstances: one of the cabinet doors had blown off, half of its contents were either smashed or spilt, and the only faint illumination was from streetlight filtering in. André's eyes stung as he peered through the thick dust to try and read labels.

'36 . . . 35.' Marielle had taken over reading Joël's pulse. 'Weakening again!'

There were normally three or four adrenalin flasks in this cabinet. *Surely* . . . Finally André found one that was intact, raced back across, measured into a syringe, and injected.

'34 . . . 33.'

'Come on . . . *Come on!*' And started a silent prayer that he wasn't too late, or that the adrenalin wouldn't kick the macaitin into overdrive to start eating through Joël's healthy cells like a rotavator; or the myriad of other possibilities that they hadn't been able to take account of in the time they had.

'32 . . . *31!*'

'Please, Joël . . . *Please!*' And as André clasped Joël's frail hand in his and felt his rapidly dying pulse, his tears flowed freely, cutting stark, ghostly rivulets through the blood on one cheek. They'd gone too far, sacrificed too much – *all of them* – for it all to be lost now.

André felt suddenly dizzy, faint, as the boiling emotions and exhaustion of the past long months finally pushed him over the edge, made him lose his last grip on reality – and with the heavy shrieking of the monkeys, he was suddenly back in the tree with the snake only a foot away, the teeth-baring of the monkeys becoming death's head grimaces. André even thought he saw a background flash of lightning, completing the picture – but it was only the electrical sparks from a train. And as the train passed and the flashing died, André feared that the tombstones would rise up again in the darkness to confront him. One final showdown.

'11 . . . holding. 12 . . . 13. Picking up again.'

But as the cloying dust of the room settled, a light started to break through: the city lights of central Paris with a backdrop of irradiated moonlight beyond a heavy cloud layer. André had never been in the labs this late at night, especially with all the lights out, and so it was a view he'd never noticed before. But in that moment, the light struck him as strangely, eerily beautiful, like the distant light of hope in Dalí's *Calvary* – and as he felt himself drawn towards it, the light striking and flowing gently through his body in a warm, cathartic wave, he knew that everything was going to be all right.

39

Wenner stood in front of Philadelphia's Justice Courts building and, with an air of dramatic relief, exhaled his first puff of Mahawat.

Five years. Could have been worse. Could have been better, too.

Danielle Stolk had survived the accident with a broken leg, fractured pelvis and only flesh cuts. The in-house joke at the Spheros – David Copell whispered in Wenner's ear as she walked into the courtroom – was that she was a witch and could walk free from any cataclysm.

Certainly, the only outward signs of her accident at the time of the trial six months later were some ugly scar tissue on her neck and a heavy limp which she aided with a walking stick. Though even that Copell said she'd exaggerated to try and draw sympathy from the judge and jury. A cripple trying to bring up a young daughter on her own.

The only area in which they found her to be severely crippled was emotionally.

While the judge accepted that she probably hadn't known about the bombings until late in the day, and her final actions in trying to warn ORI-gene stood in her favour, he pointed out that she'd been fully aware that André Lemoine's son might well die without the macaitin treatment at issue, yet had still willingly participated in stealing it.

With Chisholm no longer around to face charges, she'd also quickly seized the opportunity to blame him for everything, paint herself merely as a tame pawn with little other choice. But from the judge's summing-up, this seemed to have backfired and gone against her.

He described her as a sadly misguided individual who'd put her own ambitions above all else, bringing disgrace to her profession and providing a pitiful role model. 'Only perhaps, for what *not* to do. And when the opportunity arises, you appear eager to blame anyone and all else for your own actions. Possibly to try and convince yourself that you've done no wrong, and perhaps even to gain some sympathy: paint the picture that you too have been a victim. Even now as you stand before me, you seem to have learnt little from the events which brought you here. *Five years!'*

With no accomplice-to-murder charge on the table, only industrial espionage and property damage, probably close to the maximum the judge could have given. Certainly, it was a year more than Kiernan's sentence, a measure of how the judge saw her as more culpable.

Chisholm had hit the ground within a minute of Wenner arriving. 'When I said that he was going to go down, not exactly what I had in mind,' he'd joked cynically to Batz. But for a moment he'd worried what might await him seventeen floors up. Thankfully, Eric Lemoine's shoulder wound wasn't serious, and there'd been no charges pressed against him or Desouza. No other property had been affected, they'd merely been taking back what had originally been stolen from ORI-gene.

Wenner took another long draw of his cigarette and raised his hand for a taxi. He'd spent long enough in this city these past months; he was eager to get away.

David Copell had appeared in court two days ago to make his statement, but today he was rushing around making final arrangements for his return to Paris.

As Wenner settled into the back of a cab heading towards Philadelphia International, he took out his mobile to tell Copell the good news.

'Look . . . *look! Stop!'*

Marielle had been driving slowly owing to the snow, but because of what she knew the bridge had represented to André, she'd slowed a fraction more, and Joël had noticed the two squirrels perched on the bridge railings. One of them was trying to open a nut while the other looked on.

Predictably, as soon as they stopped and got out, the squirrels scampered off across the graveyard, their trail showing clearly on the virgin snow.

Two days after Christmas. It had been Marielle's idea to go out, invariably the one with bright, exciting ideas for outings.

'Let's go to Montmartre. It's like a big ice-castle on a day like this – and you can see over the whole of Paris.'

She quickly sparked equal enthusiasm in Joël, and so André simply shrugged. A passenger again, yet now a more willing one.

It had taken him five months to finally get round to telling Charlotte about Marielle – by which time she'd already half-guessed from occasional slipped comments from Veruschka and Joël. He needn't have worried. She was settled in her relationship with Henri Porcelet, and had in fact started to worry about how he might react to talk of divorce and remarriage. Now that she was more grounded and solid, she'd feared that he might, in turn, be vulnerable, unstable – as if one of them in the relationship had to take that role.

They'd gone down to Provence that summer as a family – himself, Marielle, Veruschka and Joël – and as part of the holiday had one day visited Gallinard.

Gallinard proudly showed them round his garden, which took two gardeners to upkeep, 'Though on days when my bones don't feel too stiff, I still do a bit myself,' and Joël looked up at one point, enquiring:

'Are you a relative?'

There was a moment's silence before Gallinard answered with a smile, gently patting Joël's shoulder. 'No. No, I'm not. Just a good friend of the family.'

André met Gallinard's smile in that instant over Joël's shoulder, and could swear he saw tears welling in the old man's eyes. The cycle that had started sixty years ago in Monteroule when his daughter died was finally complete. He'd seen another child saved: this time, his own blood.

'Monsieur Gallinard is far more than that, Joël.' André answered Gallinard's smile with equal warmth, compassion. 'Only he's too modest to admit it.'

With the macaitin breakthrough, ORI-gene was prime candidate

469

to win the main Gifford Award – the results would be announced in two months – and resultantly there'd been a healthy boost in shares and investor confidence. Four months ago they'd moved to a new building near the Luxembourg Gardens, complete with bright, pristine animal houses, and David Copell had joined them to head up a new virology department. Boisnard was riding high again. He'd even promised to cut back on his drinking.

'Only Christmas and birthdays. Oh, and weddings. And anniversaries. And Bastille Day. And when we win the Giffords . . .'

The graveyard no longer held any fears for André. Maybe because it was now covered in snow – its shadowy portent was suddenly whited-out, sanitized – but it hadn't visited him in his dreams again since the night he'd saved Joël.

Though as he held Marielle's hand and looked across the graveyard to the two squirrels trying again to crack the nut open – probably one of the last bits of food they'd find with the ground now frozen and hard – if the past year had taught him anything, it was strength of resolve.

Maybe Hervé had been right: God had meant him to save Joël. But when he thought back to the many times that the odds had been stacked mountainously against him and it looked impossible to go on, it would have been so easy then – almost a welcome release from deluding himself that he might succeed and the extra suffering he was putting Joël through meanwhile – to simply throw in the towel and say that it was God's will that Joël should die. It was only through persisting, refusing to give up, that he'd finally learned what God had planned for him.